*For Alan—who makes all good things possible—
and for Karen, Lisa, and Steve*

# · CHAPTER ·

# 1

In Rome Frobisch had a vision on the Spanish Steps. It was a wet night late in August. Rain cast a silver patina on the ancient stones. Mist shrouded the gray-banked reaches of the Tiber. In the square where Frobisch found himself, confused about the route back to his hotel, flowers massed in earthen pots bent under a pummeling of showers like pale inverted bells.

Frobisch had dressed for the inclement weather in an Irish walker's hat, tan poplin raincoat, short-sleeve silk shantung shirt, blue slacks, dark socks, and tasseled loafers. He was hurrying back to his hotel room after a dinner with his daughter, Sima, who had flown to Rome that afternoon from Tel Aviv at his request. It was over a year since he had seen her. Their meeting, a truce of sorts between two equally stubborn personalities, had been unsatisfactory. When they met—on the street in front of the apartment where Sima had opted to stay with Italian friends—Frobisch had cried. Sima had stopped shaving her legs. She was wearing brown leather sandals of the sort tourists who travel to Israel purchase, and her toes, bound by wide leather thongs, looked none too clean. She had gained weight. To camouflage the added pounds (Frobisch supposed) she had wrapped herself in a flowered cotton shift that represented pink and yellow blossoms on a field of bilious green. And her hair—her lovely hair that Frobisch himself had braided and twirled when she was small in long caramel-colored plaits—had been cut and frizzed into a burgeoning Afro.

When Frobisch moved to kiss her she quickly averted her face and offered instead her hand, the nails ragged and bitten.

"Hello, Howard," she greeted him.

Frobisch resented the use of his given name. "What's that, a new hairdo?" he'd asked, dabbing his face with a sodden handkerchief and hoping she would attribute the moisture on his cheeks to rain.

"I cut it and had it permed," said Sima. There was an odd British inflection to her words that Frobisch had found affected.

"What do you call that style? The burning bush?"

Sima told him, "You haven't changed."

"You have," Frobisch accused.

Sima sighed. "We're going to have dinner at a vegetarian restaurant, if you don't mind. It's because I'm keeping kosher."

"If I don't have to order eggplant," Frobisch said.

He'd let her lead him down the narrow street. Her dress billowed behind her like an unfolding parachute. She was carrying an umbrella of beige watered silk with a carved green parrot head for the handle. Frobisch's heart had skipped when he observed the parrot. "Is that the same umbrella I bought you for your eleventh birthday?" Frobisch called to Sima who plowed ahead, slogging through puddles as though aware the muddy water would have no effect on her already muddied toes.

She'd stopped so short that she and Frobisch almost

collided in the darkness. She held the umbrella handle out for him to see a faint trace of script embossed on the handle near the downward curving parrot beak. "No. It's Italian. Authentic Papagallo. See. I found it in the apartment."

Frobisch was stung. He resolved not to open his coat so she would not see he'd made a point of wearing the shirt she'd bought for him on Father's Day, some fourteen months ago, the last month she'd lived at home. This past June she'd sent him nothing, a fact that he'd quickly excused on the grounds that her duties at the kibbutz kept her too busy to think of shopping.

"It's nice," Frobisch said of the umbrella. "Authentic Papagallo. What do you know?"

In the restaurant Sima had ordered eggplant parmigiana, and Frobisch, making no sense of the menu printed in Italian, had done the same. When his dinner came, he picked at it morosely, raising long strings of mozzarella with his fork and letting them subside into a puddle of thick tomato sauce.

"Why do you order it if you don't like it?" Sima asked.

Frobisch shrugged. "It's a matter of expanding one's experience of food, isn't it?" He took a tentative nibble; then he set his fork down on his plate. He began kneading the inside of a piece of bread into pellets. It was very hot inside the restaurant, and he was sweating under his coat, but he would not undo it as a matter of principle. Sima was eating hungrily. She held her knife and fork in the European style, and when she had speedily consumed the eggplant, she mopped up the sauce with a bit of bread. As Frobisch watched, she licked her fingers, a gesture so reminiscent of her childhood that he had once again to fight off tears.

"Your mother will be disappointed to hear that you've gained weight," he said to Sima.

"Do you still talk with her?" She seemed surprised. She stopped licking her fingers and gazed at him in what appeared to be sincere perplexity. Frobisch noticed that she had stopped plucking her eyebrows. They had grown together in a dark line over the bridge of her nose.

She had an almost perfect nose, narrow and straight, its photogenic symmetry marred at the tip by a sudden upward turning. For years Frobisch had taken shameful secret pleasure in the fact there was nothing Semitic to its shape.

"Of course," Frobisch said. "Why wouldn't we?" He had revved up for the speech he'd known would have to be forthcoming. "Sima, when people divorce they don't stop all communication. There's a severing of marital ties, not a cutting out of tongues." Sima looked shocked, and Frobisch worried that the last analogy had been too stark. "Your mother and I still talk a lot," Frobisch concluded lamely.

"She told me you walked out." She'd nailed him with a child's accusing look. He'd confronted that solemn gray-eyed gaze before, during countless sad childhood revelations. There is no Tooth Fairy. Santa is a tale told by adults for their own secret designs.

Frobisch sighed. He began strewing pellets of bread across the checkered tablecloth as though they were marbles. He willed himself to stop. "We were getting on each other's nerves. It seemed better for us to be apart. In cases like this, I believe it's customary for the man to leave. I thought your mother concurred in this. I shouldn't have thought that she was feeling bitter."

Sima said, "She wasn't exactly feeling bitter. She wrote

me that you were being bothered by health problems."

Frobisch thought, news of my impotence has been highly exaggerated. He wondered what story Sadie had concocted for the purpose of saving face. He would have spoken of his fears aloud, but he believed one didn't mention aspects of the boudoir to one's child. As far as he knew, Sima, through nineteen years of innocence, believed she had been immaculately conceived. "Sima," he begged, "please try to understand this. I'm not sure I can explain it clearly. I began to feel—I felt—that I was living in a void."

"Mother thinks you've been having problems with your prostate."

Frobisch studied his daughter's face to see if she was joking. She looked absolutely grave. "Well, she is wrong," Frobisch said stiffly. "And since it appears she wrote you a bill of particulars about my shortcomings"—he thought he detected on Sima's face the swiftest, fleeting smile— "may I point out a few things in my behalf. She got by virtue of the settlement the house in Kensington and one of the cars. I would have been glad to let her have the Volvo, but she wanted the old Dodge Dart because she always thought it was more feisty. She even had it written into the agreement that she was to have permanent custody of the dog."

"But you always hated him," protested Sima.

"That's beside the point. When you're settling the fate of a living entity, you're at least entitled to a say." Frobisch mopped unhappily at his face with a frayed napkin. His shirt was sticking to him. He could feel a river of sweat meandering the region of his spine.

"Aren't you hot in that coat?" asked Sima. "Have you made some kind of stubborn resolution about wearing it?"

Frobisch was at once warmed and alarmed by her prescience. "The rain chilled me," he said.

Sima looked unconvinced. "Do you want to order coffee?"

"Couldn't we have it at your place?"

"We'll have it here. Shall I order two espressos?"

"Why don't you want me to meet your friends?"

"If you want to meet my friends, you're welcome to come to Israel."

So that's it. Frobisch sighed. "I have explained why I won't go back there."

Sima said, "It makes no sense."

Frobisch allowed himself the opening of his top coat button. He dabbed the napkin to his neck and chin. Then he placed it on the table squarely between them, a no-man's-land between two warring factions. He pressed both palms together like a supplicant. "Sima, the understanding was that you wanted a year off before starting school. Fine. If you remember, I made no objection. I made no objection when you took off for the Middle East. I offered to pay your air fare, but you refused. I made no objection when you wrote that you were camping on the beach. When you said you were joining the group at the kibbutz I was even pleased, though I confess I was a bit put off to hear that they had you working in a factory making gun barrels. For a child who was schooled by peaceful Quakers—I just don't know."

"I don't do that anymore," said Sima.

"Now you're in the kitchen scrubbing pots. A fine fate for a girl who dreamed of going into special education. Sima, I wouldn't lie to you; it breaks my heart. Why must you stay there?"

"When you visited last year, you said you liked it."

6

"I admit it, I was pleasantly surprised." He had expected an arid desert place—a kind of hard, desolate mesa, dotted with tumbleweeds, like a Hollywood version of the old West. Instead he'd found a pleasant settlement of cottages, shaded by palms and set in a green enclave like the Catskills resort where he'd first met Sadie, where they'd lunged, parried, and played in the mosquito-ridden shadows of the bushes. The kibbutz complex was dominated by a modern edifice with luminous wide windows and a soaring roof. Frobisch's spirits lifted when he saw it. "Who lives there?" he'd asked Sima, and she'd responded, "That's the shul." He'd been amazed. "I wouldn't have thought the Orthodox built in the style of Frank Lloyd Wright." "Even the Orthodox can have good taste," Sima had told him, and he'd detected in her voice the first rumblings of trouble.

Frobisch allowed himself the opening of a second button on his coat. He was afraid that he might faint. "Sima, I liked it as a temporary measure. When you wrote last winter that you were planning to stay permanently, that was another matter. What about college? What about your life?"

"It *is* my life."

"I've told you what I think of that."

Sima repeated tonelessly, like an obedient child assigned the recitation of a poem, " 'I will not set foot upon the holy soil of Israel until you return to your senses and come home.' " She smiled, seemingly pleased that she had total recall.

Frobisch cried, "You think that's easy? You think I don't have ties? That is my spiritual home, just like it's yours. I got trees planted in my mother and my father's name. I got trees for every relative I've ever known. Listen,

Sima, there's a whole forest in Jerusalem bearing the name of Frobisch—and on your mother's side, the Goldens, they got a few. You think I don't long to see them? You think I don't want to wander in that heavenly shade? But I promise you, I won't set foot over there until you tell me you're ready to come home."

"I won't do it, Howard. Home is a void. You said so yourself, a minute ago. If you can see that for yourself, why not for me?"

"Sima"—Frobisch, who'd sworn on the flight to Rome that he wouldn't plead, was pleading—"I think I comprehend. You like the spirit. You like the Sabras, those wild-eyed boys in khaki shorts holding their tommy guns like they were lovers. Believe me, I understand. Didn't I see *Exodus* three times, counting the times on television? You think you'll find Paul Newman? You will—I'm sure of it—if you come home. Sima, you like idealistic types, we'll find them. It doesn't have to be a doctor. Come home, I'll introduce you to one of Nader's raiders. Look at you—that frown—you're not pretty, darling, when you do that. You don't want a lawyer, we'll find you a forest ranger, what do you say?"

"Do you or do you not want coffee?" Sima asked.

"I don't want coffee. I want some air."

They had fought over the check. Frobisch, the cost accountant, was too distraught to figure the conversion of dollars to lire and had finally let her pay. He had walked with her to her friends' apartment under a silver glint of rain that fell like moonshine. They were the only people on the street. In the great square of Saint Peter's Frobisch knew throngs were waiting patiently in the rain for a sighting of white smoke that would herald the choice of a new Pope. It seemed that all of Rome had piled into the square to keep that solemn vigil, leaving the surrounding streets as silent and empty as passages in a ghost town.

When Frobisch and Sima arrived at the apartment entry, Sima stopped short and turned to face him as though she meant to hold him at bay with her parrot umbrella. Frobisch made no attempt to kiss her. "Thank you for dinner." He essayed a little bow.

"Shall I wait with you until you find a taxi?" Sima asked.

"No need to find a taxi. I want to walk."

She had seemed genuinely concerned. "Listen, you really shouldn't. There are people all around just looking for tourists. In that hat, that coat, you're a dead giveaway."

"You're thinking I'll get mugged?"

"Worse than that. They're awful people. Terrorists."

"Terrorists? In Rome, where right now the Princes of the Church are gathering to choose a Pope? What will they do? Kidnap me? Hold me for ransom?"

"It's not funny, Daddy. They shoot people in the kneecaps."

Her acknowledgment of his paternity was not lost on him. He was unnerved. "Is a broken kneecap worse than a broken heart?"

He wanted to take the words back the moment he said them. She was too smart, his Sima, to let him get away with it, that laying on of guilt. He could feel her retreating from him even before she turned to face the house. "Look," Frobisch babbled, "no harm will come to me. I love Rome. I've always loved it. Good vibes here. Happy memories. On our honeymoon your mother and I entered the city under military escort, did you know?"

He had told the tale so often he could see the scenes

unfolding like a repeating movie. His honeymoon with Sadie. They were driving south from Florence in a car he'd rented in Paris, a black Renault Dauphin that Sadie in a burst of characteristic enthusiasm had christened *Petit Pamplemousse*. Little Grapefruit. Better to call it Lemon. The gearshift balked in reverse, and the radiator overheated on the gentlest slopes. In an American-type drugstore selling sundries Frobisch had acquired a metal pail. He had fallen into the habit of stopping every ten kilometers or so, at farms and dim cafés, to beg for water. He maintained a vision of himself approaching a hostile peasant, wielding the pail and waving his arms (in nervousness over his faulty French, pidgin Italian) like a ruffled bird seeking a puddle in which to bathe his dusty feathers.

In the mountains south of Carcassonne, Frobisch detected in the swarthy faces of the villagers the look of brigands. They would as soon knife him for a diversion, Frobisch feared, as give him water. When he confided this fear to Sadie, she had laughed. The thought of danger exhilarated her. She inhaled infusions of courage with the hot breath of the mistral. While Frobisch, trembling over anticipated stabbings in the back, fed the steaming radiator with water, she tumbled from the car, danced circles in golden meadows, whirled barefoot through blazing poppies that bent like waves, collapsed in the shade of cypresses that rose like walls. Sadie sniffed out Frobisch's fear as though she were an active rooting puppy, and sensing it she mocked him for it. Frobisch consulted with mechanics in Portofino and Florence and knew that he was being taken. He made pit stops at posh hotels, tinkered with the faltering engine while Sadie shopped or cut a quick swath through the museums. The statues of naked men in the Uffizi, Sadie told him, were something else! Frobisch dreamed of Rome and the amenities he might find in an Esso station.

On the broad *autostrada* that runs from Florence to Rome Petit Pamplemousse did pretty well. But unaccountably, outside Rome the road narrows, descends to sudden dips and hairpin turns, then rises to blind hills that lose themselves in the gray-green of olive groves. The swift descents and sudden rises put stress on the car's already straining engine. The arrow on the dash was showing red. To add to his woes Frobisch found himself trapped in the center of a military convoy transporting soldiers home from bivouac. The soldiers, bearded and dark with the same ominous look of the peasants who had scared him in the south of France, hooted at Frobisch, jeered, shouted, assailed Sadie with obscene gestures, which she returned in kind. Fearless Sadie egged Frobisch on to pass the trucks, courting probable death, certain collision with platoons of speeding Fiats that dive-bombed from the tops of hills. He was in a proper fix with the radiator steaming and Sadie challenging him to take a risk and the jeering soldiers impugning his manhood with upraised fingers.

He had been paralyzed with despair when out of nowhere a jeep drew up beside them bearing a man who appeared, by the look of his natty uniform, to be the officer in charge. The officer assessed the situation and then signaled his driver to pull back into the line. In a moment two motorcyclists roared into sight and motioned Frobisch to follow them into the opposite lane. He'd thought he was being arrested. He'd chugged after the cyclists amid billows of steam. The soldiers' laughter, Sadie's cries were blurred by the ringing in his ears. The cyclists, grinning guardian angels, escorted them over a bridge and into Rome at the siesta hour.

The city slumbered like a languorous lion, bathed in green-gold haze and spread out on the banks of the calm Tiber. Frobisch noted enormous statues flanking the approaches of the bridge and had a brief moment of déjà vu when he thought he was back in Washington, D.C. Relief at being home swept over him like a rush of sweet release after sexual tension. Then he felt the bump of trolley tracks and saw on a traffic island shaded by a green umbrella a traffic cop, clad in a blazing tunic, white pith helmet, knife-creased pants, immaculate white gloves. The cop directed traffic as though performing in an antic dance. He paused midway through a balletic maneuver to stare at them. "Is he adorable?" said Sadie, who flashed the man the V-sign as they passed.

He would wonder if the troubles they had in Kensington in later years stemmed from those moments in the car when she had seen him impotent and had laughed; and he had stared at her, the object of his heart's desire, and found her not what he had thought. He had picked her for his own out of a square dance in the Catskills. She had literally do-si-doed into his heart, waving her skirts, tossing her hair, skipping in little cotton slippers that fastened over the instep with the aid of a button hook. Capezios! How lightly she had trod in them upon the grass, kicked up her heels, lured him into the deep green of the bushes where the sharp edges of holly leaves had left scratches on his arms like the marks of cats' claws. In time the bitter recollections of their honeymoon diminished, and in their place he had an amusing story, a good teaser of a beginning with which he could intrigue guests over cocktails.

"On our honeymoon Sadie and I entered Rome under military escort, did you know?"

"I grew up on that story," Sima said.

"Invite me upstairs and I'll tell it again with new embellishments," Frobisch promised.

"Daddy, I'm tired," Sima said simply. "I want to go to sleep."

"Have breakfast with me tomorrow," Frobisch begged.

"I'm catching an early plane."

Frobisch peered at her face. He could barely discern her features in the murky light. Somewhere beneath the matronly facade, the puffy sunburned cheeks, the frizzed-out hair, his lovely laughing Sima, gold of hair, supple of build, light of his life, joy of his waning years, lurked like a teasing shadow. "Sima," Frobisch whispered, "my new apartment in D.C. is very nice. There's a little den, an extra room for you, if you should care to use it."

Sima said, "Thanks." He thought, couldn't be sure, she touched his arm in a gesture both placating and affectionate. He moved to grab her hand, but she was gone, vanished in mist like a creature in a Gothic tale. He could hear the flip-flop of her sandals on the wet pavement. Frobisch stood weeping in the rain. Behind a curtain of drooping bushes a vestibule door clanged shut with a sound like broken dishes.

For a time Frobisch walked in circles, experiencing with every inhalation of the swampy air a stab of pain, tasting salt tears and the acrid mix of garlic and eggplant

on his tongue. He remembered Sima's warning about terrorists and he was afraid. He imagined figures lurking in
the dark of corners, sentries posted against walls, eyes
marking his faltering progress as he walked, less and less
certain of the route to his hotel. Twin shadows looming
near a stand of Lombardy poplars threw him into a panic
until he realized they were figures caught in an
embrace—now joining, now receding, joining again with
a pull like ocean waves. Frobisch pitied their anguished
polarity. Iron filings in the magnet's grasp. Even as he
feared them he wished them well. He watched the
shadows merge; then, overcome with tact, he glanced
away. He was ready to give up the ghost and hail a cab,
but there were no cars on the street—only a cyclist pedal-
ing a drunken zigzag in his path. Frobisch, reacting to sudden impulse, bent double and crossed protective hands
over his knees like a dancer performing a giddy Charleston.
The cyclist vanished with a squeak of tires, and Frobisch
was alone, bent double in his sodden raincoat, water dripping from his hat brim, tears flooding his eyes, the growing heat of heartburn filling his chest.

He looked up to see the familiar front of the American
Express building. Frobisch exhaled, murmured his
gratitude with the softness of a benediction. God bless the
old U.S. of A. God bless its representatives in foreign fields.
He figured he must be near the Piazza di Spagna, not far,
if memory served, from his hotel. The rain had stopped.
A shaft of moon lighted the ancient vista of the Spanish
Steps with bright theatric flair. Frobisch began hurriedly to climb the steps with no sure knowledge of where the
ascent might lead. Midway to the top a young man clad
in antique dress was standing. He wore a robe of plainest
homespun bound with a rope. He was holding what could

have been a pole, a fishing rod perhaps, a shepherd's staff. A fool done up for a party, Frobisch thought. On the young man's feet were muddy sandals. Maybe a friend of Sima's. The youth had long hair flowing to his shoulders and a full curly beard that did not hide a look of passing sweetness. Frobisch remembered a poem he'd had to learn in the sixth grade about an angel who possessed a look "made of all sweet accord." He retained the crazy notion that the young man was a friend of Sima's, come to tell him to go back; she'd had a change of heart. More likely he was a hippie, drunk or stoned. Frobisch would have passed him without another glance; but the man spoke to him in English, and Frobisch, pleased to hear his native tongue, paused to listen. The youth's words were muffled by the noise of a motorcycle roaring through an adjacent alley. Frobisch thought he'd said, "Do good. Quit messing up." Frobisch meant to respond, "That's a good costume." And "Could you possibly direct me to the Hotel Plaza?" Instead he plummeted, fell to his knees, clasped his palms before him, and in a voice that boomed over the moonlit square with the resonance of belief he cried, "Tell me, oh, tell me, please, how is it in the house of God?"

There is nothing ambiguous about a vision. To the viewer it is there, tangible as rainfall, searing as the summer heat. Nothing equivocal. No room for doubt; no reason for argument, Talmudic discourse, philosophical debate. So Frobisch, certain of what he'd seen, sank to his knees, felt the dampness of wet stone, noted a rending of the cotton in the knee of his pants (and with a part of him removed, that part of him that watched himself performing as though he were a lumbering actor in a theater of the absurd), pondered—even as he trembled—offering a few hundred lire to the brunette maid in his hotel if she would sew them. Frobisch, about to shout, "Good costume." And, "Could you possibly direct me to the Hotel Plaza?" had instead astonished himself by crying, "How is it in the house of God?" And yet was not astonished, knowing the vision to be true. Later there would be doubts—a feeling not unlike postcoital triste—but for the moment there was only a flooding of well-being. Where he had been warm he now was cooled. Where he had felt sodden and dank he experienced a warmth of heat suffusing him like a healing poultice. Ever precise, he longed to ask, "Why me?" Or "Could you enlighten me as to your religious denomination?" Instead he'd felt somewhere a gift of tongues impelling him to speak in language at once biblical and poetic. "How is it in the house of God?" The vision was not poetic in kind.

Frobisch, muddled by surprise as well as the noise of the motorcycle, had his first moment of doubt wondering if he'd heard correctly. "Do good. Quit messing up." That was hardly the stuff of prophets. Frobisch rose stiffly to his feet. The young man had vanished. Where he had stood a beam of moon lighted the spot with a circle like a spotlight. Above the light the twin belfries of Trinita dei Monti loomed mysterious behind a skein of clouds. Frobisch avoided the circle where the man had stood and continued climbing. When he reached the summit of the Steps, he began walking with a sense of certainty in a straight line back to his hotel.

The hotel was the same place he'd stayed with Sadie twenty years before. Then, as now, there was a hint of previous seedy splendor in the twisted metal of the wall sconces, the clouded crystal of the chandeliers. The walls had once been painted dusky pink. Now they were re-painted peachy terra-cotta that retained a smell of fish; and the carpet that had been oyster gray with a sculptured petal pattern to the wool had been replaced with indoor-outdoor stuff of rusty brown speckled with lint and bread crumbs. Every time he walked the halls Frobisch thought the floor would make a fine feeding place for pigeons.

His room, for all he knew, might be the same one he had occupied before. It was large and square with tall shuttered windows and furniture out of the thirties—dark, heavy pieces of varnished wood that had reminded Sadie of Mussolini. She could not say why. In his present room there was a mirrored armoire where Frobisch hung his suits on wire hangers. There was a dresser topped by a mirror that had been cracked in half and glued together carelessly so that the two pieces didn't match exactly. When he dressed, Frobisch perceived his face as bisected like a dramatic mask, half comedy, half tragedy. His right cheek didn't match his left. He surveyed his strange disjointed jaw in the seamed reflecting glass and pondered growing a beard. There was a washbasin affixed to a wall beside the bed; inside a gray-tiled bathroom there was a leaky toilet, a bidet, and a shower with a domed ceiling that made Frobisch think of Saint Peter's.

When he'd checked in on Friday, Frobisch observed that his washbasin was soiled with strands of lank, dark hair. He'd asked the maid if she would clean it for him. She had stood, uncomprehending, a woman with enormous breasts and a mass of ink-black hair that tumbled from beneath a sort of cotton dustcap. On her upper lip was the faintest shadow of a mustache. For some reason that incipient mustache excited him. He couldn't fathom why. Maybe he craved the masculine. Maybe he was a closet queen. He'd offered the maid a fistful of rainbow-colored lire and pointed to the sink, pantomiming cleaning movements. She had stood meekly murmuring, "*Prego.*" Frobisch thought she understood and was pretending not to. He fought the urge to beat her to the bed and swoop upon the soft down of her lip with kisses. He considered that he was going crazy. At last he told her, "Never mind. I'll clean it up myself." She had stood smiling shyly, examining him with dark enormous eyes in which there lurked a hint of tears, exhaling garlicky breaths of regret and whispering, "*Prego.*" It was enough to drive him mad. "*Basta, per piacere,*" Frobisch said. It was all he could remember of Italian, and he wasn't sure he had it right. Finally he told her, "*Prego,*" and ushered her to the door bearing her towels, her spotted linens, her air of sorrow. She left, leaving behind the aura of sardines.

Safe now, in his hotel room, Frobisch undressed. There were half-moons of perspiration on his shirt. He unbuttoned it quickly and let it fall on the bed. He removed his torn trousers and folded them neatly over a chair back. He sat on the bed—the dark-haired maid had turned back the cotton spread to reveal sheets of somber grayness—and removed his wet loafers, his socks. He wiggled his toes, enjoying the scratchy feel of rust-brown carpet under his soles. He got up and stood bare-chested in the gingham boxer shorts that Sadie had purchased for him at Saks Fifth Avenue in Chevy Chase. He padded barefoot to the bathroom, brushed his teeth. At a hotel where he and Sadie had stayed in Portofino there had been little ceramic toothbrush holders, fashioned like candlesticks. When they'd packed to leave, Sadie had stolen two of them. When Frobisch importuned her not to, she had laughed.

"Of course I'm going to take them. That's what they're here for. Souvenirs."

Frobisch hadn't believed her. He felt guilty still that he had let her do it—make a little bundle of them wrapped in tissue and secrete them in the suitcase underneath her slips. "Forgive me," Frobisch whispered as he cleaned his teeth. He missed his electric toothbrush, which he'd left in the apartment in D.C. fastened to a beige holder on the wall. The ceramic toothbrush holders stood on a little mirrored shelf that hung in the master bath in Kensington. For years Frobisch had avoided looking at them, but sometimes he felt dark stabbings of guilt as he flossed his teeth.

Is it possible, thought Frobisch, I have always had an instinct for virtue and I never knew it? He rinsed his mouth. Still pondering, he urinated dreamily into the toilet, noting with pleasure the full force of his spray, the bright gold of the arc rising and fizzing softly into rusty water. There was nothing amiss with his prostate. Nothing out of kilter with his private parts where he had felt mild swellings of interest encountering the maid. He had tried and tried again to explain to Sadie that he wasn't unable, merely unwilling. He had been drooping with malaise, a sense of boredom, listlessness akin to pain. Sadie, tortured, uncomprehending, suggested he was depressed, or in the grip of virus, summer flu, male menopause, lead poisoning, hay fever, allergy to MSG. Finally, the last barb, not even confided to him, she'd scrawled on airmail paper to innocent Sima, who must worry thousands of miles away in desert heat amid the threat of alien bullets about her father's failing prostate!

Frobisch finished and flushed, watched in hushed expectancy as the water rose to the rim of the toilet bowl and then subsided. For a moment he had feared he would be drowned in his own fluids. He thought again about the maid and felt the swelling of interest in his penis. He stepped out of his shorts. Naked he turned the faucet of the shower on and listened for a rumbling in the pipes. There emerged an anemic spray of tepid water. Frobisch stepped into the gray dome of the shower and stood, letting the water play against his chest. He felt somehow sacrilegious standing naked in the domed enclave and thinking lascivious thoughts about the maid. He permitted himself finally to consider the encounter on the Spanish Steps. "Oh, Lord," said Frobisch shyly, "have You paid me a visit only to invest me once again with sexual desire?" He waited to be struck dead. The pipes continued rumbling. The water suddenly ran cold. "Forgive me, Lord," said Frobisch, convinced he *would* be forgiven, as he'd been forgiven for the stolen toothbrush holders. Not an actor in that caper; merely accessory to the fact. He stepped out of the shower and groped for the towel that the maid had left him. It excited him to think that she had put it there and he was now dabbing at his naked body, rubbing hard across the shoulders, probing more delicately at those parts that were more sensitive. He strode into the bedroom bearing a massive erection, the grandest display he'd ever had. He felt at once guilty and proud, sorrowful that the sight must go unmarked. "Forgive me, Lord," said Frobisch once again. "I am, as You see me, only a poor fool with common urges." He crept into the bed, thinking he would not sleep out of excitement, out of the sheer urgency of his need. But the moment he pulled the covers to his chin he was asleep, lost in a dream of sunlit vistas, fields covered with purple clover, slopes descending to smooth streams in which there gleamed in the white sand of the shore colored pebbles. He floated in a reverie devoid of guilt or desire, a dream place filled with light and languor, harmony and joy. Absence of clamor. A gentle dream. A dream of peace.

He woke up craving cornflakes. He imagined the table set—cereal heaped in a yellow bowl under a layer of thickly sliced banana, a swift dusting of sugar, a splash of milk poured from a glass bottle in which gobbets of cream glistened at the top like bits of pearl. His mouth watered for the taste of it; he pictured his mother expertly wielding the knife—her nails blunt cut and unvarnished, her wedding ring severing a chunky finger like a strand of wire as she poured and sliced. He recognized his craving for what it was—a longing to return to the simplicity of childhood. There drifted through the open window of his room a smell like burning chicory. He thought of coffee dripping in the glass Silex on the stove.

He got out of bed and walked to the window. He had left the shutters open. It must have rained again during the night. There was a damp spot on the carpet that reminded Frobisch of the aging terrier, Gregor, that Sadie now owned by virtue of legal decree. The dog's kidneys were failing, and he had frequent accidents, which Sadie cleaned with the sweet silence of a martyr. Frobisch had awakened often to the sight of his wife on her hands and knees, plump in a flowered housecoat, working at a stain with a cloth dipped in cold water. Later she would attack the spot with foam rug cleaner and the vacuum, but something of Gregor always remained—faint jagged outlines in the sand-beige of the rug like the outline of unknown countries on a map.

Sadie forgave the dog. "We must be patient with the ones we love in their old age," she'd told Frobisch piously. He'd always thought it didn't become his bold and brassy Sadie (he had to admit it—brassy, a touch flamboyant, she was) to spout little pilgrim homilies. Like Hester Prynne.

The dog had been an early source of controversy. They had fought over his name from the day they got him from a kennel in Virginia where a woman in granny glasses and a tight gray bun had interrogated Frobisch as though she were a social worker and he a mendicant begging a handout.

"Do you have a fenced-in yard?"

"We intend to fence it in," Frobisch had told her. "Or to build a pen. Whatever seems more convenient."

"We require a fenced-in yard."

"It's a big yard for such a little dog," Frobisch protested mildly.

"It's a requirement," the woman told him.

"Then we'll fence it," Frobisch said, trapped. It was he who had researched the breed; but Sima, then only five, had made the final choice. She had picked the dog from a litter of four puppies—three of whom pranced under a picnic table with gay infant abandon. Only this one, the only male, had sat brooding and apart. Frobisch thought the puppy needed love. "My daughter wants him," Frobisch surrendered.

"Is she the only child?"

"She is," Sadie apologized.

"She's rather young," the woman said, as though youth were an ailment akin to syphilis and equal to that malady in the shame it bore by its very condition.

"She's very gentle," Sadie said.

"Old for her years," said Frobisch. "Very advanced."

"She must be taught not to abuse him," the woman said.

Frobisch had balked. "And has the dog been taught not to abuse her in turn?"

"The dog is an aristocrat," the woman said.

He had studied the compact little body, plump and round with a puppy coat that shone as though it had been rubbed with oil, and announced there was only one name possible for this pet—Gregor Samsa, after the man who had been transformed into a shiny beetle. Sima wanted to call him Blackie, and Sadie said Sammy would do her fine. Howie's choice, she had argued, was pretentious and had depressing overtones. Frobisch had the dog registered as Gregor Samsa, but nobody except him used that name, and the dog would never come to him when called—or for that matter, respond to his efforts at training. Never did the dog give Frobisch a friendly wag, a doggy smile, a lick, a shudder of welcoming affection, the time of day. He was Sadie's dog—Sadie's and Sima's. It was appropriate that Sadie should have the animal in his waning days, but Frobisch worried secretly that there was something wrong with his, Frobisch's, personality if the dog he'd raised from puppyhood didn't like him. Maybe the terrier hated the Kafka name, the likening to a glossy beetle. Its adult coat had grown in rough, a wiry black and tan, so the comparison no longer signified. No matter. Gregor was Slavic, gloomy, perfect. Everybody else called Welsh terriers Dylan or Trevor. Gregor had class.

Frobisch gazed down at awakening Rome. The city shimmered like a city under water, a wash of mellow colors—the pink of painted stucco, the green of travertine, the dun of ancient brick. The one jarring note was the blazing marble of the monument to Vittorio Emanuele II, glistening like a square of outsized wedding cake amid buildings of muted ocher. The sky was clear, wide with light that shone with the clarity of sapphires—a ring of sapphire banding the green of cypresses, umbrella pines. Frobisch thought, *It's going to be a scorcher. At least a dozen people are going to faint today waiting outside Saint Peter's. Early this evening the cardinals will choose their Pope, a popular choice, but not a practical one.*

He turned from the window, shivering with a sudden chill. What had made him think such a thing, acknowledge it with such certainty? It was something he knew, sensed through his naked skin as though he were equipped with heavenly radar. "What makes me know that?" Frobisch said. "Why even think it? What makes me sure I know?"

Moments before, homely thoughts of cornflakes, of Gregor peeing on the rug had brought him down to earth, convinced him that his vision (so-called vision) of the night before was a dream; at most, a weird hallucination brought on by his anguish, nerves. He was—he argued this, pacing the room naked and shivering as a newborn babe—obsessed at the moment with the idea of religion. Wasn't everyone in Rome sitting out the solemn business of the Papal Conclave? Everyone was ripe for odd dreams, views of saints, heavenly apparitions. So was he.

On the flight to Rome he had read avidly in his early edition of the *Washington Post* the details surrounding the Papal Conclave. There would be one hundred eleven cardinals assembled, housed in loggias in the Vatican that would be furnished simply with night tables, cots. Each night table would bear a ration of toilet paper, tissues, soap. A second table provided pen and paper. (Frobisch trembled to contemplate the sacred jottings.) When the cardinals convened for meals they would dine in a dining room that had been inhabited by a Borgia Pope—their dinners served by nuns of the Order of Saint Martha. The concise details of this had warmed Frobisch's accountant's soul, while that other part of him, the secret part that read poems and Gothic novels had thrilled to the unfolding drama.

Shortly after Frobisch had arrived in Rome he'd seen on TV the assemblage of cardinals, gorgeous in long red robes and scarlet miters, in the Sistine Chapel. The TV station had interrupted an amateur baseball game in progress to show the scene. This morning, even as Frobisch paced, the cardinals were gathered in the Chapel, seated at twelve tables, each table twenty-five feet long. They would cast secret ballots written in Latin, which they would deposit at a marble altar under Michelangelo's *Last Judgment*. At the corner entrance of the Sistine Chapel was a gray cast-iron stove. A gray stack ran from the stove to a window just below the ceiling. The addition of a special chemical stick would make smoke from the stove run black or white. All Rome was waiting, Frobisch knew, to mark the color of the smoke. All Rome was in a state of nerves.

"Should I phone the Vatican?" Frobisch wondered aloud. "Should I tell them that I *know*—that I have been told—that today they will choose a Pope. That I even know his name?" Frobisch pressed his palms together like a man in prayer. "They would never believe me. They would lock me up. For being a spy. For having access to secret documents. But how, then, do I know? I can't be sure they've even voted. I can't be sure they are awake." He felt a pressure in his bladder. No problems with prostate. "Prostate's fine. Prostate's fine," mumbled Frobisch, as though that were a talisman.

Frobisch made up his mind. He would phone Sima. He would tell her of his hallucination of the night before and the odd conviction he had this morning that he knew the cardinals would choose their Pope today. That he knew who would be chosen! That the smoke would run first white, then black, then white again—assuaging the disappointment of the crowd. He struggled to remember Sima's number. In the restaurant she'd offered to write it down for him, but he'd said, "I can remember it. You know how I am with numbers. Absolute recall." Now he could tick off swiftly changing numbers. One hundred eleven cardinals. Seventy-five votes. Six hundred million Catholics. The two hundred sixty-third Pope. All the numbers out of the *Post* article, but no connection with Sima.

"Help me, Lord," prayed Frobisch. He picked up the phone and asked the desk clerk in English if he could connect him. "Two-four-oh-six," said Frobisch.

The clerk murmured, *"Prego."*

"And to you," said Frobisch, naked and afraid.

A woman, speaking soft accented English, answered on the first ring as though she had been poised beside the table waiting for his call. Frobisch asked if he could speak with Sima Frobisch. "This is her father," Frobisch explained.

"She is left," the woman said.

"She is left?" repeated Frobisch.

"This morning. Yes. She is left on the early plane."

"But it's Saturday," protested Frobisch. "She doesn't travel on Saturday. She is a very religious girl. She makes a point of keeping kosher, don't you know?"

"She is left," said the woman sadly.

She sounded neither old nor young. Frobisch wondered if she was the owner of the parrot umbrella. Was she pretty? Her voice was sweet. Would she talk with him? Could he invite her to coffee on the Via Veneto and offer, like a sad and weary pilgrim, his confession to a sympathetic soul?

"Tell her I called," said Frobisch stupidly. "If you speak with her again, tell her her father called. Howard Frobisch."

"She is gone home," said the woman.

"Home?" questioned Frobisch. For a moment his heart lightened with hope. Perhaps last night a miracle had transpired after all. "You mean to Maryland?" asked Frobisch.

"To the kibbutz," explained the woman. "Kibbutz is home."

"Kibbutz is home," repeated Frobisch.

"I'm sorry," the woman told him kindly.

Frobisch hadn't heard. "What?" he asked her rudely.

"I'm sorry for you," said the woman.

"*Grazie,*" said Frobisch. "Tell her I called. Tell her I'm sorry, too." Gently he placed the phone in its cradle, as though fearful any sudden movement might cause a major earthquake, an explosion of volcanic heat. He walked like a man strung up by wires, gingerly, barefoot on the rust-brown carpet, as though sidestepping puddles. "What to do," moaned Frobisch. "What to do."

Someone was knocking on the door. Frobisch thought, it's Sima come to say good-bye! He looked about frantically for something with which to cover his nakedness. His torn pants were neatly folded on the chair beside his bed. He seized them and struggled into them, catching his bare toes on the cuff and cursing as he struggled to right himself. His fingers trembled as he zipped the fly.

"I'm coming, Sima," Frobisch called. "Please wait for me. I'm coming."

He hurried to unlatch the door, mindful of the pressure in his bladder. He wished that he could take a moment to relieve himself. But the knocking was growing more intense. If he kept her waiting in the hall she might interpret that as his rejection and turn away. She might leave for the airport thinking he had meant to let her go without a loving word, a sweet kiss of forgiveness.

"Hang on a moment longer," Frobisch told himself as well as the person waiting. He hurried to unchain the door.

The maid was standing with a pile of sheets pressed to her breast. Her mustache quivered as she greeted him, shyly and yet with something forward to her manner. Frobisch felt the pressure in his loins increase. "Oh, it's you." He tried to keep his voice steady, but it struck him that the words came out in an odd falsetto, as though someone else were speaking, as though some alien spirit not his own now occupied his body. His body that so longed to piss! That longed to rub up to the maid who stood, dark eyes agleam, lips tremulous, cheeks flushed. "What do you want?"

The maid answered something in Italian and held out her pile of linens as though offering a flag of truce.

"Not now," said Frobisch. "I just got up. I have to shave and dress. *Capice?* Later. Can you come back later?"

The maid stood her ground and sighed.

Frobisch thought, if I asked her to come in, if I threw her on the bed, she would not resist me. He toyed with the idea. He was aware of a new pain, hitherto unnoticed, in the region where his pants were torn. His knee was bruised where he had hit the Spanish Steps so suddenly. He had not bothered to examine it, but it was probably cut, or at least turning black and blue. It throbbed now as though it were a central source—all pain radiating from it as though it were the locus of a compass. Hurting and crazy with desire, Frobisch moaned, "Not now. Okay? Please come back later. When I've got my head together. I can't cope just now." The maid stood firm. Frobisch slammed the door in her startled face and quickly fastened the chain so she could not enter with her pass key.

He limped into the bathroom, moaning. He reached the toilet in the nick of time.

Later, freshly shaved and dressed, Frobisch paced the room in anguished thought. He had thrown his torn pants on the rumpled bed, where they lay all in a tumble of blankets and sheets like a blazing beacon—attesting to his fate, to the truth of what had befallen him. Why me, questioned Frobisch. Why me? Why pick me for a heavenly visitation? It was one thing to be blessed by heaven, to be afforded special perks. Good luck on the market. Oil in the backyard. His daughter married to a Jewish doctor. Blessings of that sort, he could handle. But the vision he had had laid down the law. "Do good. Quit messing up." He had considered that he might have had a stroke, a heart attack, a hallucination. Were there mushrooms in the eggplant? He recalled there were. Maybe they were poisonous and he was hallucinating as a result of deadly botulism. His knee ached, refuting all the arguments. His stomach burned. He felt a renewed longing for cornflakes. He would have some breakfast, and his head would clear. He seized his torn pants from the bed and stood with them, uncertain what he meant to do with them. He remembered that he'd meant to ask the maid to sew them. No chance of that, he thought. Her feelings must be hurt beyond reparation; and as for the trousers, no amount of sewing would repair that rent. He knew it, knew it, *knew it*! As surely as he'd known the night before that what he'd seen was real, and of a realm not known to man on earth.

"Why me?" wailed Frobisch.

He thought of the day they bought the puppy Gregor—the way the dog had cowered in false sanctuary under the picnic table until a great hand scooped it up, cradled its bristling haunches, set it precariously on a child's strange lap (scratchy blue plaid, box-pleated) where it had hunched too terrified to piddle! Awful to be selected while one's sisters (brazen bitches) frolicked unafraid. The one who gets picked, Frobisch decided gloomily, is the one certain of feeling pain.

"Why me?" mourned Frobisch. "Why me?" he wept, reaching for his wallet, his passport case, his keys. *Why me?* Frobisch rushed out of his room, hurling the door shut behind him and taking pleasure in the slam. Shaking less from fear than rage, he ran stiff-kneed over the spattered carpet—furious because he had been singled out!

Sadie phoned him at the office to ask, "How was your trip?"

"Going or coming?"

"Take your pick."

"Going was good. I read the *Post* as far as Metro News and we were there."

He could hear her thinly veiled exclamation of contempt. She used to get riled about the way he pored over the morning paper like a rabbi seeking deeper meanings in the Talmud. He began on page one with the vital news, and he proceeded line by line, reading every story, checking the ads, scratching pencil marks by advertised specials Sadie might wish to buy. Sometimes he clipped cartoons or funny stories to bring to work. By the time Sadie got the paper it was ripped and marked—another point for her to add to the long bill of particulars she held against him.

Sadie said, "You're sounding flat."

Frobisch explained, "Jet lag." He added, "Sima is fine."

"I know Sima is fine. I talked to her on the phone. She said you were acting strange."

"I was acting strange? I begged her to come home and got upset when she said she wouldn't."

Sadie counseled, "Give her time."

"Do I get a choice?"

Sadie's silence hung between them, heavy with untold woes. At last she said, "I didn't call to have you start in about Sima. What was so bad about the flight back home?"

Frobisch lied, "It was uneventful." His seatmate had been a merry Irish priest who had arrived in the company of black-garbed colleagues. Boarding, they looked like crows marching in twos to join the ark. They were tall men, slightly stooped as though the weight of others' sins had left them permanently bent. Oh, but they were gleeful! Their joy in the choice of the new Pope, John Paul, the former Patriarch of Venice, robbed them of any clerical solemnity. They were so keyed up with excitement they couldn't light. Once the plane was airborne, they'd roamed the aisle, saluting each other in Boston Irish accents that jarred Frobisch's nerves.

Frobisch's seatmate had finally come to rest beside him. Frobisch studied him with interest. Since his moment on the Spanish Steps it was as though his eyes were freed of scales. He was beset by tiny details he would heretofore have never noticed—the frayed threads on the priest's Roman collar, the odd aspect of his shoes, which were dull black and elaborately pointed like an illustration in the Brothers Grimm. The priest had silvery hair waved like an old-time matinee idol's and pink, scrubbed cheeks too fair to show much beard. There was a spate of oversized tan freckles on his forehead. He would have to keep out of the sun. Frobisch had groaned and clapped his palms over his eyes not wanting to know the things he knew.

The priest had looked concerned. "You're ill?"

"'Snothing, Father. Touch of indigestion from the trip."

"Ah," the man smiled. "The dago food." He had nice eyes, pale blue crinkling into laugh lines. A proper priest for christenings and weddings. Frobisch would have preferred a darker sort for giving solace.

"D'you know," the priest confided, "what I've been craving for a week? A Big Mac! And a bag of fries. I'm addicted to it, don't you know. Fast food! It's the nation's strength."

"Is it, Father?"

"It is. I was a chaplain in Korea, and I'll tell you, my son, it's how our boys got through it, eating fast food. All that good grease and plastic coating they had in high school was like a sealant on their insides. Man, you couldn't bayonet them if you tried. The holes just closed. Our boys survived 'cause they had guts of polyethylene!"

"Fancy that," said Frobisch, catching the scent of cloves.

The priest belched as though the mere thought of McDonald's was enough to arouse a turmoil in his gastric juices. Frobisch moaned. He was like some ailing Proust in whom the slightest jar, the least vibration was enough to drive him mad. He peered out of the window, scanning the clouds. *How is it in the house of God?* The sky was streaked with pink and turquoise like the lush pastels of Rome. Before leaving the Holy City he had convinced himself the vision was a mean practical joke. The hippie was a hired actor secured by Sima for reasons of her own. Why would she do that? Children are cruel. Cruelty starts with the first flow of adolescent juices and extends through sour adulthood. Frobisch envied his seatmate's childless state, the innocence of pleasures as simple as fast food.

Without understanding why, he'd nudged the priest. "Are you confident of the new Pope's health?"

"What do you mean?"

Frobisch shrugged. "He's sixty-five."

"And likely in his prime, may the good Lord bless him." The priest marked him with heightened interest. "Are you a Catholic?"

"I'm an iconoclast," said Frobisch. He'd steeled himself for a lecture. But the priest had merely grunted as though encounters with nonbelievers were a necessary hazard of his trade. In a moment he was asleep, his mouth gone slack, his hands clasped in a gesture of perfect piety. Frobisch, who would have liked to argue the merits of his case, was disappointed.

Sadie asked, "Are you still there?"

Frobisch took in the carefully chosen trappings of his office: the rosewood desk oiled to a winey luster, the pewter mug of lethally sharpened pencils, the crystal vase holding a single, tight-furled rose. A double picture frame of chaste, hinged silver displayed a posed photograph of Sadie looking gloomy and operatic and a candid shot of Sima in thinner, happier days, laughing and romping with the dog. "I guess I am."

"Come out tonight. I'll cook your dinner."

Frobisch asked, "What's wrong?" Since the divorce it wasn't characteristic of Sadie to offer gifts unless there was something she wanted in return.

"What could be wrong? I want to see you. You could give me news of Sima."

"You just told me you talked with her on the phone." It was the sort of verbal sparring that had gone on interminably in the months before they split and had finally worn him down, more than his supposed failures in the bedroom. Maybe he wasn't the stalwart consort she had wished, but the contrariness of a Sadie could work upon

34

a man like water eating away at stone. Frobisch asked, "What's broken?"

"Must something be broken for us to talk?"

"What isn't working?" He thought, if she makes some wise-ass allusion to my private parts I will hang up.

"The sink in the guest bathroom is leaking."

"Did you call a plumber?"

"Howie, it needs a twenty-five-cent washer."

"What else?"

"The air conditioning makes a rattling sound when it kicks on. And don't ask did I call the repairman, because I did, and he can't get here until next Wednesday unless I want to pay double overtime. He says most likely it's a loose filter jiggling over that fan that's in the furnace."

Frobisch scrawled busy notations on a pad. "One washer. One filter. What else?"

Sadie's voice sounded garbled. Maybe the phone was tapped. Frobisch moved the receiver to his better ear. "Say again."

"Sammy is dying."

"Gregor Samsa?"

"Yes."

Easy, thought Frobisch. Easy. The enemy is in decline. Nonetheless it's best to tread softly when one enters a mine field. "Well, Sadie, he's going on fifteen."

"Fourteen."

"What's that in human years? Something like ninety-eight?"

"I don't care about human years. He's a dog."

"What's the matter with him?"

"His pancreas is failing. His kidneys are shutting down. Once a day I take him to the vet's for I.V. feedings. I give him shots."

"*You* do?"

Sadie's laugh was brief and harsh. "I'm a regular Florence Nightingale. Believe me, Howie, it's hard. He needs to be walked maybe every ten minutes. At least it seems that much. He needs to go out a coupla times during the night. I walk him alone in the dark, and for the first time in my life I'm really scared. Last night I saw a bat, ugly as anything, circling the big trees near Rock Creek. I ran. I dragged poor Sammy by his leash until I thought he'd choke. He got as far as our front steps and fell down on his belly in a heap and just lay there wheezing. I thought he was finished, then and there."

"They don't hurt you, bats don't," Frobisch told her. "They look scary, but they don't do any harm."

"Oh, yeah?" Sadie tried to joke. "Maybe it was Count Dracula come to drink my blood."

Frobisch sighed. "What can I do?"

"Come out tonight and change the washer."

"That much I will do. And I'll pick up a new filter."

"You could have a bite of dinner and stay the night. You'd have a change of clothes. I got your suits all clean and hanging in the closet wrapped in plastic. The room is so neat since I don't sleep there, it's like a shrine. You'd have your privacy, if that concerns you."

"You moved out of our bedroom? Where do you sleep?"

"I put Sammy's bed in the den, since he can't climb the stairs. I sleep on the den couch so he can signal me if he has to go out."

"Sadie, maybe you have to consider that it's time—"

"Don't say it!"

"It sounds like he's suffering. And you're worn out."

"It's not that bad."

"It sounds it. Maybe he should just go peacefully to sleep."

"That's it? That's your best advice?"

"I have to say it. Yes."

"Maybe you got a message from a higher power?"

"Suppose I did. Would you listen to me then?"

"Not likely."

That was his Sadie. No power in heaven or anywhere on earth was likely to faze her. If *she'd* been on the Spanish Steps and was accosted by the Angel Gabriel himself, she'd most likely tell him she'd been born with perfect pitch and had noticed that he blew his horn off-key.

Frobisch told her, "I'll be out tonight. Some time after seven. No dinner."

Sadie answered, "Suit yourself."

They'd bought the house in Kensington when Sima was a baby. It was a brick Georgian colonial set on a rise of ground that sloped to meet an avenue of willows and the flat green of the park. Below them the creek flowed brown and sluggish over outcrops of gray rock. On one side of them was a sprawling glass and wood contemporary with a swimming pool set behind a redwood fence, the De Filippo place. On the other side was open land, a grassy marsh that flooded in the autumn rains and was a stopping place for wondrous colored mallards as well as homelier brown ducks and box turtles.

Frobisch would have passed up the house as too big for the three of them, but Sadie had seen the sign, For Sale by Owner, and prodded him, "Let's take a look."

It was a glorious fall Sunday. He remembered red leaves crunching underfoot. The smell of wood smoke and apple cider. A Norman Rockwell set piece. He'd warned himself he must resist; the setting was too much like theater or a magazine illustration of the good life. The owner of the house was tall and courtly with an aura of old money in the tattered elbows of his sweater, the casual patches on his slacks. He was absorbed in a Redskins game and not terribly interested in a sale. He invited Frobisch to watch the game with him. They'd sat together in the room that would be Frobisch's den—silent in perfect companionship, eating cheese doodles and sipping cokes and watching Jurgensen loft long, amazing passes toward the sun. The owner's wife took Sadie to the kitchen to show off the Spanish tiles, the wide brick hearth, the warm southern exposure, perfect for hanging plants. When Sadie came back into the den, he could tell by the look of her that she was already dreaming, planting chives and basil in a kitchen garden, replacing the pitted cement of the patio with flagstone. Frobisch helped himself to a fistful of cheese doodles and mouthed a solemn "No," which she ignored.

"There's a little boy next door near Sima's age. Maybe a little older. Wouldn't it be nice if they got to be friends?"

Jurgensen had just got sacked, and Frobisch was distracted. He and the owner groaned in concert.

"Howie, I want you to see the upstairs bedrooms."

"After the next play, Sadie."

"Howie, we are intruding on these people's Sunday as it is."

"Nonsense." The owner waved her off. "Let him watch."

At the commercial break he'd followed Sadie up the stairs, noting the frayed treads of carpet, the fingerprints of phantom grandchildren smudging the walls. Sadie pointed out the fine polished mahogany of the banister. "You don't see that anymore," she whispered.

"Sure you do," said Frobisch.

Sadie stopped midway on the landing and turned so suddenly he almost lost his balance and tumbled down the stairs. Light from a porthole window streamed through her hair, transforming her latest champagne blonde to fine white gold. She pressed her body to his as though she meant to forcibly detain him until he came around to her way of thinking. He waited, embarrassed, lest the owners find them tussling on the stair. "Howie, I want this place."

"We don't need four bedrooms, Sadie."

"Sure we do. I could have a music room. You could have a study."

"What would I study?"

"Anything you want."

He'd let her lead him through the bedrooms, even though he'd felt like a voyeur taking furtive peeks into the lives of strangers. Their preference for twin beds. Their taste for *Reader's Digest* condensations. Sadie, who seemed to have no shame, kept up a running commentary on the choice of wallpaper, the awful color of the drapes. She was somewhere beyond him, beyond good manners or tact, talking armoires and country French. Sima would have a four-poster bed with a canopy when she was old enough. Sadie would place an old-fashioned standing Victrola in the music room and play Caruso. Finally she'd taken him to see the master bedroom with its little alcove sitting room and French doors opening to a sun deck. "Go out," she'd urged. "Enjoy the view. I'm going to check out the closets."

He'd been glad to escape her, to stand quiet in the bracing air. He stared into the branches of a copper beech, the leaves like fire in a blaze of sun. Below him a young woman was walking an Irish setter, her hair the same russet as the dog's silken coat. She was wearing a green turtleneck sweater and tan jodhpurs and black boots; she carried a little crop, which she swatted playfully against the dog's slim rump. As Frobisch watched, admiring, she noticed him and waved. He waved back, feeling proprietary, as though the deck, the burnished tree, the sweep of lawn were already his. He knew, of course, it was decided and had been all along. At a point when Jurgensen ran bandy-legged down the field and hefted a mighty bullet, or when the young woman paused and smiled at him, he'd taken title in his mind.

Sadie had come out on the deck. "Well, Howie, what do you think? You like it, don't you? I can tell by looking at you."

"It's a nice house."

"You like it! Oh, Howie, we're going to be so happy here!"

He had followed her into the house, bemused. He wasn't sure if he'd succumbed to his own needs, or Sadie's pleas, or the beauty of a young girl laughing up at him, an aureole of sun framing her face. After they bought the terrier, he took long walks around the neighborhood with a reluctant Gregor Samsa, but he never saw the girl again.

He parked the Volvo in the drive behind Sadie's blue Dart. She was outside working on the lawn, tugging a length of hose and a rusty sprinkler to a dry patch on the grass. She was barefoot, dressed in white duck pants that flared out at the ankles and a red and white striped top with a deep kangaroo pocket that buttoned at her breasts. She had had her hair set, Frobisch noticed, and colored with a silvery rinse. She looked suntanned and fit.

"Let me do that," Frobisch called.

Sadie ignored him and continued tugging at the hose.

Frobisch shut the car door with a slam. He crossed the front lawn slowly, noting the dryness of the grass, the singed look of the white pines. They must have been a long time without rain. He could see beyond Sadie to the De Filippos' lawn where a jet of water from his neighbors' revolving sprinkler swept the sky in a lazy arc and descended like a pointing finger. Frobisch approached Sadie complaining, "The lawn boy cuts the grass too close. In weather this dry you got to leave it taller."

Sadie let the hose drop and confronted him, hands on her hips. "There's nobody here to tell him."

"You're here."

"I got other things to concern me. Did you bring the filter?"

Frobisch smote his brow. "I must be getting simple. It's in the car."

"'Sno hurry."

Frobisch said, "You're looking well."

Sadie patted her hair. "I think she added too much silver. I told her to tone it down some; it was looking brassy 'cause I've been out in the sun, but I think she added too much silver. What do you think?"

"It looks good." In the twenty-four years of their marriage, they had had this conversation once a month over the color of her hair, which had ranged according to fashion from yellow gold to apricot to palest beige.

"I told her I wanted a kind of ash tone, but she made it gray. You think it's aging?"

"Nah," Frobisch told her with conviction. "You're looking good."

"You're not," Sadie said sharply. "You look like you saw a ghost."

"Jet lag," Frobisch said quickly.

"Still with the jet lag? Why'd you go in to work? I thought you were taking a month's vacation."

The truth was he was feeling antsy in the new apartment. He'd meant to spend his free time puttering, hanging hooks, stocking the pantry, lounging in bed. Living the Sybarite's existence. He'd spent his first night home awake and pacing. The floor was cold parquet. The doors squeaked on new hinges. He'd started rearranging the furniture, new stuff he'd picked out in a hurry from Sloan's Clearance Center so he could load it in the Volvo and take it with him. It had struck him suddenly as harsh. Metal and glass. Steely. Too angular. He missed the gently curving wood, the soft-rubbed patina of the older stuff in Kensington. He gave up any thoughts of sleep. His bedroom was a sealed-off box, the only sound the ruthless murmur of the air conditioner recirculating dust.

He thanked God for the pint-sized balcony off the living room where he could sit and watch the lushness of the trees or mark stars flickering like pinpoints in the dark. He could discern the faint shadow of Washington Cathedral on its hill. He'd thought about the boozy priest who loved fast food and had been a chaplain in Korea. The man must spend his sober days endeavoring a dialogue with God; and he, Frobisch, who harbored thoughts of greed and lust, had been selected for some kind of heavenly visitation. He'd spent the night pondering the justice of it. In the morning it was a relief to head for the office.

He told Sadie, "I wanted to check the mail."

Sadie snorted. "Some vacation. C'mon inside. I'll give you a cold drink before you faint."

"The house looks good."

"The shutters need a coat of paint. So does the trim."

"I don't think so."

"Inside and out, the place needs sprucing up. Come in, I'll show you."

She hadn't said a word about the dog. He supposed that she was waiting out of her inherent sense of drama to spring the dying Gregor on him as a shock, startle him with a graphic illustration of the awful trials of age and its infirmities.

"You go on," said Frobisch. "I'll start the sprinkler."

Sadie shrugged and headed up the walk. He stood still for a moment watching her, admiring the way her buttocks jiggled in the too tight pants. She walked like a young girl, dawdling so he could get the full view of her nice round ass, observe the tightness of the cotton over her thighs. His heart ached, remembering Sima plodding ahead of him like an old woman, clutching the furled umbrella as though it were a cane.

"Sima gained a good bit of weight," Frobisch called to Sadie.

"Thank God she's eating," Sadie flung over her shoulder and disappeared into the silence of the house.

Frobisch moved the sprinkler to a patch of sun-browned grass that spread beyond the scant shade of the trees. He had crawled on hands and knees upon this very spot with Sima (adorable in a sky blue leotard that showed the pink flesh of her bottom, the dimpled creases of her thighs) hunting for a four-leaf clover. Watching them, the dog, Gregor, had sat tethered to a tree panting in some secret excitement. From time to time the terrier raised his muzzle to the breeze, exulting in the wave of scents—new grass, wet earth, and bird shit all in a mix heady enough to induce wobbling doggy drunkenness. If Frobisch had released him, Gregor would have bounded upward in a series of wild jumps. Like a stuffed toy propelled by springs, the dog would leap out of sheer exuberance—a mad, four-footed Nijinsky. Frobisch deplored these moves; the wasted energy seemed dumb.

He'd once questioned Sadie, "Why does he do that?"

And she'd replied, "Characteristic of the breed."

The wild jumps served no purpose except to make Sima laugh. When she'd complained that day on the grass that she couldn't find any lucky clover, Frobisch, duplicitous with love, had covertly ripped apart some stems and fashioned a bogus plant bearing four leaves.

"Here's one, sweet. How's that for luck?"

She'd viewed him suspiciously, eyes bright with un-shed tears. Oh, she was wise beyond her years, his Sima! "It's not right!" Her voice had signaled she was treading a fine line between anguish and hysteria.

"Now, now," had cautioned Frobisch. Sadie always complained that the child got too overwrought when she played with him. "What's wrong with it?" begged Frobisch.

Sima had flung his offering on the grass in a fine show of temper. As if on cue, Gregor had strained at his leash, barking his rancor.

Frobisch kicked at the sprinkler, overwhelmed by

sadness, thudding memories of defeat. If he'da got loose he'd've bit me, Frobisch thought.

"You going to be all night?" Sadie stood in the doorway framed by the glow of the hall light. Her breasts were firm under the kangaroo pocket. She stood posing sideways, a model's stance she often adopted at their closet mirror. *Am I sagging, Howie? Do I show my age?* Sometimes he woke to find her naked before the mirror, hunting for telltale signs of cancer.

Frobisch called, "Just a minute," and bent stiffly to turn on the sprinkler. The sky, which had bristled yellow heat long into evening, had dulled to streaky pewter. A mockingbird pealed a song, piercingly sweet, to the moon. Frobisch walked slowly to the car like an invalid who is just testing his legs after a bout in bed. The awful sensitivity he'd noted on the plane had heightened his perceptions. He marked the first cracks in the concrete of the drive, dust coating the dull leaves of the rhododendron, the trails of ants ending the business of the working day. The sideward motion of a spider caught his eye and jarred his nerves as though each movement of an insect leg were a heavy footfall. The curved arc of his neighbor's sprinkler glistened iridescent drops. His gaze moved to the grass. If there had been any to find he would have spotted a four-leaf clover easily tonight. He wondered what earthly good was a talent for discerning minutiae when the larger problems went unsolved. His accountant's soul should revel in detail, *did* revel in the orderliness of numbers. But what he craved now was more perfect order, all the segments of his life neatly in their proper place.

He retrieved his bag of washers and the furnace filter from the car. Slowly he trudged to the front walk, reflecting, I am not happy to be here. What I feel is neither kind nor charitable. Nothing good comes of my spending time with Sadie. What I want is to escape. Why can't she accept that?

She had vanished from her post at the front door. The center hall stood empty, gleaming with yellow light. Frobisch brushed aside a pair of pale-winged moths that had clustered on the screen door, attracted by the inside lights. They had papery, fan-shaped wings that fluttered, tremulous as beating hearts. One moth took off; the other stayed fixed on the screen, splayed like an impaled specimen. Frobisch resisted the urge to squash it. He thought of Sadie's confrontation with the bat skimming the trees that grew beside the creek. Shivering, he strode into the warm light of the hall.

He took his time changing the washer. It felt good to be handling tools. When he'd plodded downstairs to the cellar in his stocking feet (Sadie had warned, "Don't track grass into the house.") to turn off the main water valve behind the freezer, he'd discovered himself humming happily. He had been a conscientious householder in his time. He liked to make up neat lists of his obligations and tick them off with check marks as they were done. It pleased him to respond with military precision to his own commands.

*Clean gutters*, he would order himself on paper; and as the task was finished he would write with intense satisfaction beside his check mark, *Gutters cleaned*. Frobisch shivered, recalling the pleasures of his list:

| | |
|---|---|
| Chop wood | Wood chopped |
| Plant bulbs | Bulbs planted |
| Soak humidifier in vinegar | Done and done and done |

Frobisch found the water valve and turned it with some difficulty. Overhead, from the kitchen, he could hear Sadie's complaint. "What have you done? The water's stopped."

"It'll be just a coupla minutes," Frobisch called. Some perverted sense of curiosity made him peek into the freezer. He was surprised to find it stocked with steak and hamburger and cut-up chickens, as well as plastic containers of cooked food labeled with masking tape. Who was she cooking for? He spotted what looked to be a round cake encased in foil and tagged. He squinted to read the label: Howie's Birthday Cake. Guilty, he slammed the door shut and hurried to his tasks.

After he had replaced the washer, Frobisch attacked the filter. He had some trouble taking off the furnace plate. When he had exposed the old filter, he scanned the cellar Peg-Board looking for his gardening gloves. They were not on the peg where he had left them.

"Damn!" Frobisch exclaimed.

Experience had taught him never to touch the filter without wearing gloves or he would get painful strands of fiberglass in his fingers.

"Howie, I need the water," Sadie called.

"Just a second," Frobisch hollered. Hurriedly he turned the valve to On. He could hear Sadie's startled scream as the kitchen faucet exploded in a sudden gush.

"Howie, could you c'mere?"

"I'm just changing the filter."

"Can it wait? I need a hand."

"Two more minutes."

"Now!"

The woman could give ulcers to a saint. "Keep your

pants on!" Frobisch called. He started working on the filter without bothering to find the gloves.

In the kitchen Sadie removed a tray of hypodermic needles from the refrigerator. Frobisch counted five needles in the tray, each encased in its own sheath of lavender plastic. Sadie rattled the tray as though it were a tambourine and set it on the table. She selected a needle and expertly broke the plastic casing. Then she held the needle to the light. "C'mere, Sammy," Sadie murmured.

The dog lay on its side at Sadie's feet. Only the quivering of one paw, an odd tetany Frobisch had never seen, gave any indication it was alive. Sadie bent over to prop the terrier on its haunches. "Sit," she commanded. The dog flopped on its side. "Help me, Howie," she pleaded.

Frobisch drummed his fingers on the kitchen table and winced in pain. Some of the fiberglass particles must have pierced his hand. He felt the worst soreness in the fleshy ball of the thumb. It would take days, maybe weeks, for the offending particles to work their way to the surface of the skin. Every time he grasped an object he would have a painful recollection of this night. "Damn and damn again!" said Frobisch. "What was the big hurry to get me upstairs?" He licked his painful thumb.

"So you could help me with Sammy. Come on, Howie, give a hand."

"No way. That dog would bite me with his dying breath. Listen to him growl."

"He's growling 'cause he doesn't want his shot. Isn't it something that we should come to this? Would you think that I could do it? I told Van Zandt I couldn't; but he said you got to. If you don't want the animal to suffer."

"Who is Van Zandt?"

"Dummy. You know. The vet. Dieter Van Zandt. It's a funny name. I think he's Dutch."

Frobisch believed she'd said, "He's in Dutch," and told himself not to question why. Whatever troubles plagued the vet, Frobisch didn't want to hear them. His thumb smarted cruelly. He considered asking Sadie if she'd fetch him some Neosporin and a Band-Aid and then thought better of it. In spite of her attentiveness to Gregor, she was not a willing nurse.

During Sima's bouts with childhood illness it was he who had camped by her bed, keeping anxious all-night vigils. Sadie told him it was nuts the way he read calamity in every childish cough. But how, he asked, could he sleep when his darling might choke on her own phlegm or suffer burns from the vaporizer's steam or wake up frightened from a dream of ghosts?

"It's you who'll look like a ghost to her," Sadie had said. And this was true. Stubble-cheeked, in creased pajamas, and bent from lying on the floor, he must have looked like a frightening apparition to Sima in the night. If he slept, he was plagued by erotic dreams. He was the willing prisoner in a seraglio. Veiled women caressed him with their tongues. He was sprawled supine in an open boat. Naked girls with upper bodies of astounding muscularity plied the oars. He didn't know what caused his lurid dreams only on nights that he tossed cold and fretful on the floor, wrapped in an old quilt. Maybe he took joy in discomfort, like some half-mad anchorite finding pleasure in the scourge.

On one of those painful nights Frobisch woke to the sound of heavy panting and the sight of staring eyes. There was a dead weight on his chest. For the sake of sleeping Sima, he resisted the urge to cry out. He ordered himself to stay calm, to breathe deep breaths; as he did so he inhaled a familiar musty odor. Gregor's breath! Gregor! That lousy Gregor, that idiot, mange-ridden mutt who would neither come when Frobisch called nor eat from his hand was sitting on his master's chest contemplating him as though he meant to bite a choice segment of jugular. The dog's eyes gleamed yellow in the dark. His breath stank of rotting fish and bile.

"Get off me, you bastard," Frobisch whispered.

The dog sat immobile.

"Get off," threatened Frobisch, "or I'll have you altered!"

Gregor uttered a low growl but didn't budge.

Frobisch lost all sense of caution and struck out with his palm. He connected with the terrier's muzzle and felt the sharpness of a jutting canine tooth. Frobisch swore in pain, "Goddamn bastard tried to bite me."

Taking his own sweet time Gregor cleared Frobisch's body with a bound. The dog's dark shape melded quickly with the shadows. Frobisch heard the jangling of the terrier's collar tags as it retreated to the hall. Sima whimpered in her sleep. For a long time Frobisch lay awake seeing menace in the homely objects of his daughter's room. The vaporizer hissed rank steam. Silhouettes of Alice and the Red Queen leered cruelly from the wall.

The next morning he'd told Sadie about the incident with Gregor.

She'd answered calmly, "He probably needed to go out and didn't want to disturb me."

Frobisch had set down his coffee cup and regarded her

with a long incredulous stare. "You invest in that creature the ability to have rational thought?"

"You say he wanted to bite you. That's not thinking?"

"I don't know what he wanted to do. I said he startled me, is all." And they had dropped it, as Frobisch had known they must. For if she said Gregor was cute and wasn't it a funny thing to do, it would be mandatory for him to hit her, and he had never hit a woman in his life.

Sadie had propped the ailing terrier to a sitting position. She held the needle firmly and said, "Now watch." She was wearing one of her summer lipsticks, a glossy bronze that looked like metal paint. She had on eye makeup, too, and some kind of blusher on her cheeks that added the high color of fever to her tan. Frobisch wondered if she had gotten fancied up for him.

"There's a heavy fold of skin back of the neck. You hold it like so." Sadie demonstrated. "Then you insert the needle." She plunged the sharp point of the hypodermic into the fold of Gregor's skin. The dog sat unblinking. "If you do it right, he doesn't feel a thing. The first time I did it, the needle went right through the fold of skin instead of into the muscle, and the medicine spurted across the kitchen. I thought I'd die! Sammy just sat there looking at me as though he knew I was a fool."

Frobisch stared at the tray of needles. "You do this every day?"

"Once a day around dinner. In the morning we go to the vet's for his I.V. feeding."

"And on the weekend?"

"On the weekend, too."

"The vet stays open?"

"Half a day on Saturday. Sunday he sees us because

we're a special case." Sadie gestured to the dog who still sat, panting, as though he knew he had to face further indignities. "Now I've got to give him his eye drops."

"Phew, Sadie. This really is a bit much, don't you think?"

Sadie was weeping softly. The tears were tracing glistening channels in the bright red of her cheeks. "Well, it's not easy."

"I wish I could help you."

"You could. If you stayed over tonight, you could take him to the vet's tomorrow. I could sleep in for a change and then get going on some errands."

"Tomorrow's Saturday?"

"Yes, it is." Sadie summoned some of her customary feistiness. "All day."

She had started up the air conditioning again after he'd replaced the filter. Frobisch was shivering. He ought to tell her that she kept the house too cold. It was a flagrant waste of energy setting the temperature so low. The kitchen felt like winter. "You want me to sleep over tonight and take him?" he repeated dully.

"I don't like to ask."

Frobisch had stopped gnawing on his thumb. His mouth retained a sour taste. "Does it have to be me?"

"Who else is there to take him?" Sadie flared.

She had flung the used hypodermic into the trash. Now she was standing in her diva pose, swaying a bit, hands planted firmly on her hips. Frobisch had the crazy notion she might start to sing. She had a strong, untrained soprano, which she would demonstrate to anyone who asked. She loved to show her depth of range, the absolute precision of her pitch. She sang at funerals, at weddings, at PTA's—a display of exhibitionism that always made him want to run. He thought, if she starts the "Habanera" I'm going to bolt.

"Do I often bother you for favors? I haven't asked you for a goddamned thing except to fix the filter and one leaky faucet!"

"Which I did. Consider my obligations done."

"Don't start! Oh, don't start on the subject of your obligations!"

"Listen," cried Frobisch, "I didn't come out here to fight!"

Sadie laughed an octave's length of mirthless notes. "Well, that would be a change. The generosity of your spirit leaves me breathless. Catch me! I'm going to faint!"

It *was* an urge to generosity. Either she'd shamed him with the hidden birthday cake or the angel lurked in the shadows pulling strings. "If it means so much to you, I'll stay, though I'll be frank, I don't like it. It doesn't seem quite proper, d'you know?"

"You think I'll attack you in the night? Don't worry. Your virtue's safe."

Frobisch stood up. "It's getting dark. I'm going to turn off the sprinkler."

"You want a bite to eat?" Knowing he would stay, Sadie had softened her tough stance. "I got egg salad. Tuna."

"Nothing."

"I make a special plate. Little cherry tomatoes, chopped green pepper, a sprinkling of fresh mint."

"I know your specials, Sadie." She could still seduce him with her summer salads. Mounds of purple cabbage diced with sweet red onion bits; fans of crimson beets flavored with orange zest. And to go with them, her rolls! He felt the saliva rising at the memory, golden shells whorled with lines of cinnamon and nuts and nuggets of golden raisins that shocked you with their sudden sweetness. God knew what ammunition she had stashed away in rows of Tupperware in the pantry! "Thanks," said Frobisch. "Finish what you have to do with Gregor. I don't want food."

He moved slowly from the kitchen table, feeling the peculiarity in his limbs, the sense his feet were shod in lead.

"Nothing?" persisted Sadie. "Maybe a soda?"

"Nothing. Listen, we settled it. I'll stay the night. Make up the sofa in the den for me, will you?"

"The sofa in the den? Just like old times." Still operatic, she clutched both palms to her breasts. The kangaroo pocket rose and fell as though she were gathering breath to belt out a closing aria. Tosca on the battlements. He'd have to duck.

The grass had taken a good soaking. Frobisch walked gingerly across the spongy turf, resisting the urge to kick off his loafers and feel the cool ooze through his socks. His knee still felt sore from the incident in Rome. It was a dull pain, persistent as a toothache, a nagging reminder of what had happened on the Spanish Steps. Sometimes he could go for hours without remembering. Then there were times, as now, in the half-light of early evening, when the presence of something ineffable seemed so close it scared him silly. He didn't believe in ghosts, nor did he disbelieve. There had been nights during Sima's childhood when she had awakened to complain of bogeymen in the closet. Hurrying to console her, he had shared her fear. He'd peeked amid the pale smocked dresses hanging so stiffly on their padded hangers and felt the certainty something was there. The same feeling he'd had in Rome.

Someone was watching him from the curb. A tall form lounged against a car, one leg braced against the trunk of a pin oak. Limping to favor his sore knee, Frobisch moved cautiously through the shadows. His fists were clenched tight in the pockets of his pants.

"'Lo, Mr. Frobisch. Long time no see." The youth who moved to greet him had his arm outstretched. Frobisch could see in the brief and sudden explosion of the streetlight the steel blade of a penknife.

"Who's that?" He cursed himself for the trembling in his voice.

"'Sme, Mr. Frobisch. Randy. The De Filippo kid."

"Randy De Filippo!" The knife should have told him. His neighbor's son had been a comely youth who had spent most of a pointless adolescence standing in the yard flinging a penknife into the grass. A steady, mindless habit, it had seemed harmless enough until one day Sadie mentioned that the boy was frightening Sima. Huffing with embarrassment, Frobisch had gone next door to complain. Some time after that Randy dropped out of sight. There was a rumor he was in a school for wayward boys. Frobisch had worried that he'd had some hand in the boy's fate. Did fooling with a penknife land you in reform school? Frobisch squinted into the lowering darkness. "Gee, Randy, you've grown."

Randy flung his knife into the grass with the ease born of practice. He seized Frobisch's offered hand and pumped it hard. "Grew some and got gruesome, didn't I, Mr. Frobisch?"

The kid was right. He'd been the sort of child one sees in religious paintings—a cherub's face with puffy cheeks and a smile of dimpled innocence. When he was small his mother had dressed him in starched white playsuits and high white socks and sandals that were always gleaming fresh with polish. He seemed always to be going to or coming from Communion. One day Frobisch had caught him urinating into Sima's sandbox and had had to reprimand him. "Cats do that, Randy. Not children."

Randy had whipped his little dong inside his pants and said, "Fuck you," with such startling swiftness that Frobisch had to laugh, whereupon the little bastard had picked up a fistful of sand and flung it in Frobisch's face.

Frobisch gave Randy's hand an extra hearty shake to prove he bore no rancor. He peered at Randy in the dark, marveling that in the perfect cocoon of the child's body had lurked this tall, ungainly man dressed in frayed jeans and a stained T-shirt and a black wool watch cap pulled low over his ears. Frobisch pointed to the hat. "Aren't you warm in that?"

The boy's smile was sad. "Gotta cover the haircut, y'know?"

Frobisch, nodding as though he understood, wondered what jail or halfway house had meted punishment by shearing Randy's hair. It was a standard penalty these days. Barbaric, Frobisch thought, but not without its precedent in history. Like hacking off a limb. He was for once glad Sima was in Israel, spared Randy with his glinting penknife and the aura of a darker past.

Frobisch pretended interest. "Doesn't it itch in weather like this?"

Randy considered this as though it were a philosophic statement worthy of argument. "Not too bad. Better than looking bald."

Frobisch patted his thinning topknot sadly. "You got a point."

"Hey, you're still all right, Mr. Frobisch. You're still a fox."

"A graying fox, Randy." Frobisch leaned against the car in an effort to be companionable. "Nice of you to say so, though."

Randy bent over and scooped his knife from the grass. He offered it to Frobisch. "Want a chance?" Fireflies were flickering in the dark. In the first glow of moonlight Randy's face looked intent, earnest, as though in offering this gift he were a supplicant.

"I don't mind," said Frobisch. He weighed the penknife in his palm, testing the heft. Then he flung it blindly downward. It struck cement and clattered to the gutter.

"Hit the curb," said Randy. "Try again."

"Nah," Frobisch demurred. "The way my luck is going these days, I'll cut off my toe."

"G'wan, try it, Mr. Frobisch."

Frobisch took the knife and let it drop. He heard a satisfying thunk as the blade sank into the soft grass. "Where is it? I don't see it." He searched the ground.

Randy moved in on the knife as though he had a homing device. "You wan' another try?"

"Your turn," said Frobisch.

Randy laughed and threw the knife. " 'S fun," he said to Frobisch.

"So it is. Thank you for letting me try it."

"No sweat." With the darting swiftness of an insect Randy had retrieved the knife. He surveyed the blade as though it were an artifact discovered in the dirt. Frobisch watched him sadly.

"I got myself into some heavy trouble, Mr. Frobisch, y'know?"

"Sorry to hear it, Randy."

"I got myself into self-defeatin' habits."

"We all do that."

"I'm doin' better, though."

"I'm glad." Frobisch's voice resounded with false cheer. "Keep it up. You'll make it. I'm convinced."

Randy seemed embarrassed by Frobisch's declaration of faith. Sighing, he wiped the knife blade on his shirt.

Frobisch slapped at a mosquito on his neck. The bushes buzzed with insect sounds. Beyond a distant hedge a die-hard gardener coaxed the last burst of speed from a power mower. "Well, I just came out to turn off the sprinkler," Frobisch said. "Keep up the good work," he advised Randy.

"Yeah, I will." Randy rotated the knife from palm to palm as though it were a hot potato. Frobisch watched warily. He was not completely certain Randy wouldn't attack.

Still contemplating the knife, Randy asked, "How's Sima?"

"She's fine. She's fine," Frobisch said quickly. "She's on a trip. She's very far away and will be for some time."

"Izzat a fact?"

"No telling how long it will be." Without waiting for Randy's response, Frobisch turned back to the house. Careful to avoid the spongy grass, he trod slowly upon the slippery flagstones of the path.

Finally, half lying on the den sleep sofa, which Sadie had had re-covered in some kind of itchy tweed, he could massage his injured knee. Sadie had brought him a pair of fresh pajamas, never worn. He'd had to carefully un-wrap the layers of tissue, remove the pins. "When did I

buy these?" he asked her. Deep pink with dark blue pip-
ing. They were not his style.

"I bought 'em," said Sadie grimly. "Belated Father's
Day. Go put them on."

"Well, thanks," Frobisch exclaimed, still fingering the
pins. He had not thought to get her anything for Mother's
Day. He wouldn't have thought such customs remained
after a divorce. He supposed Sadie would argue that
although they no longer shared domestic bliss they were
still mother and father to Sima. Who had ignored the
whole dumb thing. "I do thank you for the thought,"
Frobisch told Sadie.

She had changed into a frilly housecoat he had never
seen—white eyelet with a border of deep ruffles.

"Fancy," Frobisch remarked.

"Some men like femininity in women," Sadie said.

"Some men?"

"Maybe you ought to know, I'm seeing someone,"
Sadie said. She was bending to caress the dog, who lay inert
in his wicker bed—a frail collage of matted hair and bone,
mouth already stretched in deathlike rictus. It barely
breathed. When Frobisch first entered the room he had
recoiled—his instant thought: do I have to sleep here with
that presence? Death hovered in the room like smoke.

Frobisch pondered Sadie's news, debating the politics
of the moment. There were no protocols he knew for
divorced couples. Maybe someone should write a book
spelling out the rituals as rigidly as one described the
mating dance. "I'm happy for you, Sadie. And"—he offered her a gallantry—"I'm not surprised."

"There's no earthly reason I have to tell you."

"True. Certainly true." He cupped the pins he'd taken
from his new pajamas gingerly in his palm. He wasn't sure

how to react. She would interpret his calm as indifference. Was he indifferent? He imagined the trappings of their house (his house as well as hers, no matter what the lawyers said!) falling to a stranger by default. Worse, Sima calling some interloper Daddy. Buying him new pajamas. The question of whether or not he cared depended on how far things had gone. If Sadie was enjoying a simple flirtation, he wished her well. If, however, she was getting serious—

"Don't ask for any more details," Sadie warned.

Frobisch agreed. "I won't presume. You're entitled to your privacy."

She was stroking the dog as though it were a sleeping baby. "I never thought he'd come to this." Her voice was choked with tears. "Isn't it something that he should be this bad?"

"He's pretty far gone, I'd say."

"Where there's life."

"Oh, true; that's true." Frobisch contemplated a test. What if he laid on hands? If he achieved some minor miracle (Gregor's imminent passing he could not regard as major), might he win certain points with Sadie? A lessening of the guilt that filled the room, clouded the air between them? He considered asking her, "If I cure the dog will you let me off the hook? Stop zapping me about the failure of my obligations?" He imagined her incredulity, her immediate response—"Have you been hitting the sauce, Howie?"—followed by his careful disclaimer: "Mind you, I don't promise anything. It's an experiment, is all. It's not a parlor trick."

"But if it worked, how would I explain it?" Frobisch surprised himself by speaking aloud.

"What's that supposed to mean?" asked Sadie.

"What? Nothing. It means I'm tired, is all."

"You ought to walk him one more time before you turn in." Bending to the dog, she was a tearful Pietà in fluffy eyelet. She stroked its head. At last she stood up, moving stiffly. Characteristically she ran her palms over her hips, smoothing the crumpled ruffles of her robe. She fished in one pocket for a Kleenex and dabbed it to her eyes.

Frobisch was astonished at the extent of her grief. If he were laid out in intensive care, would she weep over his dying carcass, bend so tenderly to stroke his hair?

"Sadie, dearest Sadie, don't take it so hard." Frobisch held out his hand. "C'mere; come sit by me. We'll talk."

She surprised him by coming meekly to his side. Frobisch moved his stiff leg to make room for her. He was still holding the pins from his new pajamas. He dropped them into an ashtray, a rainbow-striped saucer of glass they'd bought in Venice. The day they found it Sadie had been done up like a gondolier in a wide-brimmed straw hat and a sailor shirt. There were pictures somewhere that he'd taken of her posing near a gondola at the dock. He had liked Venice because they could travel everywhere by water. The Pamplemousse had been stashed mercifully in the public garage. Frobisch asked, "Do you remember Italy?"

Sadie nodded glumly. Imperceptibly she leaned toward him. She was still dabbing the tissue to her eyes.

Frobisch slipped one arm around her shoulders. Sadie relaxed against him with a little sigh. She was wearing a nice perfume, something like jasmine. Frobisch smoothed the fragrant nape of Sadie's neck. He knew better than to touch her lacquered hair. "You feel all tense," he said. "The muscles are knotted." He ran his fingers lightly down Sadie's spine. "Center of all feeling," Frobisch said.

Sadie murmured, "That feels nice."

"Does it relax you?"

"More or less."

He continued to caress her back. Her body was as familiar to him as his own. He knew the softness of her breasts, the little dark mole on one that always scared her into thinking she had cancer. He knew the way her nipples were quick to rise when he teased them with his tongue. Her belly with the pink slash from her cesarean. He caressed her without desire, only an overpowering urge to tenderness, a need, stronger than lust, to give her comfort. "Sadie," Frobisch said softly, "when I was in Rome, something happened that I want to tell you about."

Sadie laughed. "Was she nice?" She had let her hand rest absently on his zipper. Gently, as though it were a moth, he brushed it away.

"Nothing like that."

"Nothing like what?" Her hand hovered for a moment and rested on his fly.

"Don't do that, Sadie! I mean it. Don't do it!" With difficulty because of his sore knee, he struggled from the sofa. In his hurry to get up, he knocked over the Venetian ashtray. Pins scattered on the floor.

Sadie cried, "I see you're too fragile to touch there. You must have had some good time in Rome!"

He didn't want to walk barefoot in the night and tread on pins. He fell to his knees to hunt for them. The pressure on his sore leg made him wince. "Will you help me?" Frobisch asked. "I dropped the pins."

"I hope you sit on 'em," said Sadie.

Frobisch turned to her with both hands clasped. It was a gesture reminiscent of his strange moment in Rome. As he had implored meaning from the angel, he implored

Sadie to understand. "Sadie, don't feel bad. This sort of thing shouldn't happen between us. We are divorced."

"Listen, Mr. Smart Guy, if you didn't want it to happen between us, why were you loving me up?"

"I thought I was giving comfort. You were in grief."

Sadie bent forward to peer at him as though she had to assure herself that he was real. As she leaned forward, her robe parted. He could see the deep crease between her breasts, the white flesh rising as she breathed, the darker puckered skin around her nipples.

"Sadie, darling Sadie," Frobisch said.

"Listen, you turkey, don't you ever—not ever—not for a million years, ever say, 'Sadie, darling Sadie,' to me again! Don't you ever touch me with your filthy hands!"

"If you don't wish it, Sadie."

"I don't wish it. After tonight I don't wish you in my house!"

In an ill-timed move he touched her knee. Sadie swatted his arm away as though it were a fly. "I mean it, Howie. You make one more move on me, I'll have you charged with rape!"

"Sadie, I won't touch you. I wouldn't hurt you. I couldn't hurt you. I'm sorry we can't make love. It's not you, it's me. I've told you that often enough."

"Oh, it's you all right, as though I didn't know that."

"There's something happening in my life. A change."

"A change, is it?"

"I started to tell you. Something has happened. It scares me. More than death it scares me. I don't know what it means, but it frightens me so much sometimes I can hardly breathe. I pace the floor at night, thinking what I think and knowing what I know. It's awful what I know. Sadie,

I could tell you right now, without equivocation, Gregor's going to die."

"Turkey! You think I don't know that?"

"But not just Gregor. I could tell you other things."

"You know what I think? I think you're crazy! Bona fide, certifiably nuts!"

He was still kneeling. The pain in one knee made him dizzy. "I don't blame you for thinking that. If you would just help me get up, I could explain—"

"I don't want your explanations. I don't care if you spend the night crawling on your knees." Sadie straightened to her full height. The robe swung open, revealing the flesh of her upper leg. Frobisch, who was beyond caution, clasped her legs and buried his head deep between her thighs. He began to kiss her through the stiffly ruffled eyelet.

Sadie gasped, "You bastard!"

"Sadie, don't leave me," Frobisch begged. "I'm scared!"

For a moment Sadie wavered as though she found the kissing pleasant. Then she hit him with her open palm just over his bad ear. Frobisch hollered, "Ouch! What did you do? You got my bad ear!" He fell over in a heap. The sharp point of a pin grazed his cheek. "Help me," he begged. "I'm bleeding."

Sadie said, "Good. I'm glad you're bleeding. I hope you bleed to death all night. The reason I hope it is because you are a no-good bastard and crazy to boot! I'm lucky to be rid of you!"

He heard the rustling of her robe as she stepped around him. He lay still, fearing she would hit him if he sat up. The carpet was rough against his scratched cheek. When he was sure that she had gone, he struggled to his knees and clasped his hands.

"You see me, Lord, hurt and afraid, amid a shower of pins, with a painful knee and a bleeding face, an ex-wife and a dog who hate me. What is it You want of me? Why have You chosen me to hear Your voice?"

He squeezed his eyes shut in terror he would be answered. There was a tinny, painful ringing in his ear. He could hear Sadie moving through the house, slamming doors. In its wicker bed beside the sofa the dying terrier whimpered in its sleep.

It was like a no-man's-land of slippery sheets. The double bed. She imagined it was going to tilt and she would slide, like some hapless climber, into the abyss. She lay square in the middle, fearing the least move would fling her from a fragile precipice. After so many nights on the den sofa, she was uncomfortable with all this space. It was a big bed, not meant for sleeping alone. She had her side; he had his. When they met in this icy middle, it was for giving and receiving pleasure. She had provided him some comfort in her time. Now that she was sagging, finding wrinkles in the once firm flesh, he had lost interest. He had even bragged about finding somebody in Rome. Sadie wept. "That turkey." The tears coursed in a salt stream into the pillow. Impatiently, she brushed them from her cheeks with doubled fists. He was not worth her grief. Imagine, he had had the nerve to kiss her, to diddle his fingers down her spine and then react like a frightened virgin when she responded.

Well, she was no old, dried-out husk. Dieter had told her she was handsome. He had looked at her with his solemn spaniel eyes as though the force of his deep need robbed him of speech. He was like one of his suffering animals, showing his pain with sighs and movements. So far, she had opted not to understand. But there'd come a time. Oh, there might well come a time. She sighed. Kissing her there, Howie had aroused her. She'd felt her breasts grow taut; she'd felt dizzy, boozy, melting with the need to hold him. Her own husband for twenty-four good years (discounting the time that he turned crazy) and he acted like some prissy twit. Don't do that! It made her laugh. That was it, she should be laughing, not lying here like a sniveling kid abandoned by her first real crush. But she had loved him, and she had given herself to him so willingly. Why could he not love her back? "Am I so old and ugly?" she said aloud. She ran her hands down her body, feeling the fullness of her breasts, the soft flesh of her belly bisected by the wide raised scar. They were a lot neater these days with cesareans. They did a horizontal slash instead of that awful vertical incision. Women could show up on the beach in bikinis and nothing showed. Not that she would wear a bikini ever; it was unseemly in a woman her age. But she wasn't old. The blood still flowed; sure as the clock's ticking, every month—she could set her watch by her body's regularity. A waste. All those eggs manufactured and sloughed off. She'd been pregnant once; she would not ever repeat it. She had told him so.

She shuddered on the icy sheet, remembering Sima's birth. That night there'd been the worst blizzard of the winter. Howie had come to see her while she was in labor, and she had stared at him through a haze of pain and seen the large white flakes melting on his coat collar, the wet, glistening pinpoints in his hair. She'd been crazy with pain, confused to see him in his coat with that dusting of white over his shoulders, melting as he sat beside her. She'd thought it was dandruff. "Don't ever show yourself in public in that state," she'd told him.

He'd squeezed her hand, murmured, "Sadie, poor darling Sadie."

"No, Howie, I mean it," she had told him between contractions. "There are shampoos for that kind of thing. Very effective." He'd held her hand so hard that she had cried in pain, or maybe it was just the building contraction, the hurt that rose up in a wave and broke with so much fury, threatening to drown her. She'd pulled him close. "Listen." Her lips were cracked. She'd begged for water and he had offered ice—melting like the wet pinpoints of snow dotting his hair, his coat collar. Every time she thought she tasted it, it turned to slush and left her thirstier than before. "Listen," she'd told him hoarsely, "never again. Not ever."

"What's that, darling Sadie?" he had asked.

"No more after this. I don't care, girl or boy. Never again."

"What, never?" His voice had risen in a whine. The bastard, already complaining. He wanted more. Well, let *him* try it. Let *him* lie there with his insides bursting, and *she'd* do the bedside vigil. Only she'd have the sense not to go out without shampooing her hair. "Promise," she'd asked him. "Promise there'll be no more."

"What are you saying, darling? You'll change your mind."

And she had wailed—oh, she had keened—the way old women do who've lost their loved ones in a war. Lord, she had screamed so that the young, fat nurse—sleepy-eyed with floppy boobs and a bad bleach job—had come running, waving her stethoscope like a weapon. "Promise!"

"All right, darling. I promise."

"Swear it," she'd panted. "Swear to me: Sadie, there'll be no more."

He'd turned, imploring, to the nurse who was wielding the black snake of the stethoscope somewhere near her straining gut. Pulling the sheet away the nurse put the cold thing to her belly and bent low, listening as one listens to the earth for the distant rumbles of a quake. Oh, she was rumbling; she was breaking up. "Understand this," panted Sadie. "I can't stand a moment more."

"Soon it will be over," he promised; and the snow was gone, and he was standing in a melting puddle, dabbing his eyes.

She screamed again, "You have to swear!"

And he had sworn there would be only one. Maybe that was it, thought Sadie, inert in the cold smooth bed. Maybe he'd resented her all these years for not wanting to have any more after Sima. But that was enough. Twenty hours in labor, and then the assholes told her they would have to cut. Cut away! She was flying by then. Babbling about snow and dandruff. Only she'd had the sense to beg them, "Tie my tubes. While you're about it, fix it so I can't have any more."

And the assholes had refused! Told her flatly, no. You're out of your head; you'll think better of it when this is over, when you hold your baby in your arms. You're a young woman, Sadie. You'll want more.

But she hadn't. She'd had Sima, perfect Sima, and it was enough. And she would never drown in waves of pain again, never lie helpless while Big Boobs palpated her private parts and thrust the cold cup of the stethoscope into her belly. They wouldn't do it! What a waste. Every

month the overflowing rush of blood and nothing to do
about it. Now there was Dieter, too shy to ask, and sooner
or later she must make up her mind. What did you do—
at her age and having to say, "Excuse me, please; I have
to go and put my diaphragm in place." If she worked it
out beforehand, if she came prepared, he would know
she'd planned a seduction. She would be ashamed if he
believed she had succumbed to him without spontaneity.
Oh, but she *was* ashamed. A woman who cherished fidel-
ity planning an affair with another man because her own
husband didn't want her. Never mind what the decree
said, he was her husband still. She had married him
forever; not for a two-week lark, not for a brief roll in the
hay and a new adventure the next week. What was happening in this life? Vows of loyalty meant nothing. Words
of love got flung aside. She loved Howie, loved Sima, loved
Sammy—forever, not temporarily. And she was losing
each in turn. What if she and Howie had had another
baby? Would he have thought better of her? Would he
have not drifted away? No, it wasn't that; it was her body
getting older. He had found someone in Rome. "But it's
not time," wept Sadie. The juices flowed. He had kissed
her—had the gall to kiss her there; and she had grown
dizzy, would have let him have her then and there on the
floor by Sammy's bed while the poor sweet darling
whimpered in his sleep. She heard rustlings on the stair,
the sound of someone taking off the door chain. She
thought, he's walking Sammy. And she fell asleep.

The terrier woke him by scratching against the wicker
bed. A sound like fingernails scraping against a black-
board. Enough to set his teeth on edge. The fool vet—

what was his name, Van-something—should have had the
sense to clip the poor mutt's nails. It was a mean job trying to do that, Frobisch knew. He had done it once and
had cut too close to the quick; the dog had bled in terrifying spurts as though Frobisch had cut an artery. He'd
yelled to Sadie to bring some ice. The fool dog had sat there
looking reproachful, spurting blood. It was as though the
bleeding was something he did for spite.

In the dark Frobisch groped for his pants. He pulled
them on over the silky pink pajamas and left the fly unzipped. The dog's scramblings sounded urgent, as though
he might have to drop a load somewhere on Sadie's gold
shag carpet. The den had doors of sliding glass that opened
to a backyard patio. Sadie would raise hell if he let the
mutt perform out there. Frobisch thrust his bare feet into
his tasseled loafers. "Keep a tight asshole, Gregor," he advised. He couldn't find the goddam leash and finally had
to scoop the terrier up under his arm. There was nothing
to him. It was frightening to feel the fragility of his bones,
the thinness of his matted hair. Frobisch hurried to the
front door, cursing Sadie for her sentimentality. The dog
should have been filling glue pots weeks ago. What was
this crap with I.V. feedings, daily shots? It gave Sadie a
hobby—that was the gist of it.

The heat hit him like an assault. He felt as though he
and the dog were walking under water, plodding a dim
subterranean world of shadowy plants and waving
branches. The moon blazed bright as phosphorous, then
dimmed behind a cloud. Small stars flickered like lumines-
cent fish against a sea of black. He set the terrier down
on the lawn and heard him gasp as he expelled a spurt of
liquid bile. There was no need for the leash. The dog

walked slowly on stiff legs. Poor bastard, Frobisch
thought. You're already half dead and they're pumping
you full of stuff so you can squat and pour your guts out.
The dog walked a few feet farther and squatted again.
Frobisch considered it would be a kindness to take him
to the creek and weigh him down with stones. If he tossed
him out among the rocks, the poor mutt could sink to
coolness, and the welcome dank of grass and mud. Back
to the primordial, Frobisch thought. Not a bad death—
floating amid the grunting bullfrogs and the silver min-
nows. He pictured Gregor trailing a plait of dampened
weeds while Sadie wept. Still, it would be a blessing. The
dog was crouching once again, expelling liquid. Frobisch
walked beside him sighing.

He spotted Randy by a tree, slouched almost as he had
left him hours ago. He was still toying with the penknife,
weighing it within his palm, testing the blade with a
cautious finger, throwing it into the soft night earth, and
retrieving it to throw again.

"'Lo again, Mr. Frobisch." The youth touched the
knife to his cap in a salute.

Frobisch asked, "Don't you ever sleep?"

"Sure I do, Mr. Frobisch." Randy laughed. "Don't
you?"

"The dog needed walking," Frobisch said.

"Here, pooch," said Randy, flinging the knife. "Nice
dog," he said to Frobisch.

"He's a bit over the hill."

"He got the runs?"

"That's about the only thing that runs."

"Oh, yeah?" Randy threw the knife.

A sudden breeze riffled the silent bushes. The dog

raised his muzzle in seeming pleasure and appeared to sniff some wonderful cocktail—late summer roses, honey-suckle, mint. Frobisch fought tears rising in his throat.

"Guess we'll go in," said Frobisch. "Try to get a coupla hours' sleep."

"Hang loose, Mr. Frobisch."

Frobisch wondered if Randy was joking. He said, "I guess we will."

Randy studied his knife. "Mr. Frobisch, before you go, you wanna see the way it looks?"

"The way what looks, Randy?"

"You know. The haircut."

"The haircut?"

"Yeah. The way it looks without the cap."

"Sure. If you want me to."

Randy laughed and flung the knife somewhere in the dampness of the grass. He swept away the cap just as the clouds parted to a blaze of yellow moon. His skull gleamed like a naked bulb, an ivory dome, pallid and hairless. He stood upright in the light—the naked head rising like an obscene, uncovered phallus.

Frobisch gasped, "Cooler that way, I guess." He scooped the dog under one arm and called, "G'night."

Randy grinned, framed by waving trees—the moon brazenly lighting his naked head. "Thought you'd get a charge out of it," he said.

Frobisch acknowledged, "Quite a sight." Clutching the gasping terrier, he ran; his loafers made funny sloshing sounds on the wet grass. He was on the flagstone path, almost at his door, when he felt the fetid wetness on his pajama sleeve. He stared down in the light cast by the moon and saw the unmistakable smear of bile soiling his sleeve. "Damn you to hell, Gregor!" He set the terrier down on the walk and bent to find something to clean himself with—a handful of leaves or grass. The breeze shifted and he caught the odor squarely, as though he had been smacked flat across the face with something putrid. Swearing, he bent among the dark bushes and retched.

# 3

In the morning Sadie performed the cancer test, standing naked at the closet mirror with her left arm raised. With the fingers of her right hand she probed the flesh, poked the doughy mass of her left breast, tested the knobby circle of the areola, felt the pink nipple rise as though stimulated by a lover's touch. She skimmed the shaved skin of her armpit and deemed it safe. She raised her right arm next and with her left hand began a similar, cautious probing. For a moment she held her breath, feeling a hard, fleshy protuberance, recognized the mole she'd had since childhood, and exhaled a sigh so laden with relief she felt her body quiver and her legs go weak.

"Fool," she told the image in the mirror.

The towel she'd draped around her hips fell to the floor. She kicked it aside with some impatience. She was still wet from the shower. There were little drops on her arms and neck that rose like blisters. There was a spatter of freckles on her chest, the thin lines of a bathing suit etched white against her tan. In the gray light of daylight-saving she looked still young, the beginning crow's-feet, the harder lines soothed by kindly shadows. She thought, I'm forty-six and maybe could pass for forty. Thirty-nine if I stayed out of the sun and applied some Magik Stick to those dark circles. No hiding it; in spite of deceptions of appearance, she was middle-aged. She shivered with a sudden chill, retrieved the towel, and draped it around her shoulders.

"Middle age" was a euphemism for sagging flesh and the body's slow, inevitable dying. She made a face, deriding the face reflected. Her skin, with its tan, looked sallow—the circles under the eyes dark, the cheeks fleshy, the mouth without lipstick too prim. Thank God the new haircut was growing in. A pixie (silly name) devised for comfort and carefree swimming had been a disaster— more like yellow spikes. Pale spikes over the forehead meant to be bangs and more of the same, like metal filings, stuck up at the crown. She moistened one finger with saliva (thinking as she did so, disgusting!) and tried to flatten the few upstanding hairs. She might ask Marlene to change the rinse, set it to look more elegant, give it (her smile was rueful) the dignity of advancing age.

Could you be dignified standing naked, the breasts (blessedly free of lumps and knobs) swinging pendulous, the belly round, the hips too wide, the thighs mottled by veins like the careful tracings of a road map? Howie had always teased that he preferred thin women. Those models like sticks in round-necked T-shirts. No bosoms to speak of. She imagined the woman he'd met in Rome must look like that. A long neck, like an ostrich. Nothing seductive. He must be nuts.

Sadie bent to touch her toes and groaned as a sharp pain hit the back of one knee. Trouble. A muscle pulled or a tendon stretched beyond endurance, ready to snap like an elastic pulled too tight. Groaning, she hobbled to the bedside chair where her clothes were laid out neatly. The peppermint-striped shirtwaist. The new high-heeled white sandals. She would greet him in the kitchen looking poised and cool. No mention of last night's quarrel.

He wouldn't want to be reminded that he'd looked the fool, crawling on hands and knees, hunting for pins. Babbling about his secret fears. Everyone was afraid of something. Sadie was scared of getting cancer. Dying. Imagine being dead. Never singing; never seeing Sima.

The idea gave her goose bumps. When you got suddenly cold this way and felt prickles rising on your neck, it meant someone was walking on your grave. She pictured herself dead and buried; a simple stone. Maybe a bronze plaque set flush with the ground the way they did it nowadays. Dignified and starkly tasteful. A death designed in Swedish modern, without the curlicues and furbelows of sentiment to give one pain. Howie, bent and remorseful, staring at the new-turned earth and weeping that she'd been a good wife and a loving mother. Would he have the grace to light a *yahrzeit* candle for her immortal soul? Would he select a proper epitaph? Sadie Golden Frobisch, Dead of Cancer. More like a broken heart. The sum total of little aggravations broke the spirit, sapped the strength, till one died literally of sadness. That much was fact. Not yet. I'm not dead yet, thought Sadie, bending, with a litheness that belied her years, to snap her bra.

It was quiet in the kitchen. Sadie's hanging grape ivy had shed a few dry leaves. The toaster shone. Mrs. Garcia, the maid, had used a new chromium polish on it that smelled like shit. It took away the appetite. All Howie had had for breakfast was a cup of instant coffee. He had left the stained cup in the sink, and the spoon crusted with dampened granules. He might have had the wit to rinse it. Sadie ran some hot water into the cup and set the spoon to soak in it. There were no sounds coming from the den. She would not peek in lest she catch him dressing and have him think she had designs on him. *This shouldn't be happening between us. We are divorced.* The stupid fool. Could he have left so early? He would have to wait for Dieter to open the office. What was the tearing rush? It's just like him, thought Sadie. Hurry up and wait. Possibly he was walking Sammy. She peered out of the kitchen window hoping to catch a glimpse of them. The Volvo wasn't in the drive. They'd gone, then. Sadie leaned against the sink. A dull pain had started under her breastbone—not cancer, certainly—more like a stricture of the heart, a squeezing that curtailed her breath and made her dizzy. The pain passed, and she could breathe free, but she was weeping. "It's such a mess. Such a god-awful mess." Just like the days before they'd split, with Howie sleeping in the den because he couldn't bear the shame of not performing.

Before Sima left for Israel they should have talked; she should have told the child the truth about all men, how all they cared about was that segment of precious flesh and how it rose and fell, which way it pointed, right or left, whether it dangled limp and sad or projected, nobly cantilevered. In spite of what they said; in spite of the avowed importance of their work, their silly, somber posturings, that was it, right there, the central core. And if it didn't function to their specifications, they might as well be dead and buried, for all they cared. The bloody fools, wept Sadie, helpless to stanch the tears that fell, splattering the silken shirtwaist and spilling salty droplets in the brimming cup.

At first light he had awakened inhaling dust. Cobwebs on *The Complete Mark Twain*. Grime on "The Man Who Corrupted Hadleyburg." The evanescent architecture of a spiderweb clouding *The Gilded Age*. Sima's little silver cup, which she had won for being all-round good kid at Camp Sea-Sprite, was tarnished. Tarnished (Frobisch descended into bathos) as youthful hopes.

In its wicker bed the dog looked dead. Frobisch devoutly hoped that this was so. He knew what was expected of him, knew Sadie's intent, had guessed the grim, secret agenda since the moment he'd heard her voice, raspy with tears, whisper to him on the phone, "Sammy is dying." Well, let him die, prayed Frobisch, without my help and without, God willing, any more of Sadie's operatic posturings—the sighs, the groans, the tears, the brandishing of the needle as though she were playing Madame Curie to his Pierre. Oh, she had missed her calling; she should have opted for a life in opera, should have invested all the energy, the drive, in a career and left him to find someone a little softer. Someone who didn't scare him with all the fortitude, the guts. Stiff-upper-lip Sadie, like London housewives in the Blitz, singing "There'll Always Be an England" and planting flowers in the ruins.

He had awakened like this before, nursing a stiff neck and interpreting the early morning sounds—footfalls, rumblings in the pipes—as the noises made by strangers. In the weeks before he left, he'd slept here in the den, refusing Sadie's offer of an upstairs room. She'd said it was the last, unkindest cut. She could have borne it if he would at least camp in the guest room or the upstairs study till they could find some common ground. He couldn't countenance being that close. He wanted to put as much space as he could between them, to wait at ground level near an easy exit, poised for his escape when the time was right.

One morning, very early, she'd surprised him by appearing in the den. She was wearing a high-necked flannel nightgown. He fancied he could see beneath it to the heaviness of her flesh. He didn't know how long she'd watched him as he slept. In the long white gown she'd looked like Lady Macbeth, wringing her hands and grieving an irremediable past.

"What I can't abide," she'd whispered fiercely, "is that your reasons are so banal. Restlessness. Middle age. A search for the real Howie Frobisch under the pin-striped suit. Soon you'll be wearing jogging suits and neck chains. It makes me want to retch!"

He'd struggled painfully to surface from the pull of deepest morning sleep. "What do you want of me, Sadie?"

"Go or stay. Make up your mind."

He'd been a long time gone, and she still couldn't accept it—nor, at this moment, could he, waking with this awful sense of déjà vu, the conviction he was reliving all the old mistakes.

In its wicker bed the terrier was waking, stretching stiff legs before garnering the effort it would take to raise itself to its feet.

"So you made it through the night," said Frobisch and wearily began to dress.

The dog, Gregor Samsa, had one trick—not so much a trick as an aberration—which Frobisch discovered one winter Sunday when Sima was still a tyke. They had been sitting together on the living room sofa reading the comics. Frobisch remembered the paleness of the winter light and the contrasting green of Sadie's plants blooming with jungle effulgence on the sill. Sima had looked so sweet in a pink quilted robe and pink bunny fur slippers that shed tangled threads wherever she walked. Gregor was sleeping in a patch of sun. When he rose to stretch, his coat was matted with pink fuzz.

Frobisch had gotten up to put a record on the stereo, Beethoven's Third, the Eroica. The dog had perked up at the first low notes. He'd moved to sit beside the speaker where he stayed fixed with his head cocked in an attitude of unusual attentiveness. Sima had lost interest in her father's dramatic rendering of Spiderman and had gone to sit beside her pet. She tried to pick the pink fluff from his coat. She offered the last morsel of a breakfast doughnut. Gregor ignored her and sat in a seeming trance.

Sima complained to Frobisch, "Sammy won't play."

"He's listening to the music," Frobisch laughed.

The dog had stretched out on his side and lain with his muzzle fixed against the speaker. His tongue lolled lazily amid strewn crumbs. His eyes were rolled back in a look of crazy ecstasy. He stayed that way through the four movements of the symphony. When Frobisch switched to Rachmaninoff, the dog eyed him glumly and slunk away.

That afternoon Frobisch's partner, Freddy Gottlieb, and Freddy's wife, Renee, stopped by for cocktails. Sadie had set out Brie and crackers and dry-roasted cashews. Frobisch put on a recording of the Pastoral. The dog rose from a nap, somnolent, wobbly, still trailing fuzz, and parked himself beside the speaker. Frobisch tried to lure him with a piece of cheese. The terrier stayed fixed beside the speaker. When the record ended, he trotted off.

Without commenting to Sadie (who would have hooted) Frobisch began to put Gregor through tests. He experimented with New Orleans jazz, Sousa marches, Gregorian (relishing the pun) chants. Opera, with Sadie in the background delivering the recitative, caused Gregor to vanish. Bach's subtler inventions left him cold, as did Alicia de Larrocha's *Cantos de españa* and Rubinstein's Chopin. But Beethoven hypnotized him, transfixed him in a dreamy rapture from which he would not be seduced, either by rattlings of the leash or offerings of food or the temptations of a rawhide bone. It was uncanny. Frobisch described the dog's odd trait at the office and was met by jeers. He essayed a scientific explanation; something in the music's frequency, its pitch had an odd effect on canine hearing, the way high-pitched whistles made some dogs frantic. No one believed him. Frobisch showed off for dinner guests. First, Mozart. Maybe a spot of Grieg. Sadie, now privy to the secret, suggested the *Water Music*. "He should appreciate that, but make sure he's near a tree." Frobisch played Handel, and Gregor yawned his boredom. Frobisch switched to the earliest lure, the Eroica. Gregor trotted swiftly to his accustomed spot and sat down panting. "It's the percussion," offered a guest. "It's the heavy beat, the loudness, the building rhythm." Frobisch switched to a more placid string quartet. Rapturous, Gregor seemed to swoon.

People made jokes. "'His Master's Voice.' Rent him out to RCA Victor as a model, Howie."

Frobisch assented. "Maybe I will."

Frobisch had lunch with his friend, Marty Katz, who was a scientist at NIH and who had written his own version of the Passover Haggadah, explaining that the plagues in Egypt, the parting of the Red Sea, could be explained by bona fide natural disasters and geologic upheavals. Frobisch presented the case for Gregor. Marty considered this as he stabbed at his cannoli and finally posited the view that the chemical composition of the recordings, even the album dyes, offered certain olfactory sensations that were pleasing to the dog.

"Only of Beethoven?" Frobisch asked.

Marty shrugged. "'Spossible."

Frobisch said, "You're telling me my album of all nine symphonies from Deutsche Grammophon smells like a bitch in heat?"

Marty hung tough. "Maybe it does."

Privately Frobisch considered writing a letter to a dog-lovers' magazine or querying a vet. It was passing strange. It was bizarre. Through weeks of Sunday mornings, stringent tests, Gregor never missed a beat, never confused a Beethoven with a Mendelssohn, a Liszt. "The dog is an aristocrat," the kennel lady had said. Pondering this, Frobisch tempered some of his disappointment in the terrier with respect.

Driving to Van Zandt's place, Frobisch still brooded on the wonder of it. The morning had dawned less humid. Frobisch sensed a hint of autumn promise in the drier air. He had rolled down the windows of the Volvo, thinking the terrier might relish the fresh smell of the breeze. But the dog lay sprawled beside him on the seat, oblivious to scent, a sorry-looking mop of tangled fur. In his prime he had been handsome—the ears like amber silk; the tail perky, erect. The smooth puppy coat that had reminded Frobisch of Kafka's beetle had given way to a rough pelt of black and tan that needed expert plucking. Every few months Sadie took Gregor to be groomed. When he came home with his coat smoothed and gleaming, she would boast he had show quality. The dog groomer always fixed a pert bow tie to Gregor's collar; Frobisch always insisted that it be removed. A dog who loved Beethoven, who neither begged nor performed tricks, shouldn't be gussied up like a damn French poodle. There was atavistic hauteur in the terrier stance; the fool bow detracted from that classy look.

"Shall we try some decent music, Gregor?" Frobisch fiddled with the radio dial until he found the good music station playing "Listener's Choice." Cannons were booming the closing crescendo of the *Overture 1812*. Frobisch thought he heard the terrier groan. "What you have to accept, old man, is that the world doesn't quite have your discernment. I'm not saying you're a snob, but your taste for Beethoven is uncanny. If I were to criticize, I'd have to say you limit yourself a bit by not accepting Mozart. However, they tell me stubbornness is a terrier trait." The record ended with a turgid drumroll and the roar of guns. "*Vive la France*," sighed Frobisch. A girl sounding sexy and sleepy touted the merits of a local bank. The announcer revealed the next popular choice, Beethoven's Fifth.

"You know this one, Gregor." Frobisch turned up the volume. The dog lay still. "When I was a kid in good ole Bayonne, New Jersey, I learned those first four notes signified the V-sign. Dot-dot-dot-dash. V for Victory in the war, you know? I never hear them without thinking of destroyers going out to sink the *Bismarck* or the RAF setting out over the Channel on a dawn raid. Of course you don't know what I'm talking about, Gregor. You love the music, plain and pure, don't you?" The dog lay on its side; the faint rising and falling of its body showed it was still breathing.

They had entered a narrow street off Chevy Chase Circle. Trees spread a leafy canopy across the road. Frobisch pulled to a stop beside the curb.

"Can you hear it, Gregor? Don't you care?" He turned the symphony to full volume. He would wake up the whole street trying to get a rise out of the stupid terrier. "C'mon, Gregor, rise and shine. Gimme a sign, a tail wag, something to let me know you hear it. Get up, goddam you, Gregor! Gimme a sign! It's not like I'm asking you to listen to the Hammerclavier. No atonalities to hurt your ears. No dissonance. A nice familiar symphony. You know it, you stupid dog. Show me I'm wrong, that you're not half dead and ready for the dustbin!"

A jogger, running bare-chested like a gladiator, broke in midstride to stare into the car. Frobisch could picture how they looked, parked amid shuttered houses—a pale man in rumpled clothes shaking a silent dog, as the perfect notes of Beethoven's Fifth Symphony soared glorious in the morning air, melding with birdsong.

Van Zandt said, "You gotta hold him while I shave his leg. It's to find a vein for the I.V."

Frobisch said, "No."

Van Zandt squinted at Frobisch over rimless glasses. He was a tall man who loomed over the examining table with imposing girth, a colossus wearing a denim jumpsuit and rubber waders that reached his hips. Frobisch figured he would make quick work of Gregor and head out for the nearest stream to fish. "You squeamish?" asked the vet. "The girl's here this morning. I can call her in to assist."

"Not about the I.V., no."

"Then what's the problem?"

Frobisch said, "Put him to sleep."

Van Zandt sported a curly beard. When perplexed, as he now seemed to be, he pulled at the beard as though expecting some burst of reason to explode with tugs of chin hair. Frobisch longed to caution him, "Don't do that. You'll go bald."

"Put him to sleep? You mean that?"

"I do."

"Does Sadie agree?"

Frobisch said, "She's running errands. That's why I'm here."

"Does she agree?"

"Of course she agrees. The dog's in pain. He can't eat; he can't sleep; he can hardly drag himself around. If he were your pet, wouldn't you feel the same?"

Van Zandt tugged at his chin. He had strange eyes, brownish yellow. Behind the glasses they looked clouded, opaque.

"My business," the vet said, "is to prolong life."

"At any cost?"

"However I can. It's a losing battle. Sooner or later, all my patients die."

"Sooner or later won't make that much difference for Gregor Samsa."

Van Zandt studied his hands. He had broad, stubby fingers—a butcher's hands, lacking the surgeon's grace. The nails cut short; scrubbed raw. No wedding ring. Only a signet on the pinky that pinched the flesh.

"If you insist, I'll have to do it," Van Zandt capitulated with a shrug.

Frobisch coughed to hide the trembling in his voice. "That's it? You do agree?"

"I don't agree or disagree. The dog is yours. You want him put down, I'll put him down."

"It's a kindness, don't you think?"

Van Zandt removed his glasses and rubbed them on

his denim sleeve. He took his time about replacing them, as though some lingering stage business would give Frobisch a chance to change his mind. "I don't answer questions like that. I don't know that he's suffering so much. If we continue with the antibiotics and the I.V., he's got a little more time left in him, I think."

"You know his eyesight is kaput. I think he's getting deaf."

"I haven't been aware of that."

"There are indications."

"A dog can do well with its sense of smell. It can be happy with lots of loving care and attention. Sadie gives him that."

"I think you're being sentimental."

"I'm stating simple facts."

Frobisch said, "Put him down."

"You'll have to sign a release."

Frobisch felt stupid. "Release of what?"

"Consent to euthanasia."

Frobisch whistled. "Consent to euthanasia. Heavy stuff."

"I'll tell the girl to get the form."

"Yes. Please do that."

"Will you wish to claim the remains?"

"Will I—?" Frobisch had trouble hearing. His bad ear, where Sadie had zapped him, buzzed as though something, a gnat, were trapped inside.

"Speak up, would you please?" asked Frobisch. "I'm not sure I caught that last."

"Will you bury the dog yourself?"

"Do I have to do that?"

Van Zandt looked pained. "We can ask the Humane Society to pick him up."

"They'll bury him, you mean?"

Van Zandt laughed. "Not likely. They'll cremate the remains. Or you can claim the body and bury him yourself. Somewhere in the yard is what some people like to do. If you do that, I recommend purchasing some quicklime."

"Quicklime?"

"I think Sadie would prefer home burial, don't you?"

"I guess she would."

"That's it, then. The receptionist will show you what you have to sign. Do you want to be with him?"

"Do I want to be with him?" Frobisch repeated stupidly.

"When he falls asleep."

"No, I don't."

"As you wish. I'll ask you to bring him to the other examining room."

Frobisch hedged. "He really just goes to sleep?"

"I'll give an intravenous injection. He'll go to sleep. The whole process will be over very quickly."

"Very quickly," Frobisch parroted Van Zandt.

"You want to change your mind?"

"Understand this, Doctor. I mean this as a kindness."

"He won't suffer, I promise you."

"That's fine," Frobisch said. "That's the whole point, isn't it?" Frobisch set the terrier on the floor, careful to avoid touching its backside. Tugging Gregor on the leash, he followed Van Zandt to a small room paneled in pine. On one wall was a window flanked by glass cases of instruments. Atop one cabinet was a mounted skeleton of a small animal, possibly a cat. On the wall were photographs of large gray birds captured in profile. They had curved beaks and wide webbed feet.

"Interesting," said Frobisch. "Did you take those shots?"

"Yes. That was on an expedition to the Pribilofs with Save the Whales. I shot those near the Bering Sea."

"Extraordinary. What are they?"

"Sea gulls."

"Silly of me. I should have known."

"If you'll place Gregor on the table."

Frobisch hefted Gregor to the table. "Should I remove his collar?"

"It frightens some dogs to lose their collars. Leave it on him for a bit."

"Nice of you," said Frobisch.

"No sweat," answered Van Zandt.

Frobisch touched the terrier's head. "End of the line, Gregor." The dog who had been stretched limp on its side summoned a last reserve of energy and shifted to its back. It lay in an attitude of submission, the forepaws bent like a beggar's, the hind legs extended as though already stiffening with death. Frobisch scratched the terrier's belly. "With his last gasp he surprises me. It would be easier if he tried to bite me. I always said he would."

"Said what?" Van Zandt seemed distracted.

"That he'd try to bite me with his dying breath."

"Do you wish to wait outside now? The girl will give you the form."

"Yes. I wish to wait outside."

Van Zandt promised, "It won't be too long."

What to do was study the details. Strange driftwood sculptures fashioned by someone with an eye for whimsy. A freeform bench designed to follow the natural shape of the wood. Nakashima, maybe; Frobisch couldn't be sure.

88

An old-fashioned wall phone, mounted in wood. Too cutesy for Frobisch's taste. A stylized drawing of an owl, little squiggles for the feathers and eyes that looked like twin fried eggs. A framed needlepoint rendering of a squirrel. A cork bulletin board showed pictures of Van Zandt judging a dog show; photos of spotty dogs with floppy ears and feathered tails raised like banners. A rack of pamphlets. "You and Your Pet." "The Cat Fancier's Handbook." "Training Your Dog." A pile of literature about free rabies inoculation clinics and dog obedience classes at the high school or the armory—take your pick. Maybe if he had taken Gregor to dog obedience, the terrier would have learned to mind, would have bonded with Frobisch as his master. Leader of the pack. Frobisch sat down on the freeform bench. The seat was hard and hurt his rump. The girl at the front desk was a blonde with acne-mottled skin and a prim mouth pursed in a look of permanent disappointment. She asked Frobisch, "How is Sima?"

"You know my daughter?"

The girl looked sour. "We went to school together."

Frobisch said, "Small world." He wondered what was happening to teenagers. Once, the girls had all been goddesses with waterfalls of silken hair and slender figures, shining skin. The boys had towered, tall and manly. Now, there was Randy with his white, bald head, and Sima with her girdle of matronly fat and dirty toes, and this poor thing, so wan, with the angry pits and bumps of acne glaring like neon from her cheeks. Was it something in the water? The girl handed Frobisch a form. He signed it without reading it. License to kill. Van Zandt buzzed, and the girl disappeared into the inner room carrying the form. Frobisch continued his inventory. Two hanging plants thirsting for water. A lamp fashioned of a tea canister. A row of empty coat hooks on the wall. Where were Van Zandt's other patients? Probably he had none. His personality wasn't so hot. He had offered no words of comfort, had remained laconic, lachrymose, as though his own pet were dying. The best he could manage was the casual murmur of encouragement, "He won't suffer." Frobisch picked up a magazine and sat a long time staring at a picture of a fuzzy dog nudging a tennis ball with its nose. "Love your puppy," the caption commanded.

The light projected columns of dust through an open casement window. A curtain riffled in a puff of breeze. "Mr. Frobisch?"

"Yes?" Frobisch saw him through a haze of sun and panicked, thinking the tall, bearded man in rubber waders was his apparition of the Spanish Steps. "What is it?" Frobisch asked too loudly.

"It's over," Van Zandt said.

Frobisch stood up painfully. "Over?"

Van Zandt handed over Gregor's collar and tags. "He is asleep."

"Did the girl give you the form?"

"She did."

Frobisch glanced at Gregor's collar. It was a new one Sadie must have purchased recently. Electric blue. She'd even had a new name tag inscribed, My Name is Gregor Samsa. I belong to Sadie Frobisch. The woman didn't miss a trick. Frobisch stashed the collar in the pocket of his pants. "Will you tell me something, Doctor?"

"What is that?"

"Tell me it was a kindness."

"There was no pain."

"I don't mean that. Tell me I did the right thing."

Van Zandt tugged on his beard. "You can pick him up out back."

"Tell me," begged Frobisch.

"I don't address myself to that," answered Van Zandt.

Sadie's hair gleamed like a golden helmet in the sun. "I see you beat me getting back." Smiling, she'd surveyed him from the glass door of the den before stepping out onto the patio. "Isn't it too hot for yard work?"

"Necessary," Frobisch said. He wiped his mouth with the back of his hand and bent to the spade. He had picked a spot underneath a weeping cherry where Gregor had liked to lie in shade on summer afternoons. The ground was dry, and he had not reckoned with the gnarled tree roots that rose like strange humped animals above the ground.

"What are you digging?" Sadie asked.

"A trench of sorts," said Frobisch. "The spade's no good."

"I could get a pitchfork from De Filippo," Sadie offered.

"Don't bother."

Sadie asked Frobisch, "How's the dog?"

Frobisch considered this a moment before answering. "Not in pain."

Sadie lifted her face to the sun. In her striped silk dress and high-heeled sandals she looked pretty and young.

"Nice outfit," said Frobisch.

"It's so lovely today," said Sadie. "You should've let Sammy out."

"Can't do it," Frobisch said.

"Why not? Does Dieter think he's worse?"

"Not exactly."

"What do you mean, not exactly?"

"I mean he's not exactly worse." Frobisch bent to his work. He had managed an excavation about a foot deep. He had propped a sack of quicklime against the tree.

Sadie asked, "Where's Sammy?"

"Back in the car."

"In the car! What are you thinking? He'll die of heat!"

Frobisch worked another moment before answering. "He is gone, Sadie."

"Gone? How could he be gone? Did he run away?"

"You know he couldn't run. He could hardly walk."

"Then why do you say he's gone?"

"I say he's gone because he has . . . expired."

"Howie, I don't know what you mean. I don't understand you."

"Gregor died at the vet's." Frobisch concentrated on the grave. The force of his agitation was lending him some strength so that the hole was growing deeper. He dug with renewed vigor.

"I don't believe you!"

"Hush, Sadie, please."

"Don't tell me to hush. I don't believe you! Gregor isn't—expired. Dieter would never let him die. Dieter would do anything, would use extraordinary methods to keep him going. This is another of your lousy jokes."

Frobisch was suddenly so weary he was afraid he would faint. He propped the shovel against the tree beside the bag of quicklime. He wiped his dirty hands on his pants. "I asked Van Zandt to put the dog to sleep, Sadie. It seemed it would be a kindness. He couldn't see. He couldn't hear. I knew he was in pain."

"You asked! How could you ask? He wasn't yours to

ask or not to ask! I have the paper. It's spelled out very clearly. The dog belongs to me."

"Truthfully, Sadie, I never thought of that. I never stopped to ask myself was he yours or mine. I just asked was he suffering, and it seemed to me he was. It seemed humane. So I asked Van Zandt to end it."

"You killed Sammy!"

"I asked Van Zandt to put him out of his misery, Sadie."

"You had no right! I don't believe this! I don't believe my ears. I asked you to take him to the vet, just for his regular feeding. I didn't ask you to do anything else. Did we talk about doing anything else?"

"We talked about it, Sadie. We didn't agree."

"You're right we didn't agree! How could you do this? How could you decide such a thing?"

"I don't know, Sadie. It seemed right at the time."

"At the time! You killed my Sammy because it seemed right at the time!"

"Sadie, I'm sorry. Something told me it was the right thing to do."

"Something told you! You are crazy! Do you know that? You are a madman. You killed my dog!"

"I was trying to be kind. I brought him back with me, Sadie. Believe me, that was hard. I picked this spot he always liked—under the weeping cherry. It's cool here; the grass is green, and there's a lot of shade."

"I want him back!"

"I can't do that, Sadie."

"I want him back, Howie!"

"Ah, Sadie, don't carry on like that. Don't cry. Think about it a little and you'll see I'm right. I think you wanted me to do it. I felt it when you phoned. When you told me

Gregor was dying, I felt there was a favor you wanted of me, but you couldn't say the words outright. Wasn't I right about that, Sadie?"

"No, you aren't right! You killed my dog because you hated him. You hated him so much you had him put to sleep."

"That isn't true."

"It is! You always hated him. You said he was a lousy mutt. You said he tried to bite you. Probably if he tried, it was in self-defense."

"It isn't true. I didn't hate him. He was all right. He was an all right pet. He was unusual."

"You thought he was so unusual you had him put to sleep!"

"That isn't why I did it, Sadie. I did it so he wouldn't be in pain. That was all I thought about."

"What about my pain? Did you think of that? Did you think what I would feel to come home expecting to see my Sammy feeling a little better after his I.V. and have you tell me he has ex-pired?"

"I knew you would be sad."

"And you wanted to hurt me, didn't you? You wanted to hurt me because I'm seeing Dieter!"

"I don't know what you mean. This is crazy. I didn't want to hurt you or the dog. Who the hell is Dieter?"

"The vet. You hate me, and you hate him, and you hated Sammy!"

"I don't hate anyone, Sadie. I didn't exactly like the dog, but he wasn't so bad. A dog who loves Beethoven couldn't be all bad."

"There you go with your lousy jokes!"

"I'm not joking, Sadie."

"I will never forgive you for this, Howie. I will find a way to make you pay."

"Ah, Sadie, don't."

"I am going to go inside and call up Dieter and ask him what happened; then I am going to call the police and tell them you destroyed property that didn't belong to you. I'll have you put in jail or an asylum. Whichever one is worse, I'll pick for you."

"Please, Sadie, try to calm down. Look at it rationally."

"Then I am going to call up Sima at the kibbutz and tell her you killed her puppy. What do you think of that?"

"She's a religious girl. I think she would understand."

"What does religion have to do with Sammy?"

"I tried to do God's will."

"Oh, you are crazy," Sadie cried. "I'm scared to be out here alone with you. Don't follow me into the house or I'll have you arrested."

"Wait, Sadie!" He was hiccuping bitter acid; the morning's coffee bubbled in his throat. Ah, jeez, it was appropriate. The Lord afflicted Job with boils; and he, Howie Frobisch, prime fool of the Western world, dog-killer and patsy, got hiccups to keep him meek! "If you're going in the house, could you maybe bring me out a glass of water? Ginger ale? Something? I don't feel so hot."

Sadie hesitated. "Are you having a heart attack?"

"Nothing like that. Bad hiccups is all." It had happened this way once before, years ago, under the wedding canopy. He'd sipped the ceremonial wine, not what you'd call a vintage year, and erupted in a series of wild belches. Like a groggy, drunken sailor he had taken Sadie to be his bride.

"Hiccups!"

95

"I guess I'm nervous. I couldn't eat this morning. Sadie, I know you're mad at me, but just a sip of water would help a lot. If I go into the kitchen I'll track in dirt."

"I'll get you your water."

"That's good of you, Sadie."

"I'm not doing it to be good. I'm doing it because I don't want you dying of a heart attack in my yard. Go home to your playboy pad and do your dying! Be my guest!"

"All right, Sadie."

He watched her stumbling across the grass in the high-heeled sandals. It was true he hadn't stopped to think about her grief, only the certainty that he was acting out of ultimate compassion and that Gregor's death was a consummation Sadie wished as much as he. Not that she'd admit it. She would have gone on with the I.V. feedings, the night walks near the creek, the shots, until she dropped. His ever-feisty Sadie, staring death in the face and telling it, "Get lost." In six months she'd have another puppy, Frobisch bet, whereas he, the murderer, poor hiccuping schlemiel, would carry with him to his last breath the memory of Gregor Samsa dying a beetle's death, helpless on his back with his legs groping in air. When Frobisch tickled its belly, the terrier had shaken its hind leg in a last instinctive spasm of pleasure.

Frobisch sat down near the weeping cherry and stared at the trench he'd dug. He felt drained of his last strength. The hiccuping was explosive, squeezing his breath.

"I meant it as a kindness," Frobisch gasped. "I'm not the ogre she thinks. I didn't wish him pain. I wish him a happy doggy heaven, a good shepherd in charge, and the 'Ode to Joy' piped into all the kennel runs. I was trying to 'do good,' whatever that may mean!"

The sun glinted greenish gold through shadowy leaves.

The earth smelled of flowers and new-mown grass. High in the copper beech a flock of nervous starlings jabbered complaints to an interloping squirrel. The squirrel traversed a branch in a series of brief jumps and then retreated amid a din of caws and beating wings. Frobisch watched the action in the beech tree through a blur, grateful that Sadie had gone into the house and there were only the cackling starlings to see him weeping over Gregor's grave.

"You look to me," said Father Paul, "like a man who might take comfort in a drink."

"For the depth of that perception, Father, bless you!" Frobisch said and blushed, embarrassed at his own temerity. Imagine the infernal, stupid chutzpah of his blessing a priest! No matter that he meant it in the most figurative sense—the words carried no more weight than what you told someone after a sneeze. Sitting in the priest's dimly lit study amid walls of somberly bound books and chaste pastels of the saints and a crucifix of yellowed ivory bearing a slender Christ who gazed at him with a look of mild complicity, he felt bloated with pious juices. He would have followed his uttered blessing with a palm held high—a middle-aged Jewish accountant in linen slacks and an Izod shirt and Gucci loafers, miming a benediction. Better to bless the sense of tact that kept him rigid in his seat. He was trapped in a wobbly director's chair that threatened to topple whenever he shifted weight. Facing him, Father Paul loomed tall in a chair of tufted oxblood leather behind an ebony desk, massive as a grand piano. The priest was wearing faded jeans and a white tennis shirt with a blue wreath on the breast pocket. He looked boyish and fit.

Father Paul hefted a cut-glass decanter to the light and blinked. The bottle radiated rainbow prisms. Flashes of violet, pink, and gold danced on the twisted vine leaves of the rug. Reverently he removed the stopper and poured scotch into twin smoked-glass tumblers etched with the outlines of geese in flight. He handed a brimming glass to Frobisch. "Try that. It's twenty-year-old stuff. I'd offer ice, but it's a desecration." Father Paul raised his glass to toast Frobisch in Hebrew, "*L'Chaim.*"

"*L'Chaim.*" Frobisch held the tumbler in both palms and took a cautious sip. The warm scotch tasted like smoke.

"Drink up," laughed the priest. "It isn't brandy."

Father Paul had a good laugh, properly deep. There was a resonance, a mellow timbre that invoked trust. He must have developed that sonority during countless pastoral councils. It denoted humor without mockery, a shared humanity. Humble. Sincere. Look at me, said the laugh. I'm a pleasant fellow underneath the virtuous trappings. I zip my pants the same as you. Frobisch imagined the good father in the confessional startling some poor sinner with an infectious chuckle. Where a penitent might expect the weight of guilt, sad acts of contrition, assigned with gloom, he got instead a burst of glee, warm laughter rising like bubbles from the priest's vantage behind the screen. The shock of it probably shaped some people up.

Quickly Frobisch swallowed and coughed as the warm booze seared his throat and settled in an aching puddle in his gut. " 'Sgood."

Father Paul beamed at Frobisch. He had black hair he brilliantined into a dated 1950s pompadour and dauntlessly intent black eyes that could outstare a devil or a dybbuk, Frobisch was sure. Once, watching the priest perform on a noon talk show, Sadie had remarked, "I don't trust him. The man's too handsome to be good." She'd thought he looked like Tyrone Power a bit after the actor's prime.

Tonight the priest's jaws bore the shadow of a heavy beard. Frobisch wondered about all that dammed-up masculinity. What postures of ecstasy gave it release?

"You could've knocked me over with a feather when you called."

"It's been a while," Frobisch acknowledged.

Father Paul mused, "How far do we go back?"

Frobisch ticked off the names. "The Council for Peaceful Integration of the County Schools. The Fund for Culture in the Inner City. The Committee to Support Home Rule."

"Didn't we eat good off a those? Every fund-raiser a feast!" Father Paul's eyes gleamed with a Sybarite's appreciation of remembered pleasures. "Shrimp-stuffed cherry tomatoes from Avignon Frères? Those little squares—spinach quiches I think it was—from Ridgewell's? Chicken wings, sour cream dip, hummus, garbanzos, guacamole? All in the name of charity and brotherhood." He winked. "Don't you love doin' good?"

"Frankly, Father, it's good for business."

"Same here, Howie." Father Paul lost himself in reminiscence. "You always took the window seat, and during all that palaver we used to have about the black man's burden and the white man's guilt you were the voice of calm. An island of rationality in a rising, angry tide. Didn't you and I once hold off a whole roomful of Yahoos? The issue was police brutality. You and I were opting for the policeman's right to self-defense, or *offense* as the case may be, and the forces of sympathy and justice were about to beat us in with clubs!" The priest flashed the grin Sadie had damned as preternaturally sexy. "Those were good days, weren't they?"

"I guess they were." Frobisch stared at his drink as though he saw both past and future in its golden depths. He had felt shy during those meetings. Even in perfect English tailoring and Italian leather shoes he was still timid Howie Frobisch, son of a greenhorn delicatessen owner in Bayonne who'd dubbed himself the Pickle King. His fellow committee members (mostly pin-striped bureau-crats who boasted Ivy League connections) would have chortled contemptuous laughter if they'd known. So he'd hugged the fringes of the room, admiring the way Father Paul could play a crowd, circulate with a smile as daz-zling as his starched white collar, touch lips to proffered cheeks, shake hands with a perfect mix of firmness and sincerity. Pretty women flocked to greet the priest, made excuses to touch his sleeve, teetered on spiky heels to whisper confidences like children reaching for forbidden sweets. Savvy Washington gals with perfect hair, shapely in nondescript print dresses ("shiksa frocks," Sadie called them) they bought at Garfinckel's, chirped and fluttered in the tall priest's shadow, content as nesting birds. And Frobisch hunkered by a wall, burning with jealousy and indigestion. Belching crudités and sour wine.

Father Paul was eyeing him with the attentive look he gave to talk show hosts. "What's eating at you, Howie? You look like Hamlet's ghost."

"I don't know what you mean."

"You walked in and I could smell the angst. Your lips were movin' like you were deep in conversation with yourself. What is it? A woman? Cancer?"

"Nothing so simple."

"Nothing so simple? Wow!"

The tall priest sat in shadow. From the wall behind him sconces fashioned like three-branched trees cast pale lights on the green and garnet of the rug. In the soft light Frobisch studied his drink and was alarmed to see a gnat teeter on the rim and topple to a wondrous, golden drowning. He fished carefully in his glass to remove the bug.

"Can I refresh that?"

Frobisch shook his head and placed the dead gnat on his knee. He drank deep and felt the tension ease as the scotch spread like a healing poultice to the knotted muscles of his limbs. "Father, I need to know, what is the Church's position on miracles?"

Father Paul stared bleakly at his glass. "Not overly welcoming. Why do you ask?"

"I believe I may have been present at a miraculous event. In Rome. During the Papal Conclave." Frobisch drank. There was a problem with his tongue, which expanded after every swallow like a lick of flame and then curled in upon itself, a poor burned cinder. An ashy tongue tasting of heat. A log doused by liquid fire. It worried him, this swollen tongue that turned recalcitrant just when he needed to be most eloquent. He prided himself on perfect diction. His voice, disembodied in the shadowy room, was sounding British. The words echoing in his ears were clipped. Aristocratic. It occurred to him that he was getting drunk.

Father Paul had eased back from his desk. He rested an ankle on his knee and began toying with the laces of his sneaker. He was wearing white crew socks banded with purple. Above the thick ribbed cuff there appeared a span of whitish skin, mottled with black hairs and knobby veins. "What was the nature of the miracle?"

"An angel appeared to me in a pool of light. Miraculous white light shining with tremendous radiance in the night. It was like one of the wonderful old paintings, awash with chiaroscuro. I knew it was an angel because of the sweetness of his face. Serenity born of goodness. Joy out of perfect peace. He spoke in a gentle voice. He told me to do good. Quit messing up. I fell on my knees. I hurt my left knee rather badly. I tore my pants. I answered him in a voice I hardly recognized as my own. Basso profundo. The whole scene was a bit operatic, to tell you the truth. Since then, I believe everything has changed."

"What has changed, Howie?"

Frobisch shifted unhappily in his seat, overcome by dizziness at the effort of his speech. If his chair collapsed, it would bring his painful unburdening to a slapstick climax; he would tumble like a silent movie comic in a mess of shattered glass and wasted scotch on Father Paul's Oriental rug. He half expected to hear from deep within the rectory the first notes of barrelhouse piano setting the scene. "Flashes of clairvoyance."

"Clairvoyance?"

"Yes. Bulletins, as it were, of future events. I knew who would be Pope several hours before the announcement."

Father Paul suggested, "A lucky guess."

"Father Paul, you know I am a Jew. I never heard of Albino Luciani, the Patriarch of Venice, before Saturday morning in Rome."

"Saturday *morning?*"

"Yes."

"You heard talk on the street. You thought you didn't notice, but the memory remained?"

"Maybe."

"What else?"

"I have the overpowering conviction that I *must* do good. I am saddled with an urge to show compassion—like nothing I have ever known."

"*That* might be a miracle."

"It's terrible."

Father Paul asked, "What else?"

Frobisch flushed. "Forgive me, Father, if I offend you. A renewed surge of sexual power. A cure, I'm pretty sure, of impotence."

"You're pretty sure?"

"Well, I haven't exactly put it to the test. But I'm sure. And how, I'm sure!"

The priest grinned. "How old would you be now, Howie?"

"In November I will be fifty-one."

"Any domestic difficulties?"

"I am divorced."

"Kids into drugs?"

"My daughter has discovered religion."

The priest laughed his wonderful deep laugh that reestablished between himself and Frobisch the common bond of their humanity. "Almost as bad."

Frobisch nodded. "It is. Father Paul, I'm an unobservant Jew. I don't go to shul; I never did. Not even on the high holidays. And Sima has gone to Israel. To a kibbutz. When I last saw her—that's why I went to Rome—it didn't go so well."

"Ah, now, it's hard being a parent. Were your people religious?"

"My people? Good God, no! My father ran a kosher delicatessen. That's the closest he came to the faith. If he worshiped anything at all, it was a perfectly seasoned pastrami. A juicy, fat corn beef. In his spare time he studied Marx. That stuff about the opiate of the people, my father took it to his heart." Blame the scotch's potency. He could see the old man as clearly as if he had materialized to solid flesh, standing near the wall under a murky rendering of Saint Anthony in the desert. The old man looked the same, wearing the stained gray fedora he used to push back on his head to cover a growing bald spot (vanity, not piety, had governed Frobisch men) and a butcher's apron hanging to his shoes, the ties wound double around his skinny waist. He was slicing belly lox and scowling at the pink flesh falling to a mound on coated paper. Frobisch raised a palm in a wan effort of greeting, and his father faded to a maze of fine cracks in the wall that ranged the stippled plaster like the ambling branches of a river.

"My father called himself the Pickle King," Frobisch whispered to the priest. "There was a big picture of an oversize green pickle hanging outside the store. Can you imagine the ribbing I took when I was a kid? Considering the pickle's shape, the comparison to male anatomy?" If he squinted now, he could see the hated sign, chartreuse and gold, depicting a gnarled pickle topped by a three-pronged crown (like some mythic orb of Neptune) and bold block letters hurling the appellation PICKLE KING over the trolley tracks of Avenue C. He had spent a somber adolescence working weekends and evenings in the store, wiping counters, splitting rolls—poised to avert meetings with his giggling peers who came in tumbling over one another in their eagerness to buy dills and salami from their buddy, the famed Bayonne celebrity. For if Frobisch's father was the Pickle King, it followed by certain schoolboy logic that he, Howie, was the Pickle Prince, with all the quirks of male anatomy the name implied. The sign, flapping in blustery winds so that it frightened the hovering pigeons and an occasional gull that wandered inland from the port, burdened his youth. By God, he couldn't whack off in the quiet of his room without seeing it, the overblown pickle, bumpy with knobs and sickly green, the giant, elongated phallus that did indeed bear a wan pea-soup resemblance to his private parts.

Father Paul looked bored. He had picked up an antique letter opener and was using the point to clean his nails. "Anything else you want to tell me?"

Gregor's paw extending from a Hefty bag in a bizarre Hitler salute. Sadie's sobs deepening to gutturals as though she were once again in labor. The tears plowed funnels in her rouge, and the blue-gray stuff she smeared over her eyelids ran in sluggish channels down her cheeks. He'd been reminded of the old torch song, "Cry Me a River." In the middle of Sadie's weeping he'd longed to gently pat her cheek and ask if she remembered the old bar on Third Avenue, cozy and dark, where the zaftig blonde who played piano (she called herself a *chanteuse*) sang it in a whiskey contralto and Sadie hummed along. So many memories with Sadie, so many threads out of the past he had chopped off in the name of fear and impotence and the body yelping for its freedom as the hanged man begs for air. He would have cuddled her and stroked her lacquered hair and begged, "Forgive me, Sadie. For Gregor. For everything. For loving you too much and not enough. For I do love you, Sadie. Only I can't stand you. Your pillowy breasts that smothered me when we made love. Your opera voice. Your Red-Hot Mama Jewish motherliness that is an anachronism. I want somebody lean and modern—skinny, yes—who can match me in neuroses, one on one. I want one of those long-legged broads in shiksa frocks who bats her phony eyelashes and discourses on the federal budget or the District's possibilities for statehood. A trendy—did you know I was that shallow?—who shakes hands with a wrestler's grip and jiggles braless under the silky tailoring."

Frobisch told the priest, "You have the gist."

"Well, Howie, let me tell you what I think."

"No, don't tell me!" He was tired of playing the supplicant. For chrissake, they must be the same age; yet he kept up the "Yes, Father, no, Father," as though he were a child repeating the lessons of the catechism. He might respect the Roman collar but not a tennis shirt showing dark rounds of sweat under the arms and the blue laurel on the breast that branded it Fred Perry and expensive. Was the man too high-toned to wear a Gant? "I know exactly what you think. This doesn't take clairvoyance. You figure, here's a fellow, almost fifty-one. Having domestic troubles. Under a lot of strain. Somewhat concerned because he can't get it up. He goes to Rome on a little vacation. He eats. He drinks. Maybe he has a little too much vino. He feels relaxed. He discovers he still gets horny. All the equipment is back in shape. Wunderbar! A miracle! Simple as that."

"I wouldn't have put it that way exactly. But you have the drift."

Frobisch said, "I am telling you, Father. I saw some kind of ghost or apparition, a stranger from an antique land."

" 'Ozymandias.' "

"Come again?"

"Shelley. The first line of 'Ozymandias.' I don't know if it's exact but it comes close. 'I met a traveler from an antique land.' "

"I am an accountant, Father Paul. I took a degree in business at NYU. I don't read Shelley. I never heard of Ozzie what's-his-name any more than I ever heard of your Pope. I saw an angel, plain and simple. Then I started to get flashes of what was going to happen in the future. Believe me, I don't like it. I'm not enjoying it one bit. I would give anything at all to undo what has happened to me."

"Let me ask you something, Howie. Why are you telling me? Maybe you're not observant; still, you're a Jew. You're talking a sense of heavenly possession on an unwilling vessel; an urge to righteousness and purity of heart. That's very much Old Testament, a page out of the Prophets. Why don't you talk it over with a rabbi?"

"You mean the fellow at my daughter's temple?"

"Why not?"

"I couldn't. I will not speak to him. He filled my Sima's head with all this religious crap—forgive me, Father, that's the drink talking, not me. He convinced her she must make aliyah to Israel. She gave up any thought of college. She gained weight. I hardly know her. I won't seek out that man. Besides, I don't think the vision was Old Testament. It came to me in Rome, and all the portents—the ESP, if you want to call it that—concerned the Pope. I'm convinced it's a matter to discuss with Catholics."

"The Church, my friend, is not amenable to claims of miracles."

"Aren't there ever exceptions?"

Father Paul was wearing an outsized watch with a gleaming oblong face that flashed digital numbers. Sighing, he watched the numbers change like a seer watching sand shift in a glass. Once Frobisch had met him in Rock Creek Park, and he'd been blinded by the sun reflected from that monstrous watch face like a signal beaming in from outer space. When he encountered him, the priest was running in a jogging suit of cardinal red, accepting the timid smiles of pretty girls on bicycles and women pushing babies in their strollers. Frobisch, who had been walking Gregor, stepped aside, thinking that Cortez in golden armor might have struck the Aztecs thus, with the same sense of reverence and awe. He'd let the leash go slack; and Gregor, attracted by a moving target, had leaped forward to nip the priest's leg. Father Paul commanded, "Hold your dog!" Frobisch made a kamikaze leap and landed face down on the squirming terrier amid a pile of yellow leaves. "I could sue you, Howie!" The priest had stopped short on the path to hurl that threat.

Father Paul set down his glass. Mechanically, he checked his fly, ensuring the zipper's closure, the instinctive cautionary gesture of the public man about to launch into a speech. "We got enough problems with modern life. The Church is in upheaval, Howie. Has been since Vatican II. Listen, we have to take an ancient, noble institution and incorporate it into the twentieth century, right? So we simplify the mass, translate it from Latin to English so people will understand the prayers. We figure that'll draw 'em back into the faith. What happens? We get complaints. People holler, 'Change it back the way it was. No need to understand. We want to be astonished.'

"We offer the world's most beautiful liturgical music. The kids say they want guitars. And tambourines. 'Strum me a little Scripture so I can dance and clap my hands like it was old-time minstrel business. Do a little cake-walkin' before God.' Do you know, there's a group of young monks in Vermont who get maybe a thousand people every Sunday into their church—not a church, really, a big old barn—because they play and sing their own music and they dance around. I've seen pictures. Priests dancing in a circle like Indians. Holding hands. I don't believe it. A real crowd-pleaser that is. Maybe I'll have to start that soon."

Father Paul was weighing the letter opener as though he meant to fling it straight at Frobisch's heart. Frobisch shifted in his wobbly seat, prepared to duck in case the priest went crazy and attacked.

"We got young priests saying, 'I like the job just fine, only I wanta get married. This celibacy is crap'—pardon my French, Howie—same as you, it's the scotch speaking. We got nuns saying, 'I want quits with this crummy habit. It's like being in purdah. I want somethin' outa Christian Dior. A little low-cut, maybe. A shorter skirt.' Picture it, Howie, a nun showin' a bit o' thigh? That's something to think about, right?

"How about the problems I've got in this parish? Young wives wanting to use birth control. Couples wanting divorce. And don't mention abortion! We're agreed, I hope, that that's a sin; only you do the work I do in the inner city—you see little girls pregnant from rape and incest—you start to wonder about this so-called gift of life. You do, Howie, you question your own faith.

"Then you got your do-good ladies in the parish saying, "Let us open our hearts to the street people. Let's collect the poor and the deprived and bring them to our parish where it's cool and green.' So you do; you round 'em up out of the flophouses and the alleys, and you bus 'em to the suburbs. You feed 'em and you play music—yeah, you give 'em the guitars and the clappin' hands. A little old school spirit to get 'em in a pious mood. You know how they react? They stand out in the bushes and they barf!

Or they defecate in the pews! That's the kinda problem I contend with, Howie. I got my hands full without you bringing me news of miracles!"

"I know that, Father. I heard you tell it all on 'Panorama.' It doesn't change the truth. Why won't you listen? I'm telling you something that validates your whole life's work."

The priest had spotted a droplet of spilled scotch on the desktop. Carefully he touched an index finger to the spill and brought it to his tongue, savoring the taste as though contact with the wood enhanced the flavor. "I don't need your validation, Howie."

"You won't let yourself be astonished?"

Father Paul tossed his letter opener on the desk. "The Church recognizes charismata. Moments of special grace and faith that come to true believers. People who all at once in a burst of blessed insight see the way. I wouldn't think your experience qualified as something of that sort. Listen, it's not even that unusual. In this line of work we hear it all the time. Deathbed conversions where God shows up in a burst of light. Wife-beaters who all at once feel remorse and have angels pop out of the woodwork tellin' 'em to mend their ways. Convicts who chat with Jesus in their cells. Howie, half the clowns in Congress think they have God's ear and that they got their jobs by divine fiat. Maybe they did; I don't know how else some of those turkeys made it." Father Paul smiled the rueful smile of one who sees himself powerless in the face of cosmic mysteries. "My son, I'm sorry."

Frobisch leaned forward. Caught up in the intensity of his argument he ignored the ominous wobbling of his chair. "Father, if I came to you and said I was possessed of devils, what would you advise?"

"Quick trip to Saint Elizabeth's for psychiatric testing."

"Okay. Assume I'm proven sane. I bet I'd get an audience in Georgetown. An exorcism, maybe. A ticket to New York or L.A. so I could tell my story on TV. Film rights. A contract with Time-Life—"

"Ah, Howie, you watch too many movies."

"No, Father, hear me out. If I said I sighted little gnomes from outer space, I'd get a debriefing at the Pentagon and a feature in the *Post*. I'm saying I've seen an emissary of God Himself, and you imply that's ho-hum stuff. It doesn't make good copy. Hold it now, Father Paul, don't smile. I don't claim to be a messiah. I didn't meet up with Jesus Christ. I don't have notions of that kind. What I need is someone's help. I can't stand the weight of what I know. I can't stand the sympathy I feel. I see a pigeon in the park miss out on a crumb and I start to cry. I hear my sick dog whimper in his sleep and I know his pain. Can you imagine what afflicts me when I see the day-to-day agony of the human race? Can you imagine what I feel when I pick up the morning paper? I don't read it anymore. It used to be my greatest pleasure. I gave it up 'cause I'm an open wound. I'm a mess of sensitivity about the poor, the weak, the starving; and I don't know what to do with it. It's too big a burden. I can't go it alone!"

"*Mazel tov*, Howie. You have a dream and you discover human suffering. A little late, but better late than never. What else is new?"

Frobisch struggled from his chair. He set his glass down on the dark desktop next to a quill pen molting purple feathers on a brass inkstand and a miniature of the Blessed Virgin with the Infant Jesus (bearing an awesome resemblance to a younger Randy De Filippo) in her arms.

"Father, I want to show you something." Frobisch bent

to roll up his pants leg. The trouser was cut too narrow to raise above the knee. Impatiently he pulled at his belt buckle. Father Paul raised both palms like Moses trying to quell an angry tide. Frobisch ignored him and unzipped his pants. He let his slacks drop to the floor. He stood before the priest in his gingham shorts. "It's almost a month since I hurt my knee. Look at it."

The knee blazed luminously purple like the pulpy inside of overripe fruit. The skin was soft and pinkly raw on the outer edges of the bruise; the center was dark and spongy with small, hemorrhaging capillaries.

"That looks nasty."

"It doesn't heal."

"If I were you, I'd have it looked at. Matter of fact, a complete physical might not be amiss. You took quite a fall."

"You think I had a seizure?"

"Not at all, Howie. It's an angry-looking knee."

"You think maybe a series of little strokes brought me down? A heart attack? Epilepsy? A case of petit mal or grand mal, depending on the grandiosity of my delusion, isn't that so? Maybe you think I'm simply crazy?"

"I'm suggesting you have an orthopedist check the knee. Judging by the soreness, you might have broken something."

"It doesn't heal. Some days it starts to look better; the color fades. I can touch it and it's hardly tender. Then something happens. My ex-wife phones and starts to cry. I meet an old priest on the plane who's likely to get a melanoma. The thing starts throbbing like a drum. The color darkens. You see it now. It's sort of fifty-fifty. Not as bad as it can be, but not so great either."

"All right, Howie. Pull up your pants!" Father Paul

had flushed the high color of a man irked beyond all patience. "I can't vouch for my housekeeper's imagination.
God knows what she'll think if she walks into my study
and finds you in your shorts!"

"I wanted you to see the knee—"

"I've seen it. Now zip up. Listen, I want you to see a
doctor. Get something for that knee. No ifs or buts. I mean
it. I'll give you the name of the man at Georgetown who
fixed my tennis elbow good as new."

"Tennis elbow! Don't insult me, Father!"

"It wouldn't be amiss to get some counseling. I can give
you a list of names. Look 'em over; take your pick." The
no-nonsense pastoral voice. He'd heard it that day in the
park when Gregor had broken free. "Hold your dog!" And
Frobisch had made his suicidal leap, an athlete's flying
tackle, and landed on his face, covering the muddy terrier who writhed and whimpered like a mad greased pig.
They'd followed the priest back to the rectory—all of them
trotting at a heady clip—where Mrs. Laverty, the housekeeper, bathed the leg and announced the scratches super-
ficial. Nonetheless, Frobisch had grieved. He'd tied Gregor
to a lamppost and waited till the priest appeared on the
front lawn, making something of an entrance, limping and
pale. Frobisch offered to pay or shoot the dog who was
piddling yellow streams on consecrated grass. He had
wrung his hands, literally bowed and pulled upon a humble forelock—always the blundering schlemiel—Tevye,
confronting an angry cossack on the grimy cobbles of the
shtetl.

"I don't plan to consult any shrinks, Father." Muster-
ing dignity, Frobisch zipped up his pants.

Father Paul had gotten up to pace. Frobisch took
malicious pleasure noting a ring of flab under the priest's
tight-fitting shirt.

The priest rubbed the stubble on his jaw. "Friday night we hold our ecumenical outreach. The ladies do a buffet supper. You might stop by. We're havin' a rabbi who's into marriage counseling—too late for you to get much good from him—and an Episcopalian minister who fancies he's more High Church than me. He'd love a word with you. That mystic stuff is up his alley."

"No way, Father."

"Suit yourself, Howie. I'm tryin' to help. You got me worried, kiddo."

Frobisch eased back into his chair. "Father Paul, there's something else I have to tell you, even though I'd rather not."

"And what is that?"

"Something about the Pope."

"What might that be, Howie?"

"He won't live long, Father. He's going to die."

"My son, we are all going to die."

"He is going to die within the week."

"Is he, now? That's interesting. And would you say of natural causes? Or do you predict foul play?"

"I don't know, Father. I just get . . . little hints. I don't get all the information complete, so I can't exactly say."

"You say you just get little hints? From your friendly angel?"

"Don't mock me, Father. It's a hard thing to know."

"I'm sure it is, my son."

"I don't like having to tell you. I'd prefer it if you didn't know. It's hard to have advance warning of tragedy. It's better to go in jumpin' blind, as the saying goes. Would you agree?"

"I would agree that you are troubled, my son."

"I'm sorry to be the bearer of such bad news."

"Promise me you'll see a doctor."

"I'm not sick, Father."

Father Paul had retrieved the letter opener and was weighing it in his palms, surveying it as though he meant to use it to tear human flesh. It was heavy silver, ornately carved, a weapon worthy of a Borgia. How Randy would have loved it! How he would have zinged it, whistled as he heard it cleave the heavy air and plummet with a satisfying thunk into the earth. He was half inclined to challenge Father Paul to a session of Toss and Pickup on the grass.

"Who told you the Pope's life is in danger?"

Frobisch shrugged. "It's just something I know. I sensed it in the hotel room in Rome . . . when I knew who they would pick. Something told me it was all a waste. The black smoke; the white smoke; the people waiting in the square. I knew they'd have to do the whole thing over in a month. Like when Sadie cleans the chandelier."

"You've lost me, Howie."

"See, once a month Sadie, that's my ex-wife, and Mrs. Garcia, that's the cleaning lady, wash the crystal pieces on the chandelier. They do it together 'cause Sadie won't trust Mrs. Garcia by herself. It's a day-long ritual. They get these buckets of water and ammonia and clean white rags and pieces of newspaper for polishing the teardrop crystals. Newspaper's supposed to be the best for that. They work together and they fight. Always they quarrel about whether it's finished and looking all right. Mrs. Garcia says, *'Está limpia?'* And Sadie answers, *'No está limpia. Todavia no.'* Sadie got a book of Spanish so she could quarrel with the maid. Sometimes the argument gets heated and they both get upset. Mrs. Garcia threatens to quit, and Sadie has to calm her. When it's all over, they're both worn out. The chandelier looks great. That's when

Sadie starts to wonder if it's worth it. She studies the crystal from every angle, and it's all glittery and shiny; she should be content. Only all she can think of is, in another month it will be dusty and she'll have to go through the whole dad-blamed ritual again. That's what I knew in Rome. That the ceremony would be repeated. That all the fuss, the celebrating and the fainting, was for nothing."

"You have some quarrel with the tradition?"

"He's going to die, Father."

"Suppose you're right. Could you do anything to prevent it?"

"I don't know. I don't think so, Father."

Father Paul held the letter opener to his cheek as though the coolness of the metal soothed him. "Then give it up. Forget it. Don't be shootin' off your mouth."

"I can't."

"You'll be branded a loon, Howie."

"That goes with the territory, doesn't it, Father?"

"You don't know anything about the territory. What is this sudden urge to be a martyr? You'll be mocked, you know. Taken for a fool."

Frobisch clasped his hands, eternally the supplicant. A beggar with a bowl. "I don't want to be a martyr. Believe me when I tell you, Father Paul, that my biggest ambition for the summer, besides getting Sima to come home, was to drive down to Rehoboth and prowl the swingers' beach."

Father Paul guffawed. "Then do it, Howie. You're not cut out for this mystic stuff. You don't have the personality. Lookit, you think I don't understand, but I do. When I was a student at the seminary, I had in mind to be a contemplative. I'd take long walks in the woods, ponder the eternal mysteries, pray. I'd spend hours in prayer. Skip meals. Give up sleep. Some days I'd get a wonderful weak feeling, a ringing in the ears. I'd know God was there, just over the next hilltop, waiting in a clump of trees, lying low, maybe, in a field of black-eyed Susans. Blame it on tinnitis, if you choose to be clinical, low blood sugar, fatigue. Whatever the reasons, it was one grand high before the inevitable letdown. A rush, better than drugs. And like drugs, you get to crave the feeling; you don't want to let it go, even though on some level you're sufferin'. Am I right?"

"I suppose so, Father."

"Give it up, Howie. You're not the type."

"I didn't know there were specific personality requirements."

"Give it up. Do good, like your dream told you. Pray, if it gives you comfort. As for the other stuff, the predictions and prognostications, ignore 'em."

"How do I do that, Father?"

"You simply do it, Howie. It's like carnal desire. You ignore it long enough, it goes away."

"That wouldn't work for me, Father."

Father Paul threw up his hands in the gesture of one who has given more than his responsibility requires and wants to call it quits. "We're back to square one, ain't we, Howie. Nothin' to do but drown your sorrows." He pointed to the decanter on his desk. "Hair of the dog?"

"I don't mind." Unfortunate, the choice of words, the unintended cruelty. Frobisch deplored the priest's descent into the vernacular. Had he been polled, he would have voted for the Latin mass.

Over the dark of the church parking lot, stars smoldered random fires. A fat moon lit the drive. Father

Paul himself had seen him out, ushering him down a cinnamon-smelling corridor to a locked screen door that opened on the lot. The priest had voiced concern about Frobisch driving. Frobisch hastened to reassure him, outlining his itinerary in clipped Anglican speech. "Quite all right, old buddy. Got the route down pat. Connect-cut, over Bradley, to Wis-consin. Or I could go 'round the Circle, across Reno to Thirty-fourth, and thence to Mass-a-toot-sis. No prob. Hug the right lane. Take it slow. Cruise past the embassies. Do a genuflection at the mosque jus' to cover all bases. Stop and tell the Brits hello, God save the Queen, hands across the border, sink the *Bismarck*, all that stuff. Home before dark or morning, whichever fits."

Father Paul demurred. "I can have a cab here in five minutes."

"Cert'nly not. Got the Volvo good as new. Car's been gutted like a fish. New transmission, new sparks, new Carborundum. Tha'sa joke. Car doesn't run on silicon carbide, though if it did, you could say, SiC transit. Get it, Father?"

"Yes."

"And you thought I was drunk. Consider, Father, whether drunks make puns—and not just puns, but wordplay that requires a certain erudition. Do they, Father Paul? What say?"

"None that I've known."

"'Zactly." Frobisch had seized his hand and pumped it hard. "Thanks for the booze, the pleasure of your comp'ny. Not to worry." He'd grinned at Father Paul's long face. "I'm not the least bit drunk. Besides, God's watchin' over me, don't you know?" He'd bolted out the door before the priest could posit further arguments.

A row of honeysuckle cast a scent so sweet it made him stop and gasp for purer air before proceeding in a bleary zigzag to his car. His knee throbbed as though someone had clamped it in a vise. Bending to soothe it, he dropped his keys. He knelt to search for them in the weeds. Crouching on all fours he crept, careful to avoid the sharp edge of pebbles and twisted roots. He could hear the soft sound of a piano from the window of a neighboring house. A lesson in progress. The first tentative notes of "Für Elise." He paused to listen. Sima had learned that piece. Sadie had searched around until she found a teacher who would come to the house, a little guy, bandy-legged, with a goatee. He used to show up at the dinner hour, a furious martinet who made a big deal about posture. He would position Sima on the bench, pummel her spine, nag her to square her shoulders until her little button breasts showed round and firm under her blouse. When he had her sitting straight, he would arrange her chubby fists over the keyboard and hiss with the malevolence of a snake, "Attack!"

Frobisch blinked back a rush of tears, remembering how the child would sigh and toss her head so that her long braids bobbed like the tails of small woods animals. How she would struggle to build momentum for the required attack.

She used to study Paderewski's "Minuet" and falter on the trill on the third note. The teacher, who had a funny Frog accent, would shrug and proclaim to the surrounding air, to Gregor panting his impatience for Beethoven, to Frobisch lurking in a corner chair to make sure there was no hanky-panky over the positioning of Sima's back: "Zere is a problem with the mordent."

"The more-dent." Frobisch eased his aching back (the

director's chair had been death on his lower discs) against a stunted tree. "More dent." He giggled and suppressed a burp—grimaced at the taste of stomach acids rising on his tongue. "He made it sound like a disease." Then the bearded fool would take over to execute a perfect trill, repeated and repeated again, as if to hammer home a bit unkindly the flawless beauty of his touch. Frobisch remembered firm hands scurrying the range of keys with the swiftness of blown autumn leaves.

He heard the slam of a screen door and the slap of rubber soles running on the blacktop. He stood up in time to see the child cutting across the lot, a pile of yellow songbooks clutched under one arm. He was surprised the music student was a boy—thin, with lank, dark hair and a pale face bobbing above the hedge tops like a second, smallish moon. For a moment Frobisch panicked, fearing he'd seen a ghost. He stared hard at the child, taking comfort in details that argued for the reality of what he saw. The boy was wearing baggy camp shorts bristling with snaps, zippers, and chains, and a yellow T-shirt printed with black letters: Montgomery County Soccer, and high-top sneakers with the laces untied. His legs were pocked with scabs. An oversized Band-Aid flapped loosely at one knee, the gauze pad discolored with pus and blood. Frobisch's left knee throbbed in sympathetic pain.

"I heard your lesson," he told the child. "You're doing well. You're making excellent progress, I would say."

The boy afforded him a serpent's gaze, eyes as flat and dark as coins, the mouth pursed in a little grin of malice as though there were something ominous and secret about the music he had played. He didn't speak. Frobisch blundered on. "One day you'll be very pleased that you're studyin' the classics."

121

The child stared at him as though he were a freak.

"I congratulate you on the effort," Frobisch babbled. He surprised himself and the youngster with an explosive belch.

The child eyed him warily. He shifted the pile of music to his chest as though he meant to use it for a shield. When he spoke, his voice was husky, either from the effort of the lesson or from the weight of his contempt. "Fuck off!"

Frobisch watched him sprint across the lot, jumping the lines painted to mark off parking spaces as though adhering to a particular superstition would protect him from adult wrath. He bore the child no rancor for the outburst. He must have scared the poor kid, rising as he had out of the bushes with a sappy grin and hiccuping sour, boozy breath. Profanity on church grounds was a shock, but in this case, not unseemly. It seemed a logical response to give a wobbly Ozymandias looming out of the shadows in a blaze of moon.

## · CHAPTER ·
# 5

There was a letter from Sima in the morning mail. It had lain buried beneath the heavier stuff (circulars, junk ads, department store brochures presaging Christmas) so that he'd almost overlooked it, had riffled halfway through a Brookstone catalog listing exotic tools before he saw it—a miracle, the blue airmail envelope fluttering from beneath the covers of a Lord & Taylor wish book! He picked it up, marveling at the gift unsought, possibly undeserved after the shame of his past night's excesses. He couldn't make out the posted date.

The letter had gone first to the house in Kensington where Sadie had printed a bleak Not here. In a more charitable afterthought (she was too much the good sport not to) she'd scribbled his office address. Somebody there, one of the airhead secretaries, had forwarded it to his apartment. And never called! Never alerted him that a message from his darling, his own heart's blood, was on its way.

Cold women! All of them cold. All mean, unfeeling, wanton. All but his own sweet girl, writing to apologize, or ask after his health, or merely to keep in touch. No matter. The point was, she had written. He weighed the letter in his palm—it must hold at least two folded pages— traced Sima's familiar o's and a's (strong cursive taught by the gentle Quakers) as though they were symbols wrought in Braille. He held the envelope to the light. Suppose his mind was playing tricks. If he could conjure a homespun angel, a dying Pope, why not this slim, onion-skin missive scrawled with conflicting directives?

Last night Father Paul had warned him of the blurred line that exists between reality and hope. Frobisch had argued, "When you cross that line, isn't that faith?"

"Faith is one thing, Howie. I don't quarrel with faith. But you're claimin' some effin' miracle!"

They'd both laughed at the priest's inability to say the word outright. Bleary-eyed, wobbly, just this side of stinkin' drunk, Father Paul couldn't shed the cloak of clerical propriety, any more than Frobisch in his sweaty, expensive sports clothes could assume the guise of zealous mystic and make it stick.

Frobisch placed Sima's letter squarely on the glass-topped coffee table and backed off several paces. He sank into a velvet chair a safe distance from the table, still eyeing the letter warily as though the envelope contained a bomb. Suppose she'd written to renounce him. She had lived long enough with Bedouin mischief; she could disown him with a thrice-stated pronouncement, like the accepted Arab dissolution of a marriage. "I divorce you; I divorce you; I divorce you." And it was done.

He shivered in the early morning damp. The day had started with an anemic drizzle. Now the first wan rays of sun—faint, almost wintry—shone through the twin glass doors that opened to his pint-sized balcony. Even that pale gleaming was an affront. He pressed both fists to his thudding temples. There was an anvil pounding in his head— no cheery workmen's chorus, but a jumble of erratic rhythms, now a solid thud, now an offbeat tremor, like the fibrillations of an ailing heart. He fought a rising wave of nausea. Acid bubbled in his gut. He was scared to open the damned letter. To this he and Sima had come. But he adored her! He'd been a loving father to her all her life! Indeed, he'd loved her with a single-mindedness that bordered on ferocity. And he'd believed, wrongly as it turned out, that there existed between them perfect understanding.

Frobisch struggled from the cushioned deepness of his velvet seat and began to pace. Maybe, from the vantage of the Middle East, she was sending him a clear bill of particulars, citing all the times that he had erred and offering him the chance for a rebuttal—the long hoped-for truce he'd sought so desperately in Rome. If she'd done that, then he could answer point by point, acknowledge the moments he'd gone wrong, explain that the errors of paternal devotion were just that—errors derived of excess love and not of malice. He swooped on the letter with a sense of joy, his fingers already itching to frame an answer, to grab ball-point and yellow paper and start a new, important list.

The letter was two thin pages, poorly typed and dittoed in faded purple ink. It had been dated with a certain lyric candor: Autumn 1978.

A nice heading for a poem. Is it a poem, then, wondered Frobisch? He read the salutation: "Dear friends."

What's this? What is she sending me, Dear friends? Is it a joke? Am I supposed to break a code? He was choking in the stale apartment, as though a weight had settled on his heart. He slid back the glass door to the balcony and stepped outside. The damp air soothed his chest. He sat down on a metal lawn chair and quietly inhaled, as an invalid breathes steam to soothe a croup. He stared down at a row of maples, their leaves still wet with rain. Beyond the trees the grounds were landscaped like a formal garden—circles of marigolds and purple asters, day lilies, golden mums, crisscrossed by gravel walks where coveys of gray pigeons scratched for crumbs. There had been a meeting last April about the pigeons. Tenants complained someone was feeding them, luring them from the dubious joys of Georgetown to this little park where they scattered filth—pigeon shit and lice—over the pristine bulwarks of the balconies. Frobisch, innocent as a dove, had made a speech favoring the unknown benefactor ("Do we improve on nature by banning nature from the premises?") and had been jeered.

Beyond the formal lawns of the apartment complex he could see the broad sweep of Massachusetts Avenue and a slow cortege of cars, some kind of motorcade—two white cars of the District police followed by a pearl gray limousine long as a city block. "Arabs are everywhere," mourned Frobisch. He glanced back at the letter. Squinting in the brightening sun he read:

Dear friends:

As we approach the season of the High Holidays, it seems appropriate for me to take stock of my year and to share some of my experiences on the kibbutz with you, my friends. I hope you will forgive me for sending a duplicated letter. Since so many of you have expressed curiosity about my adventures overseas it seems easier to reach you in this fashion. I will begin by telling you my life is good. . . .

She sends me a duplicated letter! She calls me friend! What is this "friend" business? I'm demoted to the status of a school chum? I am her father! He hurried to the second page to see if she'd added a note to him.

> I have learned to drive a tractor, unbelievable as that may seem of one who never drove anything but automatic transmission. . . .

And recklessly at that! Too many narrow squeaks. Too many mysterious dents and scrapes of paint that showed up on the Volvo, not to mention whispered conclaves with Sadie when they thought he was out of range. She'd once bashed in the door of De Filippo's new Mercedes, and Frobisch had to plead that they settle it between them without calling the insurance people. De Filippo had let him grovel and finally waved him off, pompous as a Mafia don: "I don't need your money, Howie. It's the principle of the thing."

> Our kibbutz is an animal sanctuary of sorts. Dr. Abels is rearing two baby chimps; and we keep as mascot a female ostrich who roams at will and delights in running races with the tractor.

Who, then, is Dr. Abels? The gunslinger she loves? She finds him sexy in his khaki shorts, cosseting monkeys, showing his knobby knees. She wanted a zookeeper, I would've found her one. We got a fine zoo right here at the Smithsonian. We got a white tiger. We got the two new pandas!

There was more about the ostrich. He skipped to the final paragraph:

> As we approach the most sacred week of the Jewish calendar, allow me to wish you the happiest of New Years and the hope that God inscribe you in the Book of Life!

Happy New Year! Joyous Yom Kippur! What is this? His hands trembled as he tried to stuff the letter back into its envelope. *Erev Rosh Hashanah* she sends a goddamned Christmas letter, babbling vapid inanities about the way her life is good and she's running races with an ostrich! To me! Her father! No word of love. No little tender hint that she might miss me or wish me well. I, who offered to pay for her air fare. Second fiddle to a chimp!

It was an insult. He didn't need a travel piece from her—a Fodor guide! Blame the curse of his clairvoyance (his effin' miracle, said Father Paul), he saw the kibbutz, smelled it—motor oil and frying fish, sweet oranges, manure. A queue of visitors from the States, self-conscious in their madras shirts and stiff new jeans, admiring the shell of the planned guest house, the man-made lake. And Sima, atop the tractor—the two-toed bird streaking the browned grass at a heady clip, leaving a wake of dust and feathers. Sima was driving, singing something in Hebrew—her round face flushed, her gray eyes gleaming mischief at the chase, her frizz of blonde curls tumbling from the mashed brim of her cotton hat. Sima, no more a captive audience for his silly stories, was laughing, free. Happy because they were apart and she could mock him with a dittoed letter; because, despite the unctuous pieties of her New Year's greeting, she had disowned him after all.

"So be it," Frobisch cried. "All of it over. Sadie and Gregor. Sima, too." He tore the letter into bits and let them fall over the railing of the balcony (the tenant group be damned!) The pieces fluttered in a puff of wind, then drifted to the gravel walk, scattering amid the gray-winged pigeons like flakes of alien snow.

## · CHAPTER ·

# 6

The church basement smelled of cheese and backed-up plumbing, the same mix of food odors and faulty pipes he remembered from the old shul in Bayonne, the same old duffers clambering down the hall on canes, the same kids palming cigarettes in the shadows. In his day they'd favored Lucky Strikes. It would be pot now. (Reefers? Roaches? He was shaky on the vernacular.) If memory served, those furtive puffs on holy ground would be as exciting as forbidden sex. There was sex, too, rites of exploration and torture, taking place outside behind the floppy bushes Gregor had once marked off as canine ground.

He followed a string of late arrivals to the social hall, a long, low-ceilinged room hung with balloons and colored streamers. Along one wall was a line of serving tables covered with red and white checked paper. Cafeteria tables spread with the same paper were ranged in rows across the room. On a stage at the far end of the hall a janitor was centering a podium and three folding chairs, moving with the dreamy concentration of an actor memorizing his marks. Now and again the man paused in his labors to count the crowd.

Frobisch stood in the doorway searching for Father Paul.

A covey of females in cobblers' aprons sped by him bearing trays and clouded pitchers. Frobisch hurried to overtake a woman who was carrying a dome of jello circled by a wreath of lettuce. When he tapped her arm she shook him off. "Oh, please, not now! I've got to put this out and rescue the California spaghetti before it burns. You know they always overcook it. And this jello salad wants to melt." She was eyeing her burden with a mix of relish and defiance, Salome with the head of John the Baptist lolling on a bed of greens. Unexpectedly, she whirled on Frobisch. "You could carry in the rolls. I've got them warming in the kitchen on the Salton hot tray."

Frobisch asked, "Where is the kitchen?"

"You can't find the kitchen? Oh, Lord, you must be a guest! Are you B'nai Zion or Saint Andrew's?"

Frobisch answered, "I don't know."

"Louisa!" The woman's soprano pealed over the noises of the crowd with the stridence of a signal bell. "Louisa, c'mere and give this man a name tag. He doesn't know who he is."

"It's all right. I'm not staying." He was surrounded by flushed, beaming women bearing aromatic gifts. Their eyes radiated holy fervor; their lips parted in smiles that might turn mean if he bolted for the exit. Their breasts were rising, falling, rising, in sweetest concert under their cotton smocks. He blinked under the assault of their collected lights and glows—pink cheeks, white teeth, shimmering ruby jello studded with olive eyes.

"Of course you're staying." A firm hand tugged his sleeve. "I'll make you a name tag."

"I don't want a name tag. I won't wear one, y'see. I'm not staying. I came because I got a message on my answering machine from Father Paul saying that he had to see me, that it was urgent that we meet tonight."

What the priest had said was "Get your ass on over here! No ifs or buts. We better talk." None of the man's usual bonhomie. Frobisch discerned anger, upset, a whole sea of tribulations in the priest's terse command—even a hint of mystery that set him on his way to shower and change before heading (weary after a day's walking around the city) to the church.

"It *is* urgent if Father says so." The woman soothed, "And you don't have to wear a name tag. But you're staying. Of course you're staying. You'd be Howard Frobisch if you're the one Father called. I'm right, aren't I? He told me to look after you. He made that my special task. So, you see, you have to stay and let me perform it."

She was almost his height in flats—not so young, maybe forty—with a schoolmarm's air of stubborn certainty. You didn't cross her or she'd rap your hands. She had soft-looking brownish hair pinned up with amber combs into no particular style—an old-fashioned, messy bun. Blue eyes glinting mischief, a head-on, sexy boldness to the look that piqued him. A nose too fleshy to be perfect, but nice enough. She wasn't wearing makeup, a welcome change from his ex-wife's eye goop and the blobs of fevered rouge that afflicted Sadie with the look of lupus. This woman looked dressed for gardening in a plain white blouse and denim skirt. A gold chain with three dangling Greek letters glittered in the hollow of her neck. She fiddled with the chain, nervous under his lengthy scrutiny. When she grinned she showed white, even teeth, except for one eyetooth that was just a little catty-wampus. Orthodonture that didn't hold. They'd had the same problem with Sima, and Sadie had raised hell.

"I'm Louisa Rhinelander. I'll be your hostess—guide—whatever, if you don't mind." The woman held out her hand.

Frobisch took it, startled by the sudden raffish beauty that transformed her when she smiled. "Mrs. Rhinelander, where is Father Paul?"

"It's not Mrs., it's Miss. It's not Ms., either. I can't abide that, even though I know it's meant to be advantageous to unmarried women like myself. We don't get put down for being spinsters and I appreciate the thought, but I can't stand the sound of it. It's like an insect buzzing in the ear. Say it; you'll see what I mean. Go on, try it."

Frobisch said, "Mzzz."

"Please call me Louisa. May I call you Howard?"

"Yes, you may."

"Do you believe in ESP? Because I'll tell you something funny. When Father Paul called tonight I was rearranging some books, and I had gotten as far as Forster. *Howards End.* I was holding it in my hand and thinking what a lovely work it was and how it had been years since I'd read it but I was meaning to again, when Father Paul phoned to say he'd invited a special guest named Howard Frobisch, and would I look after him? Do you see how funny that was? I was listening to Father describe you and holding this book, *Howards End.* I had to wonder, did the name apply to you? And if it did, what did it mean? It couldn't be Howard's termination. That would be too sad. It couldn't be Howard's posterior. That would be too silly. Good grief, you must forgive me! I'm rambling on. When I have a captive audience, I just sound off."

"Howard's posterior?" He was still holding her hand. It was warm and firm, splotched with tiny freckles, the nails cut square and short. He essayed a friendly squeeze, meant to forgive the flood of chatter, and Louisa blushed.

"What happened is, poor Mr. Healy got so upset with this morning's news he went and had a stroke. The family expects the worst, and Father Paul's gone to the hospital to give the poor man the last rites. He told me I was to explain. He said he picked me because he knew I'd talk a blue streak and I wouldn't let you get away, at least until you'd eaten; and he hoped he would be back by then. I'm not sure we should have held this meeting when you consider the tragedy we've all endured, but the food was already delivered, and there was that big fuss about getting Rabbi Waldheim to come on Friday night. We couldn't send him packing after he agreed. I don't know, Howard. What do you think?"

Frobisch, pretending to understand: "I suppose the show goes on."

"Well, it does, and that's the truth." Louisa winked, and his heart almost broke for the glory of it. "You don't have to stay for the lectures after supper if you don't want to. I almost never do. I volunteer to work on cleanup. That way I can hide in the kitchen and cut out if I don't want my mind improved. I hope you don't think that's awful. Father Paul says you're a Jew, and I know they're very strong into education."

"I don't know what I am."

Louisa pondered this. "You could listen to the speakers and take your pick. Rabbi Waldheim's talking on The Eden That Is Marriage; then the Reverend Mr. Bartholomew means to zing us with The Poverty of Belief. Ah, don't smile, Howard. You think it's small-town stuff,

133

and no one would give us the time of day if we were living in the District. Well, we get a lot of real sharp people coming to these things—doctors, engineers, all those bright lady lawyers. God knows why they come. Certainly not for the food."

"I guess I don't find either topic appealing."

Louisa pressed his hand. "I tell you what we'll do. We'll get ourselves some supper. If Father Paul hasn't come by the time we finish, we'll just split. Is that all right with you?"

"Definitely all right. If you will promise to be my dinner companion."

"Yes, I will. It is my duty and pleasure." Louisa laughed.

There was that boldness to her look, the implication he'd proposed something suggestive. She had said she was a spinster, not a Ms.; still, there was something to her carriage, something in those brazen eyes that hinted at a liberation. Curious, a little excited, he followed Louisa to the serving table where the women he'd encountered at the entry stood aligned, bearing their pitchers and their vessels like maidens in an ancient frieze. Louisa glided down the line of serving tables giving regal nods, the priestess taking her due in ceremonial offerings.

"The man who had the stroke must be well liked." Frobisch nudged a soggy lettuce leaf around his plate. They had settled in a tiny classroom, where the pint-sized desks and chairs, the crayoned renderings of desert scenes, aroused in him a teary sense of déjà vu. He'd laid claim to a bare wood table positioned on a small raised platform, the teacher's desk and the only furniture that fit his height. Louisa perched in a straight-back chair beside him, poised to jump, as though to block off interference, offer sustenance or extra helpings, mop at errant gravy stains before they ruined his tie. It was pleasant, a bit unnerving, to have her bent so close, literally breathing down his neck, watching as he chewed and swallowed.

She offered him a roll. "You mean Frank Healy? I don't know him all that well."

He'd picked up bits of conversation at the serving table. "People seem gloomy—really upset."

"I suppose they sympathize with the family. I'm sure *I* do." She inched her chair a fraction closer. "Howard, you keep staring around you, as though I'd brought you to another planet."

She'd coaxed a key from the reluctant janitor who'd stared at Frobisch with suspicious eyes, the caution of the true believer who sees the charlatan unmasked. "It ain't allowed." The man trembled with stubborn loyalty. Louisa had shrugged away his fears. "It's all right. I shall take complete responsibility." When they were in the room, she'd launched into a flurry of housekeeping— opening windows, rattling shades, blowing dust from the gravely sweet visages of plaster saints.

"Not another planet. I was thinking back to when my daughter was a little girl. She went to this Jewish Sunday School that wasn't affiliated with any temple. One year they rented classrooms in a convent school. On Sunday mornings, Sadie—that's my ex-wife—and the other ladies would come early and cover all the statues of the saints with plastic bags."

"My word!"

"So the children wouldn't be confused."

"Did your daughter like the school?"

"I suppose she did. She got to play Queen Esther in the Purim play. I made her a crown out of gold paper. And

Sadie gave her one of her negligees, this pink thing with fluffy stuff on the sleeves, like feathers—what is it, eiderdown?"

"Marabou, probably."

"That's right. The marabou kept molting. It left pink fuzz over everything—the textbooks, the desks. I think, the next day, the nuns must've been upset."

"Oh, well, they can be short-tempered." Louisa pointed an admonishing finger at his plate. "Look at that. You hardly eat. That explains why you've got such bad color. Not enough protein. Don't make a face, it's true. I never used to pay attention to that stuff myself, till I put in a shelf on Diet and Nutrition. Now, when I get a chance, I read up on the latest wisdom."

"Are you a librarian, Louisa?" Frobisch stirred his pool of melting jello. There was a trap door closing in his throat. He would choke if he tried to swallow.

"You're dining with a businesswoman, Howard. I own the Aardvark. You know the store? It's on Antique Row in Kensington."

"I know Antique Row." It wasn't far from the old house if you drove north on the Parkway. At a point the architecture changed from Georgian homes of mellow brick to prim Victorian houses with porches and pointy towers. You reached a shopping center of sorts—a shoe repair, a laundromat, a Seven-Eleven. Beyond that was a rabbit warren of tiny stores displaying furniture and kitchen junk, old toys and yellowed prints, maps of defunct countries, moose heads and Borgia rings. Castoffs of the bazaar.

Sadie had found a shop where splintered wood ponies flung from carousels pranced in the cobwebbed corners

136

like phantoms of a sweeter past. Photographs of bearded men and austere women glowered from the shelves, dark with some prior knowledge. She'd dragged him there to see a black Korean chest fitted with numerous tiny drawers, the "workbench" of an Oriental pharmacist, contrived so that each drawer might hold its own herb or specific powder. In an alcove crammed with antique cradles and china dolls swaddled in splotched pink satins, she'd stood on tiptoe, tugged at his lapels, whispered with the breath of honey, "C'mon, sweetie, let's buy it." When she was covetous, she looked her best, the pampered suburban matron in silky blouse and cashmere slacks, her eyes alight with frank desire, her mouth hungry under the berry gloss. She was a masterpiece of creamy skin, of powdered, perfumed opulence—lush, pretty, sexy Sadie, mocking his poor, failed prick with that perfection of the flesh.

It jarred him the way she'd flirted. Out of an instinct to be cruel, a need to shame her before the shop's watchful proprietor (who'd sized them up when they came in and quickly shrugged them off as window-shoppers) he'd stood his ground. "Eighteen hundred clams! Don't make me laugh!"

She'd lashed back, "*Why* do you have to be so mean, so sour? You know we can afford it." There it was, she'd summed it up, a neat equation satisfying his precise accountant's heart: her extravagance plus his meanness yielded a souring of their love. Or something on that order. He must stop conjuring her up, stop summoning flashbacks heaped with old quarrels and guilt. Sadie was always there, riding his shoulder—his conscience and his devil, scarier than any angel evolving out of mist. To think he could be easily rid of her was naive. You couldn't shed the trappings of one life and start another as simply as a snake sheds its skin. There were some jolts in the transition. Aftershocks, as in a major earthquake.

"Old books," prattled Louisa. "It was something started by my father. He was career navy, but after my mother died he took early retirement so he could spend more time with me. I was an only brat, you see, just rattling around the big old house. It's that white Charles Addams monstrosity on the corner of the Parkway—you may have noticed it when you drove by. It was inherited, but don't get any ideas that I have old money, 'cause that's what my father went through setting up the store."

"It hasn't done well?"

"My father had a dream of making it an antiquarian bookshop—old, rare volumes, you know? But he didn't know enough about business, or maybe he didn't know enough about rare books. You have to have a fair amount of capital to purchase a stock that's anywhere worthwhile. I mean the sort of things collectors want. And you have to travel around a lot, I guess, and keep in touch with your fellow antiquarians. I think Papa was lazy, to tell the truth. Anyhow, he compromised by making it old books, instead of rare ones. Maybe a few treasures sneaked in from time to time. Nowadays, I make it mostly by selling romances." Louisa shook her head in mocking wonder. "Aren't they the pits?"

"I don't know. I don't read them."

"Well, they are. Papa would just die if he knew how many I have to stock to keep things going. He had this sentimental thing, I think, about dealing in old books. Other people's memories, you see. He thought they were a repository of old dreams and hopes and aspirations. A kind of 'rag-and-bone shop of the heart,' if I may quote the poet.

Do you read Yeats?" Seeing him shake his head, "Well, you should. There's so much wisdom in his poems I think, sometimes, God talked to him. Can you believe that, Howard?"

He might have known she'd be the sort who quoted poems. "I suppose so," Frobisch said glumly.

Louisa beamed. "I'm glad. Can you guess why Papa called the store the Aardvark?"

"No, I can't."

"It was his one attempt at business sense. He had heard somewhere that stores that are listed in the Yellow Pages at the beginning of the alphabet get the most attention. So he racked his brains thinking of a name. He thought once he came up with the double A he'd be top of the list. But there's an AAA wholesaler who faked him out. I don't think it made a bit of difference. But the name's distinctive, don't you think? I thought once that if we ever made a profit I could order some special wrapping paper made up—sort of a beigey peach with rows of little brown aardvarks in profile. Maybe put in a sideline of aardvark pillows and tote bags. It's not so crazy. People do it all the time with cats. And penguins. Have you seen those penguin mugs? Penguins fornicating?" Louisa slapped a palm to her mouth. "Oh, my God, I don't believe I said that! And in church!"

Frobisch laughed. "It's a respectable word, Louisa. It's the shorter version gets people in trouble."

"Oh, you're right. Howard, I like you. I believe we think alike."

"I like you, too. Very much."

Predictably, Louisa blushed, a red flush that started at the chaste V of her blouse and moved past the chain with its Greek letters to her chin, her ears, her nose gleaming with a patina of perspiration. Frobisch could have wept to think the mildness of his statement would elicit such response.

"It's such fun talking with you," Louisa said, "I'm not doing my job. Should we at least go back to meet the guests of honor?"

"Please, no. Do we have to?" Frobisch asked.

"Well, *I* don't. It's still not clear what Father Paul had in mind for *you*."

"I don't think it touched on The Poverty of Belief."

"Then we can do what we planned—have our ice cream cake and leave. Or we can skip it. We get it wholesale by the carton from Giant, and it's not so very good. The cake's dry, and the ice cream tastes like toothpaste. Say the word and we can pass it up. Maybe you'd walk me home?"

"I'd be very glad to drive you. I'm parked in the church lot."

"And give my neighbors strange ideas when they see me pull up in your car? And you can bet your boots they'll see me. They could teach the FBI about surveillance. Not on your life!"

"We'll walk, then," Frobisch agreed.

And Louisa blushed.

A breeze stirred the willows near Rock Creek. Night birds patrolled the boughs, plunging through tangled skeins of leaves to dart at insects. In the parched creek bed, pools of shallow water shone like tar amid the rocks. Along the creek's meandering course, broken boulders, flung like volcanic rubble, glistened with flecks of mica.

Louisa marveled at the brightness of the stars. "I wish I knew their names. Papa could point them out—Cassiopeia and Orion and Arcturus. He tried to show me how, but I never could pay attention. Now he's gone I figure it's too late to learn."

"He died recently?"

"About five years ago. He had cancer. People say it's some kind of virus. I think it's a giving up on life. I think people give way to despair out of loneliness or disappointment, and that's when their immune system breaks down. Father Paul says that doesn't explain the sick little ones in the hospital at Georgetown. I can't explain that either, unless maybe those children have a lot of sadness in their lives. I think cancer's a disease of grief."

"Maybe grief's a disease all by itself. We either recover from it or we don't."

"When I first saw you in the church basement, Howard, I thought you looked sad."

"I was unhappy, yes. I feel a whole lot better now."

"Really? What cheered you up?"

"When you told me that Howard's end was not terminal but posterior."

"Oh, heaven, you are a tease. I knew you were a tease. I could tell it by the way you kept grinning at everything I said. I *do* talk too much, Howard, and I don't always think before I speak; but I am not a foolish person. I don't want you to think I am."

"I think perhaps you are a miracle," said Frobisch.

"Oh, my, that is excessive. Father Paul warned me that you might say something that seemed . . . excessive."

"Did Father Paul tell you about me? About what happened to me in Rome?"

"Yes, he did."

"What do you think about it, Louisa?"

"I don't believe it for a minute. I think you imagined the whole thing."

Frobisch laughed as though a great load had been lifted

from his heart. He was a balloon relieved of ballast, flying higher, ever higher into the thin night air where the constellations known to Louisa's father glowed diamond-bright. He was weightless with the easement of his burden. This woman, so commonplace, so clever, must speak the truth, as a child speaks truly out of innocence. "Louisa, I pray you are right. I want you to be right."

"Of course I'm right. Angels don't walk the earth. They don't stop to chat with common men."

"They did in the Old Testament. An angel came to earth and wrestled with Jacob, and Jacob won."

"If you think that happened to you—well, there's a word for what I'm thinking. It's 'hubris.' Do you know what I mean?"

"I'm not sure. It's the sort of word you see in books, only you're never exactly sure of the definition."

"I'll tell you what it means. Overweaning pride. Arrogance. It's arrogance, don't you think, to believe that God would seek you out. Not just you, but me or anybody. Why would He do that? Why would He choose you, say, and not Father Paul?"

"Or Rabbi Waldheim, making an Eden out of marriage?"

"Why not? I bet he has some interesting ideas."

"I bet he does, too. Casting aside one's fig leaves. Walking nude before the Lord."

"There you go, teasing again, Howard. But that's all right. At least you're smiling. When I first saw you tonight I thought, my gosh, that man is glum! It's going to take something to make him smile. I took it as a challenge."

"And you succeeded, Louisa."

"I don't know if I did. I don't know if you're laughing with me or laughing at me."

"You think I'm here with you so I can tease you?"

"I sort of think that, yes."

"Why would you imagine such a thing?"

"I don't know. I don't know what else to think."

"Can't you imagine any other reason?"

"I don't know. Maybe I can. Maybe any other reason would be hubris." Louisa stopped before a chain-link gate overshadowed by a wall of privet. "There it is." She pointed down a walk of cracked concrete. "The old pile with the ghostly turret. Ain't it grand? Don't you expect to see Rapunzel hanging her hair down from the tower so her lover can climb up to her?"

"Yes, I do."

Louisa opened the gate and led him down the moon-washed pavement to the house.

"The term," Louisa said, "is 'lavaliered.' The letters are the Greek letters of his fraternity." She fingered the chain around her neck and held it out for him to see. He moved closer on the sofa, pretending to want a better look. "Can you remember a time when we were all that sentimental, when we practiced rituals like this? The lavaliere," she laughed, "was a statement of intent, not necessarily of action. It was the preliminary to getting pinned which, of course, was even better because that was the preliminary to getting engaged. But you know all that. Didn't you do the same when you were at college?"

"Maybe some people did. I don't remember. And the boy?"

"He went into the army and got killed. Now you look shocked. You think it's silly that I still wear it. Part of it is sentiment, you see. I keep his memory alive. I keep the thought of the potential. The other part is purely comfort.

I'm like that woman in *The King and I* who sings, 'Hello, young lovers, I'm not alone, I've had a love of my own.'"
She offered him the full candlepower of her smile.

"Louisa—"

"Oh, Lord, you're getting misty. I know the look. The spinster's tale has moved you. You're off and running on the Hollywood scenario. Greer Garson whispers *au revoir* to her soldier lover (wasn't it always Walter Pidgeon?) and then delivers a monologue into the camera about tending the home fires; then soldier boy goes off to war and Greer is left to do good works—that's better. I've got you smiling. Cheer up and drink your tea."

She had brewed tea by placing a tea bag in each cup and adding boiling water, a method Sadie (who was into Oriental rituals of steeping, straining) would dismiss as tacky. Frobisch lifted the tea bag from his cup and placed it in the saucer, careful not to spatter liquid on the pocked wood table, though he guessed Louisa wouldn't care. There was an aura to the room of alien culture, the smell of cabbage boiled too long and walls riddled with damp. In the carved frame of the sofa he had discerned furbelows of dust, trapped like life preserved in amber. There was no busy hand to plump up pillows, beat out soil. A lounge chair covered in cracked brown plastic and a clock embedded in a wood ship's wheel gave hints of the seafaring father. The other pieces—hassocks, chairs—could be rejects of Antique Row.

"The problem with leading what seems to be an empty life—notice I said *seems to be*—is that people make you the subject of their own hopes and dreams. They take the so-called empty husk and fill it with their little secret fantasies. So my neighbors think I'm an adventuress, and Father Paul supposes I'm a saint, or at the very least, a willing handmaiden, available to do his whim—which is okay, 'cause I love the sweet man dearly; and you, Howard, I don't know what you think."

"I was wondering if you'd be offended if I kissed you."

"A kiss!" The blue eyes glinted secret jokes. "Oh, mercy me, I'm flattered. A kiss. After an hour at the church and a long walk home; and you, you poor dear man, were limping—don't think I didn't notice, 'cause I did. I'm positively overcome. Because you know, my dear, you are very attractive. There's something plaintive in your eyes—and at the same time, you have a kind of charismatic aura. Don't laugh! I saw it when we first met and you were fending off those biddies at the church. Maybe it comes from being one of God's chosen people. Oh, my, I didn't mean that the way it sounded." She was twisting the gold chain at her neck.

"Hush, Louisa."

"Now you're mad."

"I'm not mad. Just please don't talk so much." Bending toward her he caught the glimmer of the lavaliere and knew with sudden, gloomy prescience that the story of the boy, killed in an unnamed war, was false. Strangely, the lie made her seem more attractive.

"You would be very wrong to vest me with qualities that I don't have," Louisa said before they kissed.

Father Paul was waiting for him in the apartment lobby. He was wearing his cleric's garb. His face was pale over the Roman collar. His eyes were rimmed by weary circles, the look of the old-time actor made up to play the grim tragedian. He was sitting rigid on a leather sofa, holding a black attaché case against his chest. When he saw Frobisch he set the case flat in his lap, quickly opened it, and drew out a folded newspaper. He shut the case with a succession of smart snaps and set it on the floor. Before Frobisch could speak a word of greeting, the priest handed him the paper, the front section of the morning *Post*. "I don't suppose you've seen this or you would've called."

"You know I don't read the paper. I steer clear of all the news." Frobisch stared at the front page. "This is terrible, Father!" Giddy, close to fainting, he sat down quickly on the tufted couch.

Almost on cue, Father Paul jumped to his feet, as though he couldn't abide the thought of closer contact. He towered over Frobisch, tall and pale. "Don't let's have any histrionics. I've been over at Sibley Hospital giving the last rites and trying to bolster up the patient's family, and I'm way too beat for any more drama. Let's just keep calm, okay?"

"I'm calm, Father. Only I'm shocked."

"It happened as you predicted. Why be shocked?"

The headline read, "Pope John Paul I Dies of Heart Attack." There was a picture underneath. A longish face. Kind eyes behind the glasses. The gaunt cheeks of an ascetic. The hair beneath the skullcap softly waved. The caption beneath the picture said the Pope had died after one of the shortest reigns in history. "I didn't know it would be his heart."

"But you *did* know."

Frobisch handed back the paper. "Do you want to come upstairs?"

Father Paul nodded. "We need to talk."

Frobisch stood up gingerly, testing his balance. He saw himself reflected in a wall of mirror tiles. Father Paul stood next to him, exuding gloomy rancor, an air of obstinate affront, as though he held Frobisch responsible for the Pope's death. "It's not my fault. I didn't have anything to do with it," Frobisch muttered.

"Don't talk nonsense. No one's making accusations."

"Will you help me, Father? I am afraid."

"No one will harm you, son. God's grace is every-where," said Father Paul—rather too glibly, Frobisch thought, as though he were still counseling the sick man's grieving family over at Sibley.

In the elevator, Frobisch asked, "How is Mr. Healy?"

"Holding his own. He can't talk, but he still has all his marbles. He knew why I was there, and he was scared." The priest allowed himself a fleeting smile. "I take it you met Louisa."

Frobisch punched the floor button and nodded. He was thinking about the kiss, the taste of lemon and sugar on her lips, her little grunt of pleasure after they'd parted. She'd been flustered after the embrace, had insisted that he leave, had expounded as she walked him to the door, a lot of sappy magazine-garnered philosophy about leaving him unsated, just a bit intrigued. He suspected she was a virgin. Driving back into D.C. he had been plotting his attack, a tender voyage of discovery that might lead them both to a salvation. Magic it was to ponder it, to savor the moment of the kiss, the princess with lips softly parted transforming the frog into a prince. He hadn't reckoned on finding Father Paul posted like an avenging judge upon the lobby sofa.

They got out at the fifth floor. Frobisch led the way down the quiet hall, limping to favor his sore knee.

"Leg hurt?" asked Father Paul.

"I walked a lot today."

"Is it worse than when I saw it?"

"Maybe the same." Frobisch stopped at his apartment door and fumbled in his pocket for the key. He undid the bolt lock and stepped aside. "After you, Father."

It was hot in the apartment. Frobisch flicked on the lights, turned the thermostat to low, drew the drapes over the glass doors that opened to the balcony. "Can I get you something, Father?"

"Maybe in a little while." Father Paul sank on the white cotton–covered sofa with a sigh. Frobisch sat across from him in the brown velvet chair.

The priest was still holding the newspaper and his attaché case. He opened the case and stashed the newspaper inside. He searched the contents of the case until he'd found a slender bottle. With great deliberation, he undid the bottle cap and placed it on the coffee table. Murmuring his satisfaction, he dabbed cologne on his hands and patted the fragrance on his cheeks. The room was permeated with the scents of spice and orange. " 'Scuse me," said the priest. "It perks me up. After a coupla hours in the hospital, you feel like Lysol's oozed into your pores." He recapped the bottle and set it back inside the case. When he had closed the case securely he set it down beside his feet.

For a moment of purest terror Frobisch had believed the priest was searching for a gun. He clasped both hands before him. "As God is my witness, Father, I don't know what is going on. I don't know what happened last night in Rome. All I know is what we talked about when we met in your study. No more or less."

Father Paul considered this with half-closed eyes. The room buzzed with the whirring of the air conditioner.

Frobisch thought the priest had nodded off. Even in repose, the priest filled the room, inhaling what was left of the existing air.

After a time, Father Paul spoke softly. "This morning I prayed for our Pope who died without the last rites of the Church. That troubles me a great deal, Howie. You told me he would die, and I didn't believe you, though if I had, I don't know what I could've done. I asked God to absolve me from any sin in that regard, and I believe He has. I asked Him for guidance on how to deal with you. In a sense, we're old friends, though I can't say I really know you. Does anyone know his friend any more than he knows the urgings of his own heart?"

"If you will listen to me, Father—"

The priest held up a palm, barring interruption. "I considered you could be part of a conspiracy. As much as I ponder that possibility, it doesn't ring true. What would it serve you? There's nothing I can see. Unless you're in the grip of evil powers. Such things are possible, I suppose, but it's hard to lend the thought much credence."

"It's nothing like that, Father!"

"You know that for certain?"

"No."

"*Was* it foul play, Howie? Was there a plot against him?"

"I don't know."

"Who will be his successor?"

"I don't know. A younger man, chosen to break an impasse. The choice will surprise you—Oh, my God!" Frobisch sat, stricken.

Father Paul had gotten up to pace. He pulled aside the balcony drape and peered through the glass doors. Above a band of trees, the faint lights of the city were flickering like wavering stars. "I have always loved this city. It's quiet now; in the summer, in the heat, it's like a sleeping beast. But when the fall comes, you can feel the energy, the hard, pragmatic spirit that takes hold. That's the mix I like. Under the surface grandeur, things get done. A lot of people think that all we do is languish under a cloud of bureaucratic inefficiency, but it isn't true. We progress a fair amount. Good things happen. Bad things, too, but I believe the good outweighs the bad. An amazing city—cynical but at the same time idealistic. And it harbors ghosts. The whole sum of our recent history packed in a few square miles. Good, bad, evil, all in a bundle. Why not a prophet in this place? A true prophet, I mean. Why not a visionary?"

"No, Father, no!" Frobisch was stunned to hear the priest arguing *his* case, even as he prepared evidence on the side of realism. "I believe I had a minor stroke. A small obstruction in an artery. Nothing to do with God."

Father Paul turned from the window. "That explains the flashes of clairvoyance, does it? The bruise that doesn't heal?"

"I don't know, Father. All I know is that it terrifies me when you talk this way."

"Ah, softly, softly; we'll work it out."

Frobisch discerned a sea change; the priest's gloomy mood had vanished. In its place there was a diffidence, a seeming eagerness to please. "When we first talked," whispered Frobisch, "you thought I was certifiable. Now you accept everything I told you as the gospel. Why?"

The priest shrugged. "I don't know what I believe. I'm thinking you could be a scoundrel. I'm thinking you could be sincere. The whole of religious history is full of stories of simple men and women who had a visionary experience, who were assailed by sudden ecstasies. Many of them unwilling. Many of them literally zapped, stopped dead in their tracks, wrestled to the ground by the force of their enlightenment. Who am I to disbelieve? If I deny your vision, I do no more than illustrate the narrow confines of my mind. In any case, the fact remains—the Pope died, and you're already getting clues about his successor. Maybe you're crazy. Maybe you're someone to be reckoned with. Which gets us to the heart of this discussion, Howie. What shall we do?"

"I'm thinking I should go away. I'm not doing any good around here. I get on people's nerves—Sadie, the people at the office. I'm like a backwards Midas—everything I touch turns to dross."

"It's self-pity we're feeling, is it?"

"It's not easy, Father. If I'd been hit by some major calamity, people would gather 'round and offer their support. In this case, what can I tell 'em? They'd all react the same. They'd tell me what you told me at the rectory—go see a shrink. Any shrink worth the price of his diploma *would* certify that I was crazy."

Father Paul had commenced circling the room, touching the objects on the shelves with the gentle deference of the connoisseur. "Nice," he murmured. "Nice." He was taking his own sweet time touring the room. Frobisch sensed he was performing, assuring himself his audience would be receptive before he spoke. "There is an order of Benedictine monks near Thurmont," said the priest. "The abbot is my friend. I could arrange for you to stay there for a time." He affected interest in a crystal ashtray.

"What would that accomplish, Father?"

Father Paul puffed at an imagined speck of dust and set the ashtray back on its shelf. "I don't know, Howie. God knows I don't. I'm a parish priest, a rich man's priest, if the truth be told. I try to expiate my taste for the creature comforts by doing a fair amount of *tummeling* in the inner city. I'm something of a media darling. Occasionally I accomplish something to be proud of. But I'm not a visionary or a mystic. That's the province of the monks. Maybe they can advise you." The priest looked wistful. "Maybe your angel will find you in those mountains."

"What you call clairvoyance could be nothing more than coincidence."

"It could."

"The fact is, I don't know so much. Tonight I heard these people talking at the church. It was fairly evident they were upset. I know now it was because of the Pope. I thought the reason was Mr. Healy."

"Maybe your next flash will tell us his condition. It would be nice to hear a good prognosis."

Frobisch stiffened with self-righteous rage. "It's not a parlor trick!"

Father Paul nodded contritely. "Excuse that as a case of nerves, Howie. You must understand, we're all traveling unknown ground."

Frobisch wished Father Paul would light. He was too weary to track the priest's meandering around the apartment. The long night was catching up with him—the priest's terse message on the answering machine that sent him scurrying to church, Louisa. There remained one more confession. "Sit down a minute, would you, Father, and listen. On the way home tonight, I was planning a seduction. I had the whole campaign mapped out—time, place, the choice of food and wine. The slow undressing.

All the sordid details. Is that the behavior of a prophet?"

The priest obliged by sinking back onto the sofa. As Frobisch talked, Father Paul broke into a grin. "Do you know the French philosopher, Péguy? He writes that everything begins in mysticism and ends in sex. Does it surprise you that I find some wisdom in that line of thought?"

"Nothing much surprises me tonight."

"Will you consider my suggestion?"

"If I went there, I'd feel obvious—some kind of freak."

"No one beside the abbot would have to know. And not him, if you didn't want it. There'd be no proselytizing. No one battling for your immortal soul. Every week there are one or two retreatants. Some come for prayer and contemplation. Some simply like the plain food and the mountain air. The monastery is near Camp David. Every so often you see the helicopters zooming in to jar the mood. But it's lovely country."

"You think that would be the answer?"

"For the time being, I do, Howie."

"I'll think on it, Father." It was a little bit intriguing— retreating to a distant mountain. Peace and quiet and no women around. "I doubt if anybody here would miss me. Sadie wouldn't care, and at the office they'll do okay." Frobisch added slyly, "It would even work out good for you."

Father Paul looked startled, as though Frobisch had nailed him for harboring unpriestly thoughts. "What do you mean?"

"You'd be rid of me for a while. No more puzzles or embarrassments. No gloomy predictions to believe or disbelieve. The responsibility for crazy Howie gets shifted to the monks."

The priest's laugh had the showman's bluster, a mix

of good humor and candor that implied Frobisch was right; if he chose to vanish to the cloister there would be no cause, on either of their parts, for sorrow. "The thought had crossed my mind," said Father Paul.

# · CHAPTER ·
# 7

There was a problem with the autumn bees who had lost the drowsiness of summer and now swooped in to sting, primed to attack anything that moved. If he beat them off, they would return, dodging and feinting like boxers who would not be denied their taste of blood. Brother Jarvis had told him the bees were drones who had been turned out of the hive by the queen who would now devote herself to caring for the new-laid eggs. These bees were crazy for nourishment; they would attack anything that had the color or the shape of food. Brother Jarvis had seen one hammering at a gray stone wall on which was caught a bit of colored ribbon. The bee had buzzed the wall like a battering ram, trying to extract some sweetness from the colored thread. Brother Jarvis thought it must have finally knocked itself senseless.

"They don't bother you," Frobisch observed.

Brother Jarvis blushed and whacked his straw hat at an imaginary bee, enacting a rebuttal. The monk was young, with puffy cheeks and a body already going flabby. A fold of belly hung above the closure of his jeans. His blue work shirt pulled tight across his shoulders as he moved. When he knelt to work the soft, dark earth, he grunted at the effort. When, through some mighty act of will, he forced himself to speak, he poked his trowel into the weeds as though beating off shyness.

"They're finding a few flowers left to ravage." Brother Jarvis pointed to a stand of marigolds and dwarf chrysanthemums planted beneath a statue of the Virgin. The sculpture depicted a woman of delicate proportions who looked down at the highway from a rocky incline, keeping vigil over moving vans and campers and big smoke-puffing semis and Cadillacs and sleek Mercedes bound for the lake resorts. The monks called the statue Our Lady of the Roads.

"If I hadn't caught sight of those flowers and the little statue, I'd still be driving around in circles," Frobisch said. "Beating off cows."

He'd seen the monastery from the road, an aggregate of gray stone buildings set on a plateau amid hills patchy with the first autumn colors, rusts and golds and reds exploding like fires on the forest slopes. Gothic spires blended with mountain mists, and the church and the surrounding buildings shimmered in what seemed aqueous suspension, remote as some celestial city. There was no sign pointing to an entry. One road that looked promising had horse-shoed back onto the highway. A second turnoff led him to a farm, an abandoned fieldstone house that might have dated to the Revolution, and a cluster of outbuildings in disrepair.

He'd parked the Volvo near a barn and clambered out to look around, picking his way through weeds and broken bottles. A dirt path led him to a fenced pasture. Without stopping to ponder, he scaled the wood rails of the fence and dropped knee-deep into a mass of goldenrod and purple clover. Sun blasted the open field with the white heat of a furnace. He headed for a clump of trees and settled in their shade, without much sense of urgency—admiring the fretwork of the boughs and patterns of sky, like blue mosaic, against the darker leaves. In the heat, amid the drone of insects, he nodded off.

He was awakened by a rush of hot breath on his cheeks and something soft, and yet insistent, nudging his temple. A dozen or more curious cows, Holsteins with steam rising from their flanks and a gleam of wonder in their eyes that did not seem welcoming, were studying him. He struggled to his feet, brushing off grass and bits of bracken. The cow that had had the brazenness to poke his face uttered a long, lowering moo; the others took it up, a muffled counterpoint of menace that sent him moving to the fence. He scaled the top with an agility he hadn't known he possessed.

The sun had dropped. A line of thunderheads rimmed the peaks of the mountains. He headed for the car, running to beat the rain. On the drive back to the highway, he began embellishing the story. A cow with the strength and menace of the Minotaur had butted him awake; it stood with great curled horns and eyes like coals, bellowing rage. Rapt with invention, Frobisch sped through the mountain passes. A mile or two down the highway, he found the turnoff, a steep dirt drive that led him upward on a twisting path, wide enough to allow the passage of a single car. In the gathering dusk he saw the Virgin's statue, circled by flowers that sparkled like the fires of a welcoming hearth.

In the courtyard of the guest house, the guestmaster was waiting, oblivious to the rain. He stood watching as Frobisch parked, nodding his head, as though he'd known about the detours, as though the cow sounds echoing through the hills like gathering thunder had alerted him a guest was coming. He was a somber man—polite, but not overly genial—wearing tennis shoes and muddy jeans that showed beneath the hem of his black cassock. He'd led Frobisch into a paneled hall lit by a single amber bulb. In the dimness, the monk looked like a figure from a Spanish painting—gaunt, his face circled by muted light, his mouth pursed in a look of hauteur. He offered to scrounge some food, although the supper hour was over. Frobisch, enjoying the virtue of the lie, invented a long, late lunch, a veritable Sunday dinner that had left him sated.

The guestmaster had looked relieved. "After you've picked up our literature, you'll want to go straight to your room, then?" And Frobisch, not clear as to his wants but grateful to be guided, had nodded yes.

They mounted a curving stairway to the second floor. He was aware of long, dim hallways, fragrant with the smells of soap and fresh-baked bread. The walls were white, newly painted. The ceiling was an arch of rough gray stones that narrowed into darkness. Trotting behind the guestmaster, who set a heady pace, he heard a sound that would become familiar, the slap of sneakers hurrying over polished tiles.

In a commons room (furnished incongruously in Danish modern that lent the place the slick, overbright aspect of a new motel) the guestmaster doled out a sheaf of rules—a schedule of meals and daily prayers, a map of the monastery (which he was pleased to say followed the plan of early medieval cloisters), and a biography of the monks' patron saint, the most revered Pachomius, who (the guestmaster allowed himself a smile) was not a household word among the list of saints, although his tablet of regulations for the cenobitic life had provided a foundation for the Benedictine Rule.

Frobisch promised, "I'll study it."

The guestmaster nodded. "You'll find the house rules straightforward and simple. No alcohol. No food in the rooms. You're expected to keep things tidy. I hope you know you're sharing a room."

"I didn't know." Frobisch, off guard, showed his dismay.

"Your request to come was so last-minute. And we're repainting. We did the best we could. The other gentleman isn't expected until the middle of the week." The guestmaster stared past him to the door as though seeking a cavalry of black-garbed monks to pound in with their affirmation he had done his best.

Frobisch interpreted his sullen stance: Gimme a break. I don't relish playing hotel keeper, and the fact is we're overbooked. Who would've thought prayer and contemplation would turn out to be trendy! I do what I am told, and it can be a bummer. You think chastity is tough? Try being obedient. Chastity's a bed of roses compared to that!

"It's all right, of course," Frobisch conceded. "It's fine."

"You'll have a private bath," the guestmaster had offered as a gift of sorts.

That night, in a room rendered lonelier by the duplication of its stark details (twin cots, twin dressers, twin night tables painted a dismal pewter), Frobisch studied the facts about the obscure saint, Pachomius, who experienced visions in the Egyptian desert and who responded to the message of an angel by building on the sands at Tabenna an edifice of humble cells, surrounded by a wall:

159

The order of this place derived from the angelic rule. All monks must learn to read so that they might participate in prayers. They must wear simple clothing and eat in moderation and assure themselves sufficient rest. All monks contributed to the communal life. In time, the monastery buzzed with the activity of tanners, craftsmen, tailors, braziers, dyers—brethren united in obedience and conformity.

During his life Pachomius suffered trials, for the elders of the clergy distrusted him for his ecstatic visions and for his claim that he had been in heaven and could read the hearts of men. He was called before the synod at Latopolis, where he defended himself successfully against the elders' accusation of presumption. His monastery thrived to the point where other communities, all subservient to the motherhouse, were established, including two convents of women.

It is said Pachomius could understand all languages, heal the sick, and drive out devils. So overpowering was his charisma that when he wished to cross a river he could stand upon its bank and summon a crocodile to ferry him safely to the farther shore.

Frobisch shivered in the gathering damp. The life, so offhand in tales of miracles and revelations, unnerved him. He felt easier examining the monastery plan, which had been rendered by a careful draftsman. It showed the entry drive curving past the statue of the little Virgin to a court closed off by buildings on three sides—the guest house, the refectory, the bakery. (That explained the tantalizing smells which had caused him to regret forgoing dinner.) The court was marked Little Cloister. Beyond the Little Cloister, at the center of the map, was the chapel, bordered on one side by the cemetery and the infirmary, and on the other by the abbot's house. A quadrangle of buildings marked Library and Monks' Cells enclosed a larger central court, designated Main Cloister. Paths from the Main Cloister led to scattered outbuildings—workshops, stables, barns.

Nice, Frobisch thought. Efficient. Neat. He sat huddled on the cot closest to the window. Rain pelted the court below him with a sound like scattered shot. He could see the silhouette of distant mountains, lit now and again by lightning. Cows with fiery eyes huddled under bending trees. A monk, poised beside a turgid river, summoned a crocodile to take him to the distant side. Myth blended with history, and the line that separated truth from fiction blurred. Dreams hovered in the air like vapor. Magic abounds, thought Frobisch, flinching as a bolt of lightning tore the sky.

"The *Farmer's Almanac* predicts a freeze. That's going to kill my flowers." Brother Jarvis surprised Frobisch by initiating the conversation. Usually, the monk spoke only when spoken to, and then his tortured grunts and sighs implied duress, as though only the bonds of courtesy and hospitality forced him to talk. Frobisch was bursting with questions he dared not ask: What made you choose this life? Don't you miss the company of women? I don't mean only sex, though God knows that's part of it. I mean their adversarial spark, their instinct for contention, the way they mix frivolity and practicality and make their choices seem so reasoned. By God, they are an education in themselves—each one a walking five-foot shelf of Great Books and cockamamie philosophy; and you and the guestmaster and all the other bustling, prayerful monks

I see crowding this place repudiate that as inconsequential and heap offerings before the statue of the Virgin. What's the point?

Brother Jarvis had confided that his main assignment was to tend the monastery sheep. He took on the cultivation of the little statue's garden as an act of love. "Like Barnaby, the humble juggler, doing his act at Notre Dame and being rewarded by the Virgin's smile?" Frobisch had read the story in high school. Brother Jarvis shrugged and blushed over the weeds.

The monk was musing to himself. "Perhaps I'll put in holly. The berries would give Our Lady a nice bright touch through the colder months."

Frobisch liked it that the monks had named their statue Our Lady of the Roads. He approved of her silent vigil over travelers—hitchhikers, runaways, students, bigwigs zooming in motorcades to the District, school kids on field trips in those old rattling buses that should have been condemned some twenty years ago. She had her work cut out for her, did the little Virgin standing amid twin stone benches and Brother Jarvis's yellow blooms. "Holly would be good. Maybe you'll let me take a few of those little mums back to my room, if they're gonna die?"

Brother Jarvis kept his own counsel, as though the sound of words spoken aloud enforced his paralyzing shyness. Frobisch had tried to counter the young monk's diffidence by spinning stories. Over the past two mornings, he'd performed like a nervous guest who is determined to be entertaining. He'd told his military escort story and his encounter with the killer cows. He'd dredged up ancient history, his boyhood in Bayonne. Bund meetings in the park. Spies watching departing freighters from the shadows of the port. Brother Jarvis grinned at the exaggerations and grunted during the pauses to show he was attending.

Today Frobisch had news. He waited for Brother Jarvis to glance up from his flowers. "My roommate arrived last night. We didn't talk. He introduced himself and then went straight to bed. I don't think he was feeling so hot." That was a euphemism invented out of deference to the monk. The man was drunk. He'd walked in wobbling dangerously to port, casing the room with a glazed look that took in everything and nothing. Frobisch divined his need and pointed to the unused bed. The man fell on it and closed his eyes. When he spoke, his speech was slurred. "Morris Gershowitz. Call me Morry." He lay still, as though the effort to tell his name had drained him.

Frobisch asked the monk, "Did you guys plan it so two of us of the same faith would room together?"

Brother Jarvis looked earnest, confused, appalled—the chubby kid at summer camp who anticipates the worst and is never disappointed. "Certainly not. That would be coincidence."

"Well, I don't mind the company." Which was not precisely true. Morris Gershowitz had kept him up most of the night with fitful turns and moans. He'd murmured imprecations to an unseen female, he'd wrestled with the sheets. Once, he'd lumbered out of bed to shed his clothes and then fallen back upon the battered pillow with a yelp of pain, the whimper of a child trapped in nightmares. Some time near dawn he'd staggered to the john to vomit. Frobisch had seen him—naked in the graying dark, dragging a sheet behind him like a lurching ghost—and he had shivered with contempt and pity.

"You'll get on," said Brother Jarvis.

"Sure we will," lied Frobisch, thinking it was a shame

to have a landsman show up potted. At first light, Frobisch got up to dress, roused by the voices of the monks chanting the sacred music of the liturgy. Gershowitz was finally sleeping. With no feeling of shame, Frobisch examined the man's discarded clothes—a plaid sports jacket of execrable taste, a wide striped tie, a pair of moccasins adorned with fringe and Indian beads. There were medicine bottles, sleeping pills and patent nostrums, strewn on Gershowitz's nightstand. Wonderful! At worst a junkie and a drunk. At best a hypochondriac.

In the bathroom, Frobisch found the dried remnants of vomit spattered on the floor. Shameful! He wet a wad of toilet paper and wiped the stains, gagging. They'd have a conversation when the man woke up. Frobisch would point out he wasn't nit-picky himself. (God knew he'd had his share of hangovers at college!) Nonetheless, they owed it to the monks, who ran a really nice establishment, to treat their lodgings with respect. And, Frobisch would add, he didn't relish cleaning up the bathroom mess. He'd headed downstairs to the guests' refectory, feeling righteous. Three days of healing quiet and he was showing patience, neatness, calm, a sense of neighborly forbearance, a reasoned turn of mind that allowed for human foibles. He'd sat down to his breakfast cereal vastly content, amid the sound of pious voices raised in prayer.

Serene on his stone bench, Frobisch waved away a bee and reveled in the unfamiliar pleasure of tranquillity. He wished Sadie could see him blinking sagely in the sun, at peace with his own thoughts and his surroundings. Sunday, before driving to the monastery, he'd swung by the old house with the hope of sitting down with her to make amends. He had rehearsed a little speech touching on bygones being bygones, slates wiped clean, the healing power of forgiveness. As he drew up to the house he saw the van parked in the drive, a beige and turquoise monster with a license plate that spelled out VET. Okay! He slammed hard on the brakes, then steered the Volvo through a perfect three-point turn. Okay! He hightailed down the street as though Randy and assorted grinning De Filippos were in pursuit, flinging their pocket knives like Frisbees. Screw Sadie's friendship! He would do okay. He had Louisa in his corner (all that untouched sexy potential waiting out his retreat); Sadie could have her vet. The man was welcome to her bed, her tantrums, her endless yodeling, her constant ruminations over the color of her hair. Frobisch mourned only for his workbench, his tools neatly aligned on pegs, his nails and nuts and bolts and screws arranged by size in jars on the shelf, his paint cans and his brushes and his lengths of rope. That solid, manly part of him, that lingering aspect of the pioneer. Sadie would give it all to the Dutchman. She dispensed his property to the first heavy-breathing suitor who came down the pike, and he was left to grapple with ghosts and creepy premonitions. Where was the fairness?

Brother Jarvis had struggled to his feet. He wiped his forehead with a dirt-caked arm. "Time to change for prayers."

Frobisch waved him off with an expansive gesture. "I'll stay and enjoy the air."

The monk nodded and began gathering his tools. He carried an old-fashioned wicker basket such as a child might use to gather Easter eggs. Before taking the path that led to the Main Cloister, he hesitated, turned to Frobisch, smiled. His face was flushed by hours of work outdoors. Now the cheeks flamed even darker, as though a sudden spurt of dye had coursed his veins. "I hope you and your roommate will be friends."

Before Frobisch could reply, Brother Jarvis had taken off with his laden basket in hand, waddling like an ungainly duck who is uncomfortable traversing land.

Frobisch closed his eyes to feel the sun. There was a texture to the silence, a bustle underneath the surface calm. Frobisch discerned the low bleating of sheep, the buzz of farm machines, the sweet clamor of birds, even the hiss and bumble of insects living in recesses of grass. The air was redolent with clover, pungent with the tang of fresh manure. Frobisch breathed deep. A bee dive-bombed his head. When he opened his eyes to swat it, he saw the man standing a bit above him where the path turned upward toward a stand of pines. The stranger, dressed in a robe of coarse brown homespun, smiled, and his eyes glowed with a light both radiant and calm.

In agony, Frobisch began to stammer; he half-rose from the bench, clasping and unclasping his hands in an anguished parody of prayer. "Is it you?"

The bee stung him on the palm, a particularly vicious attack, since Frobisch had made no move to swipe at it. He yelled, "Ow," and swung, losing his balance. His last memory before he fainted was of the angel peering sweetly from a wreath of light.

It was cool here. Pleasant between the sheets that had been washed to a pearly luster and bore the not unpleasant scent of bleach. His bed was shielded by a screen of sheets that fluttered in the draft of an open window. Through openings in the curtain he saw other beds lined in a row, each with a folded mattress resting on bare springs. On the wall facing him was a pastel drawing of a saint, with his eyes rolled upward in a look of ecstasy and his head crowned by a halo that sat atop his hair like a golden pancake. "It's the infirmary, right?"

"Yes." Brother Jarvis, unfamiliar in a hooded cassock, hovered beside the bed. He was carrying a pot of yellow flowers that bobbed and riffled as he moved, like blossoms captured by an errant breeze. He bent over the pillow, balancing the plant precariously. "You're better?"

Frobisch flexed his knees, waggled his shoulders, assuring himself of his body's solidity. "Yeah. It hurts like hell, but I'm okay." His palm, festooned in gauze, rested on his chest like an ungainly paw. With his free hand, he gestured to the flowers. "Pretty."

Brother Jarvis blushed. "I checked them over for bees." He set the flowers on the bedside table tenderly, as though regretting that such hardy blooms must be left to languish in the sickroom air.

"Why am I here?"

"You had an allergic reaction to a bee sting. You needed a shot to bring you round. Lucky I left my trowel beside Our Lady's statue, and when I went back to find it, I saw you hit at something and fall." The monk's face blazed dangerous scarlet. "I carried you back to the guest house, and then we brought you here."

"You carried me! That's all uphill!"

Brother Jarvis sank into a bedside chair as though the effort to retell his feat had tired him more than the actual performance. "I'm pretty strong."

Frobisch, slyly: "No one else around to help you?"

Brother Jarvis shook his head, gasping with what seemed terminal embarrassment. Frobisch struggled to sit upright. "I do thank you! I'm very grateful. Only it wasn't necessary. Insect bites don't bother me. It wasn't a bee that knocked me out."

"Oh, I think it was. It's true it might have been a hornet. Hornets produce severe reactions if they sting. A hornet or a wasp, for that matter, could make you very ill." Brother Jarvis's voice held a new ring of assurance, as though the donning of his habit had lent him poise. He frowned. "You shouldn't jump around that way, Mr. Frobisch. Shall I crank the bed up?"

Frobisch nodded. Brother Jarvis leaped to his feet and hurried to the foot of the bed. He bent and fiddled with a metal handle. The mattress rose in a series of creaking jolts. When Frobisch signaled it was high enough, the monk stood back and grinned, happy to be useful. "Shall I open the curtain? You might enjoy the air." He tugged at the sheets shielding the bed. Light streamed across the pillow.

Frobisch closed his eyes, frightened he'd see the angel hovering in a sunbeam like an attenuated Peter Pan. "Where's Gershowitz?" he asked.

"Your roommate? I don't know. Would you like for him to visit?"

"He should change places with me. He had a bad night, did I tell you?"

"You mentioned he was ill."

Frobisch felt the sun red-gold under his eyelids. He swallowed tears. Why me, O Lord? Why me? Why do I know the plot of every soap opera aborning? Every sob story with its inevitable unhappy ending? Every hint of failing lungs and dying flesh comes straight to me. All the bad news tied up in fancy Gucci wrapping and labeled blessing. What did I do to be so blessed? Why are there never any pleasant portents? Did Cassandra get good news, ever? Did she at least get a hint she'd show up in all those poems?

"Are you all right, Mr. Frobisch? Is there anything more I can do?"

Frobisch opened his eyes. "I need to talk to someone about a very serious matter."

"I could call Father Quentin."

"Who is he?"

"He looks after the infirmary patients. He hears confessions, offers prayers."

"I don't want the last rites!"

Brother Jarvis sat with eyes downcast, too disquieted to blush. He studied his open palms as though they, too, bore stinging wounds.

"Could you arrange for me to see the abbot?"

"That would be very difficult."

"It is important."

"Not possible."

"Why not?"

Brother Jarvis, humble keeper of sheep, tongue-tied digger of weeds, shy tender of the statue of the Blessed Lady of the Roads, spoke now as though inspired. "You must understand that the monastery is a complex community. In the variety of jobs, it's like a corporation. And the abbot, whom you might equate with the director of the corporation, bears enormous responsibility. His concerns go well beyond the religious life of the flock. There is the matter of the farm, the livestock, the making of vestments, not to mention the production of our breads and jams and jellies, which are justly famous. The abbot oversees all this, much as a chief executive oversees the daily business of a firm. He even hires and fires, so to speak. Every year the monastery receives scores of applications from people wanting to join the order. Only a fraction are accepted, and then after only the most rigorous screening. The abbot has the burden of these decisions as well; and he can't just meet with any retreatant who feels the need to chat. Do you understand me, Mr. Frobisch?"

Frobisch lay silenced by the flood of unaccustomed eloquence.

Brother Jarvis continued, "If you wish to lodge a formal complaint about the bee sting, I can call Father Stephen who is our expert on canon law."

"I'm not planning a lawsuit, for God's sake!" It was all too much. A bee had stung him. He had seen the angel on the path. He had fainted. Brother Jarvis had picked him up and carried him (the poor man, huffing, hot) to the Little Cloister of the monastery where a retinue of nervous monks had poured forth from their various cells and crannies to peer at his unconscious form—mouth open, tongue lolling, feet dragging in the dust. Where was the angel? Hovering in a puff of smoke? Sitting on a tree branch, smiling at his discomfort. There was the matter of those heavenly mandates. *Do good.* He didn't know how. *Quit messing up.* It was all he knew. "Since I can't meet with the abbot, may I confide in you?"

Bells in the chapel tower were calling the monks to late-day prayers. Brother Jarvis cast a look of longing to the window. "If you wish."

Frobisch sat up straight, testing the fingers of his bandaged hand. The pain had subsided to a quiet throbbing. He could get up soon and make his way back to the guest house. "I have to ask you something first. Do you believe that the statue of the Blessed Virgin whom you tend so lovingly really has the power to offer protection to those passing below her on the road? Give help to the fellows driving Roadway? Offer peace and charity to Allied Van? Allow God's grace to shower on the next Vista View trailer tearing up the roads with a U-Haul in tow and flea-bit dogs and nasty kids hanging out the window offering obscene signals? Do you believe she oversees them all, just like your abbot oversees the work of the community?"

"Not the statue per se. See, here's the interesting distinction that non-Catholics like yourself don't always understand . . ."

"Couldn't she move among us if she had to, and not just stand and smell the flowers?"

"The statue is merely an artistic rendering and in itself is powerless . . ."

"All right, all right." Frobisch couldn't abide more of the monk's long-winded explications. "Do you believe the Virgin, herself, could appear to you as you were working in the garden and wipe the sweat of effort from your brow? Like she did for Barnaby, the juggler? Do you think such an event is too fantastic?"

If Brother Jarvis was dismayed by Frobisch's flurry of temper he gave no sign. He seemed secure in realms of faith. Earnest. Unblushing. "It's not too fantastic," the monk told Frobisch. "Such an event could happen. Yes."

"Okay. Then hear me out. Perhaps you'll understand why I want to see the abbot."

Brother Jarvis sat composed, his head tilted to one side, as Gregor might have sat, endeavoring to understand the mix of sound and fury emanating from his master's voice. The monk had the look he'd had in the Virgin's garden— alert, polite, prepared to be amused—the caliph relishing the flavor of Arabian nights. Frobisch knew before he started he wouldn't be believed. He had worked so hard at telling stories, he had forfeited his credibility.

## · CHAPTER ·

# 8

Gershowitz retched black bile into the toilet. He was hunched low on his knees with his arms braced on the rim and his head so low it almost touched the water.

"You'll drown." Frobisch had a death grip on his roommate's temples. "Straighten up, will you?"

"Can't." Gershowitz gasped and heaved again into the bowl.

Frobisch reached over him and flushed. "Take a breather, Morry. Maybe you should get back to bed. It's freezing." He cursed himself for opening the bedroom window. If they slept with it closed, the room filled with a sickish odor, a jungle smell of overripeness, damp. Ten minutes of inhaling it and Frobisch felt he'd choke. It helped to fling the window open to the autumn air, which had turned suddenly cold—nights of curled, dry leaves and creaking branches. On her hill the statue of the Blessed Virgin glimmered white in the glow of the moon. The holly Brother Jarvis had planted trembled stiffly in the wind and scratched with pointed leaves at the Virgin's robe. Below her on the highway, the beams of passing cars transformed the asphalt briefly to a trail of light that gleamed and faded into darkness.

Gershowitz rocked back on his heels and crouched on the cold tile. He looked dumbfounded.

Frobisch let go of his head. "You think that's all of it?"
Gershowitz nodded. "For now."

Frobisch stood up stiffly, favoring his bad knee. He had
shown the bruise to Brother Jarvis who had stared, the way
children stare at the sudden horror of a freak show, and
who had not known how to answer when Frobisch asked,
"What do you make of this?" The knee was nothing to him
now, nor was the notoriety that dogged him since the
sighting of the angel near the Virgin's garden. For Brother
Jarvis, pledged to secrecy, had blabbed, had lost no time
haranguing every novice, postulant, and priest who
crossed his path, had corralled a posse of retreatants on
work duty in the barn and gossiped as they pitched
manure, had doubtless whispered in the lop-ears of his
sheep, as Midas whispered to the reeds of secret gold. Now,
when Frobisch sauntered down the twisting path that took
him to the Virgin's statue, when he paused to touch the
boughs of fragrant pines, seeking some relief for his ailing knee, he was aware of curious eyes marking his every
move. He was famous in this place, the bee-stung retreatant who'd seen an angel near Our Lady of the Roads.

Brother Jarvis had explained it, waving his plump arm
as he'd waved it to ward off bees. The day of the purported
vision was a scorcher and Frobisch hadn't taken the necessary cover. Add to that the trauma of the bee sting. The
other monks agreed. Frobisch's vision was chalked up to
allergy and the foolishness of sitting hatless in the sun.

Gershowitz had offered a different scenario. "Here's
how I see it. They could be some kind of order, like the
good buddies of Pachomius, and they wander around doin'
the Lord's bidding. And some of 'em get good duty, like
in Rome; and others, who aren't such winners, get hard-
ship posts, like maybe Vegas. Wouldn't that be a gas? Some

poor angel gets word he's billeted in Vegas, and he appeals and says, 'Hey, Lord, don't put me there. There's not much potential to work with.' And the Lord answers, after a fanfare of trumpets, drums, the whole shmear, 'Do the best with what you got!''

He had expected discussion of a more high-toned order, with monks lending credence to his claim of miracles. At the very least, he'd hoped the abbot would let up on his corporate responsibilities long enough to have him over for tea. Gershowitz's idea smacked of lousy theater. Frobisch imagined a chorus line of bland, high-kicking angels looking to the second balcony for inspiration, and a basso male lead belting his showstopper from center stage.

He'd sung out his usual refrain, "Why me?"

"Chance meeting. The schnook was heading somewhere else. The catacombs? Saint Paul's outside the Walls? How the hell should I know?"

"Some turkey got his signals crossed? That's it?"

"I figure the Man Upstairs heads a bureaucracy, and there's as much fuckin'-up up there as anywhere else."

"You're putting me on, Morry."

"No, Howie, I'm not. I gotta believe it's all monstrous confusion, 'cause if I thought my lousy luck was the result of someone's careful plan I would be pissed as hell!"

He had acknowledged Morry had a point.

Gershowitz was shivering on the icy tile. Frobisch nudged him. "You ready to go back to bed?"

"Yeah." Gershowitz let his weight fall against Frobisch's legs. Frobisch groaned as the sore knee took the pressure of the sick man's head. He grasped Gershowitz under the arms and lifted.

Gershowitz made it to his feet and began the shuffling,

sideward walk that looked like drunkenness. He was wearing striped pajamas that hung loosely on his bony frame. Frobisch steered him through the bathroom door and toward the farther bed, praying they wouldn't have to detour, as they had the previous night when Gershowitz's legs gave out and he collapsed onto Frobisch's cot. Frobisch let him sleep there. In the morning when he made up the bed he could smell the sick-sweet odor emanating from the tumbled sheets.

Gershowitz lunged to his own bed and sat down heavily. He stared at the blank wall.

Frobisch asked, "You want a pill?"

"Might help."

Frobisch picked a bottle from the jumble of containers on the nightstand. He cursed, trying to remove the childproof cap. "Gee-suz H. Christ, do they think infants get near medicine for cancer?"

"Ssh. Don't say the bad word."

"You like 'Big C' better?" Frobisch wrenched off the cap and shook a pill into Gershowitz's palm. Gershowitz swallowed it dry. "Let me get you some water or it'll come back up," Frobisch pleaded.

"Nah, I'm better. Piece of cake." Gershowitz eased down on the pillow and swung his legs onto the bed.

Frobisch retrieved a blanket from the floor and spread it over Gershowitz. He pulled one end to the sick man's chin. He tucked the far end tightly around his roommate's feet. Then he padded to the bathroom where he chose a towel, not too damp, almost clean. He let the water in the bathroom sink run in its usual rusty trickle till it got lukewarm. He wet the towel and squeezed the excess carefully into the basin. Holding the towel away from him so that it wouldn't drip on his pajamas, he went back to the bed. Gingerly, he mopped Gershowitz's forehead and the lines of dried vomit and spittle on his chin.

Gershowitz nodded his thanks. "My mother used to say that if you didn't say the word out loud you wouldn't get it."

"It's a bit late for that." Frobisch folded the wet towel into quarters and placed it on the nightstand.

"I'm protecting you, good buddy." Gershowitz laughed.

"Much obliged. You think you can sleep?"

"Yeah. Gimme that other pill."

"Too soon for that one. You'll get crazy."

"Shit. What time is it?"

"It's almost five. I gave you one at three o'clock." Instinctively, he looked to the open window. The tower of the chapel stood in silhouette against the moon. Soon a procession of black-cassocked monks would march across the dark Main Cloister to take their places in the church for the singing of Lauds, the morning prayer of the Divine Office. In the cold dawns, Frobisch often lay awake, listening to the ancient chant, sung now in English, "Glory be to the Father, the Son, and the Holy Spirit." Sometimes he dozed before the last cadenced phrases: "Let us kneel before the Lord who made us. For He is our God, and we are the people He shepherds, the flock He guides."

Mornings when he couldn't sleep he watched the mists around the purple mountains dissipate to grayish light. In time the gray lightened to gold and the sky gleamed with the clarity of serene October. Before first light, before the chattering of birds, he conjured visions of Louisa, the sweet unbridled tongue, the boniness and starch—his princess imprisoned in a carapace of cotton and no-nonsense denim. Rapunzel in the tower, she had said. He would find the key. Pondering this, he would lie shivering in his narrow cot with an erection—shameful as a monk trapped by the desires memory spawned. Exorcising lust, he composed letters he never meant to send: Dear Freddy, It is pleasant here—not unlike the Catskills, but without the cha-cha lessons, of course. . . . Dear Sadie, I wish you happiness in what appears to be a new relationship. Would it be possible for me to stop by for my tools? . . . Dear Sima, It has occurred to me that you no longer love me. I wonder why.

Gershowitz's voice rose from the muffled cavern of the blanket. "You wanna play a little gin?"

Frobisch shook his head. "No way. I'm in hock to you for a hundred forty-seven bucks."

"No sweat. I won't collect it."

"You will, Morry."

"Do your psychic powers tell you that?"

"Lately they don't tell me much."

"If you knew something I didn't, would you tell me?"

"No."

Gershowitz chuckled. "Bastard. What a waste, you havin' visions."

Frobisch got into bed and pulled the cover taut. The sheet stung like ice under his ankles. "I think so, too." He lay still, longing for sleep. He could hear Gershowitz breathing, slow and even. The quick flip-flop of sneakers sounded in the hall. Men in adjacent rooms snored, sniffled, coughed, hawked gobbets of phlegm into the toilets, flushed, dreamed, groaned. Frobisch felt the heaviness that comes from living too long without the company of women. He commenced the sweet seduction of Louisa, the slow unpinning of her hair, the tender nibbling of her earlobes—

"I gotta have me some distraction, Howie. Get the cards."

"Have a heart, Morry. I've got kitchen duty in two hours. I need to sleep."

"Listen, I got a great idea. When you finish up your work, we hop into your car and take off for the day."

"Can we do that?"

"Why the hell not? We're two adults who came here voluntarily. It's not a fuckin' summer camp."

"Where would we go?"

"I've got a mind to see my girl, Arlene."

"I didn't know you had one."

"Howie, I was married twice. Both women were the two damnedest bitches God ever put on this earth. Their mothers must've been suckin' lemons when they were conceived. I got an adopted daughter teaches history at Douglass College in New Brunswick. She's a worse bitch queen than her mama, and that is saying something. But I also got Arlene, and she is the best and the kindest woman in the world. When I go home, she will take care of me."

"That's nice," Frobisch said wearily. He was fingering the gold lavaliere and asking her to take it off, brushing his fingers softly over her neck's deep hollows—

"Whaddya say, Howie?"

"Where does she live? Arlene?"

"Bal'mer. Where else? An hour's drive. We can see her, have an early dinner in Little Italy, and be back in time to tuck you in for nighttime prayers, if that turns you on." Gershowitz managed a wicked laugh.

"How do you propose to eat in Little Italy?"

"So I'll watch. Let me call her up and tell her we're comin'. I'll have her get a friend for you."

"That isn't necessary."

"Sure it is, Howie. 'Cause me and Arlene are gonna vanish into her room and you might as well have somebody to talk to."

"You feel that good, Morry?"

"I feel like shit. It's better'n layin' here and starin' at the ceiling."

Frobisch promised, "I'll think it over."

"Could you deny a sick man's wish?"

The dark was giving way to graying shadows. The walls shone slick as gunmetal under a coat of fresh gray paint. The monks had hung no crosses or religious pictures, out of what might be an innate sensitivity—acknowledgment of guests who didn't share the faith—or simply the wish not to mar their handiwork. "The thing is," Frobisch said softly, "you take advantage."

"Sure I do," admitted Gershowitz. "I got a captive, sympathetic audience. Wouldn't you?"

"Maybe so." There was the problem of her blouse—all the tiny buttons, and she was too shy to offer assistance. He got the top one open, and then the second. She wore a simple cotton bra—

"Oh, jeez!" Gershowitz's cry rent the air with anguish. "Talk to me!"

"What is it? Are you having pain?" Frobisch flicked on the bedside lamp. Gershowitz had bolted upright. Frobisch stared into an equine face, chin covered with gray-black stubble, sunken cheeks, a jutting nose, eyes offset by sickly shadows, the irises gray-green, the whites tinged with a yellow cast, like jaundice.

"Not hurting. Scared. Talk to me."

"What shall I say?"

"Don' want a goddam editorial. Just talk!"

Frobisch wondered at what point did the body start

its inevitable dying. Was there a day of no return, a day you figuratively packed your bags, as in a marriage? Better not to dwell on that. For Morry's sake, he delved his cache of reminiscence. The old man's store. The trolley tracks in front, gleaming like ribbons in the rain. The obscene sign, flapping and banging with every gust of wind. On slow days the Pickle King sat in a booth behind a barricade of salt cellars and ketchup and dashed off letters to the Bayonne *Times* damning the capitalist conspiracy and quoting Marx. Thank God nothing was ever published, sparing the old man the label of a Commie pinko as well as something of a nut case. His father never went to shul, but Frobisch had to go with his mother on the high holidays, had to climb a rickety stair to the scorching upper level where the women sat, fanning themselves in flowered dresses and black felt hats mashed flat on their brows like the hats of matadors, he'd thought. He had to be handed down the line, had to be kissed, pinched, pummeled, pronounced a fine young man before he could shake them off and bolt downstairs. His schoolmates waited in the scraggly bushes. A girl named Dolly or Dora something-or-other, said to be a refugee from Hitler, had big boobs and an artificial leg. He felt her up Kol Nidre night, got hot groping below her waist, touching the canvas harness that strapped the false leg to her hip.

"Pervert," said Gershowitz.

"I guess so," Frobisch sighed.

"Talk!"

You could make out near the bay. Spread a blanket in the sandy weeds, light a fire, bake potatoes in the ashes. The girls let you get away with murder as long as you didn't make eye contact. You could lie there whistling

"Dixie" and get inside their bras; you could move their hands down to your pants and hear the quick gasps of surprise, as long as you didn't look into their faces. "The point was to blur the matter of identities. To simply do what you were doing and not assign a person to the deed. So it was all right then—"

"That's shit," commented Gershowitz.

"What?"

"*That is a crock of shit.*" Gershowitz enunciated carefully. "Makin' out is makin' out. That's all it was. Why do you have to make it sound so fancy? Why is it so complicated? You get where I am, you see how simple everything gets to be."

"How simple is that?"

Gershowitz heaved a weighty sigh. "You got your plain no-nonsense basics. Eatin'—for those bastards who can—sleepin', gettin' laid, playin' a little gin. That's all she wrote, bubba. That's the ball game. I don't have energy for soul-searchin'."

He felt unjustly attacked. "You don't have to be so damn patronizing. Maybe you're dying, maybe you're not; that doesn't make you a better person," Frobisch said and would have willingly cut out his tongue.

"Not better; maybe braver," Gershowitz said calmly. "I get scared shitless, but I gotta laugh it off. Smile in the face of danger; bite the bullet—that's the drill."

"You can yell bloody murder if you want to. You don't have to put on a show for me."

"I don't do it for you, you stupid prick! I do it for me. I gotta know I still got some control. When that goes, that's the clue—it's curtains. Listen, if that starts to happen and you're still here, there's something you can do for me—"

"No, Morry."

"Whaddya sayin' no for? You don't know what I was gonna ask you!"

"Whatever it is, the answer's no." Frobisch turned to face the open window.

Gershowitz was laughing softly. "You'll do it. When the time comes, if I ask you, you'll do anything I want. That's the one power I got, the power of this bum disease."

The monks had begun the morning prayers. The notes resounded cold and pure as crystal. Frobisch closed his eyes.

Gershowitz complained, "If they would stop their caterwaulin', a man could sleep."

"Leave if you don't like it. Stay with that girl, Arlene."

Gershowitz sounded surprised. "I like it here all right. I must like it, I come back every year. I'm what you'd call a groupie. I started comin' just to hide out from my ex-wives, and I found out I enjoyed it. This time, I'll stay till they kick me out."

"Suit yourself." Frobisch burrowed deeper into the pillow.

"How about that other pill, Howie?"

"Stick it out a little longer. Try to sleep."

"It's so cold."

Swearing softly, Frobisch kicked the cover to one side. He groaned when his bare feet hit the floor. He gathered up his blanket and carried it to Morry's bed where he spread it, none too gently. "I'll close the window. You'll be warm soon."

"How you gonna sleep?"

"Can't. I'll go into the commons room and write a letter." There was, in fact, one letter he meant to send, to Father Paul, though he doubted that the priest would relish hearing from him. "Try for a coupla hours' shut-eye, okay?"

The pill was taking hold. Gershowitz sounded sleepy. "You like doin' things for me, don't you? Makes you feel kinda holy. The monks like it, too. I'm everybody's fuckin' mascot."

For once, Morry was on target. As Sadie must have learned when she was tending Gregor, there were satisfactions to playing nurse. Beyond the pleasure of piling up good conduct points, there was the certainty of his own power and strength—the return of his elusive potency—in contrast to Gershowitz's growing weakness. "If you'll try to sleep, I'll consider driving us to Baltimore," he offered.

Gershowitz responded with a loud, theatric snore.

"It is a mass." The first night they talked at any length (Frobisch just back from the infirmary and feeling woozy), Gershowitz described it as a point of pride. He was propped up on his bed (having appropriated Frobisch's pillow as a second bolster) dressed in a white silk bathrobe and his Indian slippers. The room had a rank gardenia smell, a mix of paint and sweat and soggy towels. The window was shut tight. Frobisch considered opening it, but was too weary to make the effort. He sat on his cot, cradling his bandaged hand.

They had exchanged some stilted pleasantries—the mandatory facts about their lives held out like puzzle pieces offered to fill a breach. Gershowitz remained ambiguous. He had worked in sales and salvage. He had been sometimes married, sometimes not. He had lived in or around New Jersey, Phillie, Baltimore, New York. What he liked best was hanging out at private clubs, playing gin rummy, blackjack, five-card stud, whatever the members liked. If his luck picked up, he headed out to Vegas for bigger stakes. Frobisch figured he knew the type—the operator hanging out at Ocean City, playing gin for peanuts, fabricating deals, tottering on the borderline of "broke," but with enough fresh dough to stand for drinks or dinner; always with a well-built woman, though when you got past the necessary sex—come business or serious play time—these guys were more comfortable in the company of men. Gershowitz, small-time gambler and monastery groupie, got cancer and that gave him definition. He bit the bullet and was proud.

"To get to the nitty-gritty," Gershowitz told him, "it is a mass."

Plagued with bad hearing, Frobisch misunderstood. "I don't attend. I enjoy hearing the music, but I don't go near the chapel. Call it misplaced loyalty to the old religion."

Gershowitz hauled himself out of bed—a stiff rearranging of skinny arms and legs. He shuffled to a middle point between the cots, pulled at his belt, flashed open the robe's silk panels, and fanned them shut and open again, in grinning parody of an exhibitionist. He was naked underneath the billowing silk. "Take a look."

Instinctively Frobisch shielded his eyes with his undamaged hand.

Gershowitz waited. "Squeamish?"

Frobisch lowered his hand and looked up shyly. There was no meat on the man. He could count the sharp protrusions of the ribs. On Gershowitz's sunken belly, an inch wide of the navel, was a curved red scar. A stub of plastic tube projected from the scar's puckered center.

Gershowitz said, "They hook me to a tube and pump the nutrients in there. Clever, ain't it?"

Frobisch avoided looking at the shriveled genitals. He felt he had been bludgeoned. "That's how you're fed?"

Gershowitz was pleased at his ability to shock. "Yup. I bring the stuff here with me. Lay brother in the infirmary, used to be a paramedic, hooks me up twice a day. Sometimes it stays down; sometimes it don't. I figure, we're livin' together, you oughta be informed."

Frobisch, dryly: "Thanks."

"You can ask the guestmaster to switch you if you want." Gershowitz retied the robe. He rummaged in a pocket and produced a deck of cards. "Watch." He fanned the cards out in a loose accordion and snapped them back. He held the deck above one palm and let the cards drop in a steady fall into his other hand. "You play gin?" Frobisch nodded. "Let's have a game, then. High card deals; ya knock with ten; we play penny a point, for starters. I don' wanna waste you."

Fresh with visions of his angel, Frobisch took a virtuous stand. "I don't think it's appropriate to gamble here."

"Any sins come down on you, I'll take 'em on my head." Gershowitz winked. "What's the worst that could happen? The good Lord strikes me dead?" Gershowitz went back to bed. He settled against the pillows and hefted his legs onto the mattress. He was still wearing the Indian moccasins. He began to shuffle the cards.

Columns of dust danced in the twilight. Frobisch brandished his gauze-wrapped hand. "I don't think I could hold cards with this bandage."

"So take it off."

"That's not such a great idea."

"Hurts, does it?" Gershowitz eyed him bleakly.

Frobisch blushed. "It's not so bad." Gently, he eased up the strip of tape that held the bandage tight. He began a slow unwrapping, letting a labyrinthine coil of gauze drift to the floor. There was a raised welt on his palm, the size of a half dollar. At the center was a tiny black speck where the sting had entered. Frobisch flexed his fingers. "It seems okay."

"Get somethin' for keepin' score, will ya?"

Frobisch removed a yellow legal pad and a ball-point pen from the top drawer of his dresser. He drew two careful columns, marked one *F* and one *G*.

"You're nicely organized," commented Gershowitz.

"Compensation for a muddled mind."

Gershowitz beckoned with the deck. "C'mon. Move your bed up closer, and let's get on with it. I'm feelin' lucky."

They played until Gershowitz stopped winning and began making harried motions toward the bottles on the nightstand.

The next morning Frobisch found the guestmaster and asked to be assigned some useful task that would keep him outside for the major portion of the day. The guestmaster turned thumbs down on outdoor work because of Frobisch's suspected allergy and assigned him to duty in the refectory kitchen.

"There's a lesson I derive as I watch Gershowitz dying," Frobisch wrote to Father Paul. "Not the obvious one which says I'm luckier than he and should be grateful for my health and stop my everlasting kvetching. (Sadie says I'm not so much the Pickle Prince as the King of Kvetch, and as usual, she tells it like it is.) The part about my luck is taken as a given. The part that comes as a surprise is the importance Gershowitz puts on the commonplace. He is not dying with grace, nor with forbearance. He boasts that he is brave, and whimpers. He rages at his fate with the foulest language I have heard in years, and who can blame him? At the same time, he derives real joy from things I would have classed as insignificant: the comfort of a pair of moccasins, a lucky run of cards, putting one over on the monks (he runs poker games in the commons room when the good brothers are out of earshot). Last night I asked him what it was he missed the most since he got sick, and he answered without missing a beat, 'Toast.' With one foot in the grave, he accepts the idea of my angel as potential comfort, but what he really craves is his familiar breakfast.

"What all this reinforces in my mind is the wish, stronger than ever since I came here, to lead an ordinary life, to be in no way extraordinary, to live a regular routine without surprises. I think men with grandiose ambitions are either cursed or crazy. Sadie, who loves the limelight, would disagree, and perhaps that indicates why we are better off divorced."

Frobisch reread this much and concluded he was rambling. He crumpled the letter to a ball and started over:

"The sky is clear. The air is cool. Once a week the helicopters fly low heading to their landings at Camp David and scare the monastery sheep."

He continued in this vein for two close-written pages before returning to his room to dress for kitchen duty.

Brother Olivier who supervised the kitchen had a head bald as an onion dome and a pointed wisp of beard that bristled irritation whenever Frobisch hove in view. The monk dressed for kitchen work in dark brown shirts (which classed him in Frobisch's mind as a fascist) and chino pants from L. L. Bean tucked into crepe-soled hiking boots that laced to the knees. Macho as a commando, he stomped across the kitchen with a loping gait, sidestepping puddles. He spoke confused, accented English, laced with French asides that Frobisch dismissed as affectation.

From a massive central table Brother Olivier held court. Waving a knife of carbon steel, he supervised the carving and the chopping, issuing crisp directives or diatribes to novices and retreatants who hustled to his command. The monk had dubbed Frobisch *le visionnaire*. He made no effort to hide his dislike for someone who claimed to have seen—not once, but twice—a vision of an angel.

Frobisch likened working in the kitchen to duty in some last outpost of hell. It was a vast room tiled in white, in which smoky emanations wafted from a restaurant-sized stove and clouds of steam billowed from basins in a wobbly two-legged sink. The ceiling was supported by dark wooden posts, placed to bear the weight of plumbing overhead. They were directly underneath the room Brother Olivier referred to as the *necessarium*—the monks' latrine and shower room where ancient leaky pipes evoked a chilling damp that seeped under the pocked tiles of the shower floor to stain the mottled plaster of the kitchen ceiling.

Brother Olivier kept minions under his command whose sole duty was to scour and swab and keep at bay the dark patches of mildew growing on the ceiling like black flowers opening to the cloudy air. Other slaveys chopped and strained and peeled and diced, gloomy as sinners consigned to perpetual purgatory. They were a sad-eyed lot—their long faces as they went about their tasks proclaimed dashed hopes, or the chronic dyspepsia that came from tasting their own cooking. Over this lot of damned, wet-handed, snuffling souls, Brother Olivier reigned supreme, showering torrents of scathing French at hapless novices not quick enough to do his bidding.

Today Brother Olivier had set Frobisch to work in a corner husking corn, the morning's pick, still wet from the monastery fields. It had been heaped in bushel baskets coated with the remnants of the early frost. Frobisch was to strip the husks and scrape the kernels into an oversized black pot set on the floor.

Strange to the Benedictine habit of obedience, Frobisch had already protested, "Can't you cook 'em on the cob?"

Brother Olivier scowled. "If 'is tongue rattle as freely in 'is 'ead as 'is brain, *le visionnaire* wouldn' take the time to ask."

Frobisch fell meekly to his tasks, perched on a low stool that hurt his butt. When he pulled back the first green husks, he discovered fat white worms lazing on the rows of golden kernels. Frobisch picked off the first few worms halfheartedly, and then decided to ignore them. Extra protein wouldn't hurt the loose-toothed monks. He had spread newspaper on the floor for collecting the husks. The stripped cobs he stashed in a brown paper grocery bag a novice had provided. Two new retreatants labored beside him—an Indian in a salmon-colored turban that shocked Frobisch with its resemblance to a bloody bandage, and a black cop from D.C. who said his retreat was a necessary respite from the war zone. They were working in companionable silence. Frobisch had found a pleasant rhythm— rip, peel, scrape, discard—when a flash of something white-hot as magnesium flame diverted him. Grease fire, was his first thought. The light diminished to a cool blue glow, like a residue of burning gas. He looked around for a fire extinguisher and saw, as the flickering subsided, the familiar figure of the Spanish Steps, looking strangely wistful. *Believe in me*, the angel telegraphed, *or I am nothing.*

Frobisch cried, "Not here!" and toppled to the floor, where he lay belly up amid sluggish worms and scattered husks.

For a moment he lingered in that heaven which is certainty—everything seen, everything understood. There was a heavy pressure on his chest. He opened his eyes reluctantly. Blinking in the steamy light, he focused on a red, pulsating onion—Brother Olivier's bald head, flushed with rage and laced with ominous swollen veins.

"I won' 'ave this!"

"It's nothing I can control," muttered Frobisch, struggling to dislodge the monk who was straddling him as though he were a downed plow horse.

"You are an epileptic! I won' 'ave an epileptic in my kitchen! *C'est dangereux!* It isn' safe!"

"I saw a messenger of God." Frobisch was sullen. "Get off me, will ya!"

"*C'est fou! Le visionnaire* is cra-zee!" Brother Olivier kicked Frobisch in the ribs with damp crepe soles.

He responded out of buried memory. He was once again Prince Pickle, spreadeagled by a pair of thick-necked studs who wanted to unzip his pants and find out if his little thing matched the green prick on the sign. "Get offa me, you stupid goy! You narrow-minded shit! What do you know? If Christ Himself showed up in this kitchen, you'd crucify Him all over again and put the blame on me! Then you'd go play your pious act and say your prayers!"

The monk and Frobisch stared at one another in mutual astonishment. Almost meekly, Brother Olivier released him and stood up. Frobisch retrieved his paring knife and struggled to his feet, brushing off worms and strands of corn silk. He searched his fellow workers' faces for some show of sympathy. The Indian was staring past him with a look of blank detachment, as though the consciousness that dwelled beneath the bloody-looking turban had already drifted off to calmer spheres. The cop had ducked into a crouch and was moving in a cautious circle, ready to deck Frobisch if he lunged. "Hol' still," he warned. "Everythin' is cool. Jus' hand me over the knife."

The jerk was acting as though this was a standoff on Fourteenth Street. Frobisch snapped, "Don't be an ass!"

With his boots braced in familiar puddles, Brother Olivier had regained his sour equilibrium and was raising a new head of steam, calling on *le Bon Dieu* and *la Sainte Vierge* and *la mère dans le ciel* to testify he meant no harm to any man, even *"le fou—cet homme sauvage, le visionnaire."*

"Calm down, would you?" hollered Frobisch. "It's all over. I'm leaving. I'm going back to Washington. Your kitchen is safe!" The idea had been formulating in his mind since early morning when he'd sat shivering in the commons room trying to tell his thoughts to Father Paul. He'd come up with a vacant travelogue. If that was the best that contemplation afforded him, he thought he might as well go home.

The kitchen workers had gathered around him in a circle. They were waiting as though prepared to rush him if Brother Olivier gave the signal. The monk looked surprised at this unsought show of loyalty. Frobisch was mortally ashamed. He hadn't meant to fling out taunts or to cast himself as history's recurrent victim. If there was the least chance Brother Olivier would listen, Frobisch was willing to explain that his outburst stemmed from weariness and cold and the tedium of hours attending Gershowitz. He didn't want to dredge up ancient grudges. If nothing else, the angel had aroused in him a questioning spirit that was purely ecumenical.

# · CHAPTER ·
## 9

Pie-eyed on Bardolino, Frobisch staggered over a no-man's-land of shaggy carpet crisscrossed with plastic runners like the markings on a child's board game. In his arms he held a twenty-five-pound pumpkin and a jug of apple cider he had purchased at an all-night Safeway near the harbor. His jacket pockets bulged with bags of candy—Hershey's Kisses, Good 'n' Plenties, licorice, candy corn.

Arlene said, "Mind the carpet."

Drifting in a fog of wine fumes, Frobisch nodded, wavering within the runner's plastic boundaries. "Step on a crack; break your back," he giggled, listing to port. Arlene rushed to hold him upright. "Point me to the kitchen," Frobisch ordered. Arlene pointed with a red-tipped finger, bracelets gleaming on her freckled arm. Suddenly she ducked behind him and sent him forward with a shove.

He'd been surprised to learn that she was black; more precisely, sepia, of a decided ivory cast, the skin mottled with reddish freckles that dabbed her cheeks and sprayed out in a fan over her chest. Her hair was swept high in a knot, softened by frizzy bangs dyed autumn gold. Her friend Charlotte was darker-skinned, pouty, sullen; perfect features framed by ebony hair that bore the slick luster of dacron. When they were introduced, in the restaurant in Little Italy, Frobisch's eyes had moved in admiration from the sheen of the dark wig, sculpted to a rigid pageboy, to the satin gleam of Charlotte's breasts, peeping like shy woods animals from their lacy beige entrapment.

"Aren't they beautiful?" Gershowitz had grinned out of a haze of glassy-eyed euphoria, achieved by gulping a muddled "cocktail" of his pills as he and Frobisch sped east in the Volvo.

Frobisch had moved his eyes from Charlotte's chest long enough to echo, "Beautiful." A waiter silently poured wine. Frobisch drained the contents of his goblet in one long, greedy swallow.

Arlene, sipping discreetly—in a manner so chaste and nunlike Frobisch imagined she was drinking holy water— had looked pained as he drank. "Awfully thirsty," Frobisch mumbled, pouring himself a refill.

"Me three." Gershowitz twirled his glass till it overturned. Wine seeped bloodlike under a wicker basket heaped with bread sticks.

Discomfited by Charlotte's cool appraisal, Frobisch had searched the chaos in his mind to retrieve one sober thought. He'd studied the cleft between her breasts where there nestled a single drop of sweat, shiny and perfect as a pearl. "Did ya ever notice that in Italian restaurants the dish of grated cheese smells like barf?" Frobisch had offered his most winning smile.

Charlotte had murmured, "Little girls' room," and stood up, a dusky Venus rising from a weed-strewn beach. Clutching a satin evening bag crusted with tiny shells, she floated off—stiff-legged, flat-bellied, those wondrous boobs preceding her like an advance guard. Her behind was fleshier than he would have liked. She was gorgeous nonetheless.

" 'Sgoddess," Frobisch said.

Gershowitz bent to Arlene. "He's been too long among the nuns."

"Is he a priest?"

He was not so drunk he didn't notice the way they talked of him as though he wasn't there, as though his body sat, earthbound in Little Italy, while his spirit sailed—*O sole mio*—on wine-dark seas.

"Sincerely hope not." Gershowitz, who could do no more than swallow water, even more chastely than Arlene, had begged to be allowed to order. This he had done with the abandon of a man condemned—a last meal comprised of inky exotics of the deep: sea urchins, calamari, mussels, their dark shells sweetly parted to reveal the pulpy flesh. Frobisch masked the seaweed tastes with garlic sauce and mopped the last salty morsels with bits of bread.

"Makes you thirsty," Frobisch said and drank more wine.

They had paired off in the car. Gershowitz slouched in the back, lolling against Arlene and sighing, a mix of joy and profound sadness. Charlotte sat cool and quiet in the front, with enough space on the seat between herself and Frobisch to discourage any hope he might have held of familiarity. He drove in wounded silence, bound for Arlene's place. The vista of the Safeway, draped in orange streamers, roused him to thoughts of Halloween and the inevitable memories of Sima, done up like a bride for trick or treat. He owned a picture (stolen from the family album) of Sima, posed in an October drizzle, bearing a flashlight and a plastic pumpkin, Sadie's half-slip trailing frayed lace over the tops of scarlet rain boots. Whimpering nostalgia, Frobisch turned into the pitted asphalt of the Safeway lot. "You all wait here for me."

"Whatever for?" Arlene's voice had the stridence of the woman too often abandoned.

"Gonna buy a pumpkin. Gonna carve a jack-o'-lantern for my good friend Morry. Let him take it back to Saint Pachomius for company."

"The man's a prince," said Gershowitz.

"You can set it in a window. Scare the monks."

In the store he'd felt like an intruder, eyeing the unfamiliar larder of the urban poor—pork butts and salt fish and grits and gnarled, lumpish potatoes and wormy apples and pallid corn with husks stripped back to show the waxy kernels. He filled his cart with candy, wrapped in faded Easter colors, and cruised the store, searching for a pumpkin. He saw one on the floor, circled by jugs of clouded cider, and judged it perfect—properly bulbous, flagrantly bright—topped with a knob of greenish stem as though it had been newly wrested from some local farmer's vines. He hefted the pumpkin and a jug of cider to his cart. When he got back to the car, he found Morry bent double, with his head buried on Arlene's breast. Her face loomed, freckled, pale, from the back seat's purplish shadows. Frobisch met her eyes in dark complicity. "Is he okay?"

"Baby wants shut-eye." She sounded unconcerned.

In the front seat Charlotte yawned and buffed her nails.

Arlene's apartment was on the top floor of a row house built of sooty brick, the characteristic marble stoop discolored greenish gray by fumes of nearby factories. They entered through a hall reeking of insect spray. Single file, they climbed the stairs. Frobisch, following Charlotte, lamented that she suffered so badly from lordosis, the outward curving of the ass so marked he could have balanced the pumpkin on her fleshy hams. She looked her best taken head on, Frobisch decided. He struggled with his burdens on the narrow stairs. On the landing Morry stumbled, and Arlene moved, swift as a wraith, to bolster him.

They bunched at the apartment door, nudging arms and elbows, as Arlene released a series of dead bolts and locks. Frobisch held his breath, lest he offend with heady whiffs of garlic. Arlene shoved open the door and ushered them into a living room that crackled with plastic like the receiving station of an isolation ward. Plastic draped the yellow fabric of the couch, the twin red-velvet chairs, the fluted lamp shades, conical as coolie hats, that perched atop bases of simpering shepherds.

"Byootiful," said Frobisch, waddling his clumsy trail along the plastic strip that led him to the kitchen. He set pumpkin and cider on the kitchen counter and retraced his path, lifting his feet high as though he were skipping across the broken boulders of Rock Creek.

In the living room, Morry beamed in a vague narcotic daze—the benign grin of a patriarch watching his children play. Charlotte fiddled with a stereo set in a blond wood cabinet. A rush of jungle music blasted as she turned the dial, a drum's inexorable beat, countered by the nervous plucking of a bass. Charlotte bent to unstrap her sandals, revealing a physical geography of such awesome beauty Frobisch felt his eyes flooding with tears.

"How lovely is the gloriousness of God," hiccuped Frobisch.

Charlotte closed her eyes and swayed with arms outstretched. Her ample rump undulated as though it were a creature set apart, with a life support system all its own.

"Find me a pillow for my head," pleaded Morry.

Arlene grasped his arm and pulled him down a second track of plastic.

"'Two roads diverged in a yellow wood,'" recited Frobisch, and added, "Frost," although no one seemed interested. It was one of the endless list of poems Sima had to memorize in high school. He'd coached her as she practiced. He was convinced in those days that she'd be an actress, another Katie Hepburn, talking with that sort of throaty chuckle that gave him goose bumps.

Arlene tugged Morry to the bedroom. Frobisch glimpsed a turquoise-tufted headboard and imagined the cracklings of the mattress, plastic-wrapped, as the lovers tussled. The toilet in the john must sport one of those paper signs, "Sanitized," that you found now in motels.

Morry smiled from the door before gently closing it. "Just play among yourselves, little ones."

Charlotte opened her eyes, confronting Frobisch. "You wanna dance?"

"No." Too quickly he was growing sober. "I don't think so. Thank you."

"What are you? A racist?"

"Certainly not! I'd rather watch."

"What fun is that?"

"It's fun. You move well."

"White guys are strange."

"I think we probably are," Frobisch concurred. Stiffly, he walked the way he'd come, over the pale runner that led into the kitchen. He flipped a light switch on the wall and blinked at the gleam of scrubbed white porcelain. From the living room, the music's beat tempted him with a rhythm that matched the pumping of his blood. If he went back, kicked off his shoes, stepped from the careful confines of his chosen path to that wasteland of sandy carpet, and folded Charlotte in his arms, what might transpire? Would they fall together on the pristine couch and risk death by suffocation on those plastic sheets? He imagined Arlene and Morry discovering them, locked in time, like the lovers showered by volcanic ash in Pompeii. He had picked among those ruins with Sadie and shuddered at the unarguable finality of death. Better to carve the pumpkin!

He draped his jacket on a kitchen chair. Slowly he rolled his shirtsleeves to the elbows. In the aperture between the refrigerator and the wall was a folded copy of the Baltimore *Sun*. He shook the paper open and spread it on the kitchen table, a circle of butcher block that gleamed amid dark wooden cabinets like a bleached moon. He placed the pumpkin in the middle of the table and studied it from various angles.

"Charlotte," he called over the pounding music, "do you know where I can find a knife?"

"A knife?"

"Something small and sharp."

She appeared, wielding a hat pin long enough to pierce his eye and reach the deep core of his brain. "This is what I carry." For the first time since they'd met, she grinned, and her face lost its imposing beauty and took on the brazen mischief of a street kid.

"You carry that?"

"In my purse. In case some cat thinks he wants to get smart with me."

He blessed the instinct that had warned him that if he danced into her aura, took the darker road, he would meet a swift, untimely death. "I want to carve the pumpkin," Frobisch explained.

"Try any drawer."

"Arlene won't mind?"

"Judgin' by the moans I'm hearin', I'd say she's beyond caring."

Go, Morry, go, thought Frobisch. For the brotherhood of horny men. Redeem us with your dancing prick. Frobisch asked Charlotte, "Do you want to help?"

"Not hardly."

She watched him as he rummaged through drawers. Each was furnished with its sectioned tray—a model of organization even for efficient Sadie. And Louisa! The memory of her boiling water in her cluttered kitchen smote his heart.

He found a knife with a serrated blade and set to work. Charlotte leaned against the gleaming counter, arms crossed on her breasts. She was breathing noisily through parted lips. Frobisch inhaled the mix of ripening pumpkin, lily of the valley, musk, his own garlicky breath, and the stale sweat of anxiety. He carved with shaking hands. "Is there a bag or something where I can dump the pulp and the seeds?" Frobisch asked Charlotte.

Her eyes widened. Frobisch marveled at the metamorphosis women could achieve. One moment, the sloe-eyed look of an Egyptian princess; now a wide-eyed innocent, all whites and astonishment. "Man, you gonna waste it? That's good food."

"What, pumpkin? I wouldn't know what to do with it. I always dump it."

"You dump it? Isn't that just like white folks? You throw it out? Man, you got enough there to make two pies. Or pumpkin soup. Or bread."

Gentile food. Sadie wouldn't be bothered with it. "Well, what should I do with it, then?" asked Frobisch.

Charlotte shrugged. "I don't care. Throw it out if you wanna."

"I doubt Arlene would want to keep it. I venture to guess she won't be in any frame of mind to cook."

"White folks sure are strange."

Frobisch pondered the triangulation of the pumpkin's eye. He'd had long arguments with Sadie and Sima about the proper shaping of a pumpkin's features. Should the triangle rest on its base? Would the jack-o'-lantern look more formidable with a rounded eye? The women never agreed. As they discussed it, Gregor Samsa watched from a corner, waiting to retrieve spilled seeds, which he ate at awful peril to his digestion. "Charlotte, m'dear," said Frobisch, "would it be amiss if I suggested that you, not I, are the bigot?"

Charlotte uncrossed her arms and stood unshielded, breasts swelling in agitation, a motion so perilously sweet it made his head spin. "What you wanna say something like that for?"

"You've been citing the strangeness of white folks since we walked in."

"That don't make me a bigot. It just makes you some kinda fool."

Charlotte turned her back to him and ran cold water in the sink. She filled a glass and slowly drank. Frobisch watched her as she swallowed and pondered seizing her, pinning her flat-out on the floor, having his way without further argument. Only the memory of Louisa, cool and chaste, the gold links shining at her throat, kept him honorable. That and the recollection of the hat pin Charlotte carried in her purse!

Charlotte strode past him in stocking feet and flounced

out of the kitchen, every motion of her wondrous, jiggling rump betraying her contempt. Frobisch went back to his task. The eyes were out of balance, but they'd have to do. When he had carved the nose (perfect isosceles) and a snag-toothed, grinning mouth, he again rummaged in the drawers. He found a stump of candle and a box of matches. He set the candle in the hollowed pumpkin shell and lit it. Then he doused the kitchen light.

"Charlotte," he called. "Come see."

There was no answer from the living room. He stood at the kitchen door imploring, "Come see how nicely it turned out."

She was curled against the stereo cabinet as though she meant to creep inside. She had tucked her long legs under her. She looked sexy and mean. "I didn't know you talked to bigots."

"Charlotte, I didn't mean it. Let's be friends. Come see the jack-o'-lantern. We can break into the candy, have a party."

"I didn't come here to play no trick or treat."

He would have knelt beside her on the floor and braved whatever weaponry she had concealed—he was bending to her—when the bedroom door swung open. Morry stood, ashen-faced, grappling with his zipper.

Frobisch reacted as though he'd been caught in a scene of sexual abandon. Instinctively, he smoothed his hair, tightened his tie, projecting ersatz innocence, a phony heartiness. "How ya doin', buddy?" he babbled.

Morry offered a wan smile, a quick parting of the lips in a face so frozen with despair it could have been the fixed stare of a death's-head. "Okay. Looks like you two are hittin' it off."

"Better'n butter," Frobisch piped.

"He made you your pumpkin," Charlotte pouted.

"No shit? Let's pack it up and move on outa here."

Frobisch compounded stupidity upon stupidity. "You're not havin' a good time? You want to leave?"

"'Take me home, country roads,'"sang Morry.

"Where's Arlene?" asked Charlotte.

"Freshening up."

Charlotte unfolded nyloned legs in a movement that held both men rapt. Slowly she climbed to her feet. She smoothed the creases in her skirt, brushed both palms across her blouse, patted her hips. "I'll go on and talk to her." Her mood had changed. She grinned at Frobisch, even essayed a mocking curtsy. "If the gennlemens will excuse me?"

"'Scused," said Morry. "We're taking off. Tell Arlene I'll call her."

"Sure will." Charlotte ambled toward Morry. Standing on tiptoe, she kissed him on the lips. Morry swayed with arms waving beyond her as though he feared his touch would burn her. She broke away and studied his face. "Be sweet now, hear?"

"I will, baby, I will."

She looked to Frobisch. "Guess I ain't no bigot with the right sorta person." And she was gone in a cloud of lily and musk, vanished behind the door to explore the secrets of the tumbled turquoise bed with Arlene, who even now must be lighting incense, strewing petals in some cleansing rite.

Frobisch asked Morry, "Everything okay?"

"In a pig's eye," said Morry. He fell onto the golden sofa, grinding his head into the pillows. Impatiently he pulled at the plastic cover.

Frobisch warned, "Careful."

"What a bummer," Morry sighed.

"What's wrong? You feelin' bad? I don't know what we can do. You used up all your pills."

"Oh, man, Howie. I'm wasted. That's it. I'm all used up."

"That good, huh?"

"That good? Howie, I couldn't get it up! First time ever. Don't look at me like that. I mean *first time*! I am *virginally impotent*—my first, my really first encounter with that kinda fate, not counting a coupla premature ejaculations back in high school, which hadn't oughta count, considering the circumstances."

"High school! Morry, all I could ever do back then was daydream about the act."

"Daydream, night-dream, wet dream, what's the diff? I can't do it no more."

"Ah, hell, Morry. One lousy time. Don't make it such a big deal. It happens to all of us. It happened a couple of times to me."

"Not to me! Not ever! Not even with the sickness. I can't eat, I can't shit, but I can fuck. Jeez, Howie, it even got better with the cancer. It really did. For a while there—ask Arlene—I was a wild man. I couldn't tell you why, unless the body knows what's comin' and wants its last chance at life. I think that's it."

"What are you talking about, 'what's coming'? What's coming is they're gonna put you back in Hopkins and shoot you full of these experimental drugs, and you and Arlene'll be together fuckin' like bunnies before you know what hit you."

"Oh, yeah? Tell me another story, Grandma!"

"It's not a story. I know!"

"What do you mean, you know?"

"Remember who you're talking to."

"I asked you just the other night—early this morning, I asked you if you knew, and you said you didn't, and you wouldn't tell me if you did."

"I wouldn't tell you if I knew it was bad. And I didn't know. Not then. But I explained how it happens—sometimes little bits and pieces hit me. Sometimes the whole thing comes clear, all in a flash. Like now. I know!"

"You're lyin', you damn Prince Pickle. You think I'm so dumb that I can't tell when you're lyin'!"

"I'm not lying. Think what you like."

"Swear it, Howie."

"I swear."

"On your daughter's life?"

"That, too."

"Say it, Howie. Say 'I swear on my daughter's life.'"

"I swear on my daughter's life that you're going to get better."

"Show me your hands and say it again."

"What for?"

"You could have your fingers crossed. Then it wouldn't count."

Frobisch held his hands before him, palms flat and barely trembling. Moses parting the sea. "I swear on my daughter Sima's life, you will recover."

Morry pounded a ruined pillow with his fist. "Hot damn! You do know!"

"'Course I do," said Frobisch, smiling so broadly he feared his flesh would split.

Sober now, cold sober, he held the Volvo to the road— took the turns on screeching tires, floored it on the straightaway past dark bushes and waving trees. The sky was bright with stars. A car in the oncoming lane flashed its high beams, blinding him; he plowed on in a blaze of light, flicked his own brights, clicked them off. Faster, in the cold, he drove, praying to miss a turn, spin off a bridge, catapult to a wet death in the choppy waters of the bay. His life for Sima's, and God would forgive. The moon was a silver wafer.

Love me, here in the moonlight,
Kiss me, and hold me, and love me,
Or surely I'll die. . . .

Gershowitz sang rhumba rhythms to the cockeyed pumpkin in his lap.

Oh, lo-ve m-e-e,
Pretty lad-y,

Faster, something double-dared him; he switched lanes, cut off a lumbering semi, heard the horn's blast trail behind him, heard a thunder of tires, made it back into his lane in time. Everything worked. He couldn't die. He was under her protection, Our Lady of the Roads smiling from her perch amid the thorny holly and the last dried mums, frozen like flowers carved of gold.

Hold me forever,
And say I'm the one
You ad-o-r-e.

"You know I'm not staying when we get back to the monastery," Frobisch interposed before Gershowitz could launch into a second chorus.

"Wish you'd reconsider."

"Can't. My bag's in back. I've said my good-byes. The die is cast."

"Be lonely in the night without you, buddy-man."

"You'll be fine."

"I'll barf alone," sang Morry.

Frobisch laughed. "What's in those pills? Maybe I ought to get some."

"I'll retch in peace."

Frobisch groaned. "For that, a speedy death."

"Nah, Howie, life is good. The air is sweet. The good brothers are picking apples and making apple butter and Sunday pies. C'mon back with me, just till the weekend. Then I'll check out with you, if you still wanna go."

"I can't. It gets . . . wearing. I don't know why you stay so long."

"Cheaper than Grossinger's. My poker buddies say the food's not bad."

"Better than that eel and squid shit you made me eat tonight."

"Tonight was a bummer. I'll feel better next week."

"You will," said Frobisch, compounding his crimes. Forgive me, Lord, he prayed. In Your name I have taken my old dog's life and lusted after a gentle virgin and lost my cool and offended the kind monks who gave me hospitality. In Your name I swore falsely.

"Don't come to see me if I'm in the hospital, Howie. Okay? I don't want you visitin' if I'm flat on my back, stuck full 'o pins and needles."

"Arlene will see you that way."

"Arlene's a saint. She gets the hard duty. When I'm on my feet, we'll raise hell together, okay? You and me and Arlene and Charlotte. I think that little gal had the hots for you. I can always tell. When a dame acts like she's real mad at you for nothin', and she pretends she can't stand bein' in the same room with you, that means she really has the hots for you."

207

"She thought I was a racist."

"She said that? Well, she's touchy. Women are like that. All of 'em, y'know? Sensitive as hell."

He passed a trailer, hit the horn, high-pitched, too squeaky for the Volvo's stalwart character. Once before, he'd sped this way. Doing the college tour in Boston. Sima, antsy as hell, fighting him all the way. He missed a turn off Starro Drive, landed on a highway leading to the Cape. Twilight, just growing dark, they plunged through meadows gray with mist. The city glowed behind them in a rosy haze. A Coca-Cola sign shone on the Charles— arrows of neon darting like bright fish in the deep. He'd picked up speed, feeling the thrill, an unfamiliar throbbing, an unexpected pounding in the blood. Catching his mood, Sadie had laughed, which was strange because they weren't speaking.

He told Gershowitz, "I never pretended to understand them."

"Ah, I understand them, Howie. That's my curse. I understand them all too well. See, women are sex-obsessed. That's a rap they put on us, but it isn't so. A guy wants to get laid, that's for sure; but when it's done, it's done, and he can get back to important things—like who's gonna take first place in the NFL and who's gonna clinch the pennant. A fella gets on a hot roll in Vegas, he doesn't need to have some little gal draped around his neck sayin', ooh, honey, aren't you finished yet? You gonna pay any attention to me? A gal is always thinkin', is my hair okay, is my makeup right, does my dress look good, am I gainin', losin' in the right places? Am I desirable, is what she wants to know. A woman is thinkin' all the time—not to get laid—but will he want to lay me? And if not, why not? And if so, how can I torture him the most before I give in?"

"You think so?"

"I know it, Howie. I'll tell you somethin' else. Women's liberation? That's a crock. Women don't want liberation from us, Howie. What they want is to get even. See, I figure a lot of these broads, ugly as sin, got ignored by the stag line in their younger days. They got a history of bein' wallflowers, and now they're gettin' back at us. We didn't want them, so they retaliate by sayin' they don't need us. They can make out all by themselves. Next breath, they're sayin' they want to work with us, side by side. They wanna be soldier boys and bivouac with the army. They wanna play ball and change clothes in the same locker room. What is all that, Howie? That's nothin' but sexual provocation. That's wavin' a flag that says, notice me, buddy. Look at me in my little ole slit skirt and my blouse that's unbuttoned to the navel and jus' guess what I want. See, they're never able to let up on us, never for one minute. They gotta be noticed. They gotta be everywhere we are. That's liberation? My ass! That's harassment of the male. That's why I like it in the monastery. There's more wisdom behind those walls than any place I know. What are the monks sayin' but, leave me alone to think my own deep thoughts without harassment by the other gender? That's real peace, Howie. A bunch of good, serious guys bandin' together without a lot of cacklin' women to complain because you forgot to compliment 'em. That's heaven on earth when you think of it."

"I liked it there," admitted Frobisch. "Sometimes I think I have the personality to live that way for a long time. Not as a religious, but in some all-male setup. A fishing camp or something."

"Let's do it, Howie! When I'm better, let's start a fishin' camp or a huntin' lodge up in the North Woods and put up a sign: For Men Only. Admission by Invitation. Only good ole boys and card sharks need apply."

"What about Arlene?" he asked, thinking, what about Louisa?

"She could come up weekends. She could live in town. In a motel. Cook on a little hot plate. File her nails. Do whatever women do to pass the time."

"You think she'd buy that?"

"Sure she would. I'll tell you why, Howie. It's 'cause they need us. They need someone to torture. It's in their nature."

"I don't know, Morry. You could be right."

"Stop the car, Howie. I got to vomit."

He veered hard to the right and pulled to the road's shoulder, flashing his hazard lights. Morry let the pumpkin topple to the seat. Before Frobisch could set the gear in park, Gershowitz lurched out of the car. Frobisch sat frozen, counting the times they'd cheated death tonight. Morry was stumbling through the bushes. Maybe an animal would get him and effect a swift, clean kill amid dead leaves and twisted roots, under that wild outburst of stars. So Frobisch prayed. He stared at the pumpkin—empty eyes, a grin like rictus. The yellowed stump of candle like a tumor choking the brain stem. The hollow sockets of a skull.

"Soon, Louisa, soon," murmured Frobisch, rejecting death, rejecting Morry and his misogyny, rejecting the monks in their isolation. Rejecting the angel who had eyed him almost shyly through the rank smoke of the kitchen. *Believe in me or I am nothing.* His bearded angel, taking form amid chopped roots and cabbage smells, needed Frobisch if he was going to exist. "Well, I deny you," Frobisch said. Finished with that. Finished with flagellation, all that neurasthenic contemplation, all that *mea culpa*, tossing, lying awake and fearful in the night. Fearing God would find him. Fearing death. Finished with that, finished with the frozen Lady on her hill of thorn bushes. Instead, the Hebrew toast that Father Paul had offered when they drank. *"L'Chaim."* It filled him with remembrance of who he was and where he came from; where he was bound. *"L'Chaim,"* said Frobisch grasping the steering wheel so tightly his arms ached. "Back to you, Louisa," Frobisch said. "To life." And he repeated it, "To life," as Gershowitz knelt amid the dark brambles and retched.

## • CHAPTER •
# 10

The Aardvark had an air of dusty permanence, cobwebs untouched, old books, their titles not discernible, jammed rigid on the shelves. Old prints of animals and jaundiced tots stared from the walls in bleary-eyed vacuity. The place needed a sweeping, an airing, a shaking up—a dash of Sadielike vitality or Howie-nerves to spark some life. A cowbell clamored when he opened the door. Frobisch jumped a mile. There was no one in the store; still, he was embarrassed by the show of nerves. He pretended interest in a cache of paperbacks tossed into bins on a long plank table. Each bin bore a faded label: History. Philosophy. Travel. Occult. Nothing inviting there. He pondered how to weed out the deadwood, spruce up the place. If it were left to him he'd jettison the books on the Crusades or banish them out back with Nietzschean philosophy. Update travel. (Who'd buy a Fodor Guide from 1956?) Set the romances on revolving shelves for greater visibility. Title the curtained, shadowed alcove Mystery Corner and stock it with whodunits. Loving the logic of his plans, he began whistling softly, itching to start a list, to let in light, to polish up the mullioned window that could have been an illustration out of Dickens. She should capitalize on that and on the Aardvark name—

scatter a slew of plump stuffed animals on the window seat and invite children to browse.

Behind panels of faded chintz Louisa's voice rose— pedagogic, firm, without the sexy throatiness he'd conjured in the monastery. It was eerie to hear it disembodied, as he'd imagined over sleepless hours with Morry groaning in the shadows and the monks humming their prayers. In a back room she was posing chirpy questions, and a second, older woman's voice was responding, citing a litany of pains—swollen ankles, headaches, gas. Stomach pain so bad she had to walk bent over double. Frobisch, who'd experienced similar attacks in Brother Olivier's kitchen, nodded in tongue-tied sympathy.

"What you want to try is extra fiber. Lord knows, I'm no authority, and I wouldn't want to bludgeon you with my ideas, but there seems to be sufficient evidence—oh, my God!" Framed between flowered curtains, Louisa stood, his muddled goddess, spilling silver coins and books. As in dreams, she moved from shadows into yellow light, her hair askew, one amber comb caught in a twisted strand. A skirt of no marked shape or color hung to her calves; a sweater of pilled navy had a raveled sleeve; when she raised her hands to shield her eyes from the shock of his arrival, he glimpsed the pink skin of a roughened elbow, intimate as a patch of thigh. She wore a floppy smock over her clothes, like an older mother caught in a reluctant pregnancy, or a hospital volunteer. She was so much what he remembered—a woman of middle years and faded prettiness—he couldn't restrain a sigh, part disappointment, part addled lust.

Frobisch said, "Hi."

She touched the frail chain at her throat. "Mrs. Ryan and I were hunting down some early Barbara Cartlands."

Frobisch nodded. Louisa bent to gather up the books she'd dropped. Still in a crouch, she searched for coins. "Back from Shangri-la finally? How was it?"

"It was all right."

She straightened to a schoolgirl's posture, holding the books tight to her chest. "Father Paul's gone to Chicago. A meeting of the Inter-Urban Council for Racial Justice, I think it was."

"That sounds like him."

"Oh, listen." Louisa tossed her head, and a second comb flew from its moorings. "One day he's going to win the Nobel Prize. Only, I worry that he'll ruin his health with all that extra work that he takes on."

Frobisch said earnestly, "It keeps him sane. The monks know the value of the concrete task after all the muddle of abstraction. That was the genius of Pachomius, keeping his population busy with their jobs, balancing prayers with good, solid employment. If you walk through the Main Cloister, you'll see an alcove with a row of cassocks hanging on hooks. Underneath every one is a pair of work boots, stained with mud and cow dung, which illustrates my point. . . ." He saw the look that passed between the women, and he gave it up. It was apparent he had lost the art of easy banter.

"Well, the young priest who's taking Father's place can't cut the mustard, I'll tell you that." Louisa looked to Mrs. Ryan for affirmation. The old woman was eyeing him with startled joy as though she'd never in her wildest hopes believed a morning's outing would provide so interesting a diversion.

Frobisch told Louisa, "I was hoping you could help me locate *Howards End*."

214

If she read significance in that, she gave no sign. "Try fiction under Forster. In the back."

Frobisch, wounded, wobbled unbelieving, dangling his car keys in the air. "Something I want to tell you first, right off the bat. I've given up any claim to having—special gifts." When she stood unmoved, "What is it, Louisa? You hardly seem—welcoming?"

She motioned more forcefully. "Fiction is *in the back*." And Frobisch, finally understanding, plunged through the droopy curtains to the solitude of darkened shelves to await their proper meeting shielded from prying eyes, disheartened by the dust, the smells of paste and damp, the scampering underfoot that must be mice. If this place was her father's dream, the heart's repository, it was a cenotaph. He heard Louisa ringing up the sale, still prattling diet, taking her damned sweet time. She caroled a blithe "Bye now." The bell clanged as the door opened and shut. When she reappeared she was radiant with the old high color. She had taken off her smock. He read encouragement in that. "When did you get back?"

He'd thought of her as being more delicately boned, like the little Virgin keeping vigil over the highway. "Thursday morning, very early. I drove most of the night. Won't you kiss me hello, Louisa?"

"Thursday to Saturday. My, oh, my. You took your time about stopping by."

"I needed to get my head together." The truth was, there were problems in the re-entry. He was put off by the city's noise, the unexpected crush of people, the young men sporting navy blazers who bulled their way through crowded corners wielding their briefcases like shields. The women he'd once desired (wearing mannish suits this fall) now scared him speechless. When he ventured out of his apartment he clung to walls and shrank from rubbing arms with passersby. In his memory the monastery shone with sunlit purity, free of civilization's clutter; he was like a sea creature, evolving from that sweet simplicity to complex life, shedding gills for lungs and choking in the clouded air. Louisa was his only constant, and he feared she was diminished from the woman he'd contrived. "Kiss me hello?"

"Oh, well, why not?" Confronting him at eye level, she placed her palms flat on his chest, as though prepared to push him off if he got too forceful. He kissed her gently, gambling that patience would bring her around quicker than ardor. When they parted, she looked miffed. "You were gone so long, I thought maybe you'd converted."

"Not the remotest chance." He sensed trouble in the look she flashed him.

"Well, I hoped. I even brought it up with Father Paul, but he didn't want to talk about it."

"Shouldn't wonder."

"It would have made a lovely bond between us, Howard."

"There are other ways to form a bond." Her blush roused memories of Brother Jarvis. Was it something peculiar to Catholics—the flux of red rising from neck to chin, flooding the cheeks and darkening the forehead to the hair roots? If Sadie had flushed that way she could have forgone her paints and powders and lured him back to bed. "Will you have dinner with me tonight?"

"Sorry, I can't."

"You can't? I was counting on it, Louisa."

"It's Saturday, and I've made plans."

"Change 'em."

"Certainly not."

"Why not?"

"You shouldn't have to ask."

"I'm asking so I'll know the reason."

"You should've called first. If you wanted to go out, you should've given me a few days' notice."

"You won't go because I asked you at the last minute?" He might have known she'd want old-fashioned protocols observed. He suppressed a flood of rage. He had come back from a spare, cold place where men sought God with absolute sincerity. He had looked death in the face; death lay coughing in the adjacent bed. He'd renounced a gentle angel and embraced the prospect of the body's pleasure as the only sane course left to him. Spurning faith, he'd sought Louisa's womanly solace. And she was being coy!

"I'm sorry, but I have made plans. What you men don't seem to understand is that we spinsters—"

"—have a life. I know. You've told me as much before."

"Then respect it."

"All right. Dinner tomorrow. No. Dinner's too long to wait. Sunday brunch in my apartment. I want you to see how I live. Show you I'm not a weirdo. Please. What do you say?"

"I can't, Howard. I go to mass at ten o'clock."

"After mass, then. I'll pick you up. I'll meet you at the church."

"Oh, I don't know. I don't know what to say."

"Say yes. Simple enough."

"You could come to mass with me."

"Don't even think of it."

"I did hope you'd convert. I even prayed for it."

"Louisa, you must accept me as I am. A man without belief."

"That's sad, Howard."

"There are compensations. Will you come to brunch?" Bagels, thought Frobisch. Cream cheese. Lox. He'd try to get some decent Danish. The clattering cowbell startled them. Louisa clutched her throat and found the ever-present golden chain. All right, he thought. That has to go. After the second cup of coffee, after I close the blinds, I oh-so-gently unclasp it and set it on the dresser, and when she looks away I knock it off and let it settle in the dust back of the furniture.

"Customer," Louisa said. "I've got to go."

"Will you come tomorrow?"

"I don't know. Call me later and I'll decide."

"Decide right now."

"I have to go." Louisa laughed. "Two in a morning. It's a rush."

"I'll meet you tomorrow at the church. A little after eleven." She would agree. He'd marked a quick flicker of interest when he said he was a man without belief. She sniffed a soul to save and was intrigued—the thought of a potential convert was sexier 'n hell, better than all the licks and tickles he might devise, all the proved erogenous techniques. He would hint at his failing spirit and have her on the ropes, and they would both be better off for it. No guilt; only good times, and no more family reminiscences on either side. If they were going to progress beyond verbal sparring, they must devise their own mythologies.

Sunday, as church bells peeled a welcome to the faithful, Frobisch cast a wary eye over a tray of lox—too dry, too startlingly red to suit his taste, not the moist pink of his recollection garnished with lemon or a sprig of parsley if the Pickle King were so inclined. Nothing in this deli (in a bank of posh shops near Chevy Chase Circle) struck him as authentic—not the spider fern, the jugs of wine, the tins of caviar and amaretti displayed like rare jewels on the shelves. Frobisch peered over a looming plant, swaddled with good-luck bows. "Your ad says kosher style. What does that mean?"

The boy behind the counter shocked him with the resemblance to himself, fifteen-year-old Howie Frobisch, sullen and pocked with zits and glassy-eyed after a night of wicked dreams. The boy shrugged and drummed on the countertop with dirty fingernails. "I'll need time to decide," said Frobisch. The clerk yawned and retreated to the back where Frobisch guessed he'd sit in Sunday somnolence over the *Post* and pick his nose.

He studied the displays, shaking his head. What was kosher about pasta salad? Broccoli with sesame seed? An abomination. He must be going soft. When he thought now of his father's store it was with something akin to longing for its cavelike dark, the tall barrels of brine, the gnarled green pickles bobbing in the salty deeps like submarines, the trays of purplish tongue and fat salami and corn beef and salads with the zest of onion or startling bits of radish buried in the creamy depths like coins. There was a crowd of lunchtime regulars who frequented his father's place—merchants from Avenue C all dressed alike in snap-brimmed hats and painted ties and braided belts notched loose around their paunchy middles—all with a furtive glamour. They sat at favorite booths and talked of deals. They chewed on toothpicks, scratched their thighs, scrawled figures on paper napkins and tore them up, built castles of sugar cubes and knocked them down, clumsy in the heat of argument. If they noticed him at all it was to tease. "Ya gettin' any, Howie?" "Yessir." He rolled his eyes. A Jewish Willie Best. A chubby Stepin Fetchit. He was willing to endure their gibes; better these than the ladies at the shul who pinched his cheeks and viewed him as a child. The men projected quiet power, a kind of weary potency just barely held in check by the weight of their responsibilities. He eavesdropped on their fervent whispers and vowed that he, too, would excel at business. That magic jiggling of numbers. That talk of mercantile intrigues, like the quiet chant of prayers.

The counter boy was back, scratching a mop of shoulder-length black hair. "Made up your mind?"

"The bagels fresh?"

"Baked on the premises," the boy answered promptly.

Knowing he lied, Frobisch ordered a half-dozen to go with lox, then changed his mind and opted to play it safe with Nova Scotia salmon. "How're your coffee cakes?"

"Okay."

"Only okay?"

"Look, mister, this ain't the Watergate."

"Gimme the poppyseed cake. And the cinnamon Danish." He must go easy with Louisa whose morning tastes doubtless ran to Twinkies. He was happy again, contemplating an irony. *He* would convert *her*, bombard her with delicious morsels till she succumbed, not to profound theology, but to the overwhelming testament of the taste buds. That was how Jews kept the faith. The tribal memory of food—overly salty, killingly sweet, piled in tantalizing heaps on party platters garnished with fat stuffed olives and frilly toothpicks. Too bad it didn't sit well; for if it had, no one would have tortured such inspired cooks. Flatulence caused the Inquisition, Frobisch thought, and realized by the boy's quick look that he had spoken aloud.

A fountain sparkled at the Circle. The oaks lining the green were red and gold. Church traffic was picking up. Frobisch headed over Western, then backtracked south on Reno Road, enjoying the solid houses—stucco fantasies with red-tiled roofs, and brown-shingled Victorians, and sprawling Georgian boxes with grand Palladian windows softening their facades. All the Sabbath calm of Cleveland Park was culture shock after his recollections of the Pickle King. Sundays in Bayonne his folks laid low, lest some overzealous cleric whip his congregation to a frenzy over Jewish crimes against the faith. Safe in the capital of liberty, Frobisch drove home with money in his pockets and fragrant cakes warming the seat.

The phone was ringing as he entered his apartment. He could tell it was bad news by the stridence of the bell. Don't let it be Louisa canceling, he prayed, struggling to balance his cake boxes, grasp his keys, and sidestep a wad of Sunday papers jammed against the door. When he got into the living room, the ringing stopped. "Good," murmured Frobisch, carrying his burdens to the kitchen where he fell to work. He hummed with happiness as he arranged the cakes. The phone interrupted his good mood. He grabbed the wall extension, thinking he ought to air the bedroom, change the sheets.

"Hello!" He was preparing a rebuttal if she'd decided not to come.

Sadie's outburst startled him. "You're finally home! I've been trying to get you for at least a week!"

"My office knew where to reach me." The memory of Van Zandt's camper looming in the drive kept his voice cold.

"Your office knew beans."

"How are you, Sadie?"

"Do you care?"

"Of course I care."

"If you want to know, I am beside myself. Sima's home."

"Sima!"

"She flew in last night. Dieter and I drove out to Dulles to meet her."

"Dieter and you!"

"The Dodge broke down. Dieter very kindly offered transportation."

"You could have asked me."

"I called and called. You're never home. No one seems to know what you're up to. They'd love to see you at the office. Freddy's going bonkers. Maybe you should drop in from time to time."

"That's my affair," said Frobisch.

"Believe me, Howie, your affairs are something I don't need to know about. Just don't heap me with recriminations when Sima comes home and you don't hear about it first thing. I have a certain sense of what's appropriate, even if you don't. I tried to call you as soon as I knew her plans."

"All right! Enough! She's home. That's wonderful," cried Frobisch.

"Is it?" sighed Sadie.

"What's wrong, Sadie? Is she sick?"

"Her physical health is good."

"What's that mean? Her mental health is not? Stop talking in riddles and tell me what you mean."

"I ant-cay alk-tay just now."

"When can you talk?"

"I think you should come out to the house."

"Of course I'll come. Later tonight. We can all go out for dinner together. How's that?"

"I think you should come now. Matter of fact, I insist that you come now. Chop-chop. Posthaste, if you get my drift."

"I get your drift all right. What's wrong?"

"I told you. I ant-cay—"

"Enough with the pig Latin! Can we postpone it a couple of hours? I've got a date."

"Good God!" Sadie spoke in mock despair. "Did I interrupt something?"

"Not what you think. A guest is coming for brunch. I'm just setting out the stuff."

"Postpone it, Howie."

"Sadie, what is so terrible with Sima that I have to be there in the next ten minutes? I'll do it—don't get your Irish up—but tell me what is wrong."

"I'll tell you when you get here. Just get here. Okay?"

"It'll take a half an hour. Maybe a little more. I have to reach my guest to cancel."

"One guest for brunch. How cozy," Sadie muttered and hung up.


Louisa sounded flustered. "You caught me going out the door. I was just leaving for church."

"Louisa, can you forgive me? I have to postpone brunch. There seems to be a family problem."

223

"Of course your family comes first, Howard." Her voice chilled him.

"If there was a way I could avoid it."

"Don't give it a moment's thought."

"You sound upset."

"I'm not upset a bit. It's just that I postponed having breakfast because I knew we'd probably have lots to eat at your place, and now I'm practically starving."

"Grab a quick bite, then."

"Oh, no. I'm already late for mass. I'll manage. Don't waste your precious time worrying about me."

"Of course I worry. I feel terrible. Please, Louisa. A cup of instant coffee. So you don't faint."

"Howard, I certainly won't faint. I've been spending Sundays alone for a lot of years, and I'll spend this one alone without passing out, I assure you."

"Just so you're all right."

"I'm fine. Only a little weak. My own fault."

"I'll call you later today. Okay?"

"Don't trouble yourself."

"It's no trouble. I want to. I care for you, Louisa."

The anguish in his voice caused her to soften. "Howard, I'm sorry if I'm sounding mean. It's just I had a little too much wine with dinner last night, and I woke up with this awful headache. I should've eaten something, I guess, but truth to tell, I overslept. I'm feeling awful."

"Take two aspirin. A piece of toast."

"And call you in the morning? All right." Louisa laughed.

"Oh, Louisa, you are a darling. I'll phone you later today. Is that all right?"

"If it pleases you, Howard."

"You please me, sweet Louisa."

"Howard, I think you are a flirt." She no longer seemed in a hurry to leave for mass. Frobisch glanced at his watch, feeling he was trapped in an endless dialogue with resentful women who nattered on in loopy circles but never reached a given point.

"Gotta dash now, dear," Frobisch said and gently placed the phone in its cradle before she could tell him not to dash on her account. He made a quick tour of the kitchen, stashing food, retying the boxes so the cakes wouldn't go stale. He was still in shock. Sima's here. That's the good news. The bad news is something Sadie can't say over the phone. Not with Sima in earshot. Her physical health is good. As for her emotions, Sadie isn't commenting. In the hall, he stood before the mirror studying his face. He hadn't shaved. He'd lost some weight. He looked gaunt, like the martyrs pictured in the monastery's infirmary. He touched his jaw where the skin was going loose and pouchy like an old man's jowls. Enough. He sighed. Sima, Louisa, Sadie—all of 'em will have to take me as I am. No collar ad like Father Paul.

He was locking the apartment when the phone began to ring again. Hell with it, thought Frobisch. He would not go back. Probably Louisa calling to tell him she was feeling faint and the aspirin wasn't helping. Morry was right. They existed only to know you wanted them, and then they tortured you in turn.

Sadie was wearing a hostess gown of bottle green. She had darkened her hair to brown, a shade Frobisch thought was aging. "What happened to the blonde?"

Sadie patted her head, frowning concern. The gesture was so familiar it made his head spin. "It's the newest color. More natural, don't you think?"

"Go back to the blonde." He was willing to placate no one.

"You think so? Really?" Sadie smoothed her hair.

"Listen, Sadie," counseled Frobisch, "natural is the way we all start out. Blonde is the frosting on the cake."

"I didn't know you felt that way."

"The girl I fell for was a blonde."

"And the woman you abandoned."

Frobisch sighed. "Where's Sima?"

"Locked in her room. We had a fight."

As if by second nature, they were walking toward the den. In the doorway, Frobisch balked. "Not here. Can we go somewhere else?"

"Sammy's everywhere," said Sadie. "Sometimes I wake up in the night, and I think I hear his little tags jingling the way they did. They way he'd sigh, sort of, in his sleep when he was having a bad dream. I still haven't forgiven you, Howie."

"Sadie, there's something I have to ask. How come I'm still the bad guy? Not Van Zandt? He had a pretty active hand in it, don't you think? I don't remember his trying very hard to talk me out of it."

"Dieter was just the instrument. It was you made up your mind. You were the intelligence. He simply acted on your wish. I can't hold anything against poor Dieter. It was his job, and he hates that part of it. Just hates it!" Sadie said with vehemence.

"I hated it!"

"Maybe you did." She had led him to the living room, straight to the stereo cabinet, as though she meant to dredge up every vestige of remembrance—Sima in her fuzzy slippers, Gregor in an ecstatic heap, panting at the rising chords of the Appassionata.

"He's here all right." Frobisch sank to the sofa and hid his face behind his palms. Sadie sat beside him. Remembering their last encounter, he was careful not to touch her.

"I told Sima when I saw your car turn into the drive. I don't know if she'll come downstairs or not."

Frobisch uncovered his face. "What exactly is the problem?"

"She's packing her winter stuff. She's planning to move away again."

"She just got here. Where's she going now?"

Sadie's tears were quiet. They streamed slowly like the last residue of a flood that had spilled for a long time. She dabbed her eyes gently, as though the merest touch caused pain. "She's going to live with someone."

"Live with someone! Who?"

"You won't like this, Howie. Try to keep calm. I tried the screaming bit, and it didn't work. She just shuts herself away upstairs, like she did when she was younger. You remember how she'd stay locked in her room and wouldn't come out for hours? You used to be the one she'd finally talk to. Maybe she'll see you now."

"Maybe she'll see me! Who is she, royalty? Of course she'll see me. I don't like this already, and I am not interested in keeping calm—no way! Who does she plan to live with?"

"You remember Randy?"

"Randy! De Filippo's Randy?"

"Yes." Sadie fumbled in her pocket for a Kleenex. When she couldn't find one, she raised the hem of her long robe and wiped her eyes. She was wearing a flowered nightgown he hadn't seen before.

"The bald kid with the knife!"

227

"His hair's grown back a little. It's not bad. Kind of a fuzz. Like the crew cuts they all wore in the war. He's not too bad-looking, though when he was little he was really gorgeous."

"Where?" stammered Frobisch. "How?"

Sadie held the green robe to her eyes. The gown she wore was sheerer than her usual numbers. Frobisch wondered bitterly if Van Zandt had stayed the night.

"They've been writing to each other all this time. While he was in jail. While he was in the drug program. He says he needs her to keep him straight, so she came home. She told me the State of Israel's doing fine, but Randy could use her help."

The bastard! The devious junkie fink, pretending he didn't know she was away! "Have they been . . . were they screwing . . . before she left?"

"Oh, Howie, I guess so. I don't know. I didn't think he was around so much."

"She was so withdrawn. So grouchy. I thought it was on account of us."

"I'm sure it was," wept Sadie.

How quickly catastrophes assumed their proper order. All the worries of the previous weeks were nothing. His grinning angel, Father Paul, Gregor Samsa breathing his last; even Louisa nursing her maiden headache on the path to church was nothing in the face of this last true calamity. "It's nothing," Frobisch breathed. "It's Romeo and Juliet. It will pass."

"I doubt it, Howie. She's packing. She seems convinced."

"Tell her to come down."

"You'll have to tell her. She won't talk to me."

"I'll tell her all right." He stood up, hobbled by the knee's dull aching. He limped a bit to ease the pain.

"What'd you do, fall out of bed?" asked Sadie.

"I resent that, Sadie."

"Sorry. I'm not myself."

"Who is these days?" asked Frobisch, lurching to the no-man's-land above the stairs.

He pounded on his daughter's door with doubled fists. The battering hurt, but the pain was a relief—a distraction from the ache that filled his heart and burned, intractable, in his bad knee. "Come out, Sima. I want to talk to you." There was no answer. Frobisch pounded harder. "Come out!" He knelt to peer through the keyhole. Clever Sima had hung something over the knob. He pressed his ear to the doorjamb, straining to hear some movement. Supposing she'd done something unthinkable, like slash her wrists? Right now the thought of Sima lying pale, a suicide, seemed less awful to bear than the prospect of her running off with Randy. "If you're in there, listen to this, Sima. I'm going to break down the door if you don't come out. Better yet, I'll simply unscrew the hinges. You know I have all the tools I need downstairs. So come out and save me the trouble."

Sima unlocked the door. She was wearing baby-doll pajamas, a thin smock over lacy bloomers. He could see the dark circles framing pert, raised nipples and the darker patch between her legs. "Go back into your room and cover yourself!"

Sima shrugged and disappeared into the bedroom. In a moment she returned, knotting a blue flannel robe around her waist. She'd had her hair cut closer to her head in a tight-curled golden frizz. Her face looked swollen, flushed, as though she had been crying. "Hello, Howard. I hear you murdered Gregor Samsa."

Without his willing it, his hand shot out. He felt the stinging in his palm and saw the mark on her face before he realized he had slapped her. "I'm sick of taking shit about the dog! He was old, sick, and in pain. I hope someone does as much for me when I get to be the same!"

Under a splotchy sunburn Sima had turned pale. "You hurt me!" The eyes, so clear and gray that had gazed at him with childish trust over so many tender meetings, now spilled with tears. She pressed a hand to her bruised cheek; the nails were bitten short. Frobisch fought the urge to fall on his knees and beg for mercy.

"You've hurt me worse, you little bitch! Now come downstairs!" He turned, pausing to balance himself against the stair rail. A wave of dizziness engulfed him. Stiff-legged, he hobbled down the stairs, hearing Sima's sobs behind him.

In the living room, Frobisch said, "Leave us, Sadie." She hurried out, sneaking a quick glance in the mirror over the mantel to reassure herself about her hair. It was as drab and brown and stiff as the wigs Orthodox women wore. With a pang he thought about Louisa— how that tumbled mop might be spread upon his pillow even now if Sadie hadn't called him. Oh, Lord, forgive him, he wanted that more than this operatic confrontation! He turned to Sima, "I understand you've made some plans."

"I am going away with Randy. Don't try to stop me, because my mind's made up."

"Where will you go?"

"Randy's father owns a building on Eighteenth Street. He's given Randy an apartment."

"Nice," said Frobisch. "An apartment already paid for. That sounds like a good deal. No rent to hassle you. No headaches finding a place. Randy's father knows you're going with him?"

"I don't think so. It wouldn't matter if he did or not."

"He's going to support you? Because I assure you, darling Sima, I am not."

"We don't want your money. Randy's going to find a job. So am I."

"He's going to find a job? That's admirable. Tell me, my darling girl, what will he do? Hire out as a professional penknife thrower? Are there any carnivals in town? Maybe you could assist him. You stand up against a wall, and he throws the knife at you, and hopefully he misses. You could play Capital Centre. You could vary the choice of knives—ordinary penknife, Swiss army knife. As you got more adept you could work your way up to butcher knives, French carving knives. Make it a high art. Get written up in *People*."

"Could you stop your awful jokes, Howard?"

"Oh, darling. I'm not joking. Believe me, I am not. I judge, then, since you're both hunting gainful employment, De Filippo's not kicking in anything but the apartment."

"That's right. I think so. Randy's promised he's going to get his act together."

"That's nice. That's laudable. It's an interesting phrase. Getting your act together. It implies a bit of theater, doesn't it? Pretense, or sleight of hand."

"You think Randy's lying about being straight?"

"You said that, Sima; I didn't. But since you mention

it, forgive me for asking, but I have a father's natural curiosity—your mother tells me he was in a drug program. I assume he's cured, since he's home now, happily throwing his penknife around the yard and letting his hair grow."

"Oh, I hate you when you act this way! Your pretended gravity! Your pompous voice! Your stupid jokes!"

"Hate me? I guess you do. I guess you hate your mother, too. I'm looking around this room—it's a pleasant room, isn't it, Sima?—and I'm thinking of all the comforts we provided as you were growing up. I'm thinking how you must hate us. For the big house in the suburbs. The pleasant yard. The private school. Even the little dog we bought for you, poor Gregor Samsa. I suppose you hated him, too, for licking your face out of blind devotion, and jumping up and down, those wild lunatic jumps of his, when the car pool brought you home from school. I suppose you hate us all for loving you so much."

"You leaned on me, Howard! You never gave me any room! When I was sick you slept beside my bed and begged for a report every time I turned over. When I had croup, you crept under the tent and tried to breathe for me. When I was failing something in school, you trotted in to make feeble excuses. You combed my hair; you picked my clothes; you planned my weekends down to the last tortured, structured minute of them."

"What tortured, structured minutes! The concerts for tiny tots? The Trolley Museum? The Sundays at the zoo? Picnics and outings and barge rides and theme parks till some days we forgot how to talk in adult company! That was torture? Thank you very much for enlightening me. I thought it was love."

"Too much love, Howard!"

"No!" Frobisch bellowed. "Now I have you, and I protest! It is not true—there is no such thing as too much love! Not enough love is a curse. But too much? Not ever! No!"

"Too much, Howard! Too much! I needed room to breathe; instead, you did it for me. You did! If you could've managed it, you would've chewed my food and pre-digested it, like some hovering father bird!"

"Oh, I hovered, Sima! I hovered only to protect you. To give you the benefit of an experienced point of view."

"I don't want your protection and least of all your point of view! That's why I went to Israel."

"That's why? I thought you were religious! While I'm about it, let me ask, what's happened to your much touted piety? When I talked with you in Rome, it was all you thought of. Tell me, Randy's going to convert? You'll keep kosher in this apartment on Eighteenth Street?"

"Of course he's not. And I'm not keeping kosher. I've given all that up."

"Given it up? Just like that? One minute a kibbutz-nik, the next, a free spirit? Forgive me, Sima, if I appear confused. I can't keep up with you. Why have you sud-denly given it up?"

"It's irrational. Too difficult. Too many rules."

"I suppose it's difficult. I suppose there are a lot of rules. I don't think being easy is the point. And as for being ra-tional, since when was feeling rational? How do you ra-tionalize an act of faith?"

"Wait a minute, Howard. Now I'm confused. Where's my father, the practical accountant? The man who has an encyclopedia explanation for everything—moon, stars, clouds, even love?"

"No, Sima, not the last. I don't know about love. I only know when it is there."

"Well, I love Randy."

233

"What love? That is a crock! You went to bed with him? You got a thrill? You love his prick! A tussle in the hay, a coupla minutes feeling good! You call that love? You dare to compare that with something people build together over time? Like your mother and me, together all those years?"

"Aha," crowed Sima. "*Now* I have *you*! Where are you now, with your so-called love? Sadie's screwing the veterinarian; and as for your adventures, I shudder to think!"

"Don't you dare—don't you ever in my presence talk about your mother in that way! Not ever! Do you hear? Because, much as I care for you, there's no telling what I will do!"

"I'm not frightened by your threats, Howard. They don't matter to me. I'm moving out!"

"Move, then," said Frobisch. "I wouldn't prevent it even if I could. Go form your own opinions. Give up keeping kosher. Get a job. Maybe it will slim you down."

"You bastard! What a bastardly thing to say!"

"Yes, it was," admitted Frobisch. "But you deserve it, Sima. Really, you do."

He found Sadie, still dressed in her green robe, shivering beside Gregor Samsa's grave. The earth under the weeping cherry looked moist and newly spaded. Frobisch said, "You planted bulbs."

Sadie nodded. "I don't know why. Dieter thinks I ought to sell this place. It's too big for me alone, and maybe even dangerous. There were some break-ins down the street. He thinks I ought to have the place wired with an alarm, or even keep a pistol." She cocked a thumb and forefinger, pointing an imaginary gun. "Whaddya think? Deadeye Sadie?"

Someone was burning leaves in De Filippo's yard. The air had filled with dark black cinders that dipped and swirled on gusts of wind like dancing insects. Frobisch brushed a few black flecks from Sadie's shoulders. "You got to get someone to clean out the gutters. This time of year the leaves pile up, and when it rains the water sits up there. It needs attending. The furnace, too. You better get someone to check it over."

"Thanks, Howie, for what you told her in there. About me."

Frobisch held out his arms, and Sadie fell against him, weeping. "It was what I felt." He stroked the stiff cap of her hair till it loosened a bit. Lord, he hated its dun brown color. That must be Van Zandt's influence. The stolid Dutch . . . all those murky paintings, the only light around the faces . . . Puritans amid the stiff-necked tulips.

"What are you thinking, Howie?"

"I don't know. Nothing much. What are you thinking?"

"How much I miss Sammy. How I wish we had him now. Listen, I'm not making another case. It's just the way he was. When things got bad, when Sima broke her arm, and our folks died—all four of 'em over the course of eighteen months—he could make us laugh. Those crazy jumps. Waddling pie-eyed when you played Beethoven. The pretend growls if you reprimanded him."

"Were they pretend growls? They were very real to me."

"Of course they were pretend. There was nothing vicious about Sammy. He was a clown. Good for comic relief."

"I don't think Gregor Samsa in a funny hat could make us laugh today."

"No, he couldn't." Sadie cried with tiny mewing sounds, as though grief had drained her bold soprano of its power. Where was his dauntless Sadie, the laughing girl who'd reeled, drunk on joy and fragrant poppies, in a gold meadow in France? Done in. Deflated by a silly stripling child and an old dead dog.

"Let's go in, Sadie, and have you put on something warmer. You'll catch your death."

"I feel like death."

"Ah, don't say that. There is a bright side."

"There is? Do tell."

"There is. It's not all bad. I noticed when she came out in her pajamas. She shaved her legs."

In the apartment Frobisch walked on tiptoe, as though too heavy a tread would jar his studied calm, send him toppling, drunk with sorrow, to the floor. The drunkenness of sorrow—no hot shower, no steaming coffee could efface. No Gregor, hopping his crazy jumps under the trees. The phone was ringing again—a shrill, persistent blast that blared ten times or so and then let off, only to start anew. Someone was damned anxious to talk to him. He let it ring. He had no heart to babble with Louisa. If there was trouble at the office, Freddy would cope. He settled on a stool in the dark kitchen. The cake boxes he'd piled up on the counter emitted fragrances of cinnamon and yeast, a homey smell that shocked him with the contrast to his mood. How high his hopes had been this morning! How happy he had felt! And now this brutal blow from the one he loved most. Oh, she was right. He had loved her too much, cut off her air, strangled all the natural sweetness, till what was left was snarling, bitchy Sima, fighting to breathe. But with Randy? That shambling, mooning junkie, tossing his knife amid the buzzing crickets and the nighttime frogs?

When he thought of it, there had been warnings—a spate of small misfortunes—as though the household gods were spurred to mischief by his and Sadie's marital disharmony. The dryer broke. The Volvo died and needed a new part for its resurrection. Gregor's tear ducts failed, and Sadie damped his eyes with sterile cotton and dispensed drops (the same stuff Sima used with contact lenses) every hour or so. Sima messed up her SATs. They were not to see her scores. When the envelope came from Princeton, they were to leave it in the mailbox, as though the contamination of their hands would cost her points. She vowed she had no interest in attending college. Frobisch insisted that they do the tour of schools near Boston. Sadie had intimated she'd stay home and tend to Gregor, but at the last minute she changed her mind. In the matter of deciding Sima's future, she wouldn't be shut out. They boarded Gregor at the kennel. The Volvo was in drydock awaiting the new part, and the Dodge was too old to be trusted. Frobisch rented a serviceable Ford, and they took off—with Sadie in the front seat concentrating on the Triptik, and Sima, glum and silent in the back. He could see her in the rearview mirror, twisting her hair or savaging her nails or gazing through the window like a hostage. He played the radio nonstop.

At night Sadie and Sima shared a room; and Frobisch, consigned to bachelor status in a lonely single, imagined that they savaged him, that they chronicled his sins—Sadie awash in righteous tears, and Sima, stifling yawns, offering dull grunts of assent. She had no interest in the schools they visited. She glided like a sleepwalker through a dream landscape of leafy campuses—some with buildings of mellow brick and curved white cupolas; some with Gothic spires that moved Frobisch to dream. He saw his darling in an orange pinney, a short plaid kilt. She raced across a field, and sun streamed through her hair. She kicked a soccer ball; she slammed a puck; she cast an arrow in a great soaring parabola and hit the mark. She sauntered zigzag paths bearing the earth's wisdom in a satchel pressed against her sweet child's breasts. She moved in clouds of Shetland wool and softest flannel; at dusk she sipped tea in a dress of garnet velvet with a collar of Belgian lace. She breathed the air of privilege, sanctity, and peace—courtesy of himself, loving provider, doting father—Frobisch—offering a world to her of autumn smoke and russet leaves.

She was impossible at interviews. His Sima who had parroted long poems under his tutelage, who had mastered Gray and Wordsworth ("The curfew tolls the knell of parting day"; "The world is too much with us, Late and soon") now spoke in monosyllables. Sentence fragments. What were her interests? Nothing much. Her favorite books? She didn't read. Her main ambition? She strained at this, suffered so much to seize a thought and shape it till she could serve up something palatable that once Frobisch (with an ear pressed to the smoked glass of an interviewer's cubicle) had wanted to break in, grab the conversational ball, and babble on with it: She has many great ambitions. Let me list them. Finally, she stammered she might want to work with kids, had thought of veterinary medicine (Oh, thank you, Gregor!), but gave it up as much too hard. (No! Nothing is too hard! It loses points!)

The admissions officers were kind. Frobisch considered taking each of them aside and offering explanations. When Sima was small, he'd trekked to teacher conferences with a set, long face—the messenger bearing bad news and a shopping list of excuses (tensions in the home, suspected allergies), real or contrived. In the college interviewers he faced tougher challenges—the men, punctilious with courtesy and yet remote; the women, buoyant types with piercing eyes and bounding energy who stood, ebullient Minotaurs, barring his darling from the treasures of the cave. How would they rate his alibis? Her mother and I sleep apart. We rarely speak. It's likely we'll be divorced, as soon as I . . . get the impetus. It's tense, you know, setting the stage before the final break. A sensitive child, she feels it. Her grades are good. She has abounding interests. Her grandparents have died. She feels their loss. Her dog, a pet of many years, is ailing. The family car is in the shop. Take her, begged Frobisch silently, and teach her to be happy.

In Boston he served up treats. Tea at the Copley Plaza, trips to Faneuil Hall, the Common, the Fogg Museum, and lobster dinner on the docks. Driving in Boston terrified him, but he persevered, charging the traffic circles, running lights with the same crazy abandon as the natives. At night he got lost heading for the harbor, and Sadie laughed although they weren't speaking, as though the whole thing was a major lark, and he felt the exhilaration pumping him up, coursing through the blood, as though there might still be hope for them.

At the Fogg Museum, before a collection of Persian paintings so explicitly erotic he paled to know Sima was studying them, Sadie motioned him aside. "It's all a waste, you know. This trip. The way she's acted, she won't get in. No one will accept her."

He protested. "Of course she will. She's smart. She's beautiful. She looks the part. She'd be an asset anywhere."

"No," said Sadie. "Not the way she is. The way things are now."

He knew exactly what she meant. Sima would be rejected, and the fault was his. His craziness had made them crazy. They were losers, through loss of him.

Going home, they had a flat tire on the Massachusetts Turnpike. He pulled off near a toll booth adorned with silhouettes of leprechauns and shamrocks. The traffic island held a concrete planter blooming with pink impatiens. He sent Sadie and Sima to a nearby Howard Johnson's to buy some sodas. He watched them limping along the highway, fanning themselves against the heat of an unseasonably warm autumn and leaning on each other for support. They looked like waifs, he thought. Like refugees.

The phone startled him from his thoughts. Goddamn it, let it ring! He considered that it could be Sadie announcing that Sima had had a change of heart. He dived for the receiver, and the ringing stopped. Shit! What shall I do? thought Frobisch. Shall I call her? Ask for news? Take a shower? Play a record? Pray? What is the antidote for sorrow?

And again the ringing. This time he grabbed the phone. "Yes!"

"Mr. Frobisch? I'm glad you're home." The prim voice of a stranger. A junk call, worse than junk mail. They nabbed him all the time, the hucksters hawking light bulbs, storm doors, lawn care, mountain lots out in the boonies.

"Whatever you are selling," Frobisch said, "I'm not interested."

"I'm not a salesman, Mr. Frobisch. My name is Mildred Hersh." The inflection was north Jersey. There was no mistaking the nasal accent, the muffling of the *r* in Hersh.

"Should I know you, Miss Hersh?"

"It's Dr. Hersh, but that's all right. Please call me Mildred. My father was Morris Gershowitz."

"Was?"

"He died yesterday. At the monastery of Saint Pachomius. I called early this morning to let you know, but you weren't home. I've been trying on and off all day."

"Ah, no," said Frobisch.

"It wasn't unexpected. Still, I'm sorry to have to tell you. He left a letter for the abbot asking that you get word if something happened. I guess he had a kind of hunch."

"Morry? Ah, no."

"He asked that you be told and that you say a few words at the services. He said you had an *in* with certain parties. I don't know what that means."

"Paw-ties," she said, sounding like Hudson County. A shrewd New Jersey girl. Clever and tough. Frobisch blinked away a rush of teary-eyed nostalgia. "Crazy. The whole thing's crazy."

"Mr. Frobisch, this is a pushy thing to ask, but I don't know anyone in Maryland or Washington. Would you be willing to help with the arrangements?"

"You say Morry died? Yesterday?"

"Some time during the morning. Someone looked in on him. He seemed to be asleep."

The woman's composure chilled him—no tremolo of grief, no sob of filial remorse. She might have been commenting on the weather.

Why? Frobisch thought. Why didn't I know? I'm tooting around the bookstore trying to make some time and Morry dies! Every stranger on his last legs I get the scoop. That priest who likes fast food? He's going to have some trouble. The stewardess on the plane has a boyfriend in Miami who is cheating. All the sorry stories come to me. So why didn't I know? "Listen, Miss Hersh," Frobisch said fiercely. "The monks are right. There is no angel. There is no messenger of God tapping the chosen. It's craziness!"

"I'm so sorry if I've shocked you. I've expected it of course. I see it as something of a blessing."

"What blessing? One minute he's alive and raising hell. Then he is dead."

"He's not in pain. That is a blessing, Mr. Frobisch."

"Neither is Gregor Samsa! He's not in pain. I don't know, was I wrong about that, too?"

"I see that you're upset. I didn't mean to be so blunt. He was thinking of you at the end, so I should've guessed you were good friends; but he was such a strange, private man, I didn't know the two of you were close."

"I didn't either," answered Frobisch. "I didn't know."

# · CHAPTER ·
# 11

Peculiar light after a storm. Puddles of water on the paths. The grass shimmers like sea foam. A tree stands bludgeoned, bare of leaves, save for a few the wind has plastered to its blistered bark, yellow patches like incongruous blossoms against the dead brown wood. The sky is streaked—gray with wispy cloud striations, a hint of color on the horizon. Like an unsettled ocean, the blue brightens or dulls at the whim of a capricious sun. The air is raw, the last mellowness of summer wiped off with the rain.

On a rise above the grave the diggers wait—four black men leaning on their shovels, grouped like figures in a painting. The raw earth of the site has been covered with a bright green groundcloth. Here Frobisch stands with Mildred, who is shivering in a belted raincoat. When their shoulders touch, she moves away—then leans to him as if for comfort. She wears her gray hair in a single braid, a loony academic style implying middle age wedded to eternal girlhood. Morry called her a bitch queen. Frobisch pegs her as bossy, a type he'd known in high school (intelligent and obdurately plain) who dishes orders with a sergeant's vigor and assumes she will be disobeyed. Mildred tosses her braid like a nervous filly when she sees the coffin bearing her father. In the sun the varnished wood looks cheap. A carved intaglio Star of David on the lid is a garish adornment. For eight-fifty, they have been taken, Frobisch thinks.

"I could say the Twenty-third Psalm," Mildred offers.

"That would be nice."

She begins: "The Lord is my Shepherd . . ."

He remembers Arlene ushering them into the plastic-draped apartment. If he'd known her last name he'd have called, though it's possible it doesn't matter. He suspects she's someone Morry picked up; and the dinner in Little Italy, all that business afterward were services bought and paid for, nothing more. There was no tenderness between them; the projected domestic harmony was a fiction Morry devised. He hates himself for thinking this, wants to imagine Arlene is home now, wondering why Morry hasn't called. The funeral director, whose name is Curran, has said there'll be a notice in the paper. It's possible Arlene will see it. Do hookers scan the obits to find which of their johns has died? The cynicism shames him. He wonders, what have the monks done with the pumpkin he carved for Morry? The night they drove back to Saint Pachomius Frobisch stopped short on the dirt road leading to the Little Cloister and said he'd go no farther. Morry clambered from the car, hunched and gaunt, like the figure of the Headless Horseman, cradling the pumpkin in his arms. He'd shuffled a ways along the path and stopped where tall pines towered black against the stars. Frobisch had rolled the window down to yell, "So long." The air had smelled of resin. The earth gleamed white pinpoints of frost. Morry had flashed a V sign—courage and absolution in the gesture, a certain laying on of guilt. Does one friend abandon another in distress? Frobisch dumped

Morry on the path—celestial fires brightening the heavens and frost peppering the ground, so there was no clear demarcation between earth and sky. Now Morry is dead. Frobisch tests the thought out, mouths it, rolls it on his tongue, like savoring wine. A bitter wine, but not exactly vinegar. A blessing, Mildred has said.

She nudges him. "Will you say something, Howard, please?"

He has nothing prepared. Yesterday they sat together in the undertaker's study, a dim room cluttered with murky portraits and statues of stalking leopards, stiff-winged birds—travesty of a pharaoh's tomb. Rain pelted the curtained windows; wind keened through creaking branches on the outside lawn. On the undertaker's desk the six lights on a phone console flickered on and off. Workmen were drying out the flooded cables in the cellar with portable hair dryers. The sound drifted to the study, a buzz like captive bees. The lights went out. Curran lit fat memorial candles that sputtered yellow smoke. He led them through a check list—burial costs, decision as to embalming, purchase of plot, remuneration for the driver of the hearse, the grave diggers. Did they want a limo? A canopy or chairs? Frobisch and Mildred are bound forever by those awful choices, locked in dreadful intimacy as in some grim forced marriage. It is enough. He shouldn't have to speak. "I don't know what to say."

"Please, Howard. We have to show that someone cares for him."

I cared for him in the monastery. Doesn't that count? I had to choose the coffin, wandering through darkness in that nightmare room, an amphitheater of garish boxes—some satin-lined, some puckered with plush velvet. Boats of dark mahogany and capsules of space-age metal.

I signaled thumbs up or thumbs down to Curran, arguing craftsmanship and cost, while you invented a migraine
and had to run off to the little girls' room. Frobisch says,
"I'll try," and clasps his hands.

"Oh Lord." His voice squeaks, like a nervous adolescent's launching bar mitzvah greetings. His cousin Jerry
in Bayonne had once prepared a standard talk: "Oh Lord,
please get me through this so I can take my U.S. Savings
Bonds and get something to eat." He tries again. "Oh Lord,
we deliver unto You Your servant, Morris Gershowitz,
who was a faithful husband and a loving father and a good
and cheerful friend. He was a sweet man who faced a cruel
illness with great courage." Frobisch remembers something important. "It happens that I owe him one hundred
forty-seven dollars, which I will donate in his name to the
Brothers of Saint Pachomius. . . ." He breaks off, wondering if that will offend a Jewish God. Mildred looks perplexed. Frobisch shrugs. "I'm sorry. That's all I can say."

Mildred says, "That's fine. That's perfectly all right,
Howard." Stiffly, like a teacher salvaging the ego of a student whose recitation has missed the mark.

"I could've told you, I'm not so good at this."

"No, it's perfectly okay. I don't know about the 'faithful
husband.' The rest was fine." Suddenly she looks exhausted, as though she might pass out. Unabashedly, she
leans against him. "Do you think we can go now? I believe
we've done all for him that we can do."

He takes her arm and leads her on a cautious zigzag
around muddy puddles. The air shimmers aqueous light.
A leaf totters in watery sunshine and flutters to their feet.
Distractedly, he picks it up and hands it to her, as though
it were a souvenir that she will cherish. "I don't know
Baltimore too well, but I can find someplace for lunch."

She holds the leaf as though it were a fragment of an ancient culture. "I'm heading straight into D.C. I'm going to have a whole day of research at the Library of Congress. It's an unexpected opportunity for me. A feast."

"Every cloud has a silver lining." They are both stunned at his tactlessness. He endeavors to recover. "I'll bet you're a good teacher, Mildred."

She shakes her head. "No, I'm not. I think I'm probably very boring. I don't know why. Because the subject fascinates me, the whole sweep of the Middle Ages; the mounting energy; the drive. My students don't see the point. They're just not interested. Well, you know what interests them at that age."

They have reached their cars. Mildred drives a vintage blue Impala with cream and brown New Jersey plates and a bumper sticker that displays a peace sign and the slogan, I Am a Relic of the 60s. If only she were prettier, softer, the least bit flirty. Frobisch asks, "You'll keep in touch?"

She looks surprised. "I don't know. Is there any reason to?"

Frobisch says, "I guess not."

She holds out her hand. "Thank you for all your help."

Ruefully, he shakes it. "You're welcome."

"Well, *ciao*," says Mildred.

"*Ciao*," says Frobisch, feeling cheated. He had expected her to kiss his cheek. He wonders if she is punishing him for the lameness of his graveside eulogy.

Curran had given him a single memorial candle and a box of engraved stationery printed to say, "The family of _____ thanks you for your kind expression of sympathy." He'd thrown the note cards in the trash, but had left the candle on a table in the little entrance hall of his apartment. Next to the table he'd placed a pail of water and a sheaf of paper towels. When he returned home from the funeral he kicked off his shoes. He washed his hands and dried them on the paper, washing away the dark aura of death. He crumpled the paper towels and threw them in the pail. He removed his suit coat and hung it in the closet. He unknotted his tie. He was wearing an old oxford-cloth blue shirt that had been ruined by too many launderings. He pulled on the fabric of the pocket until it tore. He carried the candle to the kitchen where he rummaged to find a saucer and a book of matches. When he had lit the candle, he let the hot wax drip into the saucer; then he set the candle firm inside this waxy base until he was satisfied it wouldn't topple. He found a folding ladder in the pantry that he decided would serve him as a stool. He carried the ladder to the living room and set it down next to the coffee table. He sat on his makeshift stool and closed his eyes, relying on memory and his banished angel to help him with the ancient prayers.

"What you're doing is crazy. Shutting yourself off. Distancing people. It's selfish is what it is. And going nutso won't bring Sima to her senses, so why don't you knock it off?" Sadie circled the living room, letting in light. Ladders of sun streamed to the carpet as she tugged open the blinds. Dust rose from the windowsills in golden furbelows.

Frobisch looked up from the TV. He liked to turn the volume off during the soaps and guess the twists and turns of plot from the actors' gestures. When the commercials flashed, he flipped the sound back on and listened with rapt attention, comfortable with tangibles, the world of commerce he understood. After five days of steady watching, he knew the sales pitches by heart. "Who let you in, Sadie?"

"The super. I told him you might be sick. Was I lying?"

"I'm not sick. I'm in mourning. I believe the customary time for sitting shiva is seven days."

"Who died?"

"No one you know."

"You're sitting shiva all alone? Watching the soaps?"

"The man's family is scattered. I'm doing what I can." He gestured to the set where the actors moved like shadow puppets dancing to desired consummations. "Mostly I pray. When I get tired, I watch TV."

"God forbid you should get tired. Doesn't your lady friend stop by to keep you company?"

Frobisch turned back to the screen. She was digging again for news of his presumed affair. The truth would disappoint her. He had called Louisa once to tell her he was in mourning; and she, dear soul, had segued from a flippant greeting to instant sweet solemnity. (He'd pictured her making a swift sign of the cross over her breast.) "Come to me when you're ready, Howard." Her tenderness inflamed him. Come to me! Passion to match his own, as long as they stayed separate. Love blazed while they were parted. They were like two moony teenagers, relying on promises and whispered words over the phone to fan the flame.

"I'm worried about you." Sadie swayed above him in her Carmen pose, hands firm on her hips. He felt the usual irrational fear that she would launch into an aria. "Freddy Gottlieb says he's called a half a dozen times, and no one answers. He wants you to know that your desk is chaos. Clients are trying to get in touch with you. Your secretary's getting weepy."

249

"Tell Estelle to keep her powder dry." His secretary would take his absence from the office as a personal affront. She would barricade herself inside the ladies' room and blow into her palm to test the sweetness of her breath. She would sniff her underarms discreetly to see if she was offending. "I'll talk to her. And I'll call Freddy. But I have to mourn a full seven days. That much I know."

"You're gonna sit here in the dark with the blinds down and the dust collecting everywhere?" She ran a finger over an end table to prove her point. "Look at that. Should I send Mrs. Garcia to straighten up?"

"Don't send Mrs. Garcia. Everything's fine."

"Pardon me, Howie. I doubt that. You don't answer the phone. You don't go out. What do you have to eat?"

"I got plenty of food here. I was just going to boil myself an egg. Maybe you'd like to join me."

"No, thanks." Sadie inhaled. "Something smells spoiled."

"It does? Maybe the milk went sour. Yesterday I had to throw away a whole container of cottage cheese. You know, that must be it; it's stinking up the garbage. You could do me a big favor on your way out, Sadie. Would you take a bag of garbage to the incinerator?"

"Ask your lady friend to do it when she comes over." She fingered the fabric of the couch, then moved to touch the velvet chairs. "You got a remote control TV. You got a *white* sofa. It's a *Playboy* pad."

"The pantry's nice. You'll cream when you see the pantry."

Sadie pulled off her velvet blazer. "I'm going to heat some soup. You look like a fugitive from Auschwitz. How long is it since you ate?"

"I'm eating. Stop treating me like I was some kind of case."

"I think you're mental, Howie. Freddy told me you were acting strange. I should've listened."

"Freddy's a fool. I'm not acting strange. I'm mourning."

"Who are you mourning, Howie?"

Frobisch considered this a full minute before answering. "A friend named Morris Gershowitz. The terrier, Gregor Samsa. My parents and yours. Sima, who's as good as dead to me. Pope John Paul the First. Thank God the new fellow they chose seems hale and hearty."

"Oh, God, you are mental!"

"Easy to knock what you don't know."

"Then tell me, Howie." She was kneeling beside his step-stool. She had let her hand rest lightly on his knee.

How to explain? Within the framework of his personal epistemology, his acts made sense, though Sadie would see them as the refuge of a madman. "I can't let Morry's passing go unnoticed. His daughter is somewhere reading up on the Crusades. Neither of his ex-wives bothered to make an appearance. It's up to me." There was a more self-serving motive he couldn't say aloud. Death terrified him; solitude was worse. If he spent these days in prayer and loving contemplation, God might choose to reinvest him with His grace. If his angel returned, Frobisch would welcome him and not beg for explanations beyond the knowledge he was blessed. Since his outburst in Brother Olivier's kitchen, he had seen no blaze of light, heard no garbled messages. The dark bruise on his knee had faded. He was restored to health, to the mundane; and he would give anything to have it otherwise.

Sadie's hand dangling near his in-seam spelled temptation. He brushed it away to play it safe. She cast him a look of bleak reproach. "You got any Campbell's tomato?" She struggled to her feet. "You used to like it with a dollop of sour cream. Just the way the President ate it."

"I thought he went for southern food."

"Kennedy. He's the only President I mean."

"I could say a prayer for him."

"Oh, stop it, Howie! I think you're bluffing. It's just another of your crazy stunts, suddenly acting pious. Something to get attention."

"Sadie, I want to tell you everything that's happened to me."

"After I heat the soup."

The little gymnast on the balance beam was selling Maxi pads. Frobisch admired her moves. He considered calling Freddy and telling him they should invest in personal products. All this neurosis about hygiene. Caffeine anxiety, too. Obsession over cats and what to feed 'em. Concern for smelling good and shiny teeth. Guys doing a striptease. Women hefting barbells. The country was on the skids. The world was going down the tubes with terminal silliness, and Sadie said that he was mental! He could hear her in the kitchen, banging cupboard doors, murmuring, "Oh my, oh my," when she came upon the pantry. She was moving things on the shelves. He shifted position on the stool. All the sitting hurt his butt. Inspired by the gymnast, he stood up, stretched, bent over to touch his toes. His arms dangled to his calves. He dropped to the floor and tried a push-up, rested a bit, and tried again, keeping his back stiff and his legs taut. He collapsed onto his stomach and let his head rest on his arm.

Sadie cried, "My God, what happened?"

Hell with it, he thought. He rolled onto his side and held an arm out to her. "I'm exercising. Help me up, will you?"

She took his hand. She was wearing a frilly blouse and a paisley skirt he hadn't seen before. She'd had her hair lightened again, as he had asked. Frobisch climbed to his feet and tucked a loose shirttail into his pants, taking pleasure in the slackness of the waistline. "All of a sudden, I'm starving."

"I'll pour the soup."

He watched her as she retreated to the kitchen—the familiar undulating walk, the sensuous movement of the hips. In the years they were together, he'd never known if the gyrations she performed were conscious. He knew when she was coming on—playing it sexy when she sang, imitating Garland. She always missed the poignance. Garland was a waif, a wet puppy sometimes; and Sadie was Wonder Woman. The only time she ever showed uncertainty was when she was picking a color for her hair.

Sadie came back with a bowl of soup and a plate of saltine crackers. "That paper in the kitchen has to go. For what you pay here, and I'm assuming it's a bundle, you can do better than man-eating flowers." She set the food on the glass-topped table. "I couldn't find any napkins."

"You don't need to serve me, Sadie."

"I put your spice jars in alphabetic order. That way you'll find them faster."

"I found them okay before."

She pointed to the table. "Eat."

"You'll have some, too?" The soup smelled good. Really, he was famished. He wanted to seize the bowl and drink from it without waiting for the soup to cool.

253

"I'll just watch, thank you." Sadie eased off her shoes and settled on the sofa. She tucked her legs beneath her and smiled at him, a too-bright grin, as though she were posing for her picture. Frobisch settled beside her and stared into the soup. He felt self-conscious about eating with Sadie watching him like that. He asked, "You heard from Sima?"

Sadie toyed with the lace frill at her neck. She must have just had a fresh manicure. Her nails were painted the color of raspberries. He thought of popping her fingers in his mouth and savoring the taste.

"Sima got a job. She's a greeter at T. H. Mandy."

Frobisch crumbled a saltine in his soup, taking care not to strew crumbs on the sofa. "What the hell is that?"

"The discount store, you know? There's one over on Nineteenth Street. She stands in the door and she says, 'Welcome to T. H. Mandy.' Then she tells people what's on sale. She holds up the special outfit of the day for them to see. She's like a living mannequin, only she doesn't model dresses. She just displays them on the hanger."

"I should think not."

"Ah, don't be mean. She's dieting."

The soup was good. Frobisch spooned some up and swallowed so fast the liquid burned his throat. He blew on the second spoonful until it cooled. "And the knife-thrower? What's he doing? Perfecting his act?"

"I don't ask."

"You don't ask? Maybe you should ask. Do you stop to think about the consequences of her living with him? She could get pregnant."

"No, Howie. She's on the pill."

"You know that for a fact?"

"Of course I know it. I took her to my gynecologist when she was sixteen."

254

"You took her! You sanctioned it! What is this, Sadie, are you crazy? You took a child of sixteen and as much as told her it's okay to screw around?"

"I did not tell her that. I told her, if you're going to do it, be protected. It was more than anyone told me at that age."

"You didn't do it at that age."

"Well, maybe I would've if the opportunity arose. How do I know?" Sadie winked. "I hadn't met you yet."

"Was I that attractive?"

"I don't remember." Sadie pointed. "Eat."

"Maybe I should try to talk to her again. What do you think?"

"You could try. It won't do any good. She says we stifle her. When she's with us, she can't breathe freely. She can't be herself."

"She's herself with that junkie?" His appetite was gone. He set his spoon down in the bowl and wiped his mouth with his shirtsleeve. "The bald knife-thrower is what she wants? She's going to spend her life living in some slum, supporting him by being a greeter at T. H. Mandy. That's the real Sima? Wow. You could've fooled me all those years."

"It's not a slum. It's a nice apartment. Of course, they don't keep it too clean."

"You've been there?"

"Yes, I have. I brought them bread and salt. For good luck, moving in. Oh, stop it! She's my only daughter. What am I supposed to do? Go into mourning like you did? Pretend she's dead?"

"I am mourning for Sima as much as for Morry. I sit here and remember all the times when she was small. How sweet she was. The fun we had together. Why did that have to change, Sadie? Why can't love last forever?"

"Imagine *you* asking me that!"

"I love you, Sadie. I always have. I just can't be married to you anymore is all."

"Thanks. I got the message a while ago." She was rummaging the sofa cushions, looking for her purse. When she found it, she pulled it open with a decisive snap. She fumbled through the loose cosmetics until she found a scrap of paper scrawled with red magic marker. She handed this to Frobisch. "That's her address. Go see her if you want."

Frobisch held the paper gingerly as though it were wired to explode. "Thanks. Maybe I will."

Sadie stood up and smoothed her skirt as though she loved the silky feel of it. "If you've finished, I'm going to tuck you into bed. I want you to promise me you'll take a nice long nap; then maybe a shower. After that, call Sima. But first you need to sleep. You look like death."

"You don't need to nurse me, Sadie."

"Sure I do. I don't have Sammy to nurse anymore. I might as well nurse you."

His bedroom was non-neutral ground—too many sparks of memory charging the air. The bed loomed like new-risen Atlantis. Sadie darted around it, smoothing and straightening up, playing the nervous hostess setting the place to rights. She fiddled with his brushes, peeked into his closet to check the order of his clothes, felt the tweed of a new jacket and deemed it "nice." She spied an errant sock and placed it on the dresser. "You'll be wanting the mate to that. Shall I hunt for it?"

"Don't bother."

She turned the bedspread down, folded back the blanket, cast an expert eye over the sheets. Frobisch felt smug about the sanctity of his bed. Sadie asked, "Will you want to change into pajamas?"

"I'll stretch out as is, if it's all the same to you."

"Suit yourself."

He kicked off his slippers and lay down stiffly, already regretting the try at push-ups. Sadie looked prim and girlish standing by the bed in stocking feet. He lay with his arms crossed on his chest, staring up at her, as though he were the corpse and she, the silent mourner. She pulled the top sheet to his chin.

"Anything else I can do for you before I leave?"

Frobisch shook his head.

"It breaks my heart to see you this way, Howie. I'd stay if I thought it would help." She bent to smooth his pillow as though she were staking out a territory.

Frobisch considered the implications of this last remark. "Not necessary, Sadie." He closed his eyes.

"There is someone in your life now. I'm right about that, aren't I?"

"A friend. A woman, alone and vulnerable."

"A woman alone and vulnerable? How sweet. Is she an orphan?"

"Don't start, Sadie. I beg you."

"Maybe you think I'm not?"

"Not what?" He wished that she would go. She had already made dangerous inroads on his sovereignty.

"Please look at me when I talk to you. You can afford me that minor courtesy!"

Frobisch opened his eyes. Her cheeks were flushed, her hands back on her hips. Carmen prepared to lure Don José to the smugglers' den. "Not what, Sadie?"

"Alone and vulnerable since you walked out."

"I never think of you like that. I think of you as— indomitable."

"Sure you do, because it suits your purposes. You can walk out on a whim, do anything that strikes your fancy, and not have to give a thought to good ole Sadie. Sadie can cope."

"Don't get mad. I thought I was complimenting you." She was wearing a new perfume, something heavy, musky, doubtless chosen to entice Van Zandt. A waste. That jerk would get turned on by flea soap. The idea tickled him. He almost grinned.

"You won't be so complimentary when you hear this. I tell people you died. When I meet strangers, and they want to know was I widowed or divorced, I tell them I was widowed. That you were a heart case."

Frobisch smiled wanly. "Did I suffer?"

"No." She snapped her fingers. "You went like that." She looked stricken as she said it, as though his death were in the offing and her words were doleful prophecy. Already she seemed contrite. All he need do was show some sign of life and she would be all over him with thankful kisses. He weighed the tantalizing possibilities. Louisa had murmured, "Come to me," and the words rang with innocence and mystery. He winked at Sadie. "Next time try CPR."

"Bastard," Sadie breathed.

Frobisch closed his eyes. He heard her skirt rustling as she left, the quick tread of her footsteps on the rug. In the living room she clicked off the TV. Now she was gathering up the dishes. She might be furious at him, but she would neaten up the place, puff up the sofa pillows, brush off crumbs before she left. She carried his dishes to the kitchen, ran water into the bowl. He heard her sighing as she gathered up her purse and shoes. The outside door opened and shut. She had the grace to close it gently. He resented her forbearance. She was behaving as though he were, indeed, a case—someone to walk around on tiptoes.

He opened his eyes, blinking at the play of sunbeams on the wall. The room was stuffy, heavy with the fragrance of perfume. Steam whistled in the pipes. Sadie had left the water running in the sink. That could be bitchiness; she knew he couldn't endure a dripping faucet. He flung aside the sheet and padded out of the bedroom to shut it off, cursing her lack of subtlety, his own muddled intransigence.

Sima had printed Frobisch–De Filippo on a card and tacked it to her apartment door. Frobisch admired the neatness of the lettering. There might be something ambiguous about the status of a Frobisch–De Filippo, but there was no confusion about the writing of their names. He thought if Sima ever tired of being a greeter at T. H. Mandy, she could always get a job doing calligraphy.

He pushed the bell. Before the buzzing sound had faded, Sima opened the door. She was wearing faded jeans and a man's blue work shirt with sleeves rolled to the elbows. The resemblance to a younger Sadie startled him. "You should ask who it is before you open the door up to a perfect stranger."

"You phoned to say you wanted to come over. Who else could it be?"

"It could be anyone. A rapist. A thief."

"Are you coming in or not?"

"Yes, I am." She had said she had the morning free. Grateful she hadn't slammed the phone on him ("A quick moment of talk with you, and no coffee, no breakfast; don't put yourself out!"), he'd vowed he wouldn't criticize, however bad it was. There wasn't much for him to pick on: two backpacks tossed into a corner, a scruffy-looking chair, a sofa resurrected from the De Filippo playroom.

A folding table bore the remnants of doughnuts and coffee. The walls were bare, off-white, with the shadow of an earlier, darker color under the streaky paint. Frobisch inhaled, sniffing for drugs or incense. "Not bad. Is this all of it?"

She gestured toward a hallway. "There's a bedroom. A tiny kitchen."

"Nice. Very nice." He rocked up and down on the balls of his feet. "Nice floors."

"Parquet," said Sima.

"Not butter?" Frobisch joked.

"Why'd you come over, Howard? To let me hear your latest pun?"

"I told you, I need to talk to you. Randy around?"

"He's out." Sima folded both arms across her breast and waited. She looked sullen and mean. Over the past two weeks he'd seen her twice without her knowing it. The first time, she was sitting in the window of a Chinese restaurant near Mandy's, chatting with two women he assumed were fellow greeters. She'd seemed absorbed and not unhappy, drowsy the way one got in all that noisy warmth, dreamy-eyed and nodding over steamy soup and tea. Twice, he'd walked past the window, expecting her to see him, to whisper to her friends, "That is my father." He'd watched as she poured tea and passed round platters; and it was all he could do to keep from banging on the glass and howling out his loneliness and loss. She had no right to sit there in the shadow of a scarlet dragon, sharing food and gossip, giggling as she fussed with chopsticks, while he shivered in the dusk of chilly autumn, keeping watch lest she get sick from tainted pork.

The second time, he was heading for his office, crossing Dupont Circle in the middle of the lunchtime crush.

A group of jazz musicians were jamming near the fountain. A trio of pretty girls in French berets were offering free croissants to passersby. The lunatic of the Circle, a black man dressed in khaki, was marching double-time across the grass, barking military commands. The man saluted, and Frobisch answered with a lazy wave. "Smarten up, man!" cried the lunatic, and Frobisch said, "I will." He spotted Sima sitting near the fountain, oblivious to the crowds, her gaze fixed on a point beyond the Circle traffic. She was bundled in a shapeless jacket, hunched like someone beaten down by sorrow. Someone else's daughter, was what he'd thought. Heart thumping, he planned to rush to her and say, "Cut out this crap. You're coming home with me." Before he could get close, he sighted Randy, still wearing the black wool watch cap, shuffling across the path carrying a string bag of apples and a French bread. That flagrant domesticity alarmed Frobisch as much as if he'd stumbled on the couple's unmade bed. He'd turned and fled before they saw him.

"I can offer you some Perrier," said Sima. She was affecting her British accent.

Frobisch shook his head. "May I sit down?"

"Only if you promise in advance you're not going to lecture me."

"Scout's honor." He headed for the shabby sofa as though treading on nails. As he sat down, he detected the rustle of scurrying insects. "You got roaches!" Frobisch cried in disgust.

Sima shrugged. "They're all over these old buildings. The renovating brings them out."

"You gotta get something. Paint the baseboards. I could stop off at Hechinger's and buy you some No-Roach."

"No, thanks. After a while you get used to them."

"Sima! They spread disease!"

"You promised me, Howard."

"At least try a little Borax," Frobisch pleaded. "They don't like Borax."

"Are you finished with the household hints?" Sima had settled cross-legged on the floor. She was gnawing on one nail as though the key to her survival lay in one chewed finger.

Frobisch tried to placate her. "You lost some weight."

"Trust you to notice that."

"It's becoming. But you don't want to take it off too fast. Are you getting enough to eat?"

"I'm fine."

"I heard you were working. You like your job?"

Sima shrugged. "It's okay."

"Randy is working, too?"

"He's looking, Howard, okay? It's not easy finding a job when you're an ex-junkie. He helped out for a while on one of his father's construction sites; that didn't pan out, so he's looking for something else."

"Admirable that he's looking. That doesn't leave him a lot of extra time, I guess, to practice his knife throwing. Okay, okay, don't glare at me like that. I'm sorry. I didn't come here to start up again about the knife. You gotta admit, it's something of a strange habit. Aberrant behavior, would you say? Maybe a throwback to the time we were all hunters? Lived in the cave?"

When she was furious, the resemblance to Sadie was amazing—the flashing eyes, the full lips trembling. "You are so awful! You never change. Clever and sly. Insidious. Sarcastic. Anything for a joke and never mind whose feelings you hurt!"

Frobisch leaned forward, unhappily aware that he was upsetting colonies of insect life as he jostled the sofa pillows. "Sima, darling, I didn't come to criticize you or insult you. If anything, I came to beg your pardon, to make a penance, as it were. I have some things I want to tell you. After I do, I'll go away and leave you to your life with Randy. If it's what you want, if it makes you happy, I wish you luck. I won't interfere. I can't help the way I talk. It's me. I've always been that way. I don't say these things to hurt you—only to explain them to myself." He had talked himself into a scratchy throat. He coughed, trying to clear the passage, fearing he'd end in tears. "Could I trouble you for a glass of water?"

She cast him a long, resentful look as she got up, the old look of Saturday-in-Kensington when they were all three home together and she couldn't bear it that they breathed the same dull air. With no seeming willingness, she shuffled to the hall. She returned holding a jelly glass filled with water.

Frobisch took it gratefully and sipped. "Do you see your mother often?"

"She's very busy."

"Is that right? Busy with what?"

"She's gone out for Little Theater. She's got a part in the new Hexagon production; you know, those musical reviews they do for charity. She sings a song about a Beltway bandit. She says it's going to stop the show. She's on cloud nine," Sima added.

"That's great! That's really wonderful! I'm busy, too. It's the same rat race at the office." He wanted to be sure she knew he was working, the model of paternal probity. At the office he had eased the awkwardness of his re-entry by bringing gifts—a five-pound box of Russell Stover for

264

the secretarial pool and a potted pink azalea for Estelle, who took it with a stoic smile and said, "You have been missed." He'd had lunch with Freddy at the Tabard where, by strange, tacit agreement, they'd shied away from talk of business and softly reminisced about the old days in New York (two freshmen raising hell in Greenwich Village). They'd lingered over lunch, treating their homo waiter with elaborate courtesy as befit two men of substance. Freddy had seemed depressed. He said Renee was getting antsy, "the way women her age do," and the kids were acting as one might expect: "Vipers. All four of 'em." Frobisch believed Freddy blamed him for that. Freddy projected sadness, glum reproach—everyone in the office had looked either solemn or resentful—as if Frobisch's quirkiness had got them all off balance. For his part, Frobisch had felt a dullness; the familiar landscapes of his life gone flat without a sense of heaven's blessing, without the sightings of his vision—a funky, method-actor of an angel mumbling in his beard, but an angel nonetheless.

He hesitated before telling Sima, "There's a nice woman in my life. Nothing heavy, like you and Randy. Dinner dates, walks in the park. That sort of stuff. She's literary, y'know? You wouldn't believe what she's got me reading."

Sima cast him a look of cold aversion. Don't, the mute eyes pleaded, oh, don't regale me with your paltry middle-aged flirtations. "Is that what you wanted to tell me?"

"No." Frobisch took another sip of water. "Something happened the night we met in Rome. It was after I left you at your friend's apartment." If he breathed slow and kept up the careful sipping, he could keep his voice from trembling. Even so, his throat grew hoarse as though the

265

truth of his experience was too awesome for simple speech. The time with Father Paul he'd had that wondrous golden scotch to help him with the telling of it.

The jelly glass was chipped at one point on the rim. He was careful to drink with the rough side turned away from him. "You'd been telling me about the terrorists, and I was scared. Uptight. Very nervous. It was more than simple nerves; it was a feeling, like when you're flying and you think you're holding up the plane. You can't let go. You can't let down your guard or you're gonna crash. I could feel everything slipping out of hand. Maybe I prayed for help, though I don't remember that I did. I had gotten to the Spanish Steps. . . ." How to explain the awe and the exhilaration, the certainty that brought him to his knees; and after that, the fear, the burden of his new perceptions, the sense he was both watched and judged and not cutting the mustard! How to explain Father Paul and Brother Jarvis and Morry with the obscene stump of tubing in his belly. He talked softly, not daring to look at her. When he was finished, he set his glass down on the floor and glanced up shyly. "What do you make of it?"

"It's pretty weird."

"I suppose it is. I remember when adventures of that sort intrigued you. When I first visited you on the kibbutz, you were full of mystical pronouncements, little cabalistic tales. Do you remember how you told me that the great light of Creation had been stored in a series of bowls, and when seven of those bowls were broken the light escaped and God took on disparate countenances? Do you remember how we watched a circle of Hasidim dancing in a kind of trance, and when I said, 'Aren't they a little crazy?' you answered, 'No, they are God-intoxicated men.' Now you're a greeter, you drink Perrier at lunch, you think such things are weird."

"I have other things to think about. Did you know Sadie wants to sell the house?"

"Morry believed me right away. He never questioned it."

"You must talk to her, Howard. She's crazy to want to sell. It's a wonderful big house. For God's sake, I grew up there. Our Sammy's buried in the back. She can't just turn around and sell the whole place out from under us like that."

"Maybe because he was so close to dying."

"She's worrying about break-ins, and Dieter's telling her it isn't safe for a woman alone. If he's so concerned, why doesn't he move in with her?"

"I have a sense of something left unfinished."

"If things don't work out with me and Randy, I want to know the house is there for me."

That snapped him back into the here and now as surely as if she'd slapped him. "What do you mean? If things don't work out with you and Randy? Something is wrong? What has he done?"

"Quit harping on Randy! It's Sadie you have to talk to. Why won't you ever listen to me?"

"Why won't I listen to you? I pour out my soul—things I'd tremble to tell to Sadie, and you click off! You won't give me the time of day!"

"How should I respond? You think you saw a vision? It's another of your odd ideas, isn't it? Like when you thought the dog was listening to symphonies?"

"It's not! It's not the same. What's going on with you and Randy? You're not pregnant, are you?"

"That happens to be none of your business, but I'm not."

*O God, for Thy mercy I thank Thee. O God, Thou art great and kind. Thy wisdom is everywhere. Send me Thy bright angel that I may do Thy will!* "Then what is wrong?"

She had chewed her finger till it bled. She rubbed her hand on a shirtsleeve where it left a rust-red smear. "He's not looking for work. He pretends he is, but he never gets past Dupont Circle. He's over there right now, playing chess. That's his new obsession. He learned how when he was in the drug program. I guess you'd say it's better than throwing knives, but that's all he does. He says he likes chess because he can control things."

"I suppose he can."

"You sound like you're on his side."

"Not at all."

"He should be working, Daddy. I shouldn't have the whole responsibility of keeping us. The job at Mandy's is so boring!"

"It's a start, Sima. You have to make a start. You begin at the bottom, and you work your way up slowly. Today, a greeter. Tomorrow, a chain of stores. The sky's the limit for a young woman of your talents."

"What should I do about Randy?"

"You must decide that for yourself."

"You act like you don't care about me! Sadie, too. She wants to move to Georgetown so she can be closer to rehearsals. She's forgotten that she has a daughter who might be having problems. So have you!"

"They're problems of your own devising. You're on your own. Isn't that what you wanted?"

"I wanted a father who is sane. Who doesn't talk to ghosts. Who doesn't play around with other women!"

"Playing around's all right for you, but not for me?"

"For God's sake, you are my father! Why can't you just be ordinary?"

"Because something extraordinary happened to me." Frobisch stared at her in true bewilderment. "Am I the only one?"

"Why did you walk out on Sadie?"

"I can't give you a satisfactory answer. It's all the usual silly reasons. You turn fifty. You find out you're unhappy. Things don't go good in the sack. Don't look away! You're not so fragile now that I can't talk to you about these things! Besides, you asked me. You think about what you're missing—maybe a younger woman, a good time with someone else. That's all I wanted. I wanted to raise the devil, and I encountered God! That's either a cautionary tale for men in middle life or a cosmic joke, but it's okay. I got my glimpse of hell when I met Morry, and it's not too great. Heaven's better. There's no glamour to flirting with the devil, no matter what the stories tell you."

"I don't want my father talking like some crazy mystic!"

"I get it. The old men in broad-brimmed hats and tangled beards are picturesque. I'm an embarrassment. So be it. I don't want my daughter living with an ex-junkie who throws knives and plays chess all day in Dupont Circle. But I love you, Sima. I can't change that. Maybe that's all I really meant to tell you." He stood up, brushing his pants to shake off errant roaches. "I've got to go. These days when I'm gone too long from the office they get nervous."

"What are you going to do?"

"I think something's required of me. An act of faith. I don't know what that means. I don't know what I'll do. Whatever I decide, I hope it won't embarrass you."

"Are you going to talk to Sadie? Are you going to ask her not to sell the house? Please, Daddy, if you love me!"

The little bitch. Clever. Manipulative. Selfish. He almost pitied Randy. But he could not resist her blandishments. Please, Daddy, and she got her ears pierced. Please, Daddy, and he gave her her own phone. If he could keep her girlish, if he could ignore the relentless burgeoning of hips and bosom that consigned him to a proper distance, he would get the world for her in party wrappings. "I never know from one day to the next if your mother's talking to me. Give it a little time. In a coupla weeks, if she still has it on her mind to move, I'll go see her. Does that seem fair?"

Sima nodded. He was content to see her calmer. They were not exactly adversaries, nor were they friends. For now that was the best that he could manage.

# · CHAPTER ·
# 13

"To act rather than be acted on is a sign of mental health." He heard this on the radio as he was cooking dinner, the latest wisdom of a female pop psychologist who strewed her light like sparks upon an unsuspecting populace. Usually Frobisch flicked her off. Tonight he listened as he shed tears over onion dice. Wisdom resides in unexpected places; this dame (whom he envisioned as a whiskey-tenored Jewish princess concocting aphorisms in a rumpus room in Scarsdale) was right, for once. "To act"—to give off maundering like a lumpen blob—that was the ticket. His life, stymied on hold, dismayed him, as it did those around him—there being Freddy, wishing he'd concentrate on business; there being Estelle, trailing him with folders of unanswered correspondence; there being Louisa, attempting his conversion with books (dredged from a back bin at the Aardvark) on the Christo-mystics; there being Sima, giggling with Randy (he was sure) over his pompous attempts to state his faith; there being Father Paul, phoning after his return from Chicago to ask (with the mildest trace of sarcasm), "Had any revelations lately?" Frobisch believed he was the butt of priestly jokes: "What do you make of this, fellows? A tax accountant claiming miracles. What might they be? Foolproof shelters? Bigger deductions? A Bayonne-born messiah emerging from the Jersey swamps recumbent on a yellow legal pad or a green torpedo of a pickle? In rendering his nativity, portray him as the ass!" Frobisch took pleasure in this kind of paranoia, even as he knew the time had come to knock it off.

The only one who hadn't offered him a recent criticism or opinion was Sadie, who was too busy with Hexagon rehearsals to give a damn. He knew this because he drove out to the house in Kensington, whenever time allowed, to keep an eye on her. He was concerned about the break-ins, which likely were the work of local kids drumming up mischief, but scary nonetheless. Sadie would be too caught up in her music to take precautions, and Dieter's solution (Sadie toting a gun!) was ludicrous. Dieter, stalking the place with taciturn rigidity (poker up his ass!) would be worthless in a crisis; so Frobisch prowled, checking the locks and pulling errant weeds from the flower bed near Gregor's grave. Once, he encountered Mary De Filippo working in her yard. Both of them coolly nodded, miserable in their imposed "in-law" state, but acting civil to each other to please the kids. To act! What was required now was forward motion with Louisa. As long as sacred love eluded him, he would move to the profane.

He phoned her at the Aardvark. "Would you do something crazy? Would you throw some stuff in an overnight bag and go away with me, no questions asked?"

Her voice over the phone had a limpid, distant quality that got his goat. "Whatever for?"

"I can't breathe in the city. Simple as that."

"Should you see a doctor?"

"Please, Louisa, *please.*"

In the moment of hesitation before she answered, he

knew she would agree. She would do it! Attribute her softening to his heaven-engendered charm or that last urgent *please*, aimed like a dart at the core of her composure. "I couldn't close the store before noon on a Saturday."

"Fine. We won't go very far. Maybe the Eastern Shore—that's three hours at the most. We'll have lunch on the road, check in somewhere around five, get a great fish dinner." He was nattering. "We'll talk, take long walks on the beach. I always feel good near the ocean. Me and Ishmael. What's the line I want? Whenever I feel a dark November in my soul, I go and find a port—or something to that effect. How does it go?"

"I'm sure I don't remember."

"We can take separate rooms if you prefer."

"That gets pretty expensive. . . ."

"It does. The point, the point, darling Louisa, is that you're under no obligation . . . no prior commitment. You get my drift?"

"I'm still working on Ishmael."

"The point is . . . the point is, it doesn't have to mean anything heavy, as the kids put it. Know what I mean?"

"I believe I do."

"I won't make any demands," said Frobisch, lying in his teeth.

The motel had the musty smell of rooms rented out of season. There were two double beds covered with spreads of garish cotton, a splash of yellow roses on a tangle of green vines. There was a round table near the window and a hanging lamp shaped like a mushroom, an artifact of such inspired ugliness it shocked him to see it blaze with otherworldly orange radiance when he hit the switch.

There was a double dresser made of some light-colored wood resembling bamboo, and a portable TV, and a barrel chair that swiveled, covered in ivory naugahyde, and another deeper chair upholstered in brown stuff. There was an alcove fitted with metal hangers soldered to a rack, and a bathroom furnished with sufficient soap and towels and two paper-covered glasses. He would have to go down the hall to get some ice. He told Louisa, "It's not too bad."

"I'm wondering what I'm doing here." She had settled on the bed nearest the door with her skirt arranged around her like a picnic blanket. She was wearing a blue down jacket and shiny rain boots that reached her knees. She looked windblown, distracted.

He groped for a phrase that wouldn't rile her. "It's fun to be together—in another context."

"I shouldn't have closed the store. Saturday's my busiest day."

"We've been through that." He hefted her suitcase to the luggage rack, thinking she must have stocked it with the contents of a five-foot shelf. "What big sales are you gonna miss? A coupla paperback romances? Some old crock wanting a rehash of the Civil War? It's a nice quaint shop, Louisa, but it's not B. Dalton."

"Why can't you understand? I get all my regulars on Saturday." She had started this lament and sung it, theme and variations, since the moment they took off. Call it displacement—more than the likely danger to her virtue, the store absorbed her. Every time they passed a roadside stand, a restaurant with cars jamming the lot, even the toll booths clinking coins on the Bay Bridge, she'd begun moaning the loss of profits. He'd wanted a free spirit; he had in hand a shiksa kvetch, a Portia mourning her ducats as woefully as Shylock. He acknowledged it was maiden nerves that set her off; that didn't ease his disappointment. He'd expected easy, sexy banter in the car, a long lunch where they started out sedate and finally got foolish over wine—Louisa acting flirty once she was out of range of nosy neighbors.

"All this way and it's raining," she complained.

"The forecast calls for clearing. What's the difference? I'm gonna buy you a great lobster dinner, rain or shine."

She shook her head. "Shellfish makes me break out."

"You see? That's something else I didn't know about you." If he didn't keep busy, it was likely he would brain her! Checking the dresser drawers, he found two postcards and a Gideon Bible. Quickly, he shut the Bible out of sight, lest it start her acting pious. He wouldn't put money down on whether she'd sleep with him. When they walked in, she'd panned around the room, then said she'd take the bed nearest the door. As though it meant some sacrifice, she offered him the ocean view. To lie alone and watch the tides wasn't in his game plan. For a second of pure craziness, he pondered a swift frontal assault—slam, bang, and get it over—and leave some time for decent conversation. Mulling appropriate strategy, he sauntered to the window and pulled back the drapes. "We have a private beach. There's a stairway going straight down to the ocean. Come and see."

She had disappeared into the john. He could hear the water running in the sink and then the rumble as she flushed the toilet. She came out blushing, still bundled in her jacket.

"Are you hungry?" Frobisch asked. "Do you want to go out for an early dinner or wait a bit?"

"I don't care." She had settled in her old spot on the bed.

Frobisch flipped on the TV and scanned the channels. A quiz show. A rerun of "The Millionaire." A British flick about commandos. He stood still, absorbed in the action. Louisa watched it, too, frowning as though her fate depended on the outcome of the plot. Frobisch retreated to the bed that would be his. He pulled out two plump pillows and propped them high against the headboard. Then he lay down with an exaggerated sigh. "Why don't you come and watch this thing with me?"

"I'm comfortable, thank you."

"I'm lonesome."

Louisa stood obediently and crossed the no-man's-land between their beds.

"Kick off your boots, why don't you?"

She complied like a docile convent girl obeying the dictum of the nuns. He moved to make more room for her. She sat stiffly beside him, her stockinged legs extended next to his.

He eased off his damp loafers and prodded her foot with his toe. She answered with a hasty kick; then she inched away. "Aren't you uncomfortable in that jacket?" Frobisch asked.

"I'm a little chilly, to tell the truth."

He offered her his arm. "I'll warm you. Come and snuggle."

She leaned stiffly against him. When he moved to stroke her hair he found the usual armory of pins and combs. "Loosen it," he begged.

"Not if we're going out. It'll take me an hour to get it right again."

He traced a finger along her neck, the only naked place

276

available to him. "We can go out later if you like. We can do anything we want. Consider this." He flicked his tongue into her ear. "We're here, in a motel at Dewey Beach. No one we know knows that we've checked in. None of your friends; none of your neighbors; none of the people from the church." He nibbled gently on her earlobe. "Not the manager at Safeway or the ladies on Antique Row. Not the mailman. Not Father Paul." He whispered this into her hair.

"Oh, look!" She pointed to the television. "The sentry is going to see him. He better duck!"

Frobisch leaned close to kiss her. Her lips were cold. She kept her mouth clamped shut. "What is it, Louisa? Are you sorry you came?"

"I came of my own free will, Howard. You didn't force me. You seemed so agitated when you called. Like it was life or death for you to get away. Like we had to be somewhere together or the world would end."

"I want you to be my world. The old one is ending for me. If there are new miracles for me to discover, I want to discover them with you. Is that so strange?"

"Good Lord! It sounds like you're proposing marriage?"

He stared at the movie for a minute. The commandos were locked in hand-to-hand combat with the Nazis. The British lieutenant who was the hero rolled out of range of a German bayonet. He crouched low as the enemy moved toward him; then he whirled. His leg shot out and caught the Nazi in the groin. Frobisch grunted at the realism of the scene. "To be absolutely honest," he said softly, "the word 'marriage' scares me shitless."

Louisa had pulled an amber comb out of her hair and was raking it across her teeth with a grating sound that set his nerves on edge. "It scares me, too. My view of marriage might surprise you. I don't see it as the be-all and end-all people seem to think. I'm not that keen on sharing. I have a comfortable routine—shopping, the church, the store. All that you and I really have in common is Father Paul, and you've made it clear you won't convert."

"God is everywhere, Louisa. Why assign Him to a particular compartment?"

"It's not God so much. It's custom, ritual, tradition. What I've been born to. You're the one who started the whole fuss about God."

And he'd better give it up if he was ever going to get her to unbend. Lord, he was bored with the ritual of seduction. That was the province of the young—where uncertainty equaled excitement and every inch of territory won pointed to conquest, and the game was worth the candle. "You know, I'm starved all of a sudden," he said. "Should we get something to eat?"

"Oh, can't we just see how the movie ends?"

"The Allies win. The pretty-boy lieutenant gets wounded, but he manages to blow up the camp. Friendly planes see the fire and know where to drop their bombs. The Italian sergeant major with the cockney sweetheart gets killed."

"You've seen it, Howard!"

"Just bits and pieces. Price you pay for insomnia."

"You didn't have to ruin it for me. That was mean."

"Stick me with me, kiddo, and we'll watch Home Box Office."

"Oh, you!"

"You laughed! Praise be to heaven, you really laughed! Are you relaxing now? Have you decided it's not so terrible being here alone with me?"

"Not terrible. Just peculiar."

"I understand. And I will be patient." Gloomily, he vowed he would. If he had to sleep alone and leave her to the solemn tallying of her accounts, he would show forbearance. She was nervous, like a fractious filly who needed stroking, gentling, to calm down. He let go of the comparison as potentially too exciting. "Let me look after you. I won't ask anything of you that you don't want to do."

"Well, if you want to go to dinner—" She had turned partway toward him. His hand rested on her jacket, the touch rendered innocent by layers of puffy goose down. The thought of maiden flesh, camouflaged by all that padding, aroused him. "I guess we might as well go out," Frobisch said ruefully. His groin hurt as though he were the Nazi soldier zapped by a body blow.

Jack's Yacht Stop, the place was called. Built like a stubby lighthouse, it stood on pilings facing Rehoboth Bay. In summer the line of hungry diners started around five o'clock and snaked from the entrance ramp to the parking lot and the marina. There was a pretty cove where sailboats bobbed at anchor in the shallows, and a fishing pier where old parties in duckbilled hats dangled lines and took the sun. The dining room had wide, green-tinted windows that framed the broad sweep of the bay. They used to get there early so they could get a table with a view, and Sima could watch the gulls perched on their poles. Sadie, who'd studied Introductory Psych at Hunter College, explained to Sima about the pecking order; and Frobisch cupped his failing ear and pretended not to understand: "What's that you say? Pecker order?" And Sadie kicked him under the table with the mean spike of her heel and the pain somehow got him excited and he winked at her and leered and put on his phony Freud accent, persisting, "Please, modom. Vat is ziss pecker order? Iss beyond me to understand."

"You can't see a thing out there tonight." Louisa squinted at a wall of glass pelted by rain. The sky was black, and the water of the bay was dark and silent as a tar pit.

The dining room was almost empty. He counted three quiet couples (adulterers, he bet) murmuring over drinks. In summer the room buzzed with noisy families, and the waitresses were pretty college kids who pinned their hair up into messy topknots and showed off darling sunburned shoulders in peasant blouses. Tonight, an older hostess, sleek in tailored black and pearls, had offered them their choice of tables. Frobisch asked for the window out of habit. The Muzak was playing Chopin. The hostess lit a candle on their table and vanished like a wraith. Frobisch remembered Curran's study and the sputtering of memorial candles and the smoke hovering near useless lamps and Mildred puzzling over the list of funeral costs, shaking her head with the gray braid swinging like a hangman's rope.

Louisa said she'd like to try a margarita. Frobisch warned, "They can be strong."

"What about a mai tai, then?"

"Might as well stick to the margarita." He ordered two, although he had no taste for booze tonight. He would have been content with mariner's chowder and a quick retreat to bed and the two of them beneath the covers listening to the rain. They were sitting in a draft. He shivered.

"Are you getting sick?" Louisa asked.

"Just a little tired after the trip."

"I wish that I could drive. I begged Daddy to teach me, but he thought it was something women really couldn't do; that we weren't sufficiently mechanical. Isn't that silly?"

"Yes, it is."

"He wasn't always that dogmatic. He could be wonderful, so handsome in his summer whites, like a movie star, I used to think." She was off again on reminiscence, dredging up that childhood stuff. Louisa as a navy brat. Visits to the Navy Yard, the old weapons museum. Tomboy Louisa hanging from the mouths of cannons, hunting phantom gunboats on the Anacostia, sighting Mr. Lincoln's ghost in the room where he'd conferred with his war minister. Daddy's little girl, not quite grown up. If he got her in the sack, it would be like screwing Sima!

She was boasting of the skills she had acquired after the old man died. "Now I take charge of the furnace in the house, and I do minor repairs on the plumbing. I even fixed the dryer when it broke."

"Marvelous," said Frobisch glumly.

"It was just a broken fan belt. That's relatively simple. Oh, thanks." She flashed the hostess, who had brought their drinks, a smile of radiant gratitude. She sipped hers slowly, meditating on the taste. "It's funny. That rim of salt."

Frobisch swallowed quickly, hoping the drink would warm him. He was downhearted, remembering family dinners—Sadie, with her socko tan, and Sima, carrying her magic markers in a blue box fashioned like a suitcase, so she could color in the pictures on her place mat, or nag him for a game of dots or tic-tac-toe until their orders came. Now she was making it with Randy, and Sadie was singing in a show, and both of them must think him crazy. That was bravado, telling Sima what was required of him was an act of faith. That was mostly childish boasting, trying to capture her imagination, as he once had with bedtime stories.

"When you get that look, I know exactly what you're thinking," Louisa claimed.

"Do you?" He drank his drink.

"You're on that holy stuff again. It's like a seesaw. You believe, and then you don't, and then you do. Which is it now?"

"Right at this moment? Hard to say." He twirled his empty glass by the stem.

"Oh, balderdash, it's on again. I can always tell. It makes me sad and disappointed."

"You're happier with a heathen whom you can convert?"

"I'm happier when you're not crazy. What does this obsession get you, Howard? Does it inspire poems or paintings? Does it move you to acts of sacrifice or charity? No. It drives you nuts!"

"Should I work in Father Paul's soup kitchen? Should I donate blood? Should I give Randy a job, or hack him to pieces with his own penknife and get Sima back her life? What should I do? Tell me, Louisa, I want to know."

"How should I know? You're the one who talks with angels."

She could be bitchy as Sadie, and the eyes that so intrigued him with their bold blue gleam could flash forthright malice. He was saved from the necessity of a reply by Jack himself, the affable proprietor, costumed in yachting cap and black turtleneck sweater, a double for John Wayne in *Wake of the Red Witch*. Waddling his seaman's gait, Jack skirted islands of empty tables and bore down on them smiling. "Nice to see you and the missus."

Frobisch, half-rising, shook Jack's hand. "Nice to be back." He waved his napkin at the empty room. "Quiet tonight."

"It tends to fill up later. You're lookin' good."

"You too."

"How's that pretty little daughter?"

"So-so."

"She married yet?"

"She's shacked up with a junkie," Frobisch said.

Jack swallowed this as he might have downed a rubbery clam, not so surprised or pained as gloomily resigned. He nodded and his white hat bobbed and his gray jowls, stubbly with an aging sailor's beard, wobbled as he absorbed this. His pale eyes glinted understanding; the wisdom of the age, all sympathy and pain resided in perfect balance under the jaunty visor of his cap. He searched the room seeking some article of comfort. He scooped a dish of oysterettes from an empty table and offered these to Frobisch, who took them in the spirit they were given, with a little sigh of thanks. "I'm the one taught her to eat hard-shelled crabs," said Jack.

"Yes, you did," answered Frobisch, not remembering, but willing to acknowledge any words uttered with conviction as the truth. He ate an oysterette, which turned out to be soggy.

"You all enjoy your dinner," counseled Jack.

And Frobisch told the dark, departing back and the shoulders hunched in sadness at the sorrow that afflicts mankind, particularly fathers, "Thanks. We will."

"Do I look like the missus?" Louisa smirked.

He was tired of their sparring. The puzzle was, the

nastier she got—the more spinsterish and acerbic—the hornier he became. "He knows you're not. He says that to be tactful." He signaled to the hostess. "We'd like to order now."

Louisa wanted fillet of sea trout and french fries and rum buns and salad with house dressing. "And I'll probably order something sinful for dessert." She winked.

Determined to make the evening festive, Frobisch chose lobster. When it came, he could only poke it with his fork as though it were a great dead insect that had lighted on his plate. The Muzak had shifted to calypso, Harry Belafonte loading a banana boat eternally through time. Louisa said the trout was dry, but everything else was delicious. She'd left most of her drink untasted. Frobisch asked, "Do you mind?" and reached over for it. He finished it quickly.

"Goodness," said Louisa, picking at her salad for bits of lettuce untouched by house dressing. "Have we developed a hollow leg?"

Frobisch lathered a rum bun with butter and stuffed it in his mouth to counter the burning of the drink. The sugar in the sweet roll made him sick. He ordered another round of drinks. When they came, he drank Louisa's and his own. He was feeling happier, warmer. The couples hunched at nearby tables spoke in pleasant whispers over drinks. The candle flickering from amid a wreath of plastic roses on their table cast a softening pinkish glow over Louisa's face. A skein of nets strung on a nearby wall wavered like cobwebs. A row of old sea lanterns glimmered with the patina of well-rubbed brass. A glinting silver swordfish, anchored to a ceiling beam, reflected fixed, glass-eyed serenity.

Frobisch believed himself suspended in a green sea world, dangling between warm surface currents and ocean bottom. Above him, ferns in hanging pots tumbled like seaweed. He sighted purple sea plume wafting from a window box, and pink anemones peeping from the pearled chambers of conchs. "I'm floating." He beamed.

"Better have some coffee." Louisa nodded toward the window. "Look, the rain has stopped. I believe we're going to have a moon."

Over sobering cups of coffee he studied her, the perfect bones, the girlish flush lighting her cheeks, the soft hair tumbling around her temples however hard she tried to pull it back. She was fingering the lavaliere and smiling, a musing grin—speculative, sexy, not as innocent as he would have thought.

"It was a lovely dinner, Howard."

"More coffee? Dessert?"

"I think nothing, after all. I'd burst."

"There's mile-high pie, apple cobbler, chocolate parfait . . ."

"Don't tempt me. I'll be sick."

"New York cheesecake, rum cake, black forest torte . . ."

"You have the menu memorized?"

The litany he'd learned for Sima. "Fried ice cream, rice pudding . . ."

"*Fried* ice cream!"

"Baklava, ribbon sherbet . . ."

"Howard, stop! I'm not hungry!"

Frobisch took her hand and planted swift fluttery kisses in her palm. "Well, then, what would you like to do?"

"I dunno, Marty," she mugged. "Whaddayou wanna do?"

"I want to walk. Let's go back to our place and walk along the beach."

At the water's edge the wet sand oozed like clay under their feet and the black waves rimmed by whitish curls of foam were surprising in their warmth. Salty-warm and silky, the low waves lapped the shore like licking tongues, spilling gentle spray and coaxing the slow tide seaward. "You could swim on a southeast course, maybe to Bermuda," Frobisch mused. "Or, if you went due east and didn't get tangled up in any currents, you might hit the coast of Spain." You could do it, he thought, in this gentle ocean—just a slow, heavy trundling, and the waves pumping you along, and perhaps a friendly dolphin to nudge you on your way. "What say, Louisa, wanna swim to Spain?" They were walking arm in arm, swinging their shoes in their free hands. Louisa had removed her stockings, first insisting that he turn away, not because she was modest; removing pantyhose was awkward, and she hated to look clumsy in front of anyone. He covered his face, then peeked between his fingers and saw the leanness of her thighs. He had rolled his trousers to the knees, careful not to trigger the old pain. The bruise had faded to a yellowish semicircle, not half bad. He sensed a tenderness tonight, felt the slow blood pulsing in his knee in rhythm with the moving ocean. A faint moon hovered behind wispy clouds and lit the water to anemic silver. The waves rolled with drunken motions and broke in gray-white swirls. The wind had quieted.

"This weather's illogical," Louisa said. "Now that the rain's stopped, it's almost tropical." She dug one bare toe into the sand and burrowed a little hole. The ocean quickly filled it. "Lucky for us, or we'd both have pneumonia by now."

Frobisch said, "Why not?"

"Why not have pneumonia?"

"Why not swim to Spain?"

"I see we're feeling the margaritas."

He always felt strong by the water. Charged up and full of beans; braced by sea air and hyper with the sense of life's infinite possibilities. Summers before Sima was old enough for camp they took her to the beach because it was so great for children. The sun cured her catarrh. The sand was a perfect playground; and the boardwalk—with its tacky rides, its glorious grainy fudge and sticky taffies and crisp french-fried potatoes served up with that spattering of vinegar that is peculiar to the Eastern Shore—was exotic, noisy chaos, a child's garden of delights. At night the grown-ups took their pleasures in their rented beds, tumbling on mattresses that bore the stains of strangers, bouncing to the beat of creaky springs and the wild buzz of mosquitoes flying crazy arcs over the pillows. In the hot dark Sadie bit his neck and he squelched her cries with sloppy kisses and they rolled like acrobats and stopped, balanced on the edge of pleasure, listening for Sima's snuffles and the moans of childish dreams.

One year he took them farther south to a cottage on the Outer Banks—a wooden box on poles set on a dune that glistened in the night with bits of glass and shards of shells and the desiccated remnants of dead starfish and old, cockeyed pinwheels whirling crazily off balance in the gritty sand. In the night the wind whistled through waving sea oats, and fires burned along the beach, and their neighbors, in a house of weathered shingles, sat whooping on a cantilevered deck and shooting Roman candles toward the sky. There was no boardwalk and no television—nothing to do at night but watch the sea or sit around the wobbly kitchen table in the faint light of a twenty-watt bulb and play hearts while the radio blared songs crooned by the Carpenters or Bobby Vinton, and Sadie sang along, as Sadie would: "So we have to say goodbye . . . for the summ-mer." One night they walked along the beach and Frobisch played a flashlight in the sand and they saw a hundred, maybe a thousand, scuttling crabs, racing along the ocean's edge like white five-pointed stars alight and gleaming in the dark. And Sima cried, "Ooh, Daddy," and Sadie laughed, "Look at those little buggers run." And he flashed his light across the faces of his family. Sima's, a moon of joy and Sadie's, a smiling cipher, as she whispered, "Are they mating?" And knowing what would come when they were back together in their loft bed under knotted eaves, he'd stood, bursting with potency and addled joy, with a sense of life so fragile; life that could be ended in a sudden crash of waves or a crunch of heels against the sand. The crabs flickered like stars around them, and Sima laughed and took his hand, and Sadie squeezed his arm in a message that said, later, later, later, we'll dance around our bedroom like those crabs. We'll wave our legs in air like crazy shellfish, and the moon will light our bodies. And Frobisch, with a chill of prescience, knew that he was happy for perhaps the last time in his life.

He dropped Louisa's hand. He set his shoes square in the sand, toes aligned and pointing to the sea. Quickly, he shook free of his jacket. He unnotched his belt and zipped open his fly.

Louisa asked, "What are you doing?"

He asked, "Why not?" And let his pants drop.

"Hold it, Howard. If you make a move on me out here, I'll holler rape and we'll both be terribly embarrassed!"

"I'm going into the water. I'm going to swim as far out as I can. God will rescue me or guide me. I'm not sure which. It's in his hands."

"Are you crazy?"

He pondered this. "I don't think so. I'm a little happy on tequila, but I'm not drunk. I do this as an act of faith. I believe that God will save me. A boat will come. Or a school of porpoises will guide me toward the shore."

"Or you'll walk on water!"

"That is presumptuous," Frobisch reproached.

"This isn't funny, Howard."

"I'm serious, Louisa. I have this sense of a divine purpose. I do this, and I validate my vision. You and all the other doubters have your proof."

"You don't have to prove anything to me. You believe in what you saw, and that's enough! Let's say it's true and go back up to the room. I'm cold, and my skirt is soaked."

"It will be a miracle of a high order, Louisa. Be happy that you're here to see. When it's done, you will believe me."

"I believe you, Howard. I do. Anything you tell me, I believe. Now come inside with me and maybe have more coffee. A shower to perk you up?"

"Don't humor me! I have to do this. Once and for all, I have to show 'em. It wasn't the vino or the bee sting or an epileptic fit. It wasn't!"

"Killing yourself to prove a point is crazy!"

"Morry believed. Shall I tell you why? 'Cause it meant the promise of some comfort after all that pain—all that shitty plastic-tubed indignity. So he believed. He thought I had the scoop straight from the mouth of God, and he kneeled before me and he . . . barfed. Quite a lot of that he did, when we were at the monastery. He kept me busy cleaning up." A burst of wind whipped at his shirttails and sent him staggering to the water. He felt foolish, arguing in shirt and tie and boxer shorts with the sea licking at his ankles. The current tugged at him. There were riptides off the Carolina coast that could trap you in a fast-moving channel and bear you out to sea in minutes. Just to think of this was terrifying. If he dwelled on it, the game was up. He waded a few steps farther until the water reached his calves. If his memory of this beach was right, there would be a long expanse of shallow water with a slick, tarry bottom underfoot and then a sudden drop; it would be like stepping off a cliff.

Louisa, lumbering beside him, pulled at his arm with the strength born of desperation. The amber combs had tumbled to the water; her hair whipped around her in a crazy halo. Her face, dead-white in moonlight, glistened with spray. Over the muffled boom of waves, her voice carried with frantic urgency. "Stop right here, Howard, 'cause I'm not going another step. Now, you listen. I won't stay here and watch this. If you want to kill yourself, do it on your own time, but not with me. Pick yourself some other weekend, when I'm not here to share in the publicity."

"What publicity! There's no one here but you and me."

"I won't watch, and I won't get help. If I do, everyone back home will know I went away with you. I won't have that. What I choose to do with my own life is private."

"Sweet girl, you're still worrying about your neighbors?"

"If you kill yourself tonight, you will ruin my reputation."

"We haven't done anything. There's nothing for you to be ashamed of, unless knowing me embarrasses you."

"You bet it embarrasses me!" In the moonlight she looked crafty, almost mean. The innocence he prized had vanished in a crash of waves. "Come inside with me now, and I'll do anything you ask, Howard. Anything!"

"Louisa, darling, now isn't the time." Brusquely, he pulled free of her.

"Now or never, Howard. Come inside. You can always claim your vision. You can always put it to the test. Next weekend, next year, whenever you please. But you can't always have me. So if you want me, if that's why we came here, then come inside. I promise you, you won't regret it."

He took stock of the rolling wavelets and the soft waves of her hair, the slope of dark sand slanting to the water, and the angle of her body bending to him as she tried to grab his arm. "You want to go up now? To the room?"

"Yes. Right now, or never, Howard, I swear it."

"It can't wait a bit?"

"No, it can't. If you come upstairs with me, you won't be sorry. But if you go another step into this ocean, I promise I'll pack my things and call a cab and leave without a word to anyone that you're out here. No one will know I was with you. You'll drown alone and there'll be no one around to save you."

"I won't drown. That is the point."

"Make the choice."

"It wouldn't take so long, Louisa. If you'd wait for me."

"Make the choice."

"Listen. I believe the angel's playing possum. I have to flush him out. I don't expect another chance. I don't expect to be this brave ever again. It's now or never for me."

"Now or never. That's exactly right."

"It's not a fair temptation. The flesh is weak. You know I want you, and I'm not exactly what you'd call a saint."

"Come on," she said, pulling him shoreward.

The part that struck him as most crazy was not the wading to the sea, but the slow turning back, plodding against the tide and the warm, tugging current, setting his feet in the indentation of her footsteps as they crossed the sand. She strode ahead with her hair whipping around her like a fan and her dull blue jacket billowing oddly and her wide skirt flapping, limp, around her calves and the wet toe of her stocking dangling from a pocket like a misplaced tail. What was crazy was gathering up his shoes and coat and struggling into sodden pants and climbing the wooden stairs that creaked at every cautious step, while the wild wind bellowed and the faint sliver of moon over the ocean beckoned him back to prove his faith. Crazy to search his pockets for their room key and hand it to her and wait while she unlocked the door and issued curt directives in her schoolmarm's voice: "Get your wet clothes off. Go and wait in bed while I get ready." Crazy to shiver naked in the double bed (his bed with the ocean view), covered by a sheet like a corpse awaiting burial. Crazy to think of lovemaking after at least four margaritas and nothing much to eat and his penis lying curled and quiet as a snail while she rattled in the bathroom making her preparations.

She came out wearing a white, high-necked nightgown. He watched her fiddle with the drapes, flick on the mushroom light, and flick it off. In the pale light of the passing moon she looked girlish, so sweet he thought his heart might stop for tenderness; so timid and slender, so awkward, here in the silver dark.

Slowly, she raised her gown above her head. Frobisch watched in silence, as an audience watches, rapt, in that brief second of magic before action on stage begins. The gown fluttered to the floor like an indolent white bird.

"How lovely you are, Louisa!"

She waved this off as though his mention of the obvious bored her. "Listen," she said, "I like to be on top."

Later, it rained again. He could hear the wild drops spattering the window and the wooden stairs outside. The wind had gained velocity. He could hear the clash of waves against the shore and the screech of sea birds riding out the storm. He lay quiet, astonished, having endured something not easily defined—a kind of acrobatics, a kind of sex beyond his powers ever to imagine; having been pounded, pummeled, spent, annihilated, rejuvenated, cajoled, teased, taunted, piqued, licked, kissed, prodded, flayed, stroked, hammered, scratched, soothed, and ridden like a bucking bronco. Having been held, cupped, fondled, measured (and found not wanting), measured again (and deemed inadequate); having been lapped, sucked, tickled, squeezed, pressed, pinched, soothed, gentled; having been manly beyond his craziest hopes and embarrassed beyond his worst nightmares, and exhausted beyond his wildest fantasies; having been praised and shamed and titillated and roused to heights of joy and dashed to a pit so low, so dark, so bleak with shock and disappointment he knew his heart must break, *had* broken. He had heard it crack, like a rending of virgin tissue. *He* was innocent.

And Louisa! Who was this Louisa whom he had pat-
terned after the statue of the Virgin in the monastery
garden? Louisa, balletic, lean, a smooth-flanked nympho,
smiling astride him, raping him, battering him to ungod-
ly climax after climax. "Are you an agent of the devil,
Louisa?" he asked her once; and she had huffed, seemingly insulted and threatening to leave him somewhere
between ecstasy and death. "It's what you wanted, isn't
it?" And later, "Does this beat drowning? And this? And
this?" "Yes," he told her. Yes. *Ya wohl* and *Da* and *Oui*
and *Si*. Also *Ça suffit. Genug. Bastante.* Enough now. Sufficient. Quite enough. For the sake of Peter, Paul, and
Prick, the weary members of a tired trinity; for the well-
being of the pecker's order, those dull birds with their
wings finally clipped, their talons sheathed, their appetites
insanely sated. Enough, Louisa, you have shown your
talent; have proved beyond all reasonable doubt or foolish
claim made to the contrary: *You have a life!*

"Enough for now," Louisa told him finally and
flounced off to a steamy tub where he heard her soaking,
idly splashing, and singing in a gravelly contralto, "Smoke
Gets in Your Eyes."

She came back to their bed wrapped in a towel. Drops
of water gleamed on her shoulders. She had taken off the
lavaliere, or it had broken during the wildest of their encounters. She looked vulnerable without it—nothing on
the smooth column of neck but a spattering of freckles.
He asked, "Aren't you cold?"

"A bit. Yes." She brushed a finger across his chest. "Do
you want to sleep now?"

"In a minute. Yes."

"You look so solemn, Howard. Are you disappointed?"

Instinctively, he pulled the covers higher, in case she
meant to treat his disappointment with a round of fresh

surprises. "I'd say, confused. Why did you let me go on thinking you were inexperienced?"

"Did I ever say I was or wasn't?"

"Not in so many words, but everything in your manner made me think I was leading you down the garden path. I worried about it. I felt guilty. I *was* trying to be scrupulous, in spite of what you think."

"People believe the things they want to."

"If I could be so wrong . . . if my perceptions are so out of whack, then how can I be certain about anything? Everything I feel so sure of could be a fluke. Then I'm right back where I started. And I don't know what to do."

"Angels and visions. We're back to that again."

"We're back to that."

"And you *are* disappointed?"

"No, Louisa. No."

"Oh, you are. All the time we were together—you had this look, like what you really wanted was a watery death."

"Sex is a kind of death."

"Let's get more poetic. Call it the death of love?"

"*Are* you an agent of the devil?"

"Be serious, please."

"I think you could be. You have extraordinary talents—"

"Oh, Jesus Christ! You really are too much!" She was bouncing over him again, this time with righteous fury. Between them was the safety of his sheet and her damp towel; and every time her towel slid lower he felt an unbelievable flickering of interest in his groin. "Shall I tell you the real reason I've no interest in getting married? It's because of men like you. You're so eager to take your pleasure, and when you do, you get all gloomy and depressed because you can't be forever screwing a virgin. That must be something; some big deal, thinking you're

the first! Numero uno, that's all you want. And when that's
done, you get to feeling guilty and religious. I can imagine
what it was like being married to you! What's-her-name,
Sadie, has my sympathy, she does!"

"Are you an agent of the devil?"

"Don't flatter yourself that you're so important! If I
were, why would I want you? Why would I save your life?
'Cause that's exactly what I did. You were drunk, and you
had a notion you could swim to Spain. You were God's
right-hand man, and you offered comfort to the sick.
Maybe you thought you'd find a cure for cancer or build
another Chartres, but the truth is, you'd have drowned!
Plain and simple, if I hadn't brought you back to bed."

This was the price one paid for shunning heaven, this
taint of hell, this naked banishment to a cold room where
he lay semierect, seduced and never sated, aroused and
shamed, aroused again, his poor bent prick rising like a
phoenix and collapsing on a bed of ashes and rising again.
"Look at you," Louisa laughed. "Ready for another go-
round?" She tossed aside the towel. "Shall I tell you what
excites me? It's that first look of surprise; then the little
frown of anguish, and the puzzlement: 'What's a nice girl
like you doing in a place like this?' It's a turn-on." She bent
to him. "You like this, don't you? And this? And this, best
of all?"

Better to let her use him as she wished, to lie passive
as she played, to play back a bit (for the sake of good manners, at least) and let her think she had a convert. Given
the roster of his sins—misperceptions, clumsiness, insuf-
ficiency of faith—what was another quarter-hour of dam-
nation (more or less) going to signify? "You're right," he
said. "I would've drowned."

· CHAPTER ·

# 14

Sadie was giving a party. The line of parked cars reached around the block. Frobisch cruised the darkening street ticking off those automobiles he recognized— Freddy's ivory Mercedes pulled up on the grass for safety, and Estelle's vintage gray Buick (a tank, stuck at a crazy angle), and Dieter's van looming in the driveway with its armature of extra tires and an orange bumper sticker with the fatuous boast: I Brake for Animals. Break a foot, thought Frobisch as he passed the house.

Irrational though it was, he was hurt he hadn't been invited. His birthday was a week away, and the cake Sadie had baked for him should be safe inside the cellar freezer, wrapped in foil; although he wouldn't put it past her to scrape away the icing and present it as a gift to Dieter. They could be announcing their engagement. The idea chilled his blood. If Sadie got hitched to the vet, Frobisch and Van Zandt would be related in a peculiar way— husbands-in-law or twin daddies to Sima. Shared loves and shared experience thicker than blood. They already shared responsibility for Gregor's death. He wouldn't permit the ceremony without speaking his piece. It was Sadie's life, but it was Frobisch's responsibility to warn her that the man was flawed—a cold fish, studying the gasping dog with glassy-eyed stolidity and musing in his Nazi voice, "Sooner or later, all of my patients die."

Frobisch spun the Volvo through a U-turn and back-tracked past the house, keeping his lights on dim. There were the De Filippos, treading the slate-smooth flagstone of the walk as though traversing ice. Mary held a covered platter to her breast. A gesture of peace or payment? You never knew with the De Filippos. Her husband moved with cautious steps, a tiger poised to crouch at the first crack of the hunter's bullets. De Filippo never showed his face in public without the furtive implication there were gunmen watching from the shadows for a chance to waste him. Frobisch picked up speed so as not to feed the man's suspicions.

He spotted Katinka Turner in a froth of pink, teetering down the Parkway on metallic heels, a cloud of capes and gauzy panels bathing her goddess body in a rosy haze. She lived diagonally behind the Frobisch house, a glamour-girl British divorcée who kept twin schnauzers of daunting ferocity. In summers past, she'd sunbathed in a white bikini, and Frobisch appropriated Sima's telescope (purchased to prod the child's interest in the stars)—not out of prurient interest, God forbid, but to satisfy himself that Tinka wasn't presenting a harmful influence on the local kids. He got the best view from a dormer window in Sima's bedroom; there, of an August afternoon, he kept his patient vigil, conscious of the drone of bees and the thick heat pressing from the roof beyond the reach of air conditioning, admiring the golden skin, the legs gleaming with oil, the darling, dimpled navel accenting that suntanned belly like a punctuation mark. Carefree summers in Kensington.

Every year he and Sadie threw a party: lanterns in the

yard and booze set on the redwood table and Gregor shut up in the master bedroom and Sima, freckled from the beach, passing hors d'oeuvres. Sadie did sinful desserts and all her special salads, and he presided at the grill. Mostly, their neighbors came. If the crowd was big, Mrs. Garcia served and brought her son, Tomás, who tended bar. Nobody drank that much, but sometimes there were mild flirtations. Once with Katinka Turner, out by the copper beech, both of them drinking gin and tonics, and Tomás ran out of ice, and Katinka said, "No fear, we Brits like our gin warm." And she had cupped the glass as though it were a snifter of fine brandy and taken a long, healthy swallow, and when she paused for air Frobisch kissed her on those plum-dark lips and thought he tasted juniper. She'd looked amused, not the least bit startled. He'd wondered what to say, or even why he'd kissed her, except he'd pondered it often enough in the stuffy air under the eaves.

"Are those dogs of yours really killers?" he had asked.

Her laughter rang like sleigh bells. That's what he'd thought, standing in the late night heat and sipping lukewarm gin—those strings of bells on the doors of shops in Austria and Switzerland and Georgetown. (And the Aardvark, Frobisch thought, driving through the Sunday quiet.)

"They only attack on my command," Tinka had said.

"Would they attack if I came to see you?"

"That would depend."

"Depend on what?" he would have asked; but Sadie in a wide-striped caftan (Bedouin wildness in the desert dark) hove into sight, her face moon-pale and stricken. He couldn't guess how much she'd seen. He'd thought, not very much, that her reaction came from noting how he fluttered toward Katinka like a lost moth drunk with radiance.

Sadie called out in a chuckly voice that strove to be a mite too cheerful, "Howie. Tinka. Come on inside to the piano. By popular demand, your hostess is going to sing."

"Wonderful." Tinka had squeezed his hand; they'd both smiled secret grins that erupted into laughter. That mirth, more than the kissing, comprised an infidelity to Sadie.

To avoid Katinka's seeing him, he continued driving a fair piece, almost to the white turret of Louisa's house. Unsure where to proceed, he parked illegally beside a hydrant. Here were his past mistakes compounded in the space of a few miles—ancient history captured under Georgian bricks; and beneath that shingled tower, the recent past. His mouth went dry as he reviewed the past hours with Louisa. He couldn't label them as infidelity. More accurate to say the weekend was "an indiscretion." Desire, vanity (had he ever performed more gloriously?), a lapse of faith. He recalled the coldness of her hand as they parted at her gate. Her bleak "Thanks for an interesting time." His false "I'll call you soon."

Impatiently, she'd tugged her hair, "Oh, don't bother, Howard, okay? We'd just go on disappointing each other."

He'd stood outside the rusted gate and hollered like a braying ass, "But your books? What should I do with all those books you lent me?"

"Keep 'em," she laughed. "Nobody wants to buy them." And as a last cold afterthought, a punishment, implying there was much in them he'd never understand; or if he did, much that would lead him to despair, "Read 'em and weep." Thus passed Louisa from his sight (and likely from his life), bending to pull a dead branch from a row of barren privet, her long skirt stiff with salt, her boots caked with a residue of mud—his "virgin" love, alone and lingering wearily on the steps of her front porch.

Convinced the local cops were tracking him, he made a last slow swing past Sadie's. He saw her posed at the front door in billowing dark pants and a white sweater top, greeting approaching guests, "I hope you're hungry." At those bashes they used to give, they ended the evenings famished, too busy being hosts to eat. When the guests had left, as they cleaned things up, they both pigged out—devouring platters of dessert and salad, pasta, potatoes, bread, anything that wasn't chewed or picked apart or speckled with cigarette ash. Ravenous with relief, they stuffed their faces, gossiped, moaned about the price they'd pay in morning-after heartburn. Watching from the sink, Mrs. Garcia wrinkled her brown face in distaste; her eyes were yellow-rimmed with creeping jaundice. He always passed her a couple of extra bucks beyond what Sadie paid her, and Tomás, too.

Considering the crowd she had tonight, Sadie would be too fired up to eat; and afterward she must face Dieter, who would hang on, brushing crumbs and squashing beer cans in the trash and probably complaining if he caught Sadie sneaking treats. No after-party snacks for Dieter, who would be hoping to assuage other hungers, unless— Frobisch had a brainstorm—somebody intervened. Suppose he drove out Rockville Pike and bought a mess of Chinese take-out; and after the last guest wobbled down the walk (leaving only Dieter lurking like a stubborn child amid the kitchen chaos), he popped up at the door, bearing a feast. It was possible Sadie wouldn't be welcoming. He imagined her curt greeting, every soft word sheathed in ice: "What do you want?"

He would hold aloft the food. "I come bearing gifts of moo shu pork and other delicacies too numerous to mention." She might slam the door shut in his face, but he doubted it. She was a sucker for a tasty egg roll.

He rambled along the Parkway, conscious of the Mormon Temple rising tall above the trees, a blaze of polished marble and golden spires that moved passersby to think of Shangri-la or Oz. If you got totaled on the Beltway and stared up from the wreckage of your car to that array of dazzling stone, you might decide you'd died and gone to heaven. Atop one slender tower the angel the Mormons called Moroni wielded a gold horn, pointed to the stars.

The heater in the Volvo was emitting intermittent gasps, now turning cold, now blasting fire in his face. Cursing, he switched it off and swung west on the dark twists of Beach Drive. The moon glowed with a gold penumbra, ice crystals reflecting lunar light, he had read somewhere and passed the information on to Sima in the days they dabbled in astronomy. He turned the radio on. His nightly dinner companion, Dr. Know-It-All Psychologist, was holding forth: "Childrey *try*; adults *do*," she offered in her syrupy JAP voice, unctuous with self-congratulation at yet another aphorism spawned in the paneled vastness of her rumpus room. Frobisch guffawed. What is it adults *do*, Dr. What's-It? We grit our teeth and try to keep a grip on our composure. What's an adult, except a kid grown taller and more messed up? What do we know, except our own confusion and fragility? I'll tell you this: I've led a life of curious innocence. So has Sadie, and Freddy and Renee, too. No alcoholic parents; no tortures as a child, beyond the taunts one got as offspring of the Pickle King; no muggings in the dark. The events of our past lives would make dull stuff on TV. I didn't even make it to the army because of the bum ear.

The worst that ever happened to me, the old folks died. First, the Pickle King, arguing the merits of the old Haymarket case (as you might suspect, the old man sided with the suspected bombers) and reaching for a well-done pickle with his tongs. Paused in midsentence, I am told, and dropped dead with his hands floating in brine and his bumptious dills bobbing around him like an honor guard. A good death, people said, because it was so speedy. When Sadie and I arrived, my mother was still in shock. She had the stunned look of someone who's just been zapped across the mouth with a cream pie, a bruised cast to the eyes as though privy to a secret knowledge of human vulnerability. For myself, I felt the strangest mix of grief and sheer annoyance—the assault made on my time, my work, the endless ritual of grief and sitting shiva and making polite chit-chat with all the customers and fellow travelers who came to pay their last respects. His good friend Lippman, who was with him when he died (Lippman arguing the anarchists had botched it), engaged me with reminiscence. The Pickle King had once been an anarchist himself and had gone to live in a commune somewhere in the boonies, up by the Canadian border, Lippman thought it was; but the movement died. Could I guess why? Lippman had grinned, showing the stumps of rotting teeth but determined to employ Socratic method. When I shook my head, he giggled, something like a high-pitched scream that was out of place in that room of mourning, and said, "No one believed in government, so no one would let anyone else tell him what to do. You couldn't allot the simplest tasks. No one took out the garbage; that's why the idea failed."

There's another bright saying for you, Dr. Big-Tush: "If civilization is to survive, the garbage must be dumped." My mother would have drunk a cream soda to that and said, "How true." She lasted only six months after the Pickle King's demise, too bored without contention and his dirty looks to carry on. That's when I cried and called myself an orphan and drove out to the port and sat and watched the black eels twisting through the oily water and wrung my hands, while Sadie and my cousin Jerry—he of the cynical bar mitzvah speech—coped with the arrangements.

"*You* are the most important person in the world," caroled the therapist.

Well, acknowledged Frobisch, I grew up believing that was true. It's a province of only sons to think so, and of course your Jewish sons accept, without demur, the idea that they are chosen. They see it as their due, something that comes naturally along about the time of circumcision; no, maybe in the womb, when they already get more than their share of Mom's attentions, and the old man has to seek other diversions—business, cards, castles of sugar cubes in the back booth of the deli. No wonder the old boy was so sour. I displaced him as a household god, and all he had left was his sign, his crown, his regal pickle, flapping hapless in the wind, spattered by gull shit.

"So love yourself," the woman ended her nightly editorial.

Frobisch cackled. Given the absence of a warm bed partner, I often do. Which brings us back to Sadie, my blessed ex, and the noblest, bravest girl a fellow ever knew. A fun date. Danced the rhumba and the cha-cha as well as the Virginia reel at Beaver Lodge where I met her in the Catskills; and held the crowd (including me) spellbound when she sang (at amateur night in the casino) "Embraceable You." She told me I looked like Jean Gabin, the way I smoked with a cigarette just dangling from my lower lip (and weren't those good times before we knew the evils of tobacco?). Later, she recanted, and said maybe not Gabin. Charles Boyer, because my features were so sensitive. Well, I was hooked. That's really all it took—a little well-placed flattery and the suggestion I was loved, that here was another woman who perceived me as a minor deity. How many times I failed her, not counting the ones in bed!

Did I tell you, Dr. Unctuous, how her parents died? The good and tender Goldens, retired teachers, moving their household effects from a flat in Forest Hills to warm and lovely Florida. On their aliyah to Fort Lauderdale, the station wagon packed, they decided to take a detour down Route A-1A, see the old fort at Saint Augustine, take photographs beside the rusty cannons, send back views of sea and waving palms to the home folks freezing in New York. Out of the sun there comes some boozy cracker in a pickup; drunk or stoned, he swerves at high speed into the station wagon's lane and totals 'em. Like that! No time for Papa Golden to fix his face in that smile of warm attention assumed by good teachers of civics; no time for Mama G. to pat her hair or tug her girdle. (I'm assuming from the girth of hips that Mama wore one.) So they died, scattered across A-1A, the Frobisch-Golden wedding pictures blowing in a fine seabreeze, the ficus tree that Mama G. meant for the corner of the new co-op apartment neatly cracked, as though a minuscule Paul Bunyan had hacked it with a file and hollered, "Timber," to the palms.

Sadie took on a look. Can I describe it? You know the old colonial flags they fly at Williamsburg? The serpent

305

coiled. "Don't tread on me." And she and Mrs. Garcia
cleaned. The crystal shone. The shower reeked of Clorox,
mildew spray. You walked barefoot, you got the gritty feel
of Comet. On tiptoe Sima and I moved softly, all of us
disinfected, as though a flood of cleaning agents would
keep us safe. Lifebuoy and hexachlorophene, our totems
against death.

There came a day the soapsuds parted; that cloud of
antiseptic grief dispersed, and Sadie was standing naked
at the closet mirror probing her breasts in the usual cancer
test and even humming a little bit, "Bewitched, Bothered,
and Bewildered." I called her back to bed; we cuddled.
I think she wept a bit, acknowledging, "It's over." And
I, having been there, for once understood that she meant
more than mourning. She meant innocence and childhood
and the brazen pleasure of that entry into Rome. I tried
to give her comfort, and the damn thing wobbled to its
side and lay there, useless; and Sadie said something, trying to be funny, but mostly crude, "Tell it we're finished
sitting shiva," and sashayed off to her gleaming shower,
swishing her hips. Some weeks, a few months after, I
moved down to the den, still in mourning, mostly for me,
knowing the suddenness of death and scared without the
old folks around as buffers. I kept thinking, they are gone,
and we are next. I had evidence. Here was the pressure
in the night to go and pee; here was Sadie wanting comfort, and the poor prick, humorless and spent. Sign of the
body going, impotent and weary, to its death.

I took that baggage with me on the trip to Rome. God
knows I was feeling guilty, a little drunk that night, full
of old wives' stories gleaned from the ladies at the temple, maybe affected by the shape of old Moroni back there
on the tower with his horn. I figure I devised him out of

grief and pain, my recurrent smiling angel in his brown homespun, looking like a craftsman in the first monastery of Pachomius. I figure I enlarged him by obsession and paternal grief. I believe, Dr. Lovey-Dovey, that I'm sane and prepared for rational discourse. "But who," he said aloud as he swung into the stream of cars speeding up the pike, "would have believed that a Bayonne-born accountant nurtured in a flat over the store would have such a powerful imagination? Not Sadie. Not Sima and certainly not me."

The Chinese restaurant he found was pleasantly old-fashioned—crumbs on the dull red carpet and tabletops of stained Formica—the small room noisy, hot, replete with reassuring smells of ginger and garlic and spicy mustard. No fancy potato nests and carved red pepper blossoms to boost the prices. Waiting for his take-out order, Frobisch settled at a table near the door and sipped on tea and sampled something labeled Oriental Potpourri—mounds of sticky dough and wilted cabbage. Skewered beef. He sat prim on a straight-backed chair and fiddled with the chopsticks that came to him unasked, and ogled the teenager behind the cash register, an almond-eyed enchantress with purple fingernails and inky hair blown dry into a "do" of startling complexity. She was chewing bubble gum and watching a police show on TV, pumping away with bland-faced energy until she paused to breathe and slowly blew a rainbow bubble that hovered evanescent at a point beneath her nose and then disintegrated inward with an unromantic plop. She had a mean face, older than her years. Madame Gin Sling parting the beaded curtains to glare at Bette Davis, "Yess, I have the letter!" So Frobisch mused, admiring the girl's silky tunic and wishing she would notice him parked catty-corner to her desk. He tried an opening gambit. "Looks like an exciting show."

"Take-out will be at leas' twenny minutes." The girl managed a bubble of Venetian artistry without once glancing from the screen.

"That's all right. I'm not in any hurry," Frobisch said and smiled his worldly Gallic smile and wished he had a cigarette to dangle from his lower lip. On the screen the cops were playing piggyback on motorcycles and firing guns, a cartoon given flesh. The girl watched this unblinking and cracked her gum, dismissing Frobisch as a passing nuisance.

The Oriental potpourri was passable. The place wasn't too bad. He thought Louisa might enjoy it, till he remembered they were finished. Her icy grip. Her eyes not meeting his as she offered her bleak thanks. What did she mean, "disappointing each other"? She might remember he'd dispatched himself with honor, given as good as he got, roused her once or twice to little oohs and ahs he interpreted as passion. He gave himself high marks for boyish zest, originality, and natural talent. So where did he fall short? Unless he suffered by comparison with someone else? No wonder men wanted virgins, who might be stiff and narrow and implacable and tense (bound to be teary afterward), but couldn't be all that critical of one's performance the first time around. If he ever got it on again with Sadie (was such a thing remotely possible?), she would have Dieter to contrast. Couldn't be much. A Prussian stick, the odor of wet dog filling his beard.

"Frobisch order ready," called the girl.

"That's me. Frobisch." He winked and clambered to his feet and set aside his greasy napkin and the slippery

chopsticks and hopped clumsily into her perfumed aura—
tea rose and spearmint and Cover Girl and clingy jeans
under the tight red tunic—and wished that she would
smile and wish him godspeed on the long ride back to
Kensington.

Parked across the street on the dark grass near the
creek, he almost froze waiting for Sadie's guests to leave.
No one stayed late at Washington parties, and this was
Sunday. Most of the guests faced Monday morning work.
Katinka had to be up early to walk her second-generation
schnauzers, and Mary De Filippo would go to mass to pray
no one was waiting to shoot hubby in ambush, and Sadie,
if she ran true to form, would rise and cook a glorious
breakfast for Dieter before sending him off to further
executions.

Seeing Estelle emerge, he whispered, "Traitor." If she
spied him, all was lost. She would hasten in ungainly sandals to his car to engage him in office talk, the only chit-
chat Estelle ever allowed herself. He scrunched lower in
the seat. The mingled smells of pork and fish and garlic
left him queasy. More people left, faces he didn't know.
Sadie waved from the door, her blonde head wobbling like
a floppy blossom as she beamed and called, "See you
tomorrow. See you at rehearsal. Thanks so much for coming. Bye." Freddy Gottlieb bent to kiss her. Renee and
Sadie traded cheeks, paused to reconsider, and embraced,
sisters aligned against the craziness of men. Frobisch bet
they'd had a good session of girl talk in the upstairs powder
room. Renee's eyes, bright in a painted elfin face, widen-
ing in bewilderment. "Howie's back at work, but he just
isn't plugged in. It's making Freddy crazy." Sadie, nodding, patting her hair in the old gesture of uncertainty.

309

"Who doesn't he make crazy? What do you think, Renee? Too brassy?" He knew the drill; his heart fluttered with nostalgia for the moment of the guests' departure. He felt left out, shivering in the freezing car while lights beamed through the doors and windows of the old home place like wandering suns. He watched the Gottliebs drive away. Enough. Dieter would tough it out, however long Frobisch stayed. He fumbled in his trouser pockets searching for his old house key. Better to stash the take-out in the kitchen and go away. Sadie could guess who'd left it; maybe she'd call to state her thanks and ask him over for a talk. That would be better than waiting, slowly freezing, while Dieter and Sadie nuzzled in the hall and acted married.

He waited until Mrs. Garcia and her son came out— Tomás in skinny pants and a shirt whose starched whiteness defied reality. "She never did my shirts that good," Frobisch complained. Tomás ushered his mother to a silver Porsche. Frobisch stared in admiration as they drove away. Holding the take-out to his chest, he clambered from his car and hurriedly traversed the Parkway. He made his way across the lawn, wincing as he stepped on crunching leaves. He edged past Dieter's van and circled the dark garage, maneuvering past a toolshed where he'd stored a defunct mower and coils of garden hose. Instinctively, he checked the padlock, pulled it tight. He sprinted across the patio, swore softly when he collided with a redwood lounge stripped of its summer pillows. He sidestepped the gas barbecue and its round canister of fuel poking above the concrete like a bomb. He could strike a match and blow 'em all to kingdom come; for a moment the idea seemed attractive. He uttered a muffled cry as he plowed into the stiffened branches of a lilac bush, planted to placate Sadie who'd wanted sweet purple flowers like the ones in Portofino. Under the weeping cherry was the mound of Gregor's grave. He stared away from it. Through the sliding glass doors of the patio he saw figures moving in the den, Sadie and Dieter picking up, bending and straightening like gleaners, earnest in their task. He would have to pass under their noses to make it to the kitchen entry. There was the possibility Sadie had changed the lock, and there'd be no way to get into the house without alerting her. He set his package on the picnic table and stopped to reconsider. Something brushed past him, a cat or a raccoon. Instinctively, he hollered his surprise.

The house went dark. A moment later the glass panel slid open. Dieter stood in the door, pointing a flashlight toward the trees. "Who's there?"

Frobisch ducked behind the redwood chaise and waited.

Dieter held the light steady. He was clutching something dark and stubby in his other hand. He essayed a few steps forward, calling, "Answer, or I'll shoot!"

Stupid Sadie had let him get a pistol! Frobisch crouched low in the grass, thinking that Dieter must hear him breathing, the heavy gasps of cold and fear. A noise like an exploding firecracker resounded above his head. By God, the idiot was shooting! Frobisch rolled under the picnic table and pressed his face to the cold earth with his arms covering his head.

"Who goes there?" Dieter called. A second shot loosened a wedge of bark from the copper beech. In the Turner yard, the chained schnauzers were going crazy.

"Dieter, you're potted! Put that thing away. You'll wake up the whole neighborhood and scare everyone to death!" Sadie's voice resounded from the dark.

Dieter played his flashlight through the trees. "Whoever is prowling out there, I mean to kill him."

They were all alike, these krauts, ready to make war at the slightest provocation. Frobisch cast about for an escape. If he vaulted the De Filippo fence, he would get shot. If he headed for Katinka's, the dogs would get him. If he stayed in hiding, Dieter would likely find him; and even if Van Zandt lost interest and went inside to call the police, Frobisch would die of cold if he stayed immobile too much longer. "Don't shoot," he yelled. "It's me."

"My God, it's Howie!" Sadie screamed.

Dieter thundered, "Come out where we can see you." He moved the flashlight in a wavering circle.

Frobisch climbed to his feet and stood revealed in the white beam. "It's me. Don't shoot."

Sadie's pants billowed like harem pajamas. Her sweater was dotted with metallic stars that glittered in the night. She was shivering in her stocking feet. "What are you doing out there?"

Frobisch felt around until he found his Chinese carryout. He hoisted the greasy bag.

Dieter called, "What's that? A brick?"

"No," Frobisch said. "It's Chinese food."

"You're trespassing," said Dieter.

"Sadie, please let me in. I'm freezing."

"Go away, Howie. You weren't invited." She sounded so doleful, it gave him hope.

"Sadie, I got moo shu pork and egg rolls and shrimp Peking. I thought we'd have a little snack and drink some tea and talk."

"We have nothing to talk about," said Sadie. "Go away or I'll call the police."

"I got duck sauce and mustard and hot-and-sour soup. Maybe Dieter would care to join us."

"You heard the lady." Dieter raised his gun.

"Sadie, are you going to let him kill me because I stopped by with a midnight snack?"

"Oh, put that thing away, Dieter, before you hurt someone! Howie, go home!"

"I can't eat it all by myself."

She turned to Dieter. "You see what I mean? He is a fool!"

"Don' laugh!" Dieter bellowed his territorial rights. "He has no business out there. He's crazy and a menace. There's no tellin' what he'll do."

Sadie piped in, "If you don't go away this minute, Howie, I will not be responsible."

"Would you let him shoot me in cold blood? You'd do that to me, Sadie?"

"You're trespassing and prowling," Sadie called. "You have been warned."

Frobisch advanced slowly toward them. "Then go ahead and shoot me. If you won't accept my peace offering, if you won't even talk, I want Dieter to shoot me. Go ahead, Dieter, shoot!"

Dieter wavered. "Listen, I don't wanna hurt you."

"Shoot!" cried Frobisch. "It would be a kindness!"

"Howie," cautioned Sadie, "stop playing the fool. Don't goad him that way. He's had a lot to drink."

"Kill me, Dieter," Frobisch taunted. "You have my permission. Consent to euthanasia."

"Don't tempt me," Dieter warned.

"That's enough bluffing from both of you," said Sadie. "Dieter, give me the gun."

"C'mon, you dumb kraut coward! Do it! I'm signing a release. In the absence of pen and paper, you have my verbal agreement. Do it! I demand it! Shoot!" cried Frobisch and fell as the gun exploded in his face.

It was the same fierce blaze of light, the same deep warmth, the same sore knee that he clobbered when he toppled forward; over all, the healing glow, familiar and yet strange. No sound, and then a hum of distant voices; closer was the light and a feeling of serenity so perfect he wished never to move. If this is death, it is something largely to be wished, and Morry must find it pleasant, and the old folks, too, and Gregor Samsa. The angel, looking put-upon, tugged at his beard. "You're some pistol, Frobisch." Well, yeah, courting death by gun and drowning . . . am I alive? "Heart's strong." Frobisch, struggling to be heard: I don't know if you're guardian, keeper, jailer, mentor, friend, or casual observer, but I thank you. Owe you one, you know? Something amiss. The bearded face bending to him stinks of bourbon. A cold ear to his chest, rough fingers on his wrist.

"He's fine," said Dieter. "He's just passed out."

Wiser to fake the faint, play cagey possum. Dieter lifts him as though he were old laundry, flings him across one shoulder, staggers to the house. Careful, you bearded creep, don't hurt the leg! Drunken gangland bastard, playing cops and robbers. A man's home is his castle, only it's not yours to defend. You're too obsessed with territory, Dieter. You've been too long among your furry friends. What do you do, patrol the borders of the yard and piss in all four corners?

Familiar warmth, familiar pillows. Same itchy cover on the couch. Old dog smells in the den; odor of stale bologna crumpled in a napkin. Mrs. Garcia in too much of a hurry to vault off in the silver Porsche. Sadie, sweet, blessed Sadie, has unfolded a blanket and spread it over him. "Is he all right? Why is he so quiet?"

"He'll come 'round in a minute."

No thanks to you. The body in stress marshals its own defenses. The vessels contract and carry life-giving fluids to the vital organs. Blood rushes from the head; blood pressure drops. The victim experiences dizziness and nausea. Would someone have the wit to elevate my legs? Thank you, darling Sadie. Have I mentioned you're looking gorgeous? Don't let that sot, that murderous veterinarian, near me.

"Thank God, his color's better." Sadie, in a fury triggered by relief, turned on Dieter. "What could you be thinking of? What were you doing, shooting up the yard! You're crazy! Both you and Howie, crazy! Where's the gun?"

Dieter studied his hands, empty of weapons and the comfort of his scalpels and syringes. "Dunno. Maybe out back."

"I want you to find it and get rid of it! Bury it if you have to, but I don't want it in this house!"

Dieter, drowning, struggling for the sweet air of sobriety. "Dunno if I can find it."

"Go and look!"

Frobisch, snug in the burrow of his blanket. "Make sure he empties out the bullets."

"You're awake! Thank God! How do you feel?"

Not half bad, considering the alternative. "Good. A little dizzy, but I'm feeling good. Your friend there tried to kill me!"

Dieter attacked his beard. "Wanted to scare him."

"You were trespassing," said Sadie. "He tried to warn you off."

"Oh, yeah? He aimed right for my heart. I could bring charges."

"Please don't be stupid, Howie."

"He tried to kill me. Something . . . someone . . . deflected the bullet so it missed." For I am blessed. For surely Thou hast blessed me for no reason I can discern. Luck of the cards, Morry would say. Nothing that you deserve, any more than *I* deserved that lonely death, only a grinning pumpkin head to watch me through that last adventure.

"He only tried to scare you off. He's a little high, and he got trigger-happy, but he's had every reason to be upset. Someone's been prowling out back for the last two weeks."

"Did you tell the police?"

"Yes, but they don't believe me. Nothing's out of place. I think someone's trying to frighten me. If I open the window a crack and go off to rehearsal, when I get back, the window's shut. If I leave the shed door open, I look again and find it locked. A couple of mornings, I found muddy footprints."

"Oh, hell, Sadie." Frobisch kicked aside the blanket and pointed to his feet, shod in dirty loafers. "That would be me. Sima told me there were robberies in the neighborhood, so I've been keeping watch." He admonished, "You shouldn't leave the window open when you leave the house. It's like an invitation to a thief."

Dieter, roused from dreamy torpor: "What was he doin', sneakin' around?"

"Just checking things while Sadie was at rehearsals."

"It wasn't necessary, Howie. I don't want you hanging around the place!"

"I see you have protection." Frobisch scowled at Dieter. "He almost finished me."

"Oh, don't start that!"

"Let's ask him. Let's find out exactly where he aimed."

"Stop it! Dieter wouldn't hurt a fly. He checked your vital signs. He carried you into this house."

Frobisch had roused himself to a sitting position. "If he's so fuckin' considerate, he shouldn't mind giving an answer. Which way did you shoot, Dieter? Did you aim above me or straight for my heart?"

"Don' remember."

"You *know*! You're not that sloshed!" He'd been sober enough to hold the gun, raise it to shoulder height, and aim straight for the chest. A little snub-nosed thing, no bigger than a toy, the brilliance of the flash was startling. Someone had intervened. Frobisch closed his eyes. Singled out, then spared. And surely blessed. Familiar mumbling voice. "You're some pistol, Frobisch." Then why the swift salvation in the yard? Is it—forgive me, this is Louisa's phrase—sheer hubris, showing how quickly you can flex a muscle if you're in the mood? Is it arrogance or love that saved me? And if it's love, why me?

"Howie, I insist that you stop hounding Dieter."

"The vet gets *hounded*? Funny stuff!"

"Oh, just shut up! Dieter, I think you need to sleep it off. In the guest room," Sadie added.

"The guest room! Yeah!" Frobisch approved.

Dieter shook off this last indignity. "I will go home. I will telephone you tomorrow morning, Sadie."

"Maybe it's time you went home, too, Howie."

"Knee hurts. Don't wanna move."

"You're hurt?" Sadie, businesslike. "Roll up your pants and let me see."

317

"Nothing. An old bruise. I must have hit it when I fell."

"Should I get some ice?"

"Not necessary. A cup of tea might hit the spot." He smote his brow. "There's Chinese food out on the patio. All it needs is some reheating."

"I'll get it before the raccoons find it." Sadie wanted to know, "What made you bring it, anyhow?"

"I was thinking, after parties, we were always hungry. You remember, Sadie?"

"I remember," Sadie said. "I didn't think *you* did."

When she had left, Frobisch confronted Dieter, who had slumped into a chair beside the desk. The vet sat with his chin pressed deep against his chest. The dark curls of his beard fluttered as he breathed. "Did you try to kill me?"

Dieter squinted past him as though the thread of memory dangled just beyond his line of vision. Truth hovered in a blur at curtain height. "Don't remember."

"Did you aim straight for my heart?"

"Dunno."

"If you had, would you admit it?"

Dieter's eyes flickered with the tantalizing possibilities. "I might *want* to murder you. I wouldn' gun you down."

Frobisch hobbled to his feet, enlivened by the fervor of his argument. "I'm pursuing this 'cause it's important. I made you mad. You only meant to scare me, but you got so pissed your judgment foundered. You wouldn't hurt me consciously, but there I was—Sadie's ex-husband and Sima's father. Still a rival, so to speak. Your unconscious wouldn't mind if I was dead. Is that a possibility? Your unconscious prompted you to shoot?"

"Is this a third degree?"

"Just admit that psychologically there is that possibility."

"Psy-cho-log-i-cally?" Dieter appeared truly confounded.

"Yes?" prompted Frobisch.

"I don't address myself to that," answered the vet.

The new Sadie, busy with rehearsals, no longer brewed tea in a pot. Made do with tacky tea bags that bore the taste of soggy hemp. Ate frozen dinners and found them tasty. Had Mrs. Garcia come in an extra day, but didn't fuss over the cleaning. The new Sadie not so quick to please. "If Dieter stays over—no point in hiding the fact that sometimes he stays over—he toasts his own English muffins. Like Jerry Ford used to, you know? And better not complain." In the familiar comfort of the kitchen the new Sadie swung her hips with the old sexy movement, but walked with a new bounce and talked with a new verve; and her eyes betrayed some far preoccupation that did not touch on him. Her look suggested it was nice to have his company, but not vital to her happiness. She gazed beyond him as they talked, and he was wild for her to notice him. Take note of me, he prayed. Observe how good I think you look, how interesting I find your conversation. It intrigued him the way women—Sadie and Louisa, too—found the wherewithal to reinvent themselves, slough off their skins, alter their shapes, cast off their old personae so that hausfrau became Valkyrie and virgin evolved to courtesan and back to virgin, if she chose. The new Sadie had people importuning her—Hexagoners eager for her company. Lawyers and economists by day; show biz types by night. They had this happy camaraderie. They flipped to hear her sing. She had this funny, terrific number she did, "The Girlfriend of the Beltway Bandit." It broke them up. "Cast members. That was mostly who was here tonight. It was a lovely party until the fireworks started."

"Would it help to tell you I was sorry?"

"Just for tonight?"

"For everything. All the bad times. Gregor Samsa. Him most of all."

The waterworks again. Sadie withdrew a tissue from the pocket of her slacks and dabbed her eyes. "Oh, listen, the poor pooch was suffering. Maybe you were right."

"I don't know what is right or what is kind or even what is real. Louisa says I make my own reality." Light-years ago, that morning, in the motel coffee shop, he'd watched Louisa heap grape jam on a segment of toasted honey-wheat muffin and pop it into her mouth as though assuaging sexual hungers. "What attracted me to you initially," she'd said, "is you were different. You were muddling through some dark philosophy, and your worldview was a bit peculiar—but interesting."

"Is that the woman, alone and vulnerable?" Sadie asked. "The orphan girlfriend?"

"Not anymore. We disappoint each other." Watching Louisa eat, he'd marveled at the way she packed it in and never gained a pound. Sadie had once confided it was the special luck of certain shiksas that they could eat and not gain weight—something to do with a magic metabolism that derived from their privileged birth, like being born with Delft blue eyes and wheaten hair, and never worrying about admission into college. "Do you recall your Plato?" Louisa had asked. "How he points out the difference that resides between illusion and reality? The reflection men perceive obscures them from the real? Men can be equally blinded moving from the light or toward it?"

A woman of intelligence. Slender and widely read and wildly sexy. He'd begun mourning the loss of her before the second cup of coffee cooled. "*My* Plato?" he'd said. "You flatter me. I haven't read him. I don't know what you mean. As far as looking for the light, I'm coming to think I'm happier with a little mystery. Enlightenment isn't all it's cracked up to be."

Louisa had patted her mouth dry with a paper napkin. "Would you be surprised to know I take that as an insult?"

The family at the next table had listened openly, two stringy country types sitting with snivelly blonde twin girls who stared at them with red-rimmed eyes and brushed albino bangs from greasy foreheads. Frobisch figured they'd seen last night's seaside ballet, or they'd lain awake, marking the cries and groans and bellows from the room he and Louisa shared. "What are they looking at?" he'd asked.

"Please, Howard, don't make a scene!"

"Don't worry. Your reputation is safe."

"I thought you were different from all those others. Not just concerned with acquisitions. Open to the life of ideas."

"What does that mean, *those others*? Can I have missed the fact that you're anti-Semitic?"

"Don't be a fool! I don't even think of you as Jewish."

Fuckin' like bunnies all night, and now arguing like prim old-marrieds. "Who, if not me? Confronting messengers of God, but staying nonaffiliated? I'm the quintessential Jew, the man without a country!"

"Why is it some men, after they've had sex, have to wallow in self-pity?"

"Well, you should know, my dear." They'd finished their cooling coffees and made their weary way outside—

he walking stiffly, hurting in a hundred places after the rigors of the night, worrying about a sore spot on his shoulder where she'd raked him with her teeth. The worst bites came from humans and could get badly infected. Glumly he'd heaped their luggage in the car, and silently they'd driven west, away from the slate gray ocean and the fields gone swampy with the late-night rain. Louisa lolled in the front seat pretending to be asleep, *was* asleep, her mouth gone slack, emitting gravelly snores. He concentrated on the radio, a mix of Sunday prayers and dentist music like the stuff they played at Jack's; and when the boredom got too bad, he toyed with his idea of an all-male heaven—a fishing camp with Morry dealing gin and the Pickle King supplying eats and someone affable and guileless, like Jack in his yachtsman's cap, smiling and pointing out the dangerous channels.

Sadie was looking smug. "Sorry it didn't work out for you."

"That's my line, *sorry*."

"Sima thinks you're depressed."

"Depressed? Not crazy? We're making progress."

"Also crazy. She says you see things. Angels, visions, ghosts. They come to you in dreams. They hang around like fairy godmothers." Sadie, bug-eyed. "Do you believe that stuff?"

"Yes. No. I don't know. I thought I had a handle on it, until Dieter started shooting." In the end, he thought, it's a seduction. You get a hint of magic and you cast off logic. Questions beget questions and you're in a labyrinth. You go a little bonkers sorting out the possibilities. Father Paul, who preferred the joys of sociology, had warned him off; and the monks, abiding by the wisdom of Pachomius, submerged themselves in routine tasks—maps, histories, choirs, schedules. No wonder he'd liked it at the monastery. He was with fifty—sixty other Frobisches, all making lists.

Sadie had carried her tea, untasted, to the sink and poured it out. She'd sent the Chinese take-out home with Dieter. (Frobisch acted wounded: "It's yours. Do what you want with it.") She asked, "Should I flatter myself that you're jealous of Dieter, the way you keep accusing him?"

The man's spoor was everywhere. A box of cigarillos on the counter. A calendar marked with the imprint of the veterinary hospital was fastened to the fridge with daisy magnets. "Lookit, Sadie, I'm gonna run this through all over for the second show: Dieter shot a bullet at my heart. It never hit. Someone deflected it."

"He aimed above your head."

"Did you see where he aimed?"

"I don't know. I was watching you. He says he did."

"And I say he didn't. So who do you believe?"

"Can you prove he didn't?"

"I can't prove anything. I know that someone saved my life. That's no casual favor. I think I owe something in forfeit; I'm scared to think what it could be. An angel came to me in a vision and told me to do good."—the term "good," he'd come to realize, comprised a multitude of sins—"I don't know what that means. Maybe simple acts of kindness; maybe acceptance of a faith. Maybe I have to renounce my worldly goods and go be an evangelist. I hope not, 'cause I'm not cut out for that, and Freddy would have a stroke." The ultimate absurdity—a prophet in Gucci loafers leading the faithful to belief. In this place, in this city—with the white wine crowd, the pasta primavera—he'd be labeled a pariah. Frobisch carried his cup and saucer to Sadie and stood by as she rinsed them.

She handed him a dish towel, and he took it, grateful for the homely task of drying. "Do you know I can predict things? Listen, you'll want to hear this: Sima and Randy are gonna split. Sima will go to college."

"Thank God!"

"She'll diet until she gets too thin. We'll worry about her health."

"*We'll* worry? I doubt *we'll* even discuss it."

"She'll meet someone. An older man, already married. We'll wish for good old Randy."

"That is a lot of bull!"

"And I'm not so easy in my mind about that Polish pope."

"Well, you are crazy!" Sadie laughed.

"Don't mock me, Sadie. I don't know what to do."

Sadie stifled a yawn. "Believe in visions if you want to. You're interested in faith? Go to temple and make peace with the rabbi, even though, when he encouraged Sima to go to Israel instead of college, you tried to beat him up."

"I grabbed him by the coat, that's all. Fancy Bond Street lapels. A wimp in British tailoring, little soot smudge on his chin, calls it a beard. Rubs up to me in the market and says can we meet sometime and talk about investments? A damned entrepreneur. I don't want a businessman showing me the way to God. I want someone exalted!"

"You want to be contrary; that's all you want. In that way you and Sima are alike. You both go to extremes. You want something only if you find out you can't have it. Look at you. You couldn't wait to move yourself out of this house; now you come back every night and hang around. You say you can't stand Randy, but you're worrying because you think they might split up."

"You're not hearing me."

"I hear you loud and clear, and you're giving me a headache. So if you're all right now, I'll beg to be excused. I've just had fifty people in for buffet dinner and I'm bushed. I'm going upstairs to bed. You can sack out in the den if you're still shaky."

"I'm not allowed upstairs?"

"No way!"

"The bedrooms are Dieter's private preserve?"

"Don't be cute."

"You could stay with me downstairs. We could play some music and just be quiet. Like old times."

"Stay with you? Could you be kidding?"

Stay with me, he thought, for I need your courage. I don't know if the power that saved my life is merciful and kind or a tyrant acting out of cruel caprice. Maybe he keeps me going because I am a clown. What a show I gave last night. Those rednecks in the motel must've busted a gut laughing. I was better than the late-night news—shivering in my boxer shorts, wading merrily into the ocean, only making sure Louisa was on hand to haul me out. The Frobisch road show. Visions, prognostications, and super sex. Sex, Louisa told me once, is the last refuge of people who've run out of conversation. You and I have talked enough. Stay with me and let me show my tricks. You'll be the Blessed Lady, and I'll be Barnaby, offering my special talents. "Stay with me," begged Frobisch.

"Is that what this is all about? Showing up with Chinese food? The way you set up Dieter—"

"*I* set up Dieter? He shot at me!"

"And then the hangdog look. The piety and the contrition. Angels and visions. You're coming on with me? You're *coming on?*"

"I didn't plan it. The idea just came out."

"What is it you want exactly? A quick hop in the sack? Your girlfriend dumped you, so you want the first convenient lay?"

Frobisch, outraged. "Nothing like that! I want you back, Sadie. Oh, please, I want you back!"

"Work out another plan, Howie."

"Don't be like that. You could sleep on it. You could entertain the thought."

Sadie, rubbing the spotless counter with a sponge: "To this we've come. You're begging. I'm refusing. If I weren't so bushed, I'd be in hysterics."

"Don't make up your mind so fast."

"I'm turning in. One of us in this room is crazy, and it isn't me." The message unspoken hung between them. We're talking the woman scorned. We're talking the new Sadie. The girlfriend of the Beltway Bandit is no one's patsy.

The Pickle King used to tell a peculiar story, an event out of his youth, his one descent to sentimentality, he would trot it out at family dinners after Sadie had sung her repertoire of Yiddish folk songs and Sima had performed the "Minuet in G" on the piano. "It was when I was a boy in Russia," the Pickle King always began; and the adults rattled their coffee spoons against their cups and exchanged swift looks of pained complicity. He had been young, no more than five or six, walking across a field after a sudden shower—the grass as high as his waist, the air thick with the steaminess of early summer. He'd come to a dirt road, rutted with the tracks of wagons. The deeper ruts held stagnant puddles where horseflies buzzed and birds dabbled their beaks. In the weeds beside the road he'd sighted an odd object, cylindrical in shape, comprising many colors—violet, amethyst, pink, sky blue, and deepest rose. The thing was smooth to touch. When he picked it up, it shimmered in his palm. "It had"—he always whispered this as though it was the strangest fact of all—"the consistency of jello." Cradling the object in his palms he raced home to show his mother. By the time he reached his house, the thing was gone, evaporated into air. He felt the coolness in his palm and saw a rosy mist where the liquid stuff had transformed into vapor. He knew what the thing was: a piece of cloud, some wondrous residue of heaven fallen to the road. A treasure to be gathered up and swiftly lost, according to the natural order. Secret scholar, atheist, half-baked reformer, he had cleaved to that belief over the years.

Every time he told the story, he added some new detail, as an artist layers on paint to enhance the beauty of a landscape. Now there were houses built of logs, chimneys spewing the smoke of cooking fires, a grove of trees, a dog curled like a mat beneath their shade, a wagon hauled across the rutted roadway, a wheel sunk in the mud. Now there were smells of horse dung, peppermint, and violets. He got the seasons mixed. Mayflies swarmed. Snows came and melted. Pear blossoms quivered on young boughs. One constant shimmered from the bottom of the gully—the rounded object glowing violet, amethyst, deepest rose. The piece of cloud. His life's enchantment. Some deep mysterious link between dull earth and radiant heaven.

In the night Frobisch lay awake thinking how he and the old man had been bound in the same web of imagination, maybe the same terror of mortality. Iconoclast though he might have been, the old man set the stage for visions with his stories of a heaven trailing amethyst

327

vapors. Only the old man knew enough to keep things straight, confine his musings to the dinner table—his only public show of whimsy, the odious pickle with its three-pronged crown, whereas Frobisch set himself on a more dangerous track, hobbled between illusion and reality. Shivering on the sleep sofa, he drew a list of new resolves: to clear his head, put first things first, concentrate on winning Sadie.

Overhead, he heard her pacing. The floorboards creaked under her tread. A door opened and closed. The bedsprings rattled as she lay down and got up again. He told himself, she will be back. She will, because there is a vision of herself she must preserve—all-loving, all-giving, forgiving Sadie. She will be back because she loves me, although I am a fool, *because* I am a fool and it's her instinct to look after me. She can't love Dieter. He flatters her, nurtures her ego, consoles her for the death of Gregor Samsa, although he was the instrument, let's not forget that. A violent man, wielding a pistol. Can she recall that scene out in the yard and still allow him in her bed?

Too restless to sleep, he flicked on the light and started his own weary pacing, taking an inventory of the den— the books, the statuettes, the loving cup, the clock. In a cupboard underneath the bookshelves he found a carton holding remnants of their trips—olivewood beads and Spanish shawls, Michelin maps and postcards, a Greek fisherman's cap purchased on a stopover in Cyprus. He put on the hat, mimicking Jack as he tilted it over one eye. In a corner of the cupboard was an album dating from a time he'd dabbled in photography. He settled on the floor studying the pictures. Sadie at Great Falls, posed on a lip of rock that loomed above the waters of a chasm. Below her the wild Potomac plunged and roiled, transformed from the city's placid channel to a fall of rushing water, green whirlpools, white swirls of foam, funnels of mist dissolving to spectral vapors in the trees. Beyond her there rose a wall of cliffs, gray stone cut jagged by the flood's persistence. (She will be back because the two of us are wedded still, as much by our frustrations as by our joys. Our sparring is a necessary habit. Our anger is a kind of passion, "funny" love talk couched in sarcasm and sour jokes.) Sadie beside the C&O Canal, the water brackish, deep, dotted by yellow leaves that shone like coins. Above her the sky bristling dazzling cobalt, tempered by gold, and the sun splitting the barks of trees to planes of stripe and shadow. He'd achieved a nice contrast of light and shade. There was always trouble shooting Sadie, who either blinked or stared, got self-conscious, begged, through frozen grins, "Hurry up. I'm holding in my stomach."

Here was Sima on the steps of the school, a thin child wearing a navy peacoat and a skirt that barely brushed her thighs and white knee socks and thick-soled shoes, that year's fashion that had made children look clubfooted. A gray day, warmed sporadically by sun. A breeze blowing the new buds of the bending maples, and Sima skipping toward him, swinging her braids, popping a thick blonde plait inside her mouth as if for comfort. They'd walked to the spring carnival at Washington Cathedral; and in the shaded streets of Cleveland Park he'd snapped "artistic" shots—fanciful Victorian houses ornate with gingerbread, a rooster weathervane atop a blue gazebo, a cat pacing the wooden pickets of a widow's walk. At the carnival he'd shot a montage of displays—duck pens and flower stands, heaped banks of plants, a rabbit eating strawberries from a china plate, carvings of doves, tumblers of jam, gold pins composed of real leaves dipped in paint. They'd bought Sadie an oak-leaf cluster and planned a presentation speech. Service beyond the call of duty. Patience and industry. Love and unfailing cheer. (She will be back because she has me at a disadvantage. She knows that she can call the shots.)

Sadie must have raised the thermostat. He was feeling warm. Light flickering from the lamp fluttered through the ceiling cobwebs and glanced off the flowered panels of the curtains. Frobisch let the album slide. The angel, hunkering lotus-fashion on the desk, was eyeing him as though he were a rare exhibit. Frobisch backed up to the safety of the sofa. After a time, he found his voice. "Y'know, I'm not all that surprised. I had a hunch you might turn up again." He pointed to the book of photos. "I was looking at old family pictures. Nice times when I was married. I'm thinking I could get 'em back . . . next time, do better. Listen, there's something I have to ask. Do I imagine you? I think; therefore, you are? Is that the ticket?" The angel affected a visage of long-suffering sadness. Frobisch pressed on. "That business with Dieter. Sadie says he aimed over my head."

He could smell the musky heaviness of Sadie's perfume. She was standing at the door, holding a thick quilt to her breast. Defensively, she spoke, "I couldn't let you die of cold. I brought you an extra blanket."

The angel held the bullet in his hand. Ever so delicately, he perched it between thumb and forefinger as though it were a perfect diamond. He turned it to the light and then he palmed it. He tossed it in the air, caught it without seeming effort, dropped it in his sleeve, withdrew it from the fluted shadow of the lamp. He tossed it up again so quickly that all Frobisch could distinguish was a golden blur. The angel flipped the bullet, palm to palm in a fan of radiant light.

Sadie said, "You'd have to court me. I'm only going to say this once, Howie, so I'd be grateful for your attention. I'm willing to give the thing a try for Sima's sake, but you'd have to be my suitor all over again. Phone calls, flowers and candy, all that stuff. We'd have to date. No bedroom stuff until I say the time is right, and even then I'm not making any promises. I'm not allowing any time for contemplation, so if you want to give the thing a trial, make up your mind right now."

The bullet, sheathed in light, held him transfixed. Suppose, only suppose, he'd met certain criteria? Got pegged as a quick study. Bright, but not overly intellectual. No strong family ties. No loyalty to any one religion. A mix of sexiness and guilt that made a nice poetic tension. Quick with a quip so if his name endured in history he'd make a decent read. Suppose he offered up belief, waxed tenacious in the face of doubters, and in return got certain perks? Oh, what a grand and cosmic joke, this newest vision—a half-crazy accountant, the offspring of the Pickle King, speeding his way into the District in a tooled-up Volvo (the heater blasting hot and cold) to be reborn!

The stars on Sadie's sweater refracted points of light. "Well, Howie, what do you say?" She was standing near him pressing for an answer.

Frobisch waved her off, looking to the magic.